CRIMSON SUNRISE

KRISTIE KNIGHT

DIAMOND BOOKS, NEW YORK

CRIMSON SUNRISE

A Diamond Book / published by arrangement with
the author

PRINTING HISTORY
Diamond edition / May 1991

ISBN: 1-55773-507-7

Diamond Books are published by The Berkley Publishing Group,
200 Madison Avenue, New York, New York 10016.
The name "DIAMOND" and its logo
are trademarks belonging to Charter Communications, Inc.

PRINTED IN THE UNITED STATES OF AMERICA

10 9 8 7 6 5 4 3 2 1

For Kate Barry,
who lived to become a legend
in upstate South Carolina.
Her courage, endurance, and resilience contributed
greatly to the victory at
the Battle of Cowpens.
Merry Noelle Arledge is but a poor imitation of Kate,
who served as the inspiration for the character.

For Pa,
Mr. P. M. Steadman,
who lived for a time at Walnut Grove Plantation,
which belonged to Kate Barry.
My pa, in his ninety-first year at this writing,
instilled in me a love for our land and a pride in my
heritage and taught me that no matter how bad life gets,
tomorrow's sunrise brings a better day.
I love you, Pa.

PROLOGUE

December 25, 1774
Charleston, South Carolina

ELEVEN-YEAR-OLD NOELLE ARLEDGE GIGGLED AND PEEKED through the doorway at the grown-ups, then motioned for her cousins to join her. "Let's listen."

Charles Arledge, Noelle's father, pounded his fist on the table and glared at his brother. "Jonathan, how can you be so pigheaded? England is draining the life from the colonies and will continue to do so unless we take action."

"Charles, that's treason, and you well know it. Besides, the mother country will pay well for your services should you remain loyal."

Noelle frowned and turned to face her cousin Lilly. Jonathan Arledge, Lilly's father, was a crosspatch. Noelle didn't like to hear her father being accused of treason, especially by his own brother. Besides, she was tired of all this conversation about the possibility of war.

Erin Banning glanced at her cousins. At thirteen, she was much more mature than Noelle and Lilly, and as the eldest, she felt it was her responsibility to keep them out of trouble. "Let's go back upstairs. There's nothing to interest us here."

Lilly glanced fretfully at her father. She hated for him to be so contrary, but she could do nothing about it. At least he would leave her alone while he was involved in such a heated debate. She followed meekly along, admiring her

1

older cousin for being so considerate. Uncle Charles and Uncle Arlen often disagreed with Lilly's father, and today was no different, even though it was Christmas.

The three girls found chairs near the fire in Erin's little sitting room, and Lilly began to play with her doll. She looked at her older cousins and sighed. They seemed to know so much more than she did. Erin had even been to Boston and Philadelphia with Uncle Arlen. "Erin, when is supper? Do you think Father will want to go home immediately after we eat?"

"I'm sure supper will be served shortly." Erin gazed at Lilly with sympathetic eyes. The young girl's face was bruised. Uncle Jonathan said she'd fallen against the corner of the hearth, but Erin doubted it. Lilly often displayed bruises that were difficult to account for. "Would you like to stay overnight with us?"

"Oh, do you think I could?" Lilly asked, her eyes brightening considerably. She grinned and shook her head, sending a cascade of ebony ringlets over her shoulders.

Erin smiled. Lilly's dark eyes and hair gave her an exotic appearance even at age ten. She would be really pretty one of these days. Noelle picked up her doll and smoothed its dress. Erin thought her cousin Noelle was pretty, too. Noelle's hair was as light as the sun as it rose over the Ashley and Cooper rivers, and her eyes were as blue as cornflowers. Erin sighed. She would have loved to have the coloring of either girl. Instead, her auburn hair caused much teasing, and her green eyes were odd—or so her friends said.

Noelle placed her doll in the corner of the sofa and looked at her two cousins. Erin was staring at Lilly, and Noelle wondered why. Little Lilly seemed so fragile, even more fragile than the china cups that Uncle Arlen had given Noelle for Christmas. Her eyes glittering with excitement, Noelle slid to the edge of her seat and dangled her feet playfully. "Erin, have you ever been kissed?"

Erin glared at Noelle. "What a silly goose you are. Of

course I haven't been kissed." She considered the question for a moment and then eyed Noelle thoughtfully. "Have you?"

"No. I don't think I ever will be. You have lots of boys around all the time." Noelle fidgeted with the lace on her bodice. "There's hardly anybody who's worth kissing, even if I was old enough."

Lilly's eyes widened in astonishment. "Would you really kiss a boy?"

"Well, older women kiss their husbands, but I don't know about it. I think it would be fun to try," Erin answered before Noelle had a chance. "I've decided I'm going to kiss a boy before I'm sixteen. I have less than three years to go."

"Any boy?" Noelle asked and listened eagerly for the answer. "Or do you have somebody picked out?"

Erin shook her head and picked up her embroidery. "No, silly, but I'll make sure he's perfect. When he kisses me, he'll know I'm wonderful and marry me, but not before I go to lots of balls and parties."

"I can't wait to start going to parties," Noelle said. "I'm going to dance all night and leave all the boys hopelessly in love with me. I'll have the most beautiful gowns and the prettiest slippers in all of South Carolina." Noelle closed her eyes and imagined herself whirling around a dance floor, a red velvet gown billowing around her.

"Me, too," Erin agreed and watched Lilly carefully.

The youngest of the cousins sighed and looked at Noelle and Erin. "I don't suppose I'll get to go to many balls and parties. Father is . . . Well, we don't have too many friends."

"Oh, you goose, you'll get invited to lots of parties. You're so pretty that all the boys will want to dance with you. Your friend Mari and I will make sure you get plenty of invitations," Erin said, trying to soothe her cousin's fears. Moving to the sofa beside her, Erin hugged Lilly. "Don't you worry, you'll have plenty to do when you're old enough."

Lilly's eyes widened, and a smile teased the corners of her mouth. "Do you really think I'm pretty?"

Noelle joined her cousins on the sofa. She, too, hugged Lilly. Lilly was the youngest and the most insecure, and because of her father's poor treatment of her she was easily the most vulnerable to self-doubt. "You'll be the belle of the ball. I promise."

Erin nodded. "She's right. You'll be the most popular girl in Charleston."

Lilly smiled at her cousins and fought back the tears. Her mother had died giving birth to her, and her father had never forgiven Lilly. She wasn't sure if her cousins knew that her father treated her abominably, and she never mentioned it, but because of her mother's tragic death and the way Jonathan Arledge treated her, Lilly didn't know if she wanted to marry.

Noelle hugged Lilly again. "One of these days we'll look back on this Christmas and laugh about our fears."

"Right." Erin laughed. "We'll also laugh about our predictions. Who knows? By the time we're old enough to go to balls and parties, we may be in the midst of an awful war."

"Oh, Erin, don't say such a thing. My father's sure that war won't come." Lilly gazed innocently at Erin. "Everything will be all right."

Erin and Noelle exchanged glances. They both knew Lilly was naive and unfortunately believed everything her father said. War would be hard on her, particularly since her father was bound to remain loyal to King George.

"Well, sugar, I'm sure that whatever happens, it won't affect us very much." Erin leaned back and stared into the fire, wondering if she really believed what she had said. According to her father, war was inevitable, and Charleston would probably be an embattled city. Though she wondered how the three of them would survive during the conflict, she smiled to reassure her cousins.

Noelle patted Lilly's hand. "Lilly, we'll be safe and

sound. Charleston is a fortified city. Why, look at the batteries, and there are the two forts. Don't worry."

Lilly glanced at her cousins and smiled again. Their mothers and hers were sisters. Two of the sisters had married brothers—her own mother and Noelle's. Lilly wondered if Noelle missed her mother as much as she did. She suspected she did. "Well, if you really think so."

Breathing a sigh of relief, Noelle looked into the fire. War would come, no doubt. Realistically, any one or all of them could be killed, but she refused to think pessimistically. "Look, let's make a pact. If war does come to South Carolina, we'll all meet when it's over and celebrate."

"That's a wonderful idea," Erin agreed and cheered up considerably. "By then we'll all be married and probably have babies and our own homes. Won't that be wonderful?"

"I don't know about having babies and being married, but I'll always want us to be together." Lilly hugged her doll and thought for a minute. "We'll have a big party. Promise?"

The three girls promised, taking an oath they often used.

Noelle thought of her future. What kind of man would she marry? He'd be a strong man, firmly on the side of the Colonies, handsome, and brave. With a sense of exhilaration, she closed her eyes and tried to picture her true love. Her little girl's heart saw a tall, dark, wonderful man riding a tremendous stallion.

Would her dreams come true? Would her cousins' dreams come true?

CHAPTER
1

**October 1780
Backcountry South Carolina**

NOELLE ARLEDGE STIRRED, OPENED HER EYES, AND GLANCED about. What had awakened her? Had she actually heard a horse whinny or only dreamed it? Moonlight poured through the window, forming four bright rectangles on the wedding ring quilt that covered her. Rubbing her fingers across the neat seams, she concentrated on re-creating in her mind the noise that had disturbed her.

There *was* no noise. The crickets weren't chirping, and the frogs weren't croaking. The night was too quiet. She sat up slowly.

Peering out the window, she saw nothing extraordinary in the side yard, but she couldn't see past the huge cedar tree near the front of the house. She climbed out of her fluffy feather bed and tiptoed across the room to the corner where her loaded musket stood. Then she heard what sounded like muffled footsteps on the sandy path in front of the house.

Noelle hugged the cold steel of the musket and listened anxiously. Could it be Mandy returning to the big house? No, she reasoned, Mandy would make more noise, maybe call out to reassure her.

She eased open her bedroom door and waited. A trace of smoke taunted her. Smoke! The smell was different from the sweet smell of pine logs sprinkled with fresh rosemary that she always burned in the parlor fireplace. Fear clutched

6

her heart, and she leaned against the doorjamb for support. She breathed deeply, trying to determine what was burning; the smell seemed to be of burning oil or grease rather than wood.

Barefoot, Noelle crept down the enclosed staircase, easing her feet down onto the edges of the timeworn steps and carefully avoiding the creaky third one from the bottom. She stopped and listened when she reached the ground floor.

She knew she'd heard horses. Someone had ridden into the yard. Outside, somewhere among the tall boxwood hedges, an enemy lurked, shrouded in darkness. In up-country South Carolina, people sometimes couldn't tell friend from foe, especially now during the War for Independence, but friends didn't arrive in the middle of the night cloaked in silence.

Last month a fierce battle had been fought at Kings Mountain, little more than a day's ride away. Nobody knew exactly where the British were now, since Colonel Ferguson, the British leader, had been killed. For all Noelle knew, British soldiers could be standing outside her door.

Closing her eyes, she prayed silently that the trespassers would not turn out to be the British soldiers.

Noelle touched the smooth wood of her father's door and hesitated. It would squeak if she opened it; it always did. She decided to use the door to the keeping room—a small sitting room—instead. Almost wishing for some sound to shatter the unnerving quiet, for Mandy to drop a dish or pan, she wiped the perspiration from her forehead with the soft sleeve of her nightgown and listened to the eerie silence.

Except for Mandy, her servant, Noelle was alone in the house. She hoped her maid was safe. Mandy loved possum stew and often checked the traps before going to bed. The old slave would be terrified if she found men skulking outside, planning their attack at midnight on a house that stood more than a mile from its nearest neighbor. She was probably hiding under her bed or behind a bush in the woods. She would have been useless in a situation like this anyway. Mandy was scared of her shadow and too old to be much protection, but she was good company.

Noelle scolded herself for conjuring up trouble, and directed her attention to the problem at hand. Until this moment, she had never felt isolated. Why hadn't she insisted that Mandy move into the main house?

She wished she could see, but the stairwell was couched between the master bedroom and the keeping room. No air stirred, no light seeped in, and no noise penetrated the silence. Noelle's lungs burned inside her heaving chest. Her tongue felt as dry as a cotton boll, and her stomach convulsed into a hard knot as she waited.

Why didn't someone move or speak? she wondered. Time crawled forward, but to Noelle it seemed that hours must have passed since she heard the horse nicker. The urge to abandon herself to the encroaching panic grew stronger. She fought the desire to scream at the intruders to show themselves, to step out of the shadows, to make their purpose known.

The heavy musket hung like the muzzle of a cannon across her arms, so she rested its barrel against the floor while she attempted to formulate a plan. She'd be of no use if she fainted.

For an instant she tried to convince herself that she had imagined the noise, but she knew better. Noelle considered herself a realistic young woman, and her sensible approach to life often made her the object of unkind remarks. She remembered when . . . Noelle shook her head to rid herself of the intrusive memories. How could she have allowed her mind to wander when her life might be in danger?

Sam and Lard and the other servants would have raised a ruckus if they'd been here. As overseer, Lard made sure they were prepared for almost anything. They were always alert to the dangers of living on the edge of civilization and they would have heard the approach of the horse—or horses—but she'd sent them all to Ash Meadow in cotton-laden wagons this afternoon. Tomorrow the slaves would process her crop along with the cotton from Ash Meadow Plantation, separating the cotton from the boll and chaff and prepare it for spinning. If it hadn't been for her pride, Noelle would have gone to Ash Meadow with them. She and Mandy could have visited John Brooks and his sister Irene for a few days. Oh well, she mused, what's done is done. It was too late to change her mind. Someone had to stay and tend the few animals that remained at Tyger Rest.

Animals? The dogs! Why hadn't the dogs barked? She pictured all five of them yapping at the hooves of horses that cantered up the road in less dangerous times, and knew with certainty that their silence emphasized the grave danger awaiting her. She had to remain calm and rational, she reminded herself sternly. Panic would destroy the little advantage she had. She touched her chest where a burning sensation seemed to have invaded her heart and lungs. Was that a noise?

Noelle almost dropped the gun. For an instant the salty taste in her mouth confused her, and then she scowled as she realized she had bitten her tongue. Carefully she tested it against her teeth and found it tender.

The burning intensified until she thought her chest would explode into flame. She gasped for air when she realized that she wasn't breathing. Steadying herself, Noelle tried to breathe evenly for a few moments. Mandy, if that's you, she scolded silently, I'll . . . I'll hug you until your ribs break, and I'll make you move into the house with me this very night.

Could it be the British? Could they have reached Tyger Rest without any warning they were headed this way? Shuddering, she envisioned a detachment of British soldiers in her yard, trampling the herb garden and shrubs and waiting for her to open the door, as she knew she must.

Minutes crept on, and Noelle knew the time had come to make a decision.

Aware that she would have only one shot, she gripped the gun tighter and prayed for a steady hand and a true aim.

Noelle held her shoulders straight and raised her chin. No damn British scoundrels were going to best Merry Noelle Arledge, no, sir. She wouldn't cower behind a closed door and let them find her cringing in a corner. Seventeen years of living out here at the end of the world, within a stone's throw of the Indians, had taught her courage if nothing else.

She raised the butt of the Charleville musket to her shoulder, uttered a silent prayer, and pressed the elbow latch with her left forearm, allowing the keeping room door to swing open. Noelle peered into the semidarkness of the room. Everything appeared to be the same as she'd left it, and nothing moved.

The silence was deathly.

Perspiration dribbled into her eyes, but she refused to relax her guard long enough to wipe it away. With a shiver she wondered where the perspiration had come from. Fear, she thought. Mustering all her courage, she lifted her chin and stepped forward with a determination born of sheer internal fortitude and nervous energy.

The keeping room seemed to be too light for the hour, but not light enough to dispel the shadows. A long rectangle of moonlight fell on the bearskin that lay in front of the cold stone hearth. The light came from the front of the house.

Her gaze flew to the front door. It was open!

Before Noelle could raise the muzzle of the gun, the musket was snatched from her hands. Someone jerked her into an iron grasp.

"Let me go, you British dog!" Noelle bit into the hand gripping her arm. Tasting once again the salty flavor of blood, she kicked with all her might. Her foot did little harm, but since the bite had drawn blood, it must have hurt. She dug her teeth deeper into the smooth skin.

Abruptly the hold loosened, and she bolted across the

room to freedom. Trying to stay out of reach of her assailant, she edged along the stone lip of the fireplace, toward the dining room, hesitating only long enough to pick up the poker. If she reached the woods, she could escape. The cold iron of the poker comforted her somewhat and bolstered her courage enough to allow her to go on. Since she knew her way around, she might have the advantage even in the dark, if she didn't stumble or hesitate.

Along the walls of the room, flickering shadows puzzled her. Torches. How many soldiers waited outside? In the light of the torches she could see several dark forms huddled near the front door. She darted around the tilt-top table, scattering the marble checkers on the floor, and ran toward the back of the house.

"Stop!" a deep masculine voice commanded.

In the darkness of the dining room doorway, she collided with a wall of muscle and bare skin. A hand shot out and caught her arm. With a grip like a vise, the second man forced her hand open, and the poker clattered harmlessly to the hardwood floor. Like a snake, his hand slithered around her waist until his arm encircled her tiny form.

"Stop struggling or I hurt you," he warned.

Noelle suddenly knew that fighting this captor would be useless. The strength of his grasp sapped her energy and threatened to crush her ribs, and the cold demand of his voice frightened her. She stood as still as a statue for a moment to catch her breath and plot her next move. She prayed that Mandy would stay safely away from the house until these brigands got what they wanted and left.

Twisting around, she glared at the man whose grip almost cut her in half. He towered above her, taller than the first man, and she pummeled his smooth bare chest with no obvious result.

Cherokee, she thought, realizing he was Indian and not British.

A flood of memories—horror stories—bombarded her mind. Noelle grew even more still and hoped he wouldn't mistake her quivering for an escape attempt. Mandy's whispered conversations with Cook about women who had been captured, about the shame they suffered, came to mind although Noelle should never have heard the gossip. She wished he were British. At least the British weren't savages, as this barbarian apparently was.

"Let go of me, you beast," she ordered in the sternest voice she could muster under the circumstances and wondered if he could understand her words. "Unhand me this instant."

He said nothing but dragged her to the front door. Noelle reached out, grabbed the frame, and hung on until her fingers bled, all the while screaming at her captor. The Indian cursed, jerked her hands away, and flung her through the front door. Her momentum carried her across the wide veranda, down the steps, and into the yard. He followed and drew her roughly into his arms. Then, in response to a nod of his head, several braves threw torches onto the roof of the house and some of the barns.

"No! Oh, God, please help me," Noelle screamed, kicking once again and fighting to free herself. She pounded on his chest and flailed her arms and legs violently, but to no avail. "Stop it. I'll kill you. I'll kill you for this."

As the fire gnawed into the roof, she slowly stopped struggling. Fighting seemed useless now. A small army would be needed to douse the hellish flames that danced along the roof like satanic marionettes. Noelle felt her heart go numb with the agony of watching her heritage being converted into blackened embers.

Suddenly she was glad her father wasn't here to see this. Then her mind turned to Mandy. Noelle glanced furtively around for the slave, but knew the old woman had probably hidden in the woods when she saw the Indians—*if* she'd seen them before they saw her and was still alive.

The acrid smell of smoke filled the air, and ashes erupted into the midnight sky, mounting the chill wind that swept up the slanted roof of her home and winking out before falling harmlessly to the damp ground.

Soot consumed the cool night air like a ravening dragon from a child's tale. Noelle blinked hard to keep it from her eyes and mopped at it with her free hand, smearing it across her pale cheeks until she resembled a brave painted for war. The roiling smoke poured down over her, a black cloud that filled her lungs, choked her, and clouded her vision with tears, blurring the figure holding her into a length of bronzed muscle, hardly distinguishable from his surroundings.

"Let me go. I'll kill you, you savage!" Noelle shrieked, fighting with all her might to wriggle free. She bit into his arm and kicked as hard as she could as the realization came to her that the Indian didn't intend to release her. Her ploy didn't work with this man as it had with the first. "I demand that you . . ." Her screams faded into the roar of the fire and wind, becoming but a minor part of the horrors surrounding her. Noelle's hair blew across her face, obstructing her view, and she tossed her head, finally flicking her long curls back across her shoulder.

The Indian lifted her and strode across the cleanly swept yard to the boxwood-bordered walkway where his dappled pony was tethered. Seemingly without effort he climbed atop the unsaddled horse, pulled her up to him, and wedged her firmly between his legs.

"You can't do this." Hoping to catch him off balance, Noelle pitched forward and tried to slip off, but his iron grasp merely tightened. Even though they were sitting atop a horse, the boxwoods dwarfed them, and Noelle reached out and grabbed the thickest limb she could find. Holding on with every ounce of her strength, she tried to pull herself off the pony and scamper out of his reach.

"Stop that or I beat you," came the calm response to her actions.

Noelle stopped. Nobody had ever beaten her or even threatened to do so with such determination. Though she was courageous, she wasn't foolhardy, and she let go of the boxwood limb. This man meant every word; he wouldn't hesitate a second before beating her if it suited his purpose. Indians were known for their brutality, at least in the stories Noelle had heard, which told of their extremely brutal treatment of women, white women particularly.

The moon abandoned her. She glanced at the sky and watched the moon slip behind a wisp of a cloud, and then, as if it had given up completely, it went behind a huge thunderhead.

Why, oh, why, had she sent the servants to Ash Meadow? she wondered, feeling the weight of desperation settle on her shoulders like a wet woolen cloak. But Noelle refused to wallow in despair, and her natural optimism rebounded.

Her determination had suffered a blow but hadn't died completely. She could defeat this barbarian if she thought about it long enough under less frightening circumstances.

Noelle shivered. Her flannel gown lent little protection against the October night air, and less against the Indian who held her against his hard body. His arm beneath her breasts cut off her breath as effectively as the tree limb that had once knocked her off her runaway pony. She wriggled and squirmed in his grasp, trying to find a way to breathe without falling to the ground, but his grip tightened, and she gave up the fight. She'd find another way to escape, to outsmart him.

"Release her, Soaring Eagle," came a deep masculine voice of authority from behind them.

Relief flooded over her. She'd been rescued. Noelle twisted around and peered over the Indian's shoulder to see who spoke.

Astride a tall black horse, the man sat as stiff and erect as the sword extending from his right hand. In the firelight, she saw that he had an angry face, a face that exuded fury almost as frightening as that of the Cherokee called Soaring Eagle.

A Redcoat! She glanced around the yard. He was an

officer with no troops to back up his command, unless others were hidden in the shrubbery.

Hopes that had risen with the demand for her release wilted like roses on a hot day. His coat, the scarlet wool of the British army, told her that he was not her protector. He might be her captor.

"The woman is mine," Soaring Eagle said without loosening his grip. "Leave us."

"No."

Noelle stared at the soldier. His single word conveyed a determination she had never seen in a man. He dismounted and, with his long scarlet coat emphasizing his height, strode to face Soaring Eagle.

"I do not wish to anger you, Soaring Eagle." Flames reflected in the man's nearly black eyes, and the square set of his jaw suggested a stubborn streak that might rival Noelle's. His piercing gaze never ventured from the Indian's eyes, as if he were daring Soaring Eagle to defy his authority. "Leave the girl with me. You've done enough damage tonight."

"The woman with golden curls will be woman of Soaring Eagle." Apparently not intimidated by the red coat of the British officer, Soaring Eagle glared back at the soldier."

"I won't permit it." Sheathing his sword, the soldier strode forward a few steps and folded his arms across his broad chest. "We'll discuss this matter. Now."

Soaring Eagle glared at the tall soldier for a moment, motioned to an Indian standing nearby, and handed Noelle down to him, then dismounted. "Do not release her. She bite—like snake."

The soldier waited until Soaring Eagle reached him and then spoke to him in low, threatening tones. Noelle strained to hear, but she couldn't understand what was being said. The roar of the flames and wind drowned out the Redcoat's voice.

The wind whipped the tail of her nightgown around her ankles, and a cold rain began to fall. Thank God, she thought, the rain would douse the flames and save most of the house. Her gaze left the deliberating men momentarily and scanned the rooftops to assess the damage. Too little rain came too late to do any good.

Soaring Eagle turned to glare at her. Noelle's wet hair stuck to her face, and, wishing she could hear, she raked it back with her fingers and wiped the water from her eyes. She resented them both—they seemed to be bartering for possession of her as if she were a hen or sow.

From her vantage point, Noelle could see that the officer stood several inches taller than the Indian. The two men argued in Cherokee, and she didn't know the language, so she understood none of the discussion. She leaned forward, but felt the Indian's grip on her arm tighten menacingly and relaxed.

Minutes passed, and the voices grew louder, emphasized by expansive gestures. Both men turned occasionally to look at Noelle. The longer the argument lasted, the more she felt that Soaring Eagle would win. At any moment an arrow would pierce the heart of the British officer, and her chances of escape would dissolve as quickly as the sugar in her morning tea.

After some time Soaring Eagle stepped into the shadows. Noelle squinted as she tried to see what he was doing. The Cherokee crossed his arms, and his stance indicated his fury at the British officer, but he made no aggressive signal. The Indian began to pace, occasionally stopping to glower at her. His face contorted with rage, giving him so violent an appearance that Noelle shrank farther into the grasp of her captor.

When the men parted, Soaring Eagle strode toward her. Apparently the Indian's claim prevailed, since the soldier had no men to force the Indians to do his will. Noelle felt her hopes melt away, for although she hated the British, she feared the Cherokee more.

The tall Cherokee reached for her and held her close in his arms for a few seconds despite her squirming protests.

Noelle's muscles froze. Her fate had been set as the two men had bartered for her life. Well, she thought, Merry Noelle Arledge would not be handled this way without a fight. She wouldn't give up until there was no hope.

Before Soaring Eagle knew what she was doing, Noelle reached for his face and raked her hands down both cheeks until the blood ran in streaks. Holding her with one arm, he jerked her hands away from his face and glared at her. A glance at the British officer seemed to be all that restrained the Indian from beating her.

"Our time is not to be." Soaring Eagle lifted her, turned, and strode toward the officer, hesitated, and then handed her into the soldier's arms. "Careful. This one dangerous. She has teeth and claws like wildcat."

Snuggling in the relative safety of the officer's arms, Noelle almost smiled in exultation. He might be British, but at least he wasn't savage. Still quivering with fear from her close call, she clung to the soldier. If the officer had arrived a few minutes later, Noelle would have been kidnapped—or worse.

At least she was alive. Now she would have to look for Mandy. The old slave was probably terrified. Her fear of Indians seemed reasonable now, even though Noelle had always chided her servant for her childish feelings. For many years the Cherokee had lived in harmony with the settlers.

Drake Hastings stood holding the small, shivering girl close, trying to comfort her as best he could. He had no experience with children. He'd arrived in time to avert a disaster, for Soaring Eagle had intended to take her with him. Her life would have been no better than that of a slave.

For a moment he'd thought that Soaring Eagle would strike her. Drake admired the girl's spunk. Not many women would stand up to a renegade like Soaring Eagle and bite or scratch him as this one had. Despite her size, this girl could probably handle almost any man.

As the girl's quivering subsided a little, she relaxed

against him, and he adjusted his position to see her face better. His hand brushed her full breasts, and he stopped suddenly. Damn, he thought. She was older than he had thought.

Raindrops frosted her eyelashes and shimmered on her sensual mouth in the flickering light of the dying fire as she turned questioning eyes to him. Her face was as pale as new snow in the moonlight. High cheekbones, a deep widow's peak, and a jutting chin formed a heart to frame the lovely face. Drawn irresistibly toward her scarlet lips, he leaned forward.

Noelle's eyes opened wide. His face was so close she could feel the warmth of his breath on her cold cheeks. Entranced by his obsidian eyes, she stared at him and wondered what he intended to do with her now that he'd rescued her.

He cleared his throat, raised his head slightly, and asked in a husky voice, "Are you getting warmer?"

Though he was British and quite possibly the instigator of the raid, he had rescued her. Ignoring his question, she frowned. Rescuer he certainly was, but also guilty by association. The Indians were stirred up by the British who paid them to raid and pillage the backcountry, effectively ending the usefulness of the militia. Men who feared for their homes and families often ignored the call to battle if it would take them too far away.

Together Noelle and the soldier watched the Indians gallop noisily out of her yard and across the soft dirt of the freshly picked cotton fields until they finally disappeared down the bank of the Tyger River.

Her strength sapped by the encounter with the Indians, Noelle fell against the officer's chest, offered a silent prayer of thanks, and rested her head on his shoulder. For this moment she would ignore the color of his uniform. For this moment she would do anything he asked. For this moment she adored him and would have even if he'd been Lucifer himself. She would deal with his identity and her own mixed emotions once she was sure the Indians were truly gone.

For now she needed to locate Mandy and decide what they should do next. She wriggled from side to side, peering over his shoulder and trying to see into the edge of the woods as the officer strode toward his horse.

His hands tightened their grip, and she realized that nothing lay between her breast and his hand except her soggy flannel nightgown. A strange warmth radiated from the pit of her stomach, and color bloomed in her cheeks as she fidgeted instead of looking at him in her embarrassment. "Please put me down."

"Don't be ridiculous." He lifted her into the saddle, as if she weighed no more than a down pillow, and climbed up behind her. "Where is your family? Are they in the house? Were they . . . murdered?"

Murdered? Noelle hesitated. No, not murdered, but dead just the same. She gazed at the clouds, willing the tears not to form in her eyes and did not answer for a moment. A lump swelled in her throat, blocking any words she might have spoken.

Noelle hung on for her life, looking over his shoulder occasionally to see if the Indians were following; she didn't trust Soaring Eagle any more than Cook trusted her with an apple pie.

Her rescue seemed too easy. There had been no harsh words, no fighting, and Soaring Eagle had accepted this man's word and allowed her to leave. The officer's woolen coat scratched her face, but she didn't care. She would have gone with Lord Cornwallis himself to avoid being kidnapped by Indians.

"I . . . I have no family. My father . . ." Her voice faded as she recalled his gentle face. "My father died several weeks ago."

"What?" He stared down at her in disbelief. "You lived here alone?"

"Only for a short time." Noelle relaxed in his arms,

testing the strange touch of his beard against her cheek. Stop it, she commanded herself when she realized she liked the feel of his arms around her. This man was as much an enemy as the Indians. Color and warmth sprang anew to her cool cheeks. "I insist that you put me down."

He pulled on the reins, and the horse stopped. Rain began to fall harder, plastering her hair across her face and eyes, clouding her vision. His face, illuminated by the sizzling flames, surprised her. He was a handsome man, with high cheekbones, a straight nose, and deep-set eyes that reflected the firelight.

Admiring her courage, he gazed at her in the warm glow of the dying fire. "Look, miss, allow me to take you somewhere. Where do you wish to go?"

Noelle considered his question. Where could she go? There was nowhere. "I shall remain here."

"Like hell you will—beg pardon. How can you? Your house is aflame. Your slaves are dead or run off." He clicked the reins. "Where may I take you?"

"Dead? Mandy? No! Stop this animal!" She wriggled in his arms, beginning to panic. She couldn't leave until she knew about Mandy.

"We cannot stay here."

"We?" she repeated incredulously, knowing how the neighbors would gossip about her if they knew what had happened, although at the moment that seemed a foolish and childish concern.

"I'll take you someplace where you will be safe and someone can take care of you." He prodded the horse, and the animal moved forward.

"No. I . . . I have servants," she lied, knowing that only Mandy needed to be accounted for. "Besides, I can take care of myself."

Drake nodded. He understood her desire to assure herself of the safety of her people, and he didn't doubt her ability to take care of herself. If Soaring Eagle had succeeded in kidnapping her, the Cherokee would have gained more trouble than he'd earned. Drake didn't relish the idea of forcing her to leave when she didn't want to go. "We'll see about the servants and then find someplace for you to stay. With a little work you can live here again."

The fire had eaten into the roof of the main house, and many of the barns and cabins lay in smoldering embers. Anger welled up in her, and she sat erect, staring at the damage and thinking of her dear father.

"Too bad it didn't rain sooner," Noelle said wistfully, remembering how he had loved the house. "Papa and Sam worked hard building our house. See the flat boards? They were hewn from the timber by the river. Our house was the first around these parts not to be a chinked log cabin."

"He did a fine job." Drake stopped the horse by the blacksmith's barn. "Run in there. It looks dry. I'll find you some shoes and a cloak."

He dismounted and helped Noelle to the ground in front of a wide barn door. She ran into the barn and turned to watch him as he busied himself with his horse. When he returned with the cloak and shoes, she would go to find Mandy.

Lightning split the sky, and Noelle backed away from the door and sat down. Rain fell harder, but the rough-hewn timbers of the blacksmith's barn provided some protection against the elements. The storm grew louder and closer until the lightning and thunder came almost simultaneously.

Wind whistled through the building, rustling the leaves outside and shaking the walls and roof. From her vantage point, sitting on the hay, she could see slashes of lightning fly across the sky as if the clouds were taking sides in the Revolution.

Made of split logs, the building was better than nothing and was dry. The fireplace on one side still smoldered from the workday but provided little warmth. In her damp gown, Noelle shivered and was almost delighted when the officer came in and threw a log on the fire.

She slid nearer the fireplace as the fire warmed up

slightly, and she pulled her fingers through her hair to help it dry faster. The knowledge that she had been close to death sobered her, maybe aged her as she thought about it, and a shiver touched her slender body.

"I am Captain Drake Hastings of the British army." The officer bowed slightly and gazed down at her. He knew that big trouble sometimes came in small packages.

"Captain Hastings, I am Noelle Arledge," she answered, forcing a tight smile to her lips. Her mind wasn't prepared for idle chatter from this officer. She lifted her chin proudly and wished he weren't so tall.

"Did he . . . Were you harmed in any way, Miss Arledge?" He paused, as if waiting for her to answer a specific unasked question.

"No. Only my property has been damaged," she replied, trying desperately to remain calm. "I am merely tired and cold. I have to find Mandy. She must be terrified."

Relieved, Drake nodded. He felt a little more like questioning her now that he knew she wouldn't burst into tears or collapse in hysterics. "I ran into an old black woman in the woods. When I could calm her down, she told me the devil had come to Tyger Rest. She refused to return with me."

Noelle sighed with relief and smiled more naturally. Mandy was safe. "That sounds like my Mandy. She'll show up for breakfast."

Feeling her tension ease a little, Noelle drew back, for the first time alone and face to face with a British officer. She scrambled to her feet. Her pride demanded that she meet this soldier on equal ground, though she stood more than a foot shorter in her bare feet. For a long time, they stared out into the dark, rumbling night, watching the rain soak into the earth until it would hold no more, and then deep puddles began to form.

Dawn neared, and the storm raged on, the thunder grumbling deep and long as if it were unwilling to give up and pass by. Fatigue forced her to sit down again when the soldier walked out the door. She lay back against the hay, staring at the rough crossbeams overhead. Exhaustion crept into every muscle and bone until she could hardly keep her eyes open any longer. She decided to rest her eyes for a moment and, within seconds, dozed off.

When she awoke, it was still dark, and the storm lingered. In the flashes of lightning, she saw a man squatting inside the shack. He said nothing, but seemed to stare at her as she slept.

His dark form was invisible, except during the brief light provided by the storm, and she saw that he was the man who had rescued her. What was his name? Hastings? She said it again in her mind: Drake Hastings—a nice name.

Noelle sat up, crossing her arms over her bosom. "What do you want? Why are you staring at me?"

"Am I?" Drake refused to meet her gaze. He *had* been staring. He had been about to cover her with the cloak he'd found when he noticed the gentle rise and fall of her bosom as she slept. The sight of the lovely young woman, innocent and alone in the world, touched him more than he wanted it to. "I apologize . . . Miss Arledge."

Noelle flushed and cast her gaze down. After recovering from the way his voice seemed to caress her name, she looked back at him and studied his face. With hair as black as the sky on a cloudy night and eyes almost as dark, he stared ahead, as if he wanted to avoid her eyes. His skin told of hours spent in the southern sunlight, and the dark color flattered his angular features. She sensed an anger in him, brimming and roiling like a caldron of broth over a fire.

Vacillating between anger for the crimes committed against her and gratitude to him for his daring rescue, she said, "I'm sorry to have caused you so much trouble."

He gazed at her a moment, his eyes narrowing beneath his heavy brow. "You have no reason to apologize. What kind of man do you think I am? Do you believe I would ride away, leaving a defenseless girl to the Indians?"

Noelle didn't answer. She turned away and considered

the situation. What kind of man? The kind who instigates a raid on helpless women. Did Captain Hastings happen along, as he said? Or was he there all along, lurking in the shadows, waiting for the outcome of the raid?

She had no answers, but she felt safer with him than with Soaring Eagle. Captain Hastings rose and went to the stall where his horse now stood. After several minutes he returned with his saddle.

"Here, lie down, put your head on this, and rest. You've had a terrible night." He placed the saddle on the floor near the fire and put her cloak down beside it. "I'm sorry there is no bed."

Noelle watched him make a place for her to lie. "And you? Where will you rest, Captain?"

"I must remain alert." He sat down by the fire and motioned to her. "Go ahead. Lie down, Miss Arledge. I shall protect you."

Wondering what she should do, Noelle decided that she must rest before she could even think clearly. The fire had dried her nightgown, and she lay down trying to cover her ankles and bare feet. Silently she thanked Mandy for the yards of cloth in the nightgown, which provided her with some decorum in this embarrassing situation.

"Captain Hastings," she began, "how did you happen by my house? I didn't realize the British army was so near."

"I am an intermediary between His Majesty's army and the Loyalists in this territory. On this trip, however, I was to contact Soaring Eagle."

"I see. To initiate more attacks on the Colonists, I presume." Noelle saw that her words surprised him and was glad. For the first time in hours she had bested the enemy.

Drake Hastings looked at her. Her words were very close to accurate, but his orders were secret. Somehow serving his country had seemed like a noble task before he left London, but now, when that service threatened the life of such an innocent as well as thousands like her, he wondered if there wasn't another way.

He had no idea how long she had been alone with Soaring Eagle and his renegades, but she denied being harmed. Her nightgown remained intact, but that signified nothing. Drake knew that pain didn't always originate from a visible wound.

"Sleep now. I haven't much time, and I can't guarantee that Soaring Eagle won't change his mind. He didn't give you up willingly. I can't be sure he won't come back."

Noelle gazed at him through a flutter of eyelashes, partially closed and feigning sleep. One question burned in her mind and refused to remain unasked. "What did you say to him to obtain my release?"

Drake had hoped she wouldn't ask that question, although he knew the possibility of slipping by without answering it was slim. He could think of no reasonable explanation, especially in view of Soaring Eagle's plans for her. Only the truth would suffice.

"I told him the only thing that would ensure your freedom," he replied, wondering how she would react to his explanation. "I told him we were betrothed."

CHAPTER
2

"BETROTHED? WHY WOULD YOU TELL HIM SUCH A THING?" Noelle sat up and stared at him, astonished by his revelation. The blacksmith's barn felt suddenly warm, as if the color that sprang to her face emitted heat stronger than the fire.

"Soaring Eagle and I . . . Well, I have some influence with him, but unless I could give him a good reason for releasing you, he would simply have kidnapped you." Gauging her response to his words, Drake gazed at her face, heart-shaped and fraught with emotion. She seemed too young and innocent to be alone out here at the frontier during this dreadful war.

Her skin was like fine porcelain, and her nose turned up slightly beneath eyes of sapphire fringed with gold. Her face was well shaped, not quite as angular as her wet hair had first suggested, and framed by honey-colored curls that hung in a tangle to her waist. If he had met her at a reasonable hour for callers, her hair would have been twisted into a tight bun, and he would never have seen its true beauty. He didn't doubt that she was beautiful with her hair pulled up, but he loved the soft appearance that made her look very young. "How old are you?"

"Nearly eighteen. My birthday is on Christmas Day." Noelle thought his question a peculiar switch of topic and wasn't ready to abandon the subject. "You changed the subject. How did you convince Soaring Eagle that we were betrothed?"

"He has no reason to doubt me. I never lie to him." Drake avoided her question as gracefully as possible without seeming to be evasive. His gaze rested on her upturned face, and he wondered how much he could tell her without alienating her completely.

"But surely he must know that we've had no opportunity to know each other. You're from England, and I've never been there." Noelle considered Captain Hastings's profile. She admired his handsome face, with its sharp bone structure and the thought wrinkles etched in the sun-bronzed skin above his thick dark brows. His eyes were deep brown and authoritative. Yes, a quick glance at Captain Hastings instilled confidence. Perhaps that was why he had been chosen for this mission to the Cherokees.

"As I said, Soaring Eagle has no reason to doubt my word." He stood up, placed another log across the andirons, and looked down at her. Her sharp eyes seemed to miss nothing, and Drake wanted to end this conversation, divulging as little as possible to her. "Now rest. We still have to get you someplace safe."

Noelle hardly heard him. The warmth of the fire and her companion's vigilance provided an atmosphere of safety that lulled her senses until she relaxed in the soft, fragrant hay. Her eyelids closed, and she was rapidly losing the battle with sleep. The exhaustion of her traumatic evening and the lack of sleep took their toll.

When Noelle awoke, Drake Hastings was still sitting by the fire. Her eyes met his, and she wanted to like him. Papa would have liked Hastings—if he weren't a British soldier. He had been so kind and had saved her life, but he *was* a British soldier. Damn this war, she thought.

Dawn began to break across the horizon, sending ribbons of orange and gray slicing through the parting ebony clouds. Fog rose in smoky wisps above puddles of clear rainwater and joined the mist that shrouded the scarlet and purple clarity of the sunrise. Thunder still rumbled in the distance, but the morning sun promised to chase away the fog and clouds before midday.

Noelle and Hastings walked toward the kitchen without conversation. She didn't want to talk about the Revolution. She didn't feel like chattering with him about her friends and acquaintances to see if they might know some of the same people. Inane conversation seemed out of place between them. She didn't want to get to know him. She didn't want to care about him. She mustn't, if she intended to help the Patriots, and years ago she had vowed to do so.

Her earliest recollections of the British were tainted with her father's hatred. The Revenue Act and the Stamp Act were thoroughly discussed on cool evenings before the fire as the neighborhood men passed around the churchwarden, each man smoking the long kaolin pipe for a few seconds and then handing it to the next man, who would break off the used tip and take his turn. It didn't matter that the repressive laws were later repealed; the insults and the damage had been done. Then had come the Townshend Acts, which added fervor to the summer evening discussions on the porch in 1767. Noelle was hardly more than a baby, but she remembered the anger, and Charles Arledge, with his own rage, had always kept the memory of those discussions alive in his daughter's mind.

Her father and their neighbor, John Brooks, had been members of the General Provincial Committee in 1775, and even though the concerns of the backcountry farmers were different from those of the rich Charleston planters, their indignation had inspired them to become unified into the Provincial Congress, which enforced the Resolutions and Nonimportation resolutions of the Continental Congress.

Whenever the men gathered on the porch, Noelle sat by the front door and listened. During the winter she hid in the stairwell to hear—until Mandy found her and ushered her off to bed. The anger over the arrival of British troops in Boston swelled into fury. The rage of her fellow Carolinians nested in her breast and flourished like a fledgling eagle—

helpless today but a threat tomorrow. She had vowed then to find a way to make a difference in this war.

Tomorrow had arrived for Noelle.

With conflicting emotions Noelle returned her attention to the man walking beside her. She did care about him, in spite of his heritage and loyalties. He had saved her from a threat to which another British officer had subjected her by striking a deal with the Cherokee Indians. Captain Hastings was different from the others—he just had to be.

Noelle left him surveying the yard and entered her damaged house. Knowing that he awaited her return, she ran up the stairs and into her bedroom. Her feather mattress looked damp and heavy, but she paid almost no attention. Dressed for sleep, she could hardly do what this day would require of her.

With a moment's hesitation Noelle opened the wardrobe and instinctively felt the fabric of her remaining gown for moisture. Satisfied that it was reasonably dry and safe from exposure, she stepped into a chemise and then withdrew a muslin petticoat trimmed with box pleating and slipped it over her head. She grabbed the royal blue chintz gown and put it on over the petticoat. While she looked for slippers, her fingers flew along the row of hooks and eyes that ran down the front bodice.

Donning black leather shoes lined with linen, she glanced at the pattens under the wardrobe and sighed. With as much rain as had fallen during the night, she would probably need them. Thank goodness Mandy had cleaned them yesterday, Noelle thought as she reached for them. The paths close to the house were hard from constant use, but she needed to walk to all her buildings today and assess the damage. The wooden platforms would come in handy in some of the muddier spots.

She hurried down the steps and out the back door. Drake stood where she had left him, staring across the fields at the V-shaped rock formation at the edge of the forest. He glanced at her and smiled.

Daylight settled across the sky in a somber gray, obliterating the colorful evidence of dawn that had been promised earlier. As they walked through the yard behind the kitchen, rain began to fall, and as they approached the weathered building, hail pelted them. Squealing from the sting of the ice pellets, Noelle ran for cover on the back porch and reached it steps ahead of Drake.

"I can't believe this is happening," Noelle called, laughing breathlessly and brushing the ice from her shoulders and hair. "I thought the day would be bright and clear."

Drake gazed at the horizon and noted the lighter clouds that had gathered there. "I'd bet everything I own that the weather clears up before noon."

"And just what do you own that is worth a wager?" Noelle asked with a curiosity she didn't quite understand. Whatever it was would be beyond her reach, even if she ignored the sin of gambling and accepted the wager.

"I own a—never mind. Suppose we make this wager worth something priceless."

"Priceless? And where would I find something priceless to wager?" Noelle gazed at him suspiciously. In the past, she'd been a good judge of people, even as a child, and she rather liked Drake Hastings. Had she been wrong? Could he be a thief and a robber? The sensible Noelle asked, noting that the hail was stopping, "And if I did have something priceless to wager, why would I risk losing it to you?"

Drake laughed at the petulant pose she assumed. Like many women, she considered only worldly goods to be priceless. "I refer to friendship."

"Friendship?" Noelle repeated with a question in her voice. His soft brown eyes held hers until she could look at him no longer without blushing. She reached down beside the steps where the wild mint grew and picked several sprigs before glancing at him again. "Tell me how we can wager something that we don't have?"

"If you win," he explained and wrapped his arms around

the wooden porch post, "I'll walk away and never come back. If I win, we'll be friends."

"Friends with a British officer? Do you take me for a fool?" Noelle's thoughts were scurrying like squirrels preparing for a cold winter. What would her neighbors think? What would Mandy think? Of course, if she and Hastings became friends, Noelle might be in a position to find out British secrets, but to whom would she tell them? "How could I ever explain a friendship with a man I hardly know who's a British officer, on top of everything else?"

Drake's eyes twinkled. He knew now that she'd taken the bait. A young woman who lived alone in an isolated area like this would have to be a gambler at heart. "Of course, if you're afraid of losing."

"Wait. Not so fast." Noelle glanced at the lightening horizon and chewed her lip. There was a good chance he was right, but with the temperature rising and the air growing humid, she might win by a few minutes. The clouds didn't appear to be moving very quickly. She smiled and batted her eyelashes coquettishly. "May the better person win. You, Captain Hastings, have a bet."

Laughter lines crinkled the corners of Drake's eyes as he grinned at her spunk. Since she'd put on the blue frock, her eyes appeared to be an even deeper blue than before. "Well, miss, noon will be the telling. Friend or foe?"

Her gaze darted to the horizon, and she willed the clouds to slow their approach to protect her investment. Noelle didn't know if she could be friends with a sworn enemy, but she would never welsh on a wager. "I say foe."

"And I predict that before the day is out, we'll be fast friends," Drake said confidently, wondering what a friendship with this Colonial beauty would be like. For a moment, his thoughts ran ahead to where such a friendship might lead in normal times—to a sweet shared kiss. Recognizing the spunky young woman in her, he also envisioned the resounding slap that would be the likely result of a stolen kiss.

"Mandy's here. She's probably frightened. When she sees who we are she'll come out." Noelle thought Mandy might be hiding in the loft over the separate kitchen cabin, waiting until this officer left. Once she thought she heard a muffled sound coming from upstairs but couldn't be sure. When she glanced at Drake, his pensive gaze caused her to avert her eyes once more to avoid the blush that would surely have resulted from continued eye contact. "Well, I have a lot to do today, and here I am dawdling."

Drake took her lead and looked around. A horseshoe lay on the edge of the porch, and he reached down to pick it up. He toyed with the horseshoe, twirling it around in his strong hands while he thought of a way to continue the conversation that she obviously intended to end. "From my observation your house needs considerable repair. The walls remain, but much of the roof is burned. You were fortunate it rained last night."

"Yes, it seems so." Looking at the roof in the dim light, she saw the gaping hole over much of the dormitory room that had been built for a large family that had never materialized because of her mother's early death. The smell of smoke clung to the house, the oak that shaded the porch was scorched badly on one side, and ashes shrouded the grass like a dull gray snowfall. Noelle turned away, not wanting to see the extent of the destruction, not trusting her emotions in front of this stranger. "Let me fix some breakfast. Neither of us is likely to be in a hurry to accomplish our tasks on an empty stomach."

Noelle opened the door and went inside. Her glance confirmed that if Mandy was here, she had taken refuge in the loft. After stirring the coals in the fireplace and adding a log, Noelle moved to the cupboard and prepared to make breakfast. She cut slices of ham, placed them in an iron skillet, and stood it on a trivet in the hearth. While the ham sizzled, she cut thick slices of bread and spread them with butter.

"You appear to know what you're doing," Drake remarked, watching her place the bread in a toasting rack and stand it before the fire.

"I should," Noelle replied, slicing an apple into the ham skillet and sprinkling cinnamon over it. "I've watched Cook do this often enough."

"Watching doesn't necessarily make one a good cook," Drake observed and inhaled the sweet aroma of the apples and cinnamon. "Although in your case it seems to have worked."

Noelle smiled and stirred the apples. "Sit down, Captain. I'm almost done here."

With a final swirl of the wooden spoon in the frying apples, Noelle sighed. She took two pewter plates from the cupboard and laid them on the table. Between them she placed the platter of steaming ham, apples, and toast. "Help yourself while I get some milk."

Noelle scurried out to the smokehouse and down into the vegetable cellar. She dipped cool milk into her pail and hurried back to the kitchen. When she returned, Drake was eating hungrily.

"This is the finest meal I've tasted since I returned . . . came to the Colonies," he corrected hastily and turned his attention to his breakfast.

For a moment Noelle gazed at him, wondering if she'd just heard a slip of the tongue or if he'd simply erred in his choice of words. Something about him drew her to him, and yet there seemed to be a secret part of him, a guarded little area that he protected fiercely. Suddenly she was intrigued. She was interested in him merely for the information she might obtain from him, she rationalized. After all, she had vowed to aid the cause of the Patriots, and a friendship with a well-placed British officer might offer numerous opportunities to gather details that could be beneficial to the Colonial army. A smile teased the corners of her mouth and, if possible, her nose turned up a bit more.

"Why, thank you, Captain Hastings," she answered and fluttered her eyelashes. "I'm certain this is a mean breakfast after all the traveling you've done. Surely you're just teasing me because I'm a simple country girl."

Drake studied her face for a minute and grimaced inwardly. She hadn't seemed the sort of girl who'd flirt with any man who happened by, and she'd made it plain enough that she wasn't really pleased at his presence. For a moment he thought she might be ingratiating herself for a reason, but he decided that was probably his imagination. He had, after all, saved her life. He spooned the last of the slightly tart apples into his mouth and returned her smile. "Thank you for a fine meal. I'll look around before I go."

"That won't be necessary, I'm sure." Noelle rose and removed his plate. Mandy could wash it later while Noelle gathered a few things to take with her.

Drake strode to the door and opened it. He hesitated. Her heart-shaped face seemed to draw him, but he resisted. "Nevertheless, I'll make sure everything's safe."

Noelle watched him leave and sank into her chair. Dropping her face into her hands, she wondered what she'd gotten herself into. This man was not a foolish farm boy from backcountry Carolina; he was sophisticated and well traveled.

She heard a noise and whirled around to find Mandy descending the ladder from the loft. "Mandy! I'm so glad—"

"Never thought I'd see the day the British army be settin' at my table," Mandy scolded as she ambled across the room. "Your pa be turnin' in his grave."

Noelle rolled her eyes and shook her head in consternation. "He saved my life, Mandy. Was I to send him away hungry?"

"He coulda et on the back porch," Mandy rebuked, setting her wrinkled face in a self-righteous scowl. "Coulda et that cold corn pone Cook left. Ain't fit to set at the table with my baby."

Noelle shook her head in dismay. Mandy would never

understand why this soldier was different. "I declare, Mandy—"

Before she could finish, a knock interrupted them, and the door swung open. Drake Hastings stepped into the kitchen. "Oh, hello. I'm glad you returned safely."

"Harrumph!" Mandy snorted and turned to stoke the fire.

Smiling an apology, Noelle shrugged. "Yes, Captain Hastings?"

"I looked into the remaining slave cabins." He turned away, unable to face her for fear she'd believe he had some part in this ghastly nightmare. He'd found the cabins deserted; Soaring Eagle must have taken all the slaves with him. "I found nobody. Some of your stock is still here—a cow, a mule, a small filly, and a flock of chickens. If you wish, I'll escort you somewhere, to a neighbor's house or an inn." Drake looked around, hoping that she wouldn't choose to remain here alone. "I wouldn't like to think of you ladies alone here."

"We can manage, thank you." Noelle looked at him, hardly able to discern his features in the dim light. She had nowhere else to go. Her neighbors were in much the same situation as she; some were moving to a small town that was developing around the fort at Ninety Six.

She didn't want to like Drake Hastings—he was the enemy—but it was difficult to hate the man who had saved her life, even if he was British. And Mandy's immediate dismissal of the soldier made Noelle want to be even nicer to him.

"Miss, if you want me to stay, I will."

"No. Mandy and I will take care of each other."

"As you wish. Shall I bring in some wood?" he asked, reluctant to leave.

"No." Noelle gazed at Mandy and then looked out the window at the house. She wanted to be alone, to examine the damage. "I appreciate your kindness. I can mamage."

"Then I'll be on my way." He strode out the door and across the porch.

For a moment Noelle wanted to call him back. The isolation of Tyger Rest seemed to close in on her, but she remained silent.

He reached his horse and mounted quickly. With a broad smile and a wave, he called, "Good-bye, miss, and good luck."

Noelle bent down to pick a late-blooming marigold, then watched him ride away. She felt a strange sadness that reached farther than the damage surrounding her; it stemmed from the loss of a friendship that was forbidden because Noelle and Captain Hastings were on opposite sides during a time of war.

Twirling the single marigold stem, she caught its strong scent and heard a sound behind her. Mandy collapsed into a chair and sobbed now that the soldier had gone.

One glance at Mandy convinced Noelle that she was right to send Captain Hastings away. She'd take Mandy to Ash Meadow. Its warm security beckoned to her as the only refuge available now. John Brooks would gladly take her in.

Tears burned against the golden flutter of lashes as Noelle watched Captain Hastings ride away. She'd been taught to hate all British soldiers. She dropped the marigold, squeezed her eyes tightly shut, and refused to allow a single tear to fall. Though she was only seventeen, Noelle had witnessed—lived through—the results of war.

Almost as if it were yesterday, she remembered standing at Blackstock Road and watching her childhood friends march jauntily off to fight a war she believed in, only to return mutilated, both physically and mentally, or not return at all. The romance of war had been short-lived for Noelle. An intelligent young woman, she soon realized the glory of war quickly translated into destruction, injury, starvation, and death.

As Noelle watched a sliver of sun stretch over the horizon, she recalled her wager. Was the weather going to clear? Perhaps she hadn't seen the last of the captain after all. While Mandy worked in the kitchen, Noelle looked into each of the cabins, assessing the damage and items worth saving. Today would be a sad bu

Noelle and Mandy could go to John Brooks's p this afternoon, as soon as she could gather her belong and a few items she refused to leave behind. He wouldn't be expecting her, but he would take her in.

Noelle and John Brooks were to be married in a week.

HAPTER
3

SHIELDING HER HAIR AND CLOTHING AS MUCH AS POSSIBLE with the frilly parasol her father had brought her from Charleston, Noelle poked her head into every remaining cabin and outbuilding at Tyger Rest. The rain had dwindled off to a drizzle that threatened to cause her to lose her bet well before noon, and she cast a disgusted glance at the horizon to the west. She grimaced and continued her search, finally reaching the dog pen. Before she entered the open gate, the smell of death permeated the air. She looked around, her eyes filling with tears at the horrors she saw.

Noelle choked back the rising gall and ran out the door and into the woods. She fell to her knees and retched until her stomach muscles ached.

"Why, God? Why them?" she asked, angry with the British, the Indians, and with God for letting this happen. "They were just animals, pets."

She lay back on a bed of soft green moss skirting a large oak tree and stared at the leafy bower overhead. Tears flowed freely, obscuring her vision and releasing the rage in Noelle all over again.

Abruptly she sat up and wiped her eyes with her skirt. A smear of black scarred the bedraggled fabric, and she suddenly felt filthy. The sound of the river beckoned her. She needed a bath.

Without a moment's hesitation, she hurried to the banks ₁f the Tyger, stripped, and hung her gown on a bush. As she ⸱ ᵈed into the river, the cool water teased her ankles and then her legs. Noelle dived below the surface, submerging her body in the water and rinsing the soot and smoke from her skin and hair. The salty tears that streaked her flushed cheeks blended with the fresh stream, and she felt much better, purged and clean again, with no trace of the Indian's hands on her body. If only she could cleanse the memory from her mind as easily.

With a reluctance that tempted her to stay, she waded out of the refreshing water. Her hair hung to her waist and drizzled water down her legs; she had nothing to dry herself on except her gown.

She slipped the dress over her glistening body and started up the bank. A noise startled her, and she glanced furtively around. A short distance away, a Redcoat sat on his horse. Her heart stuttered briefly when she recognized Drake Hastings.

How much had he seen? She couldn't bring herself to ask. Noelle chose to believe that he had arrived at precisely the moment when the hem of her gown touched her ankles, covering her thoroughly.

"What are you doing here?" Noelle spoke first, unable to stand the silence any longer. "I didn't expect you back so soon."

"I've returned to help you do whatever you feel you must." He slid down from the saddle and led his horse over to where she stood. "As stubborn as you appear to be, I can't allow you to stay here alone."

"You can't allow . . ." Noelle recalled the dogs, life-less with their throats cut, and her anger manifested itself, striking out at the only possible target. "I don't know what you mean, but you can just take yourself off my land. The destruction around here is—"

"Hold on, hold on. Don't get excited. I didn't come to fight." He took her arm, and they walked toward the house. "I'm here to help."

Noelle jerked her arm away. "And what makes you think I need or want your help?"

Drake stopped and looked down into her eyes. He could have sworn they were blue when he left. Now, with her fury striking out at him, they seemed to have darkened to the lovely deep shade of the wild violets he'd seen this spring in the forest. He decided to proceed gently. "I realize you don't need or want me here, but I would like to help. You may wish to pack something heavy."

Angry as she was, Noelle couldn't argue with his logic. She wished he'd stop staring at her. "You can help if it will make you feel better. After all, this is probably all your fault anyway."

Noelle wished she could take back the words the moment they were spoken. She realized the raid wasn't his fault, but she had to lash out at the enemy somehow, and Captain Drake Hastings was here.

Drake closed his eyes briefly, trying to shut out the sight of the destruction on this plantation. Yes, perhaps it was his fault to a degree, though he hadn't issued the orders to the Indians. His protest to Lord Cornwallis had been ignored, but he felt he could have stopped the attack if he'd worked hard enough. "I apologize for all my shortcomings, Miss Arledge."

His contrition surprised Noelle. She wanted a fight; nothing less than animal brutality would appease her, she thought, clenching her fists. Then she forced herself to save her energy. There was no point in wasting it on this man when she had a slave's work to do today. "Mandy's fixing dinner. It won't be much, but you can eat with us."

Noelle and Drake returned to the kitchen and sat down at the table. She nearly gagged at the sight of food after all she'd seen, but she knew Mandy well enough to know there was no chance of skipping a meal.

The old woman hovered near the fire, never getting close to Drake throughout the meal. Noelle knew that Mandy hated having a British soldier here, but there was nothing she could do about it.

After eating, Noelle and Drake buried the five dogs near

the small family plot where her parents were laid to rest. Drake did the bulk of the work, while she sat on a rock in the sun and stared.

She watched him dig. After a while he removed his shirt and wiped his brow. Tossing the shirt aside, he resumed his task. Noelle forgot her antipathy for the British and stared. With each fall of the pick, the muscles in his bare back rippled in the sunlight, fascinating her. He dug the graves deeper than she thought necessary, but she didn't question him.

After a few moments of silence he apparently felt her eyes on him and looked up at her questioningly. "Is something wrong, Miss Arledge?"

"Wrong? No, I . . . well," she stammered, "I'm thirsty and I know you must be. Let me fetch some water."

Drake nodded and resumed his task. Noelle scurried to the well and drew a bucketful of water, thankful that he hadn't noticed the warm splotches of color in her cheeks. When she returned, once again controlled and calm, she plunged the dipper into the cool well water and handed it to him.

Though Drake had done most of the work, she felt drained and worn. Burying the animals had taken most of the afternoon.

While Drake washed the perspiration from his body in the river, Noelle sat in the sun and stared across the now barren fields. Her anger was doubled by the fact that she felt so helpless. Even though she'd had a gun, she had not been able to prevent the senseless attack from taking place.

Tears of frustration stung her eyes as she acknowledged her vulnerability. One woman at the edge of civilization could hardly fend off an attack, but in this case, a man would have fared no better.

Next time the Indians would find her better prepared. Even the well-equipped British army would find her hard to deal with. Her heart was filled with resolve even though she had no solid plan. She vowed this wouldn't happen again.

She would do something to help end this war, to defeat this bloodthirsty enemy.

When she spotted Drake standing a few feet away, watching her in silence, Noelle felt her anger return in full force. "You've done your duty, and I thank you. Now get off my land."

"Let me escort—" Drake began, apparently confused by her startling change of mood.

"Never." Noelle jumped to her feet and glared at him, venting her rage again. "We don't need to be escorted by British murderers."

The moment the words were out, she regretted them, but the British officer provided the only outlet for her mounting frustrations. Drake Hastings didn't deserve such treatment. After all, he'd spent the entire day doing everything she asked of him and more, but he was British, and that made him a target for her animosity.

Noelle made a mental note to try to curb her quick temper. She'd vowed to do so before, with little result, but she was a lady now, and ladies developed control of their emotions.

"Miss Arledge, I wish you would . . ." Drake's voice trailed off as he realized that reasoning with her was out of the question. "I'll be back soon. Oh, and this may be a bad time to mention this, but I believe you lost the wager. I'm delighted to count you among my dearest friends." He chuckled, slipped on his shirt, and gave her a casual salute as he strode toward his horse.

Noelle's anger and determination mellowed as she watched him mount, and doubts began to assault her. Friend, indeed. "Captain," she called.

He turned in the saddle to look at her. "Yes, Miss Arledge?"

"Thank you for what you've done." She swallowed, blinked, and faced him with her chin jutted out in defiance. Noelle Arledge had never welshed on a bet, and she wasn't about to begin now, no matter how difficult the matter. "My . . . my friends call me Noelle."

"And I'm Drake. Until another time, then . . . Noelle." He grinned and flicked the reins.

The tall black horse cantered away, leaving Noelle alone in the cotton field. She dropped down to her knees. The tears she wanted to shed refused to fall, but the pressure of the events last night and the sudden feeling of abandonment took their toll.

Knowing she must look a mess, she gazed into the darkness that had settled around her.

Noelle jumped to her feet and hurried toward the kitchen. Mandy would be worried. The supper hour had passed long ago, and Noelle hadn't even thought of hunger while she grieved for her losses.

When she reached the kitchen, she smelled the aroma of frying bacon and smiled. Mandy was cooking supper.

They ate quickly, Noelle nodding as Mandy scolded her for being gone so long. She listened absently while her mind worked on a plan. They shouldn't stay here. They could go to Ash Meadow. Although it wouldn't be quite proper for her to stay with her fiancé, she felt that the war made a slight difference, and the rules could be relaxed a bit.

"Mandy, after supper we're going to Ash Meadow," Noelle said aloud.

"No'm. We ain't goin' out in the dark with them Injuns hidin' behind every tree. No'm, we ain't," Mandy replied with finality.

Noelle nodded her head. "Yes, Mandy, we're going and we're going tonight. Who knows when the British might arrive? We must seek refuge with the Brookses at Ash Meadow."

"Them Redcoats is scary, but they ain't nothin' next to them Injuns and devils." Mandy looked around as if she expected the doors to burst open and admit an army of

Cherokees and devils. "We ain't temptin' the powers of the night."

For a moment Noelle fought to keep from laughing. Mandy had acquired a horror of the unknown during the night, and Noelle hardly knew how to combat it. "We're going. Please get ready."

Mandy glowered at her young mistress and went to the fireplace. "Injuns and devils hidin' in the dark jus' waitin' for ole Mandy. If'n it ain't a Injun hackin' off my scalp, it be a devil waitin' to toast my toes."

Noelle shuddered at the reference to scalping, but she refused to be swayed from her decision. Staring calmly at the scared slave, Noelle sighed. After a moment she jumped up and hugged Mandy. "Mandy, Indians or no Indians, devils or no devils, you and I are going to Ash Meadow tonight. You have nothing to fear. I'll protect you. We're going, and that's that."

Her mind made up, Noelle ate to satisfy a real hunger that she hadn't felt for days. Convinced that she was doing the right thing, she urged the dawdling Mandy to hurry with her tasks. By the time they reached Ash Meadow, the moon would have risen, and she wanted to arrive before John Brooks and Irene, his sister, went to bed.

As darkness fell, Noelle raced up the stairs to fetch her pelisse, a deep blue woolen cloak with fur trim. As she pulled it around her shoulders and started to close the door of the wardrobe, she noticed another cloak. Without hesitating, she pulled it from its peg and draped it across her arm. Mandy could wear it.

At long last Noelle straightened her slight five-foot frame, hitched the mule to the wagon left at Tyger Rest and led Mandy to the vehicle. The wizened old slave appeared to be close to fainting from fright, and her shoulders sagged from the weight of the heavy cloak, but Noelle urged her on.

After settling Mandy comfortably in the wagon bed and tucking the wool and fur cloak around her to keep out the cold air, Noelle climbed into the seat and flapped the reins. The long kid gloves did little to warm her hands, but she tried to keep one hand in her muff and the other on the reins. The old mule jerked into a steady pace. Noelle cast a last glance at her charred home and wondered wearily if she would ever return.

"Save me, Lord. Don't let the heathens get me. Save my little Noelle. Save us, Lord." Mandy chanted the words in a singsong rhythm, emphasized by the creaking of the wagon.

Noelle had no time to vent her raging emotions. The anguish gripping her heart with ever-tightening fingers of iron seemed unstoppable. Mandy's chant heightened Noelle's anger. The poor slave expected to be killed. Surely the Indians would not kill two helpless women, Noelle thought. The destruction of her home was inexcusable, but the Cherokees had left them unharmed, thanks to Drake Hastings.

Rain started to fall. Noelle heard the splat of raindrops on the bed of the wagon and urged the mule on. Afraid that the Indians might return, that their generosity in leaving her unharmed might have been due solely to the intervention of the British officer, Noelle snapped the reins, and the mule plodded on. Nothing else could happen, she thought.

Though she had listened to each snatch of conversation and rumor about the war, she longed to escape the reality for a time, for a chance to breathe freely, to live without fear. But still she would make a difference in this unwanted fight for freedom.

The bright moon split an ebony cloud, edging it with silver, and the rain slowed to a mist, well on its way to ending. Raindrops glistened like cut glass on the blades of grass and softened the dried leaves on the road, making the wheels squish along rather than crunch.

She knew the way well. The emerging moon helped her to see the road, and she could travel faster. John Brooks had been her father's friend for many years. Her father had arranged her marriage when he found out he was dying. Noelle had resisted him, but he had made her promise to marry John Brooks. Though her father had died sooner than the doctor had anticipated, Noelle felt grateful for the Lord's kindness in taking her father before the destruction of Tyger Rest. Charles Arledge would have abhorred last night's horrifying events. Noelle could not have withstood seeing the agony he would have felt watching Tyger Rest in flames.

Though John Brooks was a good deal older—at least forty-five—he would be good to her. That was all her father had asked, someone who would take care of his only child, someone who would provide stability and protection.

Noelle trembled as the night air knifed through to her bones despite her cape. Soaring Eagle's attack was so swift and unexpected, she'd had no time to grab any of her remaining clothes. The nightgown and woolen cloak were all that remained of her wardrobe, except for her wedding gown and some items already moved to Mr. Brooks house.

Noelle wasn't easily frightened. She had gumption. This war and its atrocities would not best Merry Noelle Arledge. She flapped the reins to speed the mule on its way, and the wagon jolted but didn't seem to move any faster.

A light breeze whispered through the tall boxwoods that bordered the long dirt road circling the wide lawn of Tyger Rest. Beyond the boxwoods, two rows of crepe myrtles, now bereft of their fragrant magenta flowers, reached all the way to the main road leading to John Brooks's property.

Startled suddenly by the nearby whinny of a horse, Noelle tightened her grip on the reins. She heard no other sound but knew that she hadn't imagined it. She wondered if she was being followed. Or were the Indians lying in wait for her ahead where the path grew darker, under the oaks?

The satiny white branches of the crepe myrtles had been a favorite play area for Noelle as a youngster. She glanced at the place where she had whiled away many hours, dreaming of her future and playing out her fantasies.

Now the fickle moonlight, which danced along the silvery edge of a rapidly moving cloud, and the wind, which had brought the first scent of roses in spring, combined to cast an eerie glow on the spindly myrtle branches and rattle them like bleached bones. Gone forever were the pleasant childhood memories, replaced now by the ghostly reminder of this horrible night and the night before.

The moon hid behind a towering thunderhead, and fat drops of rain began to pelt Noelle, sending shivers up her spine. She had no shelter. Heavy drops beat down relentlessly, soaking into her woolen cloak until the wrap was drenched and leaden.

As they neared Ash Meadow, Noelle's heartbeat quickened. A soft yellow glow radiated from the downstairs windows. Cold rain drizzled down her face and matted her eyelashes with crystal sparkles that rimmed her sapphire eyes like diamonds on a velvety frame. She clicked the reins, eager to reach the safety of the house. Once there, she jerked hard on the smooth leather and cooed, "Whoa, Luke."

After jumping down from the wagon, Noelle paused for a moment to compose herself before bounding up the wide steps. As she grasped the brass knocker, the door swung open, and John Brooks stood before her.

"Noelle? What are you doing here at this time of night? Come in out of the cold." He took her arm and led her inside.

"Mr. Brooks, Indians set our house on fire. Mandy survived. I was rescued . . . Mandy's in the wagon. Those men . . . it was terrible." Realizing that she was babbling, Noelle hushed and looked at the floor. "I'm sorry. If we're imposing, we can go on to . . . to somewhere."

John Brooks's gentle blue eyes searched her face. "Of course you're not imposing. This is where you belong. I'll send Joseph after Mandy. Come inside and sit by the fire. Tell me all about it. But first, let me call Irene."

Noelle watched as he quickly dispatched Joseph to take care of Mandy. The brisk echo of his footsteps on the staircase reassured Noelle, and she relaxed in a large comfortable wing chair. The fire warmed her body but not her soul. She was reminded of the towering flames of her burning home, of a searing heat that threatened to singe her hair and skin. Her father had built that house, its slave cabins, and outbuildings in 1765, and now much of his work lay in a pile of charred rubble. She rested her head against the back of the chair, wishing ill to all Indians and British soldiers, and hoping for a hasty conclusion to this war.

With eyes still burning from unshed tears, Noelle glanced around the familiar room. A neat rack of churchwardens hung by the fireplace, ready for company. She imagined the laughing men, sitting around the room, passing the gleaming kaolin pipe from one to the other while the women sewed, the same as in her own sitting room.

She'd spent many afternoons here while her father engaged in the cheerful art of storytelling and the fury of discussing King George's latest travesty of justice. The Brooks family Bible lay open on its stand, as if someone had just been reading. These were comforting items, familiar to her from childhood.

The unbidden image of a stranger's finely chiseled features silhouetted by flames swam before Noelle's tired eyes. The gentle understanding she had seen in those near-black eyes forced a warm flush to her cold cheeks. He was one Britisher who didn't seem to deserve her hatred, yet why had he come to her house? The compassion he displayed intrigued her. But in her unforgiving young mind, he became the same as the others because he was one of them. Noelle's tired mind tottered on the edge of hysteria, and with conscious determination she chose to hate. The depth of her emotions would provide strength to live through the coming days.

In the brief moments before she nodded off to sleep, Noelle forced herself to remember the dogs. The Indians had stripped her of everything she loved. And, if accounts were accurate, they were working with the British. No, she would neither forgive nor forget.

She jerked awake as Irene Brooks shook her gently. "Come, Noelle. John has lost all thought of his manners to keep you here. You must be exhausted."

"I'm sorry. I didn't know exactly what to do." John rushed into the room and took Noelle's hand. "Please forgive me. I should have taken you to a room immediately."

"It is I who should be sorry. My intrusion on you at this hour is unforgivable." Noelle drew herself erect, once again in command of her manners. Living in up-country South Carolina did little to test her education in the finer graces, but Mandy had insisted that her upbringing include the customs of polite society. The rustic atmosphere touched but did not affect her gracious manner.

Noelle longed for her own warm feather bed and hand-made quilts. Once she was settled in the familiar surroundings of Ash Meadow, she could forget the tragedies she had been forced to live with during the past few weeks since her father's illness had grown worse and resulted in his death. In the span of a few days, she had been catapulted from the innocence of youth into the disillusionment of adulthood.

"John, I'm going to see that Noelle is taken care of. You do whatever you were doing. You can see her tomorrow." Irene Brooks took Noelle's hand and led her to the stairs. "Joseph! Bring me some hot water immediately. Tell Mandy she can sleep with Ardelia." The older woman smiled reassuringly at Noelle. "They've been friends for a long time. Ardelia will be glad to see her. Now, don't you worry, Noelle." Irene turned and addressed her servant. "Oh, there you are, Ardelia. Take Mandy with you. She can help you with the wedding preparations. We have much to do this week. You two should have a lot to talk about. Come, Noelle."

The frail-looking black woman Irene addressed as Ardelia folded her arms around Mandy as Irene led Noelle up the stairs. Noelle felt comforted somewhat, knowing that Mandy was in good hands and that Irene was going to take care of everything. It was a relief to allow the burden of decision-making to be lifted from her young shoulders. Ever since her father's death, Noelle had shouldered all the responsibility of running a household. Now she had no household to manage since John's house was run by his sister.

Irene led her through an open door and closed it firmly behind them. "Now take off those wet clothes while I lay a fire." She quickly laid kindling on the andirons and soon had a warming blaze.

Noelle stood self-consciously at the foot of the huge bed and stripped herself. Mandy was the only person who had seen her unclothed since her babyhood. "I . . . I don't have anything to wear." She crossed her arms over breasts.

"I'll get you something of mine to wear to bed tonight. We'll worry about a dress in the morning. You have some really pretty nightgowns in your trousseau, but you shouldn't wear them yet. I'll be right back." The graying woman closed the door as she hurried away.

Noelle smiled, listening to the authoritative timbre of Irene's voice as she continued to issue instructions to the servants and to her brother. For an instant Noelle almost forgot her problems and the war. Thinking of her wedding seemed so normal and happy, and Irene's kindness was so warming after the horrors of the past two days.

In moments, Irene returned with a voluminous flannel nightgown and robe, which easily swallowed Noelle. "Here, put on this robe. Joseph is coming up the stairs with bathwater."

As if on cue, a loud knock resounded on the door. At Irene's bidding, Noelle moved into a shadowy corner and waited while Joseph poured water into a washtub in front of the fire. After two more trips, the tub brimmed with steaming water for Noelle's bath.

"Come. Don't be bashful." Irene spooned scented flakes

from an ornate silver bowl into the tub and tested the water with her finger. "Just perfect to warm you up. I'll order you some chocolate."

Noelle still shivered from the bone-chilling cold and exposure. "Thank you, Miss Brooks. You have been most gracious."

"Nonsense. You're a part of the family. Call me Irene. Now into the tub with you." The smile that spread across her face wrinkled the corners of her mouth, and touched her eyes. Noelle felt a rush of affection for this gray-haired woman who dealt so calmly with the strange turn of events.

Irene was older than Noelle's mother would have been. Her sweet, soothing voice recalled the longing that often haunted Noelle. The fever that had claimed Brenna Arledge had left Noelle motherless at the age of two. Noelle remembered nothing about the woman who had given birth to her, save the portrait that hung over the hearth in the sitting room.

Smiling indulgently, Irene helped Noelle into the hot water and strode to the door to send for the hot chocolate. As she sat down in the tin washtub, Noelle imagined that her own mother would have done the same thing many times if she had lived. She closed her eyes and pretended that Irene was her mother. For a moment she felt good relaxing under Irene's motherly ministrations. How Noelle longed for a mother, someone to talk to, someone to understand the changeable emotions she frequently experienced.

When Noelle opened her eyes, Irene smiled. Perhaps, Noelle mused, Irene sometimes daydreamed too. Never married, the older woman quite possibly wished for a daughter of her own. The two women smiled knowingly at each other, as if each could read the other's mind, and neither was disturbed by the thoughts she discovered.

Though they would be sisters-in-law, their relationship grew much deeper as they got acquainted. In Irene, Noelle found someone who would care about her in a way she desperately needed at this point in her life. A knock sounded at the door, and Irene hurried to open it a bit. She accepted a tray through the small opening, turned, and closed the door with her foot.

Her feelings for this young woman had become very tender and maternal. Tears sparkled in Irene's blue eyes and she cleared her throat. "Time to get out. You will be too tired to help tomorrow if I keep you up any longer."

Noelle dried off quickly before Irene dropped the nightgown over her head and straightened its voluminous folds. "Irene," Noelle said tentatively, accepting a cup of chocolate from Irene's slender hand. "Thank you for being here. Things are so much easier than I thought, with you here to help. I wish there was something I could say to let you know how glad I am."

"Don't. I'm glad I was here to help you. Now into bed with you. Tomorrow will be a busy day for both of us." Irene threw the covers back and waited while Noelle climbed in. "Drink up and don't worry about anything. Everything will be fine."

Noelle drained her cup, placed it on the table, reached up impulsively, and clung to Irene for a moment. "Will you wake me early?"

Irene nodded, blew out the candle, and left. After snuggling down into the feather mattress, Noelle fell asleep more quickly than she imagined possible. Her heart felt lighter, as if Irene had lifted some of the awesome burden Noelle had borne for weeks. She slept, deeply and dreamlessly.

The next few days sped by. Noelle and Irene spent hours overseeing the polishing of silver, the polishing of furniture, the preparation of food, and the moving of furniture to accommodate the few guests who were expected to attend the wedding.

She didn't have much time to think about her recent terrifying experience, although she confided in Irene. Listening quietly, Irene nodded with understanding and occasionally dropped her forehead onto her hands. Noelle saw tears glistening in Irene's eyes but looked away to avoid embarrassment to either of them.

Noelle looked out the window. A fat yellow cat lay on the edge of the veranda sunning herself and swishing her tail. Noelle smiled and listened as a blue jay scolded the cat.

Across a field scored with rows of dry and leafless cotton plants, with wisps of fluffy cotton still clinging to gaping bolls, John Brooks pointed to his barn, and Life, his overseer, nodded.

How many times had Noelle seen her father walk the furrows of his fields? Not enough, she thought and missed her father more acutely than she had in weeks.

The specter of homesickness fell across Noelle like a shadow, and she longed for home. It didn't matter that Ash Meadow was her new home; she wanted to see Tyger Rest, to walk its lustrous floors, to smell the hot bread baking in the kitchen, to hear Mandy yell at Cook.

Tears stung her eyes as she remembered the happy days she had spent there, never realizing they'd end so soon or so tragically.

"I've got to go. I must," she mumbled. "Irene!" she called and ran up the stairs. "Irene!"

Irene stuck her head out of a doorway and smiled. "What is it, dear?"

"I . . . I need to walk," Noelle stammered. "I'll be all right. I'll be back in time for dinner."

"Noelle, you can't seriously consider . . ." Irene stopped in mid-sentence, obviously touched by the anguish apparent on Noelle's face. "Of course. Why don't you take one of the servants with you?"

"No. I need to be alone." Noelle hurried down the stairs and pulled on a shawl before Irene could object further.

Irene's face was lined with worry as she followed her to the foot of the stairs. She cast a nervous glance out the window. "Noelle dear, are you sure? It's coming up a cloud. Why don't you wait?"

Noelle hugged Irene impulsively and smiled reassuringly. Eager to be away, she called over her shoulder as she tied a shawl across her breast, "I'll be careful. Don't worry."

CHAPTER
4

BEFORE IRENE COULD PROTEST, NOELLE SNATCHED A BONNET from its peg and hurried out the door. As she crossed the porch, she tied the ribbons under her chin, feeling giddy with action, with anticipation, with adventure.

She scurried past the beds of mauve and bronze asters and under the fragrant cedar. Feeling free and inhaling the crisp fall air, Noelle strode through the archway and onto the road to Tyger Rest. She wondered where Drake was and what he was doing. He'd been kind to her, far kinder than she expected a British officer to be.

Why was she thinking of him? She shook her head to banish his face from her mind. Her thoughts should be directed to her upcoming wedding and her fiancé, even though her husband had been chosen for her.

The distance had never seemed so far to her. When Noelle neared the bridge across the North Tyger River, she paused and felt almost lighthearted. She knew that she was coming home, but what was she coming home to?

How could anything be wrong on a day like this? she wondered. The vibrant colors of fall would soon set in, and the verdant splendor of summer would fade, a summer that she would never forget for its atrocities.

Noelle refused to dwell on her problems on such a wonderful day. Her thoughts turned involuntarily to Drake Hastings once again, and she closed her eyes.

Why had he helped her? He had no reason to offer assistance to any Colonist, and in fact, his mission would be realized only when the Colonists were defeated. Soaring Eagle's raids served the British purpose admirably. The intermittent destruction wreaked havoc with the morale of the upstate South Carolinians.

Despite his service with the British, Drake seemed a kind sort. He could have taken advantage of her as easily as Soaring Eagle had.

Drake's face swam before her closed eyes, and her heart hammered in her chest. Noelle opened her eyes suddenly. Why did he affect her this way? Her behavior and frivolous thoughts made no sense to her. "For goodness' sake," she muttered, shaking her head in consternation. "He's the enemy . . . and probably miles away by now."

Avoiding a shimmering puddle, she edged around the higher shoulder of the road and strode on full of purpose. She had no time to waste on the daydreams of a silly girl on the peculiar actions of men. Time was passing too quickly, and she needed to be on her way. Deep in her heart she was reluctant to see Tyger Rest in the shambles she'd left it.

The last honeysuckle of summer clung to a dead tree trunk beside the red clay road, and Noelle stopped to pick a sprig. Its fragrance entranced her, and she closed her eyes as she sniffed. Twirling the stem between her fingers, she moved on, tucking the delicate blossom into the knot of her kerchief.

One experience with the Cherokees was enough for her. With watchful eyes, Noelle continued her journey, but she couldn't help enjoying the warm sunshine on her back and the heady scent of autumn. As she drew nearer Tyger Rest, the fragrance of fall gave way to the odor of smoke, and her joy fled at the reminder of her near escape.

Noelle paused. She looked ahead and behind. Had she heard horses? A lump of fear materialized in her throat, and she reached up unconsciously to stroke her neck.

The clay road was usually packed hard, but the rain had softened it during the night. The sounds were muffled, but she could hear more hoofbeats and now a whinny.

From which direction were the sounds coming? And who was making them?

The British? Soaring Eagle and his braves? It couldn't be. Not again.

Noelle chewed her lip. Too far from Ash Meadow to return and too far from Tyger Rest to run for shelter there, she scurried to the edge of the road and glanced furtively in both directions. The riders weren't close enough for her to see yet. Panic thickened and roiled in her stomach until she felt nauseated and weak.

The blackberry vines on either side of the road blocked her from escaping into the woods. There were no thick-trunked trees close enough for her to hide behind. Where could she go?

Still close to the river, Noelle turned and stared at the wooden bridge. Desperation lurked in the corners of her mind as she searched mentally for a hiding place.

"My old hiding place," she muttered. Her childhood hiding place under the bridge might be safe if she reached the spot before the riders came into view.

The horses were coming closer.

Lifting her skirts, Noelle ran as quickly as she could in the slippery mud of the road.

At the bridge she hurried down the steep slope toward the river. Thorns from young honey locust trees and blackberry vines tore into her dress and pricked her arms, but she couldn't stop and she didn't care—she just wanted to hide.

The horses hammered closer. From the noise she judged that several riders were approaching. They had to be Indians or British, she decided. There were not enough Patriots left around here to ride in groups.

The sound of the horses grew louder. She could hear their hooves in the soft mud on the road—at times, a splash, at others a muffled clippety-clop.

She was almost there, she told herself, as she scampered over a smooth boulder, lost her footing, and fell to a grassy ledge below.

She scraped her knee on a sharp stone and cried out in pain. Blood seeped through her skirts as she rocked back and forth trying to keep from crying out again.

She hardly paused, but climbed between two huge stones and behind them to her little space. It seemed much smaller than she remembered, for she had grown a great deal in the last three years. Still, she felt safe.

The riders were heading east, from Tyger Rest toward Ash Meadow. Noelle squeezed her eyes shut. She wrapped her arms around her shoulders, hugging herself gently.

Hooves struck the wooden bridge. Noelle shuddered. She'd barely reached her hiding place in time.

Noelle lay back on the bed of weeds and prayed that whoever was crossing the bridge overhead would not see her. The spaces between the planks that formed the bridge allowed her to see the bellies of several horses, but not much else. Dirt and debris from the bridge sifted down into her eyes, and she grimaced as her eyes watered. She couldn't tell who the riders were, only that there were seven or eight of them.

If she could see them, however, they might be able to see her! The thud of the horses' hooves on the bridge matched the thundering of her heart. Noelle clenched her fists.

She lay for a long time, listening, until the sound of the horses completely faded away. Still she waited, afraid to quit the safety of her hideout.

The afternoon had started out as a pleasurable jaunt, but in the span of a few minutes her terror had returned. She didn't know whether to go on to Tyger Rest or back to Ash Meadow. If she continued on to Tyger Rest she might run into a group of British soldiers. If she returned to Ash Meadow, she might run into the same threat. She realized that she couldn't remain in her hiding place forever, so she crawled out and resumed her journey. Both directions offered danger to her.

Noelle decided to approach the house through the forest rather than by the road, so that she could watch the house unobserved, before approaching it. Today had been an eventful day so far, and she hoped that the remainder of her trip was much less so.

Striking out through the evergreen forest across a bed of pine needles, she followed the path she'd played on as a child. She forged a route that paralleled the trail but remained hidden by brush and undergrowth.

Shrubs, tree falls, and rocks littered her way, slowing her progress much more than she anticipated. The cool shade of the tall pines made her glad she'd brought a shawl, and she pulled it closer across her shoulders and breasts.

The fragrance of pine was wonderful. Memories of her childhood outings brought a smile to her face for the first time since the episode at the bridge. She remembered meeting her best friend, Kathleen Foster, here to exchange gossip or to plan activities. The war had brutally disrupted their plans for the future.

But Noelle always bounced back, and she would this time. She felt like a cat—always landing on her feet.

She started up the hill that rose on the western end of the cotton field. At the top, a formation of granite created a peak from which she could observe her home and property.

Taking care not to scuff or damage her slippers, Noelle climbed the smooth stones. As she neared the two sharp rocks that jutted into the sky and overlooked Tyger Rest, she hesitated. This would be a perfect place from which to keep a lookout.

She got down on her hands and knees and crawled forward, listening carefully for any sound that would betray the presence of anyone else. As silently as possible, she moved to the narrow chasm between the tall stones looming above her and edged ahead, glancing to the left and right.

Noelle soon realized she was alone. She rested her back against one of the pillars and her feet on the other as she surveyed her property. The evenly drawn squares of cotton fields and food crops were red, gray, and black now. Here and there a bright orange pumpkin dotted the kitchen garden, along with a melon or two, a few spikes of gumbo okra, and some tomatoes blushing with late color.

Now grayed with smoke and soot, the whitewashed exterior of her house emphasized the black scar across its roof. Many of the slave cabins were gone, leveled by separate fires, and some of the trees were scorched above burned buildings; but the oak in front of the house was untouched on this side, as was the old cedar.

Part of her mind urged her to break into a run, wanting to reach the home she loved and the safety she associated with home, but the rational part of Noelle knew that the danger was greater there than here in the woods. She sighed and rose. The time to go on had come.

The distance was shorter if she climbed down the hill from here, but safer if she took the gentler path the way she'd come. She took the slope.

About halfway down the slope, she began to slide on the rain-saturated earth. She tumbled through a patch of blackberry vines and rolled to a stop against a flat rock. The scream that escaped from her throat as the thorns tore into the soft flesh of her arms echoed in the quiet afternoon air.

She lay there for a moment, thankful that nothing felt broken, and then scrambled to her feet. Drops of blood appeared along the scratches and punctures inflicted by the thorns, and she pressed a finger to the deepest scratch, hoping to stop the flow of blood before it ruined her dress. She used the tatted edge of the shawl to dab her damp lashes and cheeks, musing that by now she must look like a hoyden.

There was no time to waste on self-pity. She couldn't postpone this forever. If she didn't reach Tyger Rest soon, she would have no time to look around.

Noelle made her way to the cotton field and edged carefully around it, among the spindly cedars and chinaberry trees that marked the boundary, instead of crossing in the open where she could easily be seen. She strode purposefully across the lawn, now punctuated with the hoof prints of the Cherokees' horses and dusted with a layer of gray and black soot and ash.

"I'm probably walking into a trap," she muttered, pausing at the front door and wondering if she might find herself face to face with Soaring Eagle. Noelle had to find out; she could wait no longer. The smell of smoke permeated the air, and she coughed as she reached for the doorknob.

The front door, the door to the sitting room, opened easily when she turned the knob, and she stepped inside. She was sickened by the layer of soot that covered her treasures, the floor, everything. The family Bible lay open, its words obscured by large flakes of ash. She walked to the table where it stood and stared at it for a moment, then bent down and blew the offending particles away.

She closed the Bible, then shut the wooden Bible box, slipped the latch into place, and tucked the large box under her arm to take with her to Ash Meadow. This was one treasure, the evidence of her heritage, that the marauders wouldn't destroy. The Bible had been her father's and listed six generations of Arledges, dating back to Ireland.

Her father's room appeared to be undamaged. The door to the stairs hung open, and she gazed at the staircase, wondering if she should go up to her room. She looked around, listening, heard nothing, and stepped onto the landing, closing her father's door from habit and smiling at the familiar squeak.

Suddenly, Noelle wanted to get out as soon as possible, but she summoned her courage and ascended the stairs. The house in its present condition, with its pervading silence and black drape of death, seemed to be rejecting her for some unknown reason, and the warmth of Ash Meadow, and Irene, beckoned.

When Noelle reached the top of the stairs, she looked into the dormitory room. The black scar she'd seen from the hill was over this room. From here she could see a large patch of mottled sky that threatened to produce rain later in the afternoon. She needed to hurry if she wanted to beat the storm as well as alleviate her uneasiness.

From her room Noelle grabbed her boots and a pair of slippers and headed for the stairs. A sound coming from the keeping room stopped her before she stepped from the landing onto the first stair, and she moved quietly into the dormitory to listen for the noise again.

She heard the door to her father's room squeak. An intruder was walking through her father's room, possibly tracing her steps in the soot. She heard the sound of footsteps—a man's footsteps.

There was no place to hide in the dormitory room. She couldn't cross the hall and hide in her own room because anyone coming up the stairs would see her. Her eyes scanned the room for a weapon, something with which to bash in the intruder's head.

The quilting frame hung securely from the ceiling, and it would take too long to loosen its fastenings. The neat room offered no help. Her only weapon was the wooden Bible box under her arm.

She stood beside the open doorway, hoping to surprise the intruder before he saw her. She placed the boots and slippers on a small table and flattened herself against the wall, holding the sturdy box over her head.

Inhaling deeply, Noelle hoped her arms wouldn't give out before she could bash the man over the head. Her wishes were granted when she heard the creak of the third step from the top.

The intruder reached the landing and stopped. Noelle waited.

She exhaled and quickly gulped another breath of air. The heavy odor of smoke tickled her nose and throat, threatening to make her cough as she waited for him to step into the room. She bit her lip to stifle the noise.

The sound of his feet shuffling told her that he had made his decision. One step brought him into the room, and he stared at the ceiling, looking at the same gaping hole she'd looked at earlier.

As the Bible box was on its downward swing, Noelle recognized Drake Hastings, but not in time to stop the blow. About the same time, Drake spotted her and whipped around to defend himself.

The Bible box landed a glancing blow on his left shoulder. Drake jumped out of reach, and the box crashed to the floor. Instinctively, he flung himself at his assailant, and they fell to the floor. He pinioned her to the damp and dirty pine floor and drew one hand back to strike her.

His fist missed her cheek and smashed into the floor beside her. "Damn!" Drake shouted. "What are you doing here?"

"This is my house. What are *you* doing here?" Noelle replied, her cheeks flushed with relief and excitement.

"I asked you first." He relaxed his grip somewhat. "I heard someone walking up here and came to investigate."

"I thought you were going back to join your regiment." Noelle hardly breathed. His body lay across hers, and she couldn't move. "So you could plot the death of more of my people."

"I came back to see that Soaring Eagle didn't finish what he started." Drake stared down into the sapphire eyes that seemed to be turning violet while he watched.

"There's nothing you can do here now," Noelle said, wishing he would let her up. The pine flooring had bruised her back, but there was more. She felt warm, different, as if she really wanted his body on hers, and she couldn't feel that way about the enemy. "Get off me this instant."

"Not until I'm sure you don't intend to do me bodily harm." He moved slightly, apparently trying to relieve some of the weight on her.

"Me? Why should I hurt you?" Noelle was shocked that he thought that she might want to injure him. After all, he'd saved her life.

"You tried to kill me with that wooden box." He shifted

his weight further, so that his upper body lay across her chest and freed her legs. "I've never been threatened with bodily injury from a Bible before."

"I thought you were Soaring Eagle," Noelle explained. "I wouldn't intentionally hurt you. You've done nothing to me." Noelle hardly paused to breathe. She did want to find out exactly what he was doing in this area. Was the Ninety-Six District about to become the main battlefield of the war? She softened her words and smiled. "We're, well . . . we're friends. Remember?"

Drake smiled for the first time, a genuine smile brought by her words. He released her hands, stood, and helped her to her feet. Her brown skirts were damp and torn. "Of course. But I've had enemies who inflicted less pain."

"Look what you've done." She pointed to her damaged skirt. "Why didn't you make yourself known?"

"And let Soaring Eagle know I was here? He could have been here as easily as you." Drake glanced around. "I saw you leave. Why did you return?"

"I came to get some of my clothes and to assess the damage." Noelle picked up her boots and held them toward them as proof of the innocence of her mission.

"You're on your way back now?" he asked, dusting off his white breeches as best he could.

"Within the hour. I promised my friend I'd return in time for supper." Noelle followed his gaze to the hole in the roof and then looked into his eyes, trying very hard to hate him and unable to do so even though he was British. "I'm not sure I can salvage much."

"I'm sorry. I wish I had arrived sooner. Maybe I could have prevented . . . Soaring Eagle might not have . . ." His voice drifted into silence. Conjecturing at this point seemed useless to him. He couldn't be everywhere at once. "At least he was unable to rob you of everything. You still have a few animals and some meat and vegetables in the smokehouse and root cellar."

"There was nothing you could have done. There were too

many of them, too intent on destroying Tyger Rest." Noelle stopped. She was about to remind him that the British put them up to it.

"Look, Noelle, let's gather your things and get out of here before Soaring Eagle does return, or perhaps the rain begins again." He pointed to the hole in the ceiling. "Or, if you wish, we could make another wager."

Through the open roof Noelle saw that the clouds now dotted the sky and loomed over the property, as black and threatening as the smoke that had hung over Tyger Rest several nights ago. "I believe my gambling days have come and gone. I seem to have run upon a season of bad luck."

Noelle returned to her room and selected a few items that seemed to be the least damaged.

She found a quilt and wrapped her meager belongings—two pairs of shoes, a dress, a comb and hand mirror, and her Bible box. Noelle then went downstairs, closed the front door, walked through the keeping room, and moved into the dining room.

Drake stood by the window, looking across the kitchen garden. "Where to now?"

"I just want to look around." She hesitated at the back door.

"Noelle, we really need to go." He touched her elbow, and they stepped outside into the rising wind.

"But, I can't go. Not yet. I—I need . . ." Noelle stammered, unable to express her emotions.

"What? What do you need?" Drake stopped and looked down into her eyes, his hand still on her arm.

"I need to see my father. I may not be back for a while." The words tumbled out of her mouth.

Exasperated, Drake snapped, "Perhaps another time, when Soaring Eagle has settled down, when the weather—"

"No," Noelle interrupted, refusing to be diverted from her intention. "Go on if you must. I'm going to see my father."

"Very well." Drake walked with her the several hundred

yards across the yard and through the edge of the forest to the family burial plot. If he lived to be a hundred years old, he'd never understand women. He gazed down at her and acknowledged to himself that he would never understand this woman particularly. "Go ahead," he conceded. "I'll wait here."

Noelle was silently glad for his company. At least she felt safe with him around. She walked the short distance to the small stone that marked her father's grave and knelt down, brushing away some of the debris strewn there by the storm.

Across the grave, she looked at the others, fresh mounds of red dirt that reminded her of the devastation wrought by Soaring Eagle. "Rest in peace, dear Papa," she whispered. Her eyes were dry. She'd cried enough in the past few weeks to last a lifetime. A drop of rain splattered on the back of her hand and brought Noelle from her reverie.

She gazed again at her father's grave and when she looked up, Drake was standing nearby. "I'm glad he's gone," she said, wiping a drop of rain from her nose. "He could have never lived through this." She indicated the direction of her house. "He really loved this place."

Drake's face registered the anger he felt as thunder rumbled somewhere off behind him. It was grossly unfair that war should affect this beautiful young innocent in such a dastardly way. Her agony, her spirit, her strength, and desire to survive against monumental odds touched him, and his admiration for her grew. "Come on. I'll take you back."

They walked along in silence until they came to his tethered horse. "I'm afraid we'll have to ride together again. I believe you've met my horse? Nightmare?"

"Nightmare?" A smile touched Noelle's lips, and she nodded. She handed Drake the quilt, and he tied it to the saddle. With a gentle touch he lifted her and deposited her in the saddle before climbing up himself. They rode for a while without speaking.

As they trotted along closer to Tyger River, the wind

rose, fluttering the leaves on the tall oaks and birches skirting the road. The bottoms of the leaves showed, and she knew that it would rain again soon. Clouds roiled overhead, black and threatening, skimming along on the howling wind that bent the trees to its purpose.

Noelle leaned back against him, resting in the security she derived from his presence and his touch, sheltering her face from the sharp wind. Friends, she thought, wondering why she'd allowed herself to settle the friendship with the enemy in her mind. To find out what he was doing here, she reminded herself. Maybe one day the information she acquired would make a difference in the war.

Just ahead she saw the beginning of the rain approaching like a moving wall of water. "Looks as if we're in for a dousing."

He flicked the reins, and Nightmare broke into a canter as fat drops of rain began to fall. "I believe you're right. Come on, Nightmare, let's challenge the rain."

Drake urged the horse on, and they were soon galloping along the dirt road through huge puddles that reached from one side to the other. Noelle clung to Drake for her life. Her face was nestled in the crook of his neck, and she inhaled the scent of his body, a masculine scent, invigorating and inviting.

Her hand touched his neck, and he looked down at her as if he understood her gesture, but he simply said, "Hold on."

Noelle pressed her body closer to his, savoring the protection his wide shoulders provided from the onslaught of the storm. Lightning bolted across the sky and struck a tall pine not far from them. Flames shot into the sky, and the ground shuddered beneath Nightmare's hooves.

"We need to find shelter quickly." Drake urged Nightmare on, pressing him to gallop faster.

"There's nowhere to hide between here and Ash Meadow," she yelled against the screeching wind.

Nightmare's hooves clattered across the Tyger River bridge, and Noelle felt better. They had only a half mile to go. Then she had an idea. She twisted to face Drake and yelled, "Under the bridge!"

"What?"

"There's a place we can take shelter under the bridge," she called, pulling her shawl closer and burying her face against Drake's chest. "Stop!"

Drake drew back on the reins and dismounted. "Stay here."

He led Nightmare down the riverbank to the rocks that formed Noelle's hideout. Rain swept under the bridge in cold sheets, and Noelle felt the first sting of ice on her cheeks. The wind howled down the riverbed and ambushed Noelle and Drake with a bruising assault of pebble-sized hailstones.

"Help me down!" Noelle shouted so Drake could hear her over the rumbling thunder and roaring wind.

He drew her down into his arms, shielding her against as much of the storm as possible. "Go on."

Leading him by the hand, she threaded her way among the boulders and entered her hiding place. Although the ground was damp, the rocks encircling the narrow space protected her from the fierce storm. Drake crawled in and sat beside her. She realized too late that the tiny space forced them to sit with their hips touching. The granite enclosure was long but narrow.

"Let me take care of Nightmare." Drake disappeared through the slit in the rocks.

Noelle looked around. There wasn't much room, but at least they'd survive the storm. Outside, lightning crackled and flashed while the thunder boomed in reply. The cracks between the planks of the bridge allowed a little water to drip in, but thanks to the wind, most of the rain blew farther across the bridge and fell over the side.

"Well, this is cozy and dry." Drake drew the length of his body into the small space. "I hope the river doesn't rise too much."

Noelle nodded. "I'd forgotten how little space there

was." She watched as Drake tried to find a comfortable position in the small hideaway formed by the rocks.

Drake removed his red coat. "Here, let me put this down. We'll have something to sit on."

Noelle nodded and raised her hips so he could slide the coat beneath her. It was still warm when she sat back down.

He put his arm behind her and twisted to allow them a little more room. "At least we're safe and reasonably dry. That hail strikes a painful blow."

"That it does," Noelle agreed.

"I'm glad I decided to check your house before I left. You might have been stranded out here alone." Drake looked down at her and felt a tightening in his groin. Her hair peaked on her forehead, and the gentle slope of her jawbones formed a perfect heart, accented by two wide sapphire eyes—undoubtedly the most intriguing face he'd ever seen. Her golden lashes fluttered, dislodging a drop of rain onto her pink cheeks.

Was her face flushed? Her cheeks were always a pale pink that made him want to touch them to see if they were real. Her eyes met his. Could he read them? If he did, would he see hate? Or trust? Friendship, or perhaps more?

Noelle was disturbed by the way Drake was looking at her. He appeared to be angry with her; his jaw worked, and his black eyes glittered with each flash of lightning. "Are you angry with me? Have I said or done anything . . . ?"

"Angry?" Drake averted his eyes and stared at one of the beams supporting the bridge overhead. "No. No, I'm not angry."

She stared at him, puzzled by the expression on his face. "What is it, then?"

"Noelle," he began, settling his gaze on her face once again. "Noelle, you're a . . ." His voice trailed off as he searched for words, an explanation of his behavior. How could he tell her that she was beautiful, that he desired her in a way he'd never experienced before this moment, that her luscious scent drove him to distraction? He couldn't. It wouldn't be fair to her. He still had a war to win. "Noelle, I—"

"You're looking at me as if I were the very devil." Noelle bristled, interpreting his continued perusal as evidence of his disdain.

"No, no. It's not that at all." He seemed to be getting deeper into trouble, whether he said anything or not.

"What is it?" Noelle asked impatiently. "I'm beginning to feel like a hen without feathers among a covey of peacocks."

"A hen without feathers?" Drake threw his head back in laughter and raked his fingers through an errant lock of thick black hair. He propped his elbow on his knee, his face closer to hers than ever.

"I fail to see the humor in the situation." Noelle became self-conscious and smoothed her brown skirt, wishing her gown were of gossamer instead of plain homespun. She felt the sting of his stare, of his laugh, and suddenly she didn't want that from him, she wanted something else, something indefinable to her. "Don't make jest of me with your stare, sir. I've done nothing to warrant such ill treatment."

Drake stopped laughing. "Jest?"

"Yes. I'm very well aware of your feelings. You can't hide them from me now with an innocent face." She lifted her chin, knowing her remarks struck the heart of the matter. Somehow she had allowed him to worm his way into a friendship that she never thought possible, and now, in the span of a few minutes, Drake Hastings had dashed her regard into bits and pieces.

Noelle felt his breath on her face, warm and sweet. His face was in shadow so she could not read his response to her accusation, but she felt triumphant, as if she'd achieved a victory over the enemy. Was he really an enemy? He didn't act like one.

His face was so close to hers. His lips were parted as if he wanted to speak but didn't know what to say. Her eyes met his. "Well, have you nothing to say?"

Drake offered no answer. He lowered his mouth to hers and brushed a kiss on her lips. The velvety texture of his mouth thrilled her, and Noelle stared at him for a moment. This was her first kiss, her first real kiss. Her blood sang with energy as it raced throughout her body, rushing the excitement to every inch of her.

She reached up to touch his face, to feel the roughness of his unshaved cheeks, to caress him as she realized she'd wanted to do all afternoon. From the crescent of his cheek where the stubble of whiskers flourished, to the softness above, Noelle's gaze followed her fingers. She slowly moved them to his lips and felt the moist, gentle mouth that had brought such a thrill to her body.

Drake caught her hand in his and held her fingers to his lips a moment, kissing the tips gently. His mouth moved to the center of her palm and placed a kiss there, lingering a few seconds while his eyes held hers.

Noelle gasped. Her gaze moved to her palm and back to the satiny shine of his dark eyes. Nobody had ever told her that a simple kiss in her palm could spark such a burst of emotion. She wanted him to do it again and again. She wanted his lips to touch hers. No, she wanted to do it, to see if she could elicit the same reaction from him.

His hand still held hers close to his lips, and she moved hers slightly, turning his palm toward her mouth. With a tentative touch, she placed her lips on his palm, trying to emulate his kiss.

He groaned and withdrew his hand. Flushing with embarrassment, thinking she'd done the wrong thing, Noelle began, "Drake—"

His lips covered hers. His hand caressed her neck, and he drew her closer into an embrace that shattered her composure. As he leaned toward her, pressing her back into his arms, the tip of his tongue touched her teeth, and her mouth opened to him.

Exploring the recesses of her mouth with his tongue, Drake pulled her completely into his embrace. Her spirits raced, and she abandoned all hope of regaining her dignity. The pressure of his body against hers increased, and Noelle felt an exciting suffocation; she couldn't breath and didn't care. Her fingers moved across his broad chest; her hands sought his neck, encircling the straining muscles, as she eagerly embraced a man other than her father for the first time.

Her pulse flew to heights she'd never imagined, and her breath came in erratic snatches when he pressed her body fully against his and she felt the tight muscles of his stomach and legs. He turned slightly, drawing the length of her under him, and deepened his kiss until Noelle thought she would faint.

Drake pulled away and looked around.

Noelle's eyes followed his bewildered gaze. "What's wrong?"

He stared at her and then back at the bridge overhead. "Water."

"Water?" she repeated dumbly.

"It's dripping on my head."

Noelle looked at the steadily dripping water and laughed breathlessly. She clung to him, feeling the chill October air thrust itself between them when he raised himself on his elbows and glanced around.

Twilight was settling around them. The storm had lost its fury, and lightning flashed in the distance, a mere reflection of the rage it had exercised a short time ago.

"I've got to get you back." Drake sat up and pulled Noelle to a sitting position. "Come on. If we don't hurry, I'll be drawn and quartered."

"Drawn . . ." Noelle felt the warmth of color creep into her cheeks. She was as much a wanton as the woman she'd seen in Charleston whom her father refused to discuss. "Yes. Let's hurry."

Their words became clipped and short in the conversation that burdened them as they traveled the rest of the way to Ash Meadow. She spoke only to give directions to John

Brooks's house. Noelle felt self-conscious of each incidental touch as they rode together on Nightmare, but the dreamy memory of the kiss accompanied her, salving her raw emotions.

They reached the crossroad that abutted the perimeter of John Brooks's property, and Noelle became acutely aware of how they must look. "Stop."

"Why?" Drake peered at her in the darkness. "We're in a hurry."

"Yes." Noelle wondered how she could explain without embarrassing Drake or hurting his feelings. "You can't . . . I'll walk the rest of the way."

Drake slowed Nightmare and finally pulled back on the reins. "Whoa. Are you sure?"

"Yes. They wouldn't understand if they saw me on this horse with you. You see, I'm to be . . ." Her voice trailed off. She'd almost told him she was getting married, but couldn't say the words, not to him, not after his kiss. Besides, he would never know. The kiss hadn't meant anything to him.

He dismounted and turned to help Noelle. Gripping her waist firmly, he drew her down into his arms. They hesitated, gazing at each other.

"You're so tall," she whispered breathlessly. Frustration gnawed at Noelle's composure. She wanted him to kiss her once again, but couldn't ask him. Taking matters into her own hands, she stood on tiptoe and brushed his lips lightly.

Once her lips touched his, Drake drew her completely into the warmth of his embrace and returned her kiss as she hoped he would. His kiss was lingering, deep, and thrilling, and Noelle wanted it never to end, but it did.

"Good night, little one." Drake kissed her turned-up nose. "I'll see you again."

Noelle took her precious plunder and ran. Tears welled in her eyes, but still she ran. Dear God, but she hated war.

CHAPTER
5

THE DAY BEFORE NOELLE'S WEDDING DAWNED GRAY AND somber with thunder rumbling ominously in the distance. Though she had slept well, she now worried about the events that were to come. Irene had done her best to plan a wedding to be held in the midst of a revolution, but there would be no gay houseguests happily dressing across the hall, no loud, guffawing old men telling bawdy stories downstairs, and no young, handsome groom waiting for Noelle.

John Brooks was a kind man whom Noelle had known all her life. Obviously a handsome man in his younger days, he looked distinguished now, but there was no love between Noelle and him. There was respect and friendliness, even the fondness of a child for a near neighbor, but no passionate love. Many young women married older men, Noelle reasoned. Maybe love would grow between her and John. She closed her eyes and thought of kissing him. Would his kisses rouse her and take her breath away?

The memory of Drake's kisses intruded on her thoughts, and Noelle blushed as she recalled the hunger that had flared inside her and now stirred once again. Would anybody know that the blushing bride's thoughts were of a man who was probably miles away by now and who had charged into her life only days ago—a man who was her sworn enemy and yet, because of a reckless wager, was now her friend?

A smile touched her lips, and she fingered the edge of her

dressing table, absently allowing her thoughts to wander. Drake's image flooded her mind, and she tried to remember the details of his face. Sharp planes, high cheekbones, and a square jaw combined to form a ruggedly handsome face framed by black hair tied neatly at the nape of his neck.

Noelle realized she wasn't breathing and inhaled deeply. How could she ever forget the moment he'd kissed her? Because of that kiss and its effect on her she would compare every man she met to Drake Hastings.

She was confused. What had seemed perfectly clear from the beginning of the war now seemed clouded. She questioned her own beliefs and loyalties. Her father had supported the Patriots' efforts with money, equipment, and spirit, and Noelle had always believed in the revolution as fiercely as he did and at times had wished she could join the actual fight.

Now she wasn't so sure of herself. Drake seemed like a fine man, an intelligent man, and yet he was the enemy, fighting as valiantly for the British as she wished she could for the Patriots, even though he admitted to having been born in the Colonies.

Noelle suddenly wanted the war to end more than anything she could think of. She didn't want to hear any more war news—nothing of the victories and defeats, nothing of the injuries and deaths. She wanted peace to return to South Carolina.

But what about her planned marriage to John Brooks? Before tomorrow night she would be his wife, and Drake Hastings would be only a memory.

Should she have told him she was getting married? That she was marrying a man almost thirty years older than she? That it was a marriage arranged by her father? Noelle didn't know. She wanted to be honest with Drake but couldn't find a way to say the words.

"Noelle darling," Irene called from the hallway, "may I help?"

"Yes. Come in." Noelle walked toward the door as Irene entered.

Irene smiled and crossed to Noelle. "Poor Mandy and Ardelia are scurrying about downstairs. Tonight's party is quite an affair for Mandy, to say nothing of tomorrow's wedding."

"Do you think many people will come? It looks as if this rain will last for several days, and those horrible renegades are still rampaging about." Noelle peered out the window at the ever-threatening black clouds obliterating the usual cornflower blue of the autumn sky as thunder rumbled in the distance.

"I can't answer that. Everyone who comes is taking a risk. Try not to worry. What will be will be." Irene gently pulled the fine lawn gown from its box. "It's a blessing your mother's dress held up so well over the years."

Mandy had taken it in at the waist and let it out at the breasts. "Isn't it lovely? Mother stuffed it with cotton and sealed it in a cedar box with wax. I guess if she hadn't been so careful, I would be getting married in your nightgown." Noelle tried to laugh, but it sounded strained and shrill and seemed to echo in the resounding thunderclap that punctuated her words. "Let me try the dress on to make sure it fits."

"It's lovely, and you are a beautiful bride. John will be very proud of you, as I am." Irene held a cluster of mauve asters over Noelle's head for a moment. "You're going to be the loveliest bride ever, war or no war."

Noelle looked at herself in the mirror. "I hope the storm blows over soon. Do you think it will?"

"It's just an evening shower. Should be gone before supper." Irene stood behind her, fluffing the full skirt and fussing over the placement of the tiny flowers at the waist.

For a few minutes Noelle really studied her reflection. Her face seemed to be different, more mature. Could the horrors of the past few days have changed her demeanor so radically?

Or could the change be the result of an embrace? Color stained Noelle's cheeks, and her gaze darted to Irene to see if the older woman had noticed.

"Noelle, I'm sorry we have to use asters, but the unusually cold weather has killed all my other fall flowers. And these cast a lovely pink glow on your cheeks." Irene brushed back a strand of Noelle's hair that refused to be held by her braid. "I think tomorrow we'll make a circlet of these for your hair. Yes, that will be perfect."

Feeling a sense of growing panic, Noelle hardly listened to Irene. Something inside her revolted against the picture of herself in the gown, and she suddenly wanted to tear it off. Perspiration lined her forehead, and the more Irene fussed and clucked over the gown, the more ill at ease Noelle became.

Gazing through eyes narrowed with alarm, she saw only a shadowed reflection. Her eyes sought Irene's. "I'm so scared."

"Don't worry. John will be a gentle, loving husband. He is a kind man." Irene held Noelle close and patted her back lightly.

"I know he's kind, but I can't help being scared." Noelle pulled away and began to remove the dress. The comfort Irene offered was welcome, but now Noelle needed to be alone, to consider the changes that had sculpted the new face staring back at her and the new maturity wreaking havoc on her emotions.

"I have something for you." Irene reached into her pocket and drew out a strand of pearls, then fastened the lustrous beads around Noelle's neck. "These were my mother's. They were . . . they were to be passed down to my daughter . . . if I had one."

Tears sprang to Noelle's eyes, and when she looked at Irene, the older woman turned away. "I don't know what to say . . . how to thank you."

Irene turned to face her, hugging her briefly. "Say nothing. I can think of no one I would rather give them to."

With nimble fingers, Irene unbuttoned Noelle's dress and strode from the room.

Noelle waited a moment and then let the gown drop to the floor. Mandy would brush and press it carefully so that no hint of discoloration or wrinkling could be seen. Sighing, she picked it up and looked at it with sudden pain, as if it symbolized the agony of the world as well as her own anguish.

Tomorrow would be a difficult day. Weaving the pearls between her fingers, she crossed the room and sat down at her dressing table. How could she go through with this wedding? Ever since her father had first suggested the marriage between Noelle and John Brooks, she'd had reservations. Now she knew the cause of her reluctance. Deep inside her, lodged in some secret place yet to be fully awakened, dwelt an emotion barely touched by Drake Hastings.

Noelle didn't assign that emotion to Drake as love, but instead credited him with teaching her of its existence. One day, when war became a memory, she would find the man who could breathe life into that place. Love and passion would result—a love and passion that Noelle hadn't known existed until Drake kissed her yesterday under the bridge.

Her first kiss had revealed many things to her, but the most important revelation was that she couldn't marry John Brooks. Downstairs in his sitting room with their guests, he awaited her arrival, but Noelle didn't want to face him yet. She'd have to find a way to tell him she couldn't marry him. Right now she needed to go downstairs and greet their guests. In spite of the war, Irene had insisted upon hosting a dinner honoring Noelle. A ball would have been given in less uncertain times, but Irene refused to forgo the festivities and traditions completely.

The door opened, and Mandy walked in. She went over to the wardrobe and removed a white silk underskirt embellished with artificial rosebuds at the pleated flounce. Noelle sighed and stood. The evening wore on, and she knew that people were waiting for her. She tucked her camisole into the waistband of her petticoat and threaded her arms through the long sleeves of a pale pink satin polonaise, a dress that had been among the items in her trousseau and sent to Ash Meadow earlier.

Mandy pulled the tape loops up, buttoned them at Noelle's waist in back, and examined the effect to make sure the fluffs of satin formed by the bunching lay gracefully. "Looks pretty good. Dat's the finest dress I seen since the war started."

Noelle looked at herself in the small mirror and nodded. "It's the prettiest dress I've *owned* since the war started."

She dipped and swayed, holding the skirt out in a feminine manner, and then twirled around. Stamping her foot in an unladylike gesture, she cried, "Oh, Mandy, I hate this war."

"We all hates it, chile," Mandy replied, fussing with an errant curl at the nape of Noelle's neck.

"I know, but . . ." How could she explain to Mandy how awful she felt? Would the old woman understand when Noelle refused to marry John Brooks? "But war makes people do things . . . things they wouldn't normally do. I think that up here, you know, in the backwoods, we should . . . we should just live our lives."

"Ain't that what we doin'?" Mandy used a brass hairpin to attach a sprig of artificial roses to Noelle's coiffeur.

"Of course it is, but . . . What difference can a few farmers make in a war we didn't start? I mean, we want freedom, too, but . . ." Noelle's voice dwindled off. Mandy would never understand, no matter how long Noelle talked, and she wasn't even sure she understood her own feelings. "Never mind. Tell Irene I'll be down in a minute."

Waiting for Mandy to leave, Noelle sat down at her dressing table and stared at herself in the mirror. Could she summon the courage to do what she had to do tonight? How could she approach John Brooks? Should she tell him before she joined the others downstairs, approach him immediately after their guests left, or wait until morning? No, Noelle told herself sternly, it had to be tonight. She'd never work up the courage again tomorrow. And since their guests were already arriving, she could hardly ask to speak to him now.

With no choice left to her but to make the most of what promised to be a trying evening, she descended the stairs. When Noelle entered the ballroom, people she had known all her life greeted her with hugs and kisses.

She was surprised at the gaunt faces of those she hadn't seen in a while. As she glanced around the room, Noelle noticed their clothes: yesterday's finery, today's tatters, yet still the best of their depleted wardrobes. Here and there, touches of gray hair showed where before there had been none. Some wore the black garb of mourning.

Across the room, John smiled at her as he took some good-natured ribbing from his friends who envied him his young bride-to-be. "Ah, here she is now."

John crossed the room and took her elbow. "How are you this evening, my dear?"

Noelle glanced at his eyes, clear blue and glittering with happiness. She couldn't face him squarely. "I'm fine. Please don't let me interrupt your . . . your conversation."

"Nonsense," he replied and led her to Irene. "Allow me to fetch you a glass of punch."

As he strode toward the refreshment table, Noelle smiled at Irene and wondered how the broken engagement would affect her. *Oh, Irene,* Noelle cried silently, knowing that she valued Irene's friendship and feelings more than John Brooks's. Would her change of heart destroy everything she and Irene had built between them?

Noelle's friends gathered around her, giggling and teasing, and Irene moved aside and sat down to let them get closer. None of them were escorted by beaux. All of the young men of the area—indeed, most men between sixteen and sixty—were off fighting the British. Those who had remained behind to provide some protection for the area were gathered here today, trying valiantly to ignore the reality that lay beyond the doors.

The matrons seated near Irene wore waxen smiles that betrayed anxiety for husbands, brothers, and sons. Noelle loved every one of them for putting aside their own problems to wish her and John well. Before the night was out, their efforts would prove to have been made for nothing.

"We're so happy for you, Noelle," Agnes Foster began. "You're a lucky girl, marrying John Brooks. Poor Kathleen will be twenty next month, an she's still unmarried."

Noelle forced a smile for her best friend's mother, but the words stuck in her throat, and she mumbled, "Excuse me."

The door seemed to be miles away, and Noelle hurried through the milling guests. Kathleen followed her onto the porch.

"You goose, it's cold out here." Kathleen shivered. "Why did you run like that?"

"Run? Did I run?" Noelle asked, hardly able to remember her escape.

Kathleen shrugged and rubbed her bare arms. "Not exactly, but you're as pale as a hant. Look, let's go back inside and talk. It's too cold to be chatting out here."

"No!" Noelle shouted and clapped her hands over her mouth. More gently, she whispered, "No. You go back if you want to. I need the fresh air."

"If you need fresh air—this much fresh air—then I need fresh air too," Kathleen concluded and eyed her friend suspiciously. "This sounds more serious than pre-wedding jitters. I'll get us a shawl."

"No, Kathleen." Noelle felt desperation settle heavily on her shoulders. "Irene will see you and wonder what happened. She's a love, but she'll probably insist that we return to the party."

"You know me, I'll sneak in. She'll never know I've

come and gone," Kathleen assured Noelle, squeezing her arm. "Don't go away."

Noelle watched her best friend head toward the back of the house and grimaced. She'd have a hard time getting past the hawk-eyed Mandy with Noelle's shawl.

Lifting her skirts, Noelle rushed down the steps and into the yard. Raindrops still glistened on the grass and in the plants of the kitchen garden as she strode among them, hardly seeing where she was going. When she reached the grape arbor, she stopped and looked around. Had she heard a sound?

Her gaze swept the yard and nearby fields, but she saw nothing. She was just nervous, she told herself, still searching the darkness around her. "Kathleen?" she whispered. "Is that you?"

"No," came a masculine voice from behind her.

Fear struck Noelle, and for a moment she felt rooted to the damp ground beneath the arbor. Inhaling deeply, she spun around as a hand shot out in the dark and grabbed her wrist while a second hand covered her mouth. Noelle scrambled to free herself, but found her strength lacking.

"Don't fight, Noelle," Drake whispered to the struggling woman in his arms. He felt a tightening in his loins as her wriggling ceased and she relaxed against him. He moved his hand slowly away from her mouth.

"Drake?" she asked, turning slightly to look over her shoulder. "What are you doing here? If the men inside find out you're . . ." She couldn't finish her sentence.

The situation had reached a crisis she couldn't resolve without someone getting hurt. She felt torn. Her loyalty demanded that she call out and alert the men to the presence of a British officer. Her heart wanted to protect him.

Without thinking further, he drew her into his arms and kissed her. His mouth closed gently on hers, and then he kissed her more forcefully as the hunger of the last day surged forth. He realized he'd missed her very much, and now clung to her as if he would never see her again.

Mentally cursing the darkness, he gazed down into her eyes and tried to gauge her reaction. Her response had been eager, passionate, but was it a result of relief or desire? "Noelle, tell me how you are."

"Drake," she whispered, barely able to contain her joy at being in his arms again. "I'm fine. Why are you here?"

"I can't tell you." He glanced over her shoulder toward the gaily lit house. "Who's there? What's going on?"

Noelle recalled the ballroom, filled with her neighbors and friends, and her mouth fell open. Was he here to do battle? Were the British planning to attack a civilian gathering in the darkness of night? "Drake, you can't . . . These people are my friends. They're here . . . I mean, tomorrow . . ."

Noelle stopped. She was babbling like a frightened child in front of her governess. "Please, Drake, what are you doing here? You must tell me. I can't go on being friends with someone who's plotting the destruction of my world."

Through the windows Drake saw several men gesturing and laughing. It didn't look like a military meeting, but things were seldom as they seemed these days. He was glad he'd adopted the loose-fitting shirt and buckskin coat of the upcountry Carolinians. Dressed as such, he could travel more freely. Ignoring her question, he took Noelle by the shoulders and pulled her farther into the darkness. "What's going on in there?"

"It's a dinner party," Noelle answered breathlessly as if she were pronouncing a death sentence on her friends.

His refusal to answer her question about his part in this war confirmed her fears. He must be a spy. But why was he here? Nothing was going on this far west of civilization. There were but a few settlers here and none of interest to the British.

"A party?" He stared at her, once again cursing the darkness for shrouding her eyes from him. "A party during the war? I find that a bit hard to believe."

Noelle lifted her chin. He'd snatched her as if he intended

to kidnap her, and now he was questioning her honesty. "People's lives do go on, Captain Hastings. We're not close to the fighting," she whispered angrily and paused, wondering how true her statement was. His presence seemed to imply otherwise. "Why shouldn't we gather to wish happiness to a couple getting married tomorrow?"

His gaze dropped from the window to her gown and then sought her face. Could she be getting married? Drake wondered. What a silly thought, he chided himself. If she were the bride, the groom would never have let her out of his reach on the eve of their wedding. Besides, there were no men in the area young enough for her to wed now. His scouting had confirmed that. Every man fit for Noelle would be at a battlefront somewhere.

What was she doing here? Could this be where she'd run last night when he'd left her at the crossroad? His heart lifted a little at the thought. She'd be safe here at Ash Meadow. Drake's uncle John owned this plantation, and his aunt Irene would care for her. "Noelle, are you staying here?"

"Yes," she answered and then glared up at him. "Why do you ask? Are you about to seize the property? Invade it? Burn it?"

"Of course not. I . . ." How could he tell her that John Brooks was his uncle? Would she believe him? Or think it was a ploy to gain her trust? "I was born here. John Brooks is my uncle."

"Your . . ." The words dried up in Noelle's throat as the impact of his statement gripped her. Tomorrow this stranger who'd come to mean so much to her could be her nephew. The situation grew worse every minute, and Noelle wondered whether or not to tell Drake that she and his uncle were to be married the next day. "Drake," she began. "I am—"

"Noelle, where are you?"

Noelle looked over her shoulder and saw Kathleen

wending her way across the yard toward them. "You must go. Run!"

Drake gazed down at her a second and then lowered his lips to hers. The kiss lasted only a moment but conveyed his message and gained her response. He would come back; she would be waiting. "Take care. I'm tracking Soaring Eagle again. Tell Uncle John I'll be back soon."

He brushed her lips again and then disappeared into the boxwoods behind the grape arbor. Hidden among the dense foliage, he waited and watched. For a few moments Noelle didn't move. She stared after him wtih her hand outstretched as if she wanted to say something before he left, but it was too late. A young woman reached the arbor and touched Noelle on the shoulder.

"Noelle, for goodness' sake. What are you doing out here?" Kathleen tapped her friend on the shoulder to get her attention. "Did I see someone? Were you talking to someone else? Where did he go? Who was it?"

Noelle spun around and faced Kathleen. Drake was still hiding among the trees, she knew, and she couldn't give away his position, not even to Kathleen. "What? Nobody. You must be seeing things that aren't there."

"Ridiculous. My vision is perfect, and you know it." Kathleen peered through the darkness and smiled. "Come on, Noelle. Who is it?"

Shrugging, Noelle took the shawl out of Kathleen's hands and pulled it around her shoulders. Without speaking, she glanced back at the boxwoods and strode toward the veranda. "You must be seeing things," she said again. "Maybe you'd better sit down."

"You're trying to keep something from me," Kathleen called as she ran to catch up with Noelle. "You know we don't keep secrets from each other."

Running now, Noelle lifted her skirts to keep from tripping over them and raced up the steps. She had to give Drake a chance to get away before Kathleen realized that Noelle had been talking to a British soldier. Gasping for breath, she fell into a cane-seated rocker and laughed softly. Her ploy had worked. Instead of searching the bushes for a hidden beau, Kathleen had followed Noelle to the porch.

Kathleen dropped into the rocker next to Noelle. "All right," she said, gripping Noelle's arm as if to prevent her from escaping again. "Tell me everything, or I'll announce that you sneaked out to see a British soldier on the eve of your wedding."

Noelle's laughter died. "No!" she said, louder than she intended. "No. You can't."

"Calm down. I'm only teasing you," Kathleen replied, grinning and lifting her eyebrows. "What's gotten into you anyway?"

"Kathleen. promise me. None of your shenanigans," Noelle pled, staring directly into Kathleen's eyes. "Don't ever say anything like that to anyone, even in jest."

"Oh, no," Kathleen whispered, as if the reality of her jest had taken life. "Tell me it's not true."

Noelle bowed her head. In her earnest attempt to protect Drake, she'd done the opposite. Somehow she had to make Kathleen understand the truth, if she could discover the truth herself. "Kathleen, this is difficult. I want you to listen carefully to me."

"Noelle, you couldn't!" Shock registered in Kathleen's voice.

Glancing at the door, Noelle waited a moment to be sure nobody had heard them. "Kathleen, several nights ago a renegade band of Cherokees came to Tyger Rest to burn it and . . . well, you know."

"I know. But what does that have to do with you and a British soldier?" Kathleen's brown eyes glittered with excitement. "Forget all the other stuff and get to him."

"I'm trying." Noelle smoothed her skirt and picked at a dark spot that looked like mud in the dim light. For a few seconds she re-created the scene in her mind and blushed when she recalled the touch of Drake's lips on hers.

"Noelle?" Kathleen sounded like a petulant child. "Come on. Tell."

"Well, Miss Inquisitive, Captain Hastings rescued me and—"

"*Captain*!" Kathleen exclaimed. "Do tell. This is so romantic."

"I assure you it wouldn't seem so romantic if you were in danger as I was." Noelle rolled her eyes. Sometimes Kathleen ignored the obvious and focused on a minute segment of an incident that was completely irrelevant.

"Being rescued? Not romantic?" Kathleen's eyes narrowed as she gazed at Noelle. "You're telling a fib. It is too romantic."

"Will you stop being such a twit and listen?" Exasperated, Noelle crossed her arms and stared straight ahead. The only way to get through to Kathleen now was to pretend to ignore her.

"If you don't tell me what's going on, I swear I'll tell everybody I know that you kissed a Tory." Kathleen gloated as if she'd found the perfect threat.

"Kathleen, if you do, I'll never speak to you again," Noelle parried. Drake's words suddenly sank in. She needed to speak to John privately, to let him know that Soaring Eagle was still around. "The captain happened by and kept the Cherokees from kidnapping me. What's the big deal?"

For a moment Kathleen said nothing, and then she brightened. "If that's all there was to it, then why did he come looking for you tonight?"

Noelle didn't know exactly how to answer her friend. She, too, wondered if he had guessed where she was staying and followed her here. It didn't really matter; what mattered was that she needed to tell John the news. "Look, Kathleen, I've got to find John. I have vital information for him."

Kathleen gripped Noelle's wrists. "Not until you tell me if I saw you kissing him."

A flush stained Noelle's cheeks. She'd hoped that Kathleen hadn't seen the embrace. "Kathleen, swear to me that you'll never tell a soul you saw that. It was . . . it was a sisterly kind of kiss anyway."

"Didn't look sisterly to me," Kathleen said. "What I saw was definitely a romantic kiss."

Noelle jumped up and stepped out of Kathleen's reach. "You're seeing things. I've got to find John."

CHAPTER
6

SHE RACED INTO THE BALLROOM AND SCANNED THE FACES. John stood by the fireplace, his arm resting on the oak mantel. "John, may I see you for a moment in private?"

"Certainly, my dear." John beamed at her and then faced his friends. "You'll excuse me?"

Amid a flurry of remarks about his young bride's eagerness, John joined her, and they walked to the library. "What is it?"

Noelle stared at him for a moment, unable to speak. The presence of Drake stood squarely between them, and she didn't know how to approach John with the information. How much should she relate to him now? Slowly she began, telling him as little as possible. There would be time later for the entire story. "Your nephew, Drake Hastings, has been here."

"Drake? Here?" John headed for the door, apparently eager to see his nephew.

"Wait!" Noelle called, grateful that Drake had told her the truth about his relationship with John and Irene. "He's gone."

"Gone?" John turned and gazed at her. "How do you know him? Where did you see him? When was he here? Why did he leave?"

Sighing, Noelle touched his arm. John apparently cared deeply for his nephew, even though he was loyal to the king. "I'll tell you everything later. This you must know now. I've waited too long to tell you as it is. He left minutes

89

ago. He came to warn you that Soaring Eagle is still in the area and on a rampage."

John's face reddened in anger. "That bas—confounded Indian. Where is he?"

"I don't know. Drake has been tracking him for days." Noelle sat on the edge of a leather chair and smoothed her skirts while John thought about the situation.

"Noelle, my dear, I must inform our guests of the danger." He took her hand and waited as she rose. "I apologize for ruining your party, but I believe many of our friends will want to hurry home. Some of them are already talking of seeking shelter at the fort in Ninety Six."

"No, John," Noelle began, recalling the number of Indians who rode with Soaring Eagle. "Ask all of them to stay here. Together we may have a chance against them. There are too many Indians for us to deal with in small groups."

"But their property!" John considered her argument. "I believe they'll leave. None of them can afford to lose their homes."

"But, John, ask them to stay," Noelle begged. "Tell them Soaring Eagle is out for blood."

John slipped his arm around Noelle, and she flinched. Why couldn't she be comfortable with him? They moved toward the ballroom, their faces drawn with worry.

When they entered the room, many of the guests smiled and greeted them as if assuming they'd been sneaking a kiss in some darkened corner of the house. John seemed not to notice, but Noelle felt the warmth spreading over her cheeks.

Moving toward the knot of men at the fireplace, John guided Noelle along with him. When they reached the group, he hesitated, as if weighing his words. "Gentlemen, I fear I have received bad news."

"Tell us, John," Angus Foster answered almost immediately, and the group nodded in agreement.

"I've received word from a reliable source," he began,

and looked at the faces of his friends one by one, "that the Indian Soaring Eagle is once again in the area. We believed he'd left after burning Tyger Rest, but that is not the case."

Angus glanced at his friends and spoke for them once again. "I think we should leave now."

"Noelle . . . we believe you should remain here." John released Noelle and gripped the arm of Angus Foster. "Together, perhaps we have a chance. Separately, I fear we're beaten. He has many braves in his murderous band."

Several of the men mumbled and muttered, but at last they decided to leave. John glanced at Noelle and recognized the despair in her eyes. "Please, I beg you men to reconsider. This band of renegades is ruthless," John said.

Angus eyed his friend for a moment but shook his head. "I can't chance it. I've got too much at stake. My cotton's just in. I'm going home."

Noelle stood on the veranda as her guests began to take their leave. Wedding feasts usually lasted into the wee hours and sometimes went on for days, but Noelle's was no ordinary wedding, and these were not ordinary times. The house was soon empty again except for Noelle, Irene, John, and their servants.

After a quiet dinner John joined Noelle and Irene alone in the parlor. They sat for a while talking about their guests and the wedding. Noelle was acutely aware of every sound, every gesture, and every word.

"You know, Noelle," John began, "Angus Foster told me something I think you'd be interested in hearing."

Noelle wondered if Kathleen's father ever said anything interesting, but she gave John her attention anyway. "Yes, John? What did he say?"

"Well, he had it from a dependable source that the British surrendered to a Patriot force at Thicketty Fort without us firing a single shot."

Laughing, Noelle thought of Drake. Did he know of this ignominious defeat? What would his reaction be? Then she remembered John. "Does that mean they're giving up? And going home?"

"No. No, not at all." John rose and strode to the fireplace, staring down at the logs as they crackled and popped with a cheerfulness that belied the reality of war.

Her heart went out to him. He, too, was worried about Drake. For a minute she didn't think John could continue.

He turned to her. "In August a battle took place near Camden."

Feeling his pain, Noelle whispered, "What happened?"

"Cornwallis annihilated Gates's forces." John dropped into his chair again and hung his head. "Of four thousand men, only seven hundred were fit enough to rally at Hillsboro, North Carolina."

"Oh, John, that's horrible." Noelle wondered if she knew any of the dead or injured. What had happened to the injured? Had they been left to die on a field somewhere, or had they received medical care? The import of that battle struck her with sudden clarity. "We're losing, aren't we?"

John tried to smile. "Who's to say? But we have a new force to be reckoned with. Francis Marion and his men freed one hundred fifty American prisoners at Nelson's Ferry. Then he defeated a larger Tory force at Blue Savannah."

"Then there's hope?" Noelle asked, feeling a little better.

"There's always hope," John replied and gazed down at his hands.

After staring at the fire for a moment, Noelle closed her eyes, and Drake Hastings's face appeared in her mind. What was he doing here? she wondered, wishing he would return. He should be here protecting his relatives, instead of fighting against them. Perhaps he would return now that their guests were gone. She listened acutely, hoping to hear the sound of a single rider. The memory of his kisses stirred a new warmth in her that seemed to permeate every cell, and she longed for the comfort of his arms around her.

"Stop it! She scolded herself silently for continuing to have such thoughts.

Nevertheless, she knew she'd feel much safer if he returned. She glanced at Irene. How did she feel about her nephew's loyalty to the king? Instinctively Noelle realized that Irene hated Drake's decision but would never question his right to make it.

"Noelle?"

She jerked back to the present. John Brooks was staring at her. "I'm sorry. I was just thinking about . . ."

John strode toward her. "Come, Noelle, it's bedtime. I'll walk you upstairs."

"Good night, Irene," Noelle whispered and bent to kiss her friend.

Irene caught Noelle's shoulders briefly and squeezed them. "Sleep well, my dear."

Noelle followed John and took his arm as they mounted the stairs. When she reached the room she had occupied for the past few days, she paused. "It was a lovely evening, don't you think?"

He stopped outside her door. "Yes, lovely, but pale when compared to you."

"Thank you, John." Noelle turned away from his penetrating gaze, puzzled by the flush that crept up his neck and into his pallid cheeks. "You're very kind."

"Well, my dear, we're to be married tomorrow. We mustn't be so formal." He cupped her chin in his hand.

"It seems so strange," she stammered, inwardly cursing herself for being a coward. Now was the time to tell him she couldn't marry him.

Would he be angry, perhaps throw her out? Would he attribute her sudden change of heart to mere girlish fears? He could, she supposed, force her to marry him if he chose. No matter what his response, she had to tell him her decision. John Brooks was entitled to know at the earliest moment.

"John," she began, hardly knowing how to broach the subject.

"Now, don't be concerned. I've alerted the servants to the danger of the Indians." He beamed down at her. "You have nothing to fear, now that you're . . . home."

Relieved to hear of the precautions he'd taken, she almost let the subject drop, but her heart refused to allow her any peace until she told John the truth.

"That's wonderful, but—"

"Noelle," he interrupted, "you've made me the happiest man alive. You can never know how I feel at this moment. Men my age rarely find happiness, but I've done so. I know you don't love me now, but do you feel some affection for me?" His voice broke with emotion.

"Yes, John. I have always held you in high regard." Noelle faced him, willing her fears to be silent. *Tell him*, her conscience urged. She had never willingly deceived anyone, and now she felt terrible. "John, I . . . I need to talk with you."

"The hour is late, my dear." John smiled and took her elbow gently. "Tomorrow is going to be exhausting. Rest. We shall have a lifetime to talk."

"No!" Panic rose in Noelle, and she almost shouted. This business had to be attended to tonight. There could be no further delay. "No, John. Perhaps we could sit somewhere for a few minutes."

"Of course. I didn't realize you were so troubled. My study is down the hall."

"That will be fine." Noelle followed him into a masculine room, decorated heavily with leather and hardwood furniture. She chose a leather armchair and almost collapsed onto the edge. For the moment she felt too tense to relax.

"Now tell me what is disturbing you." John moved to the chair opposite her and sat down.

His smile taunted her. Noelle despised herself for what she had to do, but knew that she could never live a lie with this man. "John, I'm very fond of you . . . but I can't marry you."

His smile seemed to deflate, and he reached out as if to touch her, to see if she was really telling him what he'd heard. "Noelle, my dear, what do you mean?"

Unable to sit any longer, Noelle rose and strode across the room. She couldn't bear to see the hurt that registered on his face. Of all people she had to hurt, she hated it to be her father's best friend. "I've been unfair to you."

The word "unfaithful" almost tumbled out, but she managed to retain her dignity. "During the excitement of the past few days, I've discovered that . . . that I'm unwilling to cheat you of the love you truly deserve."

"Come, Noelle, surely this must be a case of jitters that can be attributed to the distress of your encounter with the Indians combined with the upcoming wedding," John argued, sagging back into the plush leather upholstery of his chair.

"Perhaps," Noelle conceded, unwilling to hurt him any more than was necessary. "But I'm convinced that we . . . that my feelings . . ."

Tears stung her eyes, and she paused a moment to regain her composure. If only he would not fight her. She didn't want to mention the awakening of her desires, nor did she wish to bring Drake's name into the conversation.

"My dear, why not sleep on this? Surely in the morning you'll see the folly of your thinking." John stood abruptly, as if he'd resolved the issue. "Yes, sleep on it. That's always best."

For a moment Noelle almost gave in. Her courage sagged as he approached her and touched her arm, but she refused to allow him to labor under a misconception. "No, John. I can't allow you to persist in believing that I may change my mind. I am unworthy of your love."

"Unworthy?" he repeated, gazing into her eyes. "How so? I can't believe that."

Sighing, Noelle closed her eyes. If only the matter were so simple. "No, John. It's not that—"

"Then what? What can have come between us?" he asked, releasing her arm. "I was so happy. I thought you were happy."

"John, it isn't a matter of being happy or being unhappy," Noelle explained. "It's a matter of honesty. And I've been dishonest with you as well as with myself."

"Nonsense," he concluded. "I've always known that you don't love me, but you will. Many girls marry—"

"Many girls do marry older men, men they don't love," she interrupted, turning to stare out the window. "But, John, are you willing to deprive me of ever knowing true love? If I come to love you, it will be as a substitute for my father, and not as a husband."

"Is there someone else?" John dropped into his chair again and watched her as she turned to face him.

"No, John. I love no one else," she replied honestly. "I am going to be entirely truthful with you because I believe you deserve nothing less."

Noelle moved back to her chair and sat down, taking one of his hands in hers. "John, you've done everything humanly possible to make me happy. I regret that it hasn't succeeded."

"No more than I, my dear, no more than I," he whispered.

"On the eve of the raid at Tyger Rest, a young British officer saved my life," she stated flatly and held his large hand between her own, trying to comfort him in some small way. "That officer was Drake Hastings."

John Brooks stared blankly at her, a smile of pride touching the corners of his mouth. "My nephew? Why didn't you say something? Why didn't he bring you directly here?"

"I never knew he was your nephew until this evening," Noelle confessed. "I . . . I wanted to hate him, but I couldn't. I wanted to dismiss him as just another overly zealous pawn of the king. His . . . his kindness and concern touched me more than I was willing to admit."

A realization of what Noelle was saying seemed to dawn in John's eyes. "Are you in love with my nephew?"

"In love with Drake?" Noelle considered this idea for the first time. Could she be in love with him? "No, John, I am not. But he . . . he made me realize that I could marry for no reason other than love."

"I see." John's smile broadened, and a twinkle returned to his eyes. "But given the opportunity, you might fall in love with him."

Noelle dropped his hand and stood again. Studying the thought, she paced back and forth across the floor. "I can't answer that. There are many differences between us that would make life together . . . demanding, to say the least."

John vaulted to his feet and embraced Noelle. "My dear, this information makes me as happy . . . happier than if you had remained silent and married me tomorrow. Drake is special to me. I held him moments after his birth. I walked the floor, carrying him in my arms, when he had colic. I love him as my own son. When his mother took him away, I mourned for him as if he were dead."

Noelle listened joyfully. The details about Drake's birth mattered little to her, but John's acceptance of her refusal to marry him delighted her. "I never knew about him."

"Noelle, is there even the slightest chance that you and Drake could find happiness together?" John asked and then rushed on. "You are the perfect choice for him. I spoke to him last year when he was assigned to the Colonies, uh, America, and he plans to remain here no matter the outcome of the war."

Happiness welled inside Noelle, and she smiled gratefully at John. He had given her a bit of useful information that might color her feelings for Drake. "I can't predict the future, John."

"No matter," he concluded. "It's enough that you have

some tender feelings for my nephew, and it's readily apparent that you do."

Noelle blushed, embarrassed that John could read her so easily. She decided to change the subject. "Then I'll be going home tomorrow."

"Nonsense. Ash Meadow is your home." John tucked his arm around her waist and hugged her. "Until the end of the war, you can remain here with Irene and me. Drake will always know where to find you, if he should have a mind to."

"Thank you for your kindness, but I can't stay." Noelle allowed herself to breathe easily for the first time since entering the room. They walked from John's study to her door. "John, you've been wonderful. Irene is truly a dear friend to me, but I must return to Tyger Rest. At the end of the war I must be ready to market my cotton and take my place among the planters of South Carolina."

"But, Noelle—"

"No, John," she interrupted, feeling in charge of her own destiny once again. "I won't impose on you any longer. I am convinced that I'm making the right decision."

He gazed at her for a moment and whispered, "My dear, I believe you are. If you should change your mind, however, your place is always here with us. Irene and I love you."

Touched by his kindness, Noelle stood on tiptoe and kissed him lightly on the cheek. "Thank you for everything."

"Go in. I'll send Irene to help you dress." He kissed her lightly on the forehead. He had to jiggle the doorknob for a moment before it would turn. "That needs to be repaired. Somehow it never bothered me before, but now with you here, it seems to matter a great deal. I'll see you in the morning."

Noelle wondered about the kiss and absently compared it with Drake's kisses. John had never kissed her before. She had never been kissed at all, except by her father and by

Drake. Kathleen had been kissed once by Billy Joe Hammond, and she had confided to Noelle with a bright glow in her eyes that kissing was wonderful. Noelle recalled her response to Drake's kisses. She had to agree with Kathleen.

Drake's image swam before her eyes, and her lips parted as she remembered his kiss. Would another man's kiss stir her as Drake's had? She had to stop thinking of him. He had no place in her life anymore, no matter what John wanted for her.

Noelle removed the artificial roses and placed them carefully on the bonnet chest. She wondered if John had bought the chest especially for her? She ran her fingers along the satiny top and inhaled the heavy scent of cedar.

By the time Irene came in, Noelle was glad for her assistance. The buttons down the back of the gown were impossible for her to reach. Irene gently unbuttoned them and pulled the gown over Noelle's head. "You were beautiful this evening. I am very proud to be your friend."

As Noelle slipped into a white lawn nightgown, she marveled at its translucence. She had never owned anything so sheer. All of her new undergarments had been made of a fine lawn that Mandy had hoarded over the years in anticipation of Noelle's wedding, but the nightgown now had no significance other than for sleeping. The blue satin ribbon threaded through the lace trim had been a gift from her father on her birthday.

Her birth on Christmas Day had inspired her father to name her Merry Noelle. At times Noelle thought it rather silly, but at others she liked her name because it set her apart from all the Marys, Peggys, and Sallys.

She fiddled with the clasp of the pearls, and when it opened, she removed the necklace and gazed at it for a moment. The pearls meant a great deal to Irene. Noelle hesitated before handing them to her friend. "I want to return these to you, now that . . . since John and I . . ." Her voice trailed off into silence. She didn't know if John had mentioned their decision to Irene yet.

"You are wonderful. If I'd ever had a daughter, I would have wished her to be like you." Irene turned away, but not before Noelle had seen tears on the older woman's cheeks.

"And you are like I imagine my mother would have been," Noelle said, finally voicing her feelings.

Irene turned to face Noelle and hugged her firmly. "I insist that you keep the pearls. John says that you and Drake may . . . well, that you've met and are fond of each other. Drake is like a son to me. I never wanted my sister to take him to England. I felt he should grow up where he could at least see his father occasionally. I . . . well, there will be time to talk later. Go to bed, my child."

Noelle's fingers curled around the pearls, and she stared at her closed fist. Clasping her hands to her heart, she whispered, "I'll treasure these always."

Irene smiled. "We'll be as close as mother and daughter. Now climb into bed and I'll tuck you in." Irene pulled the coverlet up to Noelle's chin. "I wish there had been more time for us to talk. Please remain with us for a while longer."

"I can't, Irene." Noelle tried to think of the words that would convince Irene of the rightness of returning to Tyger Rest. "Right now I have so many questions, so many things I need to think about and do."

"Speak to John about your fears and questions. He will help you in any way possible." Irene smiled and turned to leave. "God be with you, my dearest."

John tapped on the door. "Irene?"

"In a moment," Irene called out, and then she whispered, "We'll talk tomorrow." Irene strode back to the bed, kissed Noelle gently on the forehead, and quickly left the room. "John, I want to talk to you. I won't keep you long."

The door closed, and Noelle was once again alone. She glanced around the big room. It smelled of cedar, burning candles, and beeswax.

Noelle unclasped her hand and looked at the pearls, fingering the satiny beads one by one. Their luster picked up the flicker of the candlelight. Each gem was perfect. She looped the strand around her fingers as she had done earlier in the evening, enjoying the cool feeling of the pearls and touching them to her cheek.

Noelle had no family except her relatives in Charleston. She could not manage alone, or so her father had thought. Her marriage to John Brooks must have seemed to be the only reasonable solution. Now Noelle had flouted her father's wishes and disappointed a good friend. She hoped she'd made the right decision and wondered if she would ever sleep soundly again.

But she did. Noelle fell asleep before she had time to consider the consequences of her decision. Later she was awakened by a loud noise she couldn't identify.

There it was again. A shriek of terror split the night. Then she heard John yelling at someone downstairs. Surely he couldn't be arguing so loudly with Irene!

A gunshot resounded through the house, and Noelle leapt from her bed. With quivering fingers she twisted the doorknob frantically, noticing distractedly that the pearls were still wrapped around her hand. She was suddenly aware of the scent of candle wax mingled with cedar, usually a pleasant smell. But tonight it only served to heighten her frenzied emotions. Every sense became acute. The cold brass doorknob finally gave, and Noelle jerked the heavy wooden door open and bounded out.

Running at full speed and barefoot, she reached the landing. Indians!

The knot of Cherokees at the bottom of the stairs stunned her. Irene stood in the parlor archway, her face blanched and strained. The wine and mauve asters from the party still decorated the foyer. Noelle's eyes scanned the scene in a slow arc, then stopped in sudden horror.

John lay sprawled in a pool of blood at the foot of the stairs, unconscious, his blue eyes staring blankly at the ceiling.

Stunned, Noelle couldn't pry her gaze from the gory scene, from the ever-increasing circle of scarlet around

John's quivering body. The combined odor of burned gunpowder and blood filled the air, and she turned to stare in disbelief at Irene who had knelt on the floor beside her brother. Irene's face was chiseled from stone. Noelle's eyes moved to the figure by the doorway.

The man holding the gun on Irene stared at Noelle for a moment. She recognized the Indian—Soaring Eagle.

"No!" she cried plaintively. Noelle rushed down the stairs as the Indian aimed a gun—Noelle's gun—at Irene. For a moment there was silence.

"Run! Run, Noelle! Out the back! Don't stop!" The report of the musket sent a wave of fear and horror through Noelle as she watched Irene crumple into a heap on the floor beside John.

Irene's warning was to no avail. Noelle couldn't run. Her bare feet refused to move from the cool wooden landing. She faced Soaring Eagle with a look of pure, undisguised hatred.

Though the bitter taste of nausea threatened to make her retch, Noelle refused to lower her eyes. When he shot her, she would be staring directly into his eyes. He had taken the lives of the only remaining people she cared for.

Screams from the back of the house were followed by gunshots, confirming her fear that the Indians intended to kill everyone in the house. Silence surrounded her as she faced certain death. She wouldn't scream, nor would she cry and beg for mercy. Raising her chin defiantly, Noelle forced herself to walk slowly toward her executioner.

"Come. That's it. Come down. We meet again without Hastings to interfere." Soaring Eagle laughed and slapped the back of a companion, who stepped inside the door.

Noelle paused. He wasn't acting the way she thought he would. She had expected him to fire as soon as he reloaded. Uncertainty gripped her heart with cold fingers. She decided to confront him with his deeds. "You are the killer of helpless men and women. Aren't you proud?"

She stepped down to the hall floor. Soaring Eagle loomed

over her, but she wouldn't be intimidated by this wild beast. Noelle kept her eyes focused on his.

He appeared startled by her brash accusations. "I'm as good as any white man, but this is easier than trapping. And more money." The Indian smiled wildly.

Noelle didn't understand what he meant, but felt the threat in his words. She stood her ground proudly. Suddenly his hand shot out and grabbed her wrist like a striking rattler. He jerked her body against his. Terrified, Noelle wrestled to free herself, but to no avail. The savage embrace crushed her breasts to his chest as his lips bruised hers unrelentingly. Noelle twisted and fought. Angrily she bit his probing tongue until she tasted blood.

"Aaaaagh! You must learn ways of Indian women." He slapped her and dragged her outside as he motioned for his men to set fire to the house. Torches arched through the air, landing on the roof, and others were tossed through the open door. Once again grinding his mouth on hers, he threw her to the ground and fell on her, pinning her beneath him.

The cruel curl of his lips and his raucous laughter suddenly stilled the fight in Noelle. He would most certainly kill her, but first, a greater torture was in store for her. Instinctively she knew that before she drew her last breath, she would suffer at his hands. In the glow of the blazing house, she renewed her struggle, hoping to postpone the inevitable horror.

Rough hands plundered beneath her gown, which had risen to her waist. Her breasts ached from his coarse fingers' pinching and kneading. Terror gripped Noelle, and she screamed, only to have the sound muffled by another bruising kiss.

Suddenly the sound of a horse coming toward them arrested the Indian's movements. A voice commanded, "Move one muscle and you're dead."

Soaring Eagle obeyed, but the crafty look in his eyes told Noelle that he was biding his time, thinking of a way that would allow him his perverse pleasure and let him destroy his enemy, too.

"Get up," Hastings commanded, glowering at the Indian.

As the weight lifted off Noelle, she scrambled to her feet and ran behind her rescuer. Drake Hastings had saved her *again*. In the firelight, his face, full of fury, was the devil's own. But she would have welcomed Lucifer himself if he stopped the Indian's assault.

"If you weren't the son of . . . a chief, I'd kill you," Hastings snarled. "Be warned. If I find you in this vicinity again, I will. By God, I don't care if we are . . . I won't tolerate such treatment. Leave the premises immediately."

"One day, Hastings, we will meet again. And then I shall be victorious." The Indian left quickly. His men followed with murderous glances for Hastings, who sat astride Nightmare as he had on the last occasion Noelle had seen him.

"I . . . I don't know what to say, except thank you. I realize it's far from adequate, but . . ." Noelle shivered and tried to straighten her nightgown.

"Say no more. Noelle, my uncle and aunt . . ." Drake's voice trailed off as he climbed down from his tall horse. "Are they . . ."

Tears burned her eyes, and she gazed at him, understanding and feeling his pain as her own. "They're . . . they're both dead, I think. Shot by Soaring Eagle."

Drake gazed at her in disbelief a second before racing into the burning house. Noelle followed at his heels. Time froze as she stared in horror at the sight before her. Fire engulfed the parlor and the staircase. The hem of Irene's gown smoked a moment and then burst into flame.

Hesitating only a second, Drake looked from his aunt to his uncle as he gnashed his teeth in indecision. "I'll kill that—"

He knelt between them, agonizing over the decision he had to make. Noelle touched his shoulder. "You take John. I'll bring Irene."

"You can't . . ." Drake began, but his voice dwindled off. He had no time to argue.

Already Drake had stamped out the fire on Irene's gown, and Noelle was lifting her by the shoulders. Flame spurted from a second spot on the cotton fabric and Noelle pounded it with her hands. The flames creeping closer and closer nearly roasted her as she moved between Irene and the fire. "Move, Drake. I can't drag her over you."

Drake lifted his uncle's deadweight and prayed silently that they might still be alive. Doubt creased his brow, and the smoke wrenched tears from his eyes as he pulled John Brooks across the threshold and over the veranda. Drake never hesitated, nor did he look back. When he reached the shelter of a cedar, he laid his uncle gently on the grass and turned to help Noelle.

Coughing and crying from the stifling smoke, she struggled to drag the heavier woman across the veranda and down the steps without killing her, if she was still alive. Drake raced to her side and lifted his aunt easily. Within seconds Irene lay beside John.

Drake felt for a pulse and found John's weak but still apparent. "Thank God, Uncle. Don't die."

With tears in her eyes Noelle placed her arm around Drake, comforting him and seeking solace for herself. She could feel no pulse in Irene's wrist, nor in her neck. There was nothing Noelle could do for Irene now.

"Drake, my son," John whispered, obviously in pain.

"Yes, Uncle?" Drake slid his legs under his uncle's head and bent to shelter him from the falling ashes. "Don't speak. We'll find a doctor for you."

"No time," came the raspy reply. His eyes sought Noelle. "Are you injured, my dear?"

Fighting to keep her voice from quavering, Noelle took John's hand and held it to her breast. "I'm fine, John. Don't worry about me. It's you that—"

"My darling, Noelle. I do love you dearly." John coughed, and blood spattered on the stark white of her gown. "I give you into Drake's care. Protect her and care for her. Drake and . . . Noelle . . . blessings . . ."

"John!" Noelle exclaimed, gripping his wrist as his eyelids fluttered shut. "No, John. Don't die. Please."

Even as she spoke, she knew John had joined his sister. Tears streamed through the ashes on her face, streaking it with black. Pure anguish wrenched at her. She could have waited to tell John of her decision, and he would have died a happy man. Racked with sobs, she hung her head and clung to John's hand. A part of this was her fault. If she hadn't told him her feelings earlier, he might have fought harder, might somehow have defeated Soaring Eagle.

Not understanding the significance of his uncle's words, Drake looked from his uncle to Noelle. What was going on here? he wondered. Uncle John had called Noelle his "darling." What could he have meant?

"What are you doing here? Why did you come here?" Drake asked vehemently, as if seeing Noelle for the first time.

Without warning, the occurrences of the past few days assaulted her—images of fire, blood, and death. A light-headedness blurred the images in her mind. Slowly she raised a shaking hand to her head. Everything was spinning and whirling about, displaced. Drake seemed to sway crazily. That was Noelle's last thought before she crumpled to the ground at his feet.

CHAPTER
7

WHEN NOELLE AWOKE, THE REFLECTION OF THE FLAMES danced along the wall of the barn. For a moment she was startled. How had she gotten into John's barn? Then she recalled Drake Hastings. He must have carried her, but where was he now?

Shivering in the cold, she realized that she was wearing a strange garment that was much too large. In the flickering light, she could see the fringe and feel the rough buckskin of Drake's coat. Though she was freezing, she wanted to rip the vile garment from her body. Noelle wanted nothing the British offered, not their coats, not their soldiers, not their rule, not even their precious tea.

She could believe he "happened by" once in time to rescue her, but not twice—and the second time just after appearing to "warn" the inhabitants of a soon-to-be-ravaged household. Drake Hastings must have instigated these raids that burned her home and slaughtered her friends; nothing else seemed logical. But then, his aunt and uncle had died in the attack. Had he no heart at all?

"You'd better keep that on if you want to live through the night. It's freezing out. That wisp of a gown you're wearing will provide little warmth." Drake sat down in the hay beside her and glared at her.

"I'll wear nothing of yours. I'd rather freeze." Noelle flung the words at him, hating him for his duplicity and hating herself for venting her anger and frustration at him. Mandy had been right about him all along. Where was

Mandy? She would probably show up as soon as Drake left again.

"Do as you wish. I can attempt to protect you from the Indians but not from yourself." He lay casually back on one elbow to study her. He didn't understand her yet, and her sudden change of attitude disturbed him. Earlier in the evening, she'd accepted his kiss eagerly, but now her demeanor was colder than a peak in the French Alps in midwinter. He found her new contempt more puzzling than the aloofness she'd demonstrated when they first met.

"What reason have I to expect kindness from you? You're fighting for the British. You hire Indians to do your killing." Noelle wanted to hurt him, had to hurt him. In order to live with the terrors of the past few days, she felt compelled to lash out at someone.

"I don't hire Indians. Neither do I ravish helpless women, even though they tempt me sorely. If you won't wear my coat for warmth, please wear it for my sake. I am not a stick of wood." Drake turned away suddenly as if her appearance was abhorrent to him. "With his last words, my uncle asked me to protect you, and protect you I will."

Noelle pondered his profile without replying to his harsh words. Did she indeed tempt him—and Soaring Eagle? Were the horrors of the past few days somehow her own fault? Had she unconsciously invited the attacks?

Irene could have helped her find the answers that plagued her. Maybe Irene could have explained the strange feeling this man caused in the pit of Noelle's stomach. It was different from anything she had ever experienced. It must be a reaction to all this horror, she thought. "I don't understand what you mean."

Why had she said that? Why did she even bother to converse with him?

His ebony glare moved steadily across her face, and Noelle edged away. Along the line of his jaw, a thin white scar caught her attention. Had he been injured in the war?

His gaze traveled down her scantily clad body at a

leisurely pace and back again. "You must be jesting. Or maybe you're toying with me." His tone became almost vicious. One way or another he would find out what was going on here.

Noelle gasped. She did not understand her own emotions, and she didn't comprehend his meaning. His tone suggested that he meant she was evil, bad—like the bad woman she had seen once in Charleston. "If you think I'm bad, then please be on your way. I can take care of myself." That should set him on his heels. "I don't need any help from a Tory."

Instead, he threw back his head in disdain. "You don't know what you think. One minute you're an innocent child. The next, you're snapping at me in anger. The next you're a Jezebel with tempting lips. Which role are you playing now?"

"I beg your pardon! I'm not an actress. Actresses are bad. Father told me so. I saw one once in Charleston." Her voice sounded shrill against the keening of the wind that fought its way through the cracks in the barn.

Noelle recalled the flamboyantly dressed woman. Her skirts, which were red taffeta, came above her ankles. The paint on her face was unlike anything Noelle had ever seen. Her own lips blushed like cherries when they began to ripen, but that woman's lips were as red as the skirts she wore. And they were greasy-looking. Two large circles on her cheeks matched the undignified scarlet of her lips. Noelle's cheeks heightened in color as she shifted under Drake's unflinching gaze. "Perhaps your mother was an actress. Is that how you know so much about them?" For a minute Noelle thought she had gone too far. He seemed to be about to strike her.

"My mother was a sweet home-loving woman who was true to my father until her death." Hastings rose quickly and, muttering with every step, strode to the door of the barn.

His reference to his mother caught Noelle's attention.

Both Irene and John had spoken briefly about Drake's birth, but neither had said anything specific about his father. Irene had mentioned that she would have liked for Drake to remain in the Colonies to be near his father. Now Drake said his mother remained true to his father until her death. She glanced up to find him staring at her.

Taking the lantern that hung by the door, he passed from her sight. When he returned, the lantern was lit. He hung it on the nail and closed the door.

"No! Leave it open." Panic seized Noelle. After her recent experience with Soaring Eagle, she didn't want to be alone with any man. The memory of the Indian's cruel lips on hers frightened her, and she closed her eyes with the horror of the recollection.

Mandy would have fallen into a dead faint if she had known Noelle willingly stayed all night in the barn with a British soldier. With that thought, her mind turned to Mandy. Was she safe? Could she have escaped once again? Noelle closed her eyes and uttered a silent prayer for the old woman's safety.

"Don't be foolhardy. You may wish to freeze to death, but I don't intend to do so just to please you. If you wish, you may go outside to freeze. I'm trying to keep us warm." With those gruff words, Hastings ignored her and began searching the immediate area.

Noelle shivered and snuggled closer in his coat. Let him freeze, she thought. She would wear his coat. Watching him speculatively, she wondered if he was married and if he had children somewhere in England. Why had he joined the British army? Perhaps he was patriotic. Pooh, she sniffed, still shivering. He was loyal to the wrong people. Even one as ignorant as he should realize that, after witnessing the Indians' handiwork.

"I could find only one blanket and I'm afraid it smells rather horsy. We'll have to share the blanket whether we're still friends or not." He dropped down beside her and said in a serious voice, "Please, Noelle, trust me. I only want to protect you."

"Friends? Protect me?" She wanted to believe him, but how could she? Her mind raced. What could she say to him? What should she do? The prospect of sharing a blanket with this handsome rogue petrified her. The memory of his lips on hers brought fresh color to her cheeks. If she could keep him talking, everything might work out favorably. Words began to tumble out of her mouth, and even though she knew she was babbling, she couldn't stop them. "Where do you come from? Is your family still living? Do you have brothers and—"

"Whoa, one question at a time," he interrupted, cocking an eyebrow at her. What was she up to now, chattering as if they were old friends who'd been apart for too long? "I'm from just outside London. Have you been to London?" Once again, Drake settled on the hay beside her and spread the blanket over them both.

Noelle shivered as the fluttering blanket stirred the cold air beneath it. When it settled, the wool scratched Noelle's nearly bare legs, but she was glad for its warmth. "No. I've never been away from here, except for trips to Charleston. Is this your first trip here, to this area, I mean?" She realized that she sounded like those women who chattered incessantly about nothing. She didn't really care if he'd ever been here before. She wished he and all his soldier friends would go back to England.

"Yes, I've been here before. I was born in the Colonies, if you recall, not so very far from here." He leaned slightly closer and tucked the blanket under his hips.

"That's right. You were born here! How can you fight against your own countrymen?" Aghast, Noelle scooted farther away. The cold tongue of air that reached through the narrow space between the blanket and her hips gave her cause to think practically again, and she returned to the spot she'd already warmed.

"It seems we've met under extremely awkward circumstances. You must admit our situation is quite remarkable, Noelle," he continued without waiting for her comment. "Though I was born here, my countrymen are British. *Your* countrymen are British. Have you forgotten that you live in the British Colonies?"

"Balderdash!" she exclaimed. That should shock him from his ridiculous attitude. "These colonies *were* British. Papa said the British forfeited all rights when they enacted that silly tea tax and committed atrocities like the Boston Massacre. Word travels slowly, but it reaches even tne backcountry."

Noelle knew there were other reasons for the war, but the most frequently mentioned grievance in her home was the silly tea tax. Other reasons were probably more important, but tea had been very important to her father when he could obtain it. And the lives lost were invaluable.

Drake laughed. "You echo the words of your father, I'll wager. Do you ever think for yourself?"

Incensed, Noelle spat, "Of course I do. Do you think I'm ignorant just because I'm not from London? My father insisted that I be educated, not only in womanly interests but also in geography, mathematics and science."

"I see. If you had been a man, you'd have been educated at Oxford, no doubt," he replied dryly.

"I'm sure of it." That should put him in his place, she thought.

"And what of your womanly interests? Do you excel in them as well?" Drake stretched lazily.

"I do. I am considered an artist of some talent. I play the piano exceptionally well. I am not a singer, though. I wish I were. My father had such a lovely bass voice that he often said we should sing together. I always refused. I screech like an owl." As she remembered her father's gentle voice, Noelle choked back a sob.

The past few days—in fact, the past few weeks—had been nearly intolerable for her. She had lost her father, her home, and the friendship of Irene, who was more like a mother than anyone Noelle had ever known.

The taste of death and destruction rose like bitter gall in her throat, all because of these hated British soldiers. And now here she was, talking with one of them as if it were teatime. Leaning down, she pressed her forehead into her hands and closed her eyes to blot out her feelings and memories. What was wrong with her? Noelle knew that without Drake, she'd be completely alone and cold. He'd been kinder to her than she expected or even could have asked of an old friend. For a moment she toyed with the idea of running, anywhere, because her conflicting emotions distressed her more than she even imagined possible.

She could go back to Tyger Rest. Though much of the roof was burned, the kitchen was intact. At least it had been when she left. When her father had first brought her to upstate South Carolina, they'd slept in the loft above the kitchen until the big house was finished. Her frontier practicality returned, and Noelle decided to wait until morning to return to Tyger Rest, to begin rebuilding her home.

"Why don't you go to sleep? You've had a long, hard day." Drake's gentle words surprised him. This girl, his sworn enemy, touched feelings never before awakened, and for the moment he didn't understand them well enough to cope with them.

He stared at the rotting wall of the barn above her head and through a crack he could see the moon rising. This was a good night to ride. He wished he could tell her the truth, that he was not what she thought, but he was sworn to secrecy. Drake damned Tarleton and his secret missions as he watched her stretch and yawn.

For the past few weeks Drake had ridden at night and slept during the day. Stealthily he moved from place to place, contacting local Tories, summoning support for Tarleton's Green Jacket Brigade. The Ninety-Six District could be a strategic point for the coming battles, and

Tarleton wanted to know where his assistance lay. Scouting the territory, Drake encountered Soaring Eagle, the Cherokee hired by the British to wreak havoc among the back-country settlers.

Noelle wanted to go to sleep. She wanted to wake up in the morning in her own feather bed. This had to be a nightmare. She wanted Mandy's comforting presence.

Nothing this bad had ever happened to anyone Noelle knew. Her response was simply to close her eyes. Many decisions would have to be made soon—tomorrow, perhaps—but tonight, exhaustion, and tension, and melancholy lulled her and lowered her eyelids into narrow slits. The conversation and her choices had become too much for her to handle.

The sensible Noelle knew that she needed to consider her options, few as they were, but the frazzled part of her mind refused to accept reality. Sleep offered the only viable solution for the present, and her eyelids closed.

Suddenly, she awoke again with a sense of disorientation. Where was she now, and whose hand rested on her stomach? Awful memories flooded back like the muddy water that rushed over the banks of the Tyger during the spring rains. Drake had kept the Indian from hurting her, perhaps from murdering her as he had Irene and John Brooks. Her eyes adjusted to the darkness, and she noted through the unchinked logs of the barn that shards of pink split the dawn sky. Terrified that if she moved she would awaken the sleeping giant who lay beside her, Noelle remained frozen in the cramped position of her sleep. The chill of the morning bit at her exposed face, and she carefully snuggled beneath the woolen blanket until her head was covered.

Groaning, Drake shook off the last vestiges of sleep and pulled Noelle closer to him. During the night, he had crept closer until their bodies were entwined for maximum warmth. Now he drew her nearer still. His masculine scent gently teased her nostrils, and Noelle thought about her reaction. Unquestionably, she had snuggled closer to him and had allowed him to pull her into his arms. In her mind, she insisted that it had been for his body heat, but the flush that warmed her numb face betrayed her. His touch inflamed her. The security that surrounded her was unmistakable.

Noelle knew it was improper for her to lie with this stranger, yet she reveled in the emotions his nearness elicited, as if she belonged in the arms of this British soldier. Yesterday she had been engaged to her father's best friend and this man's uncle, and she had lost him to Indian cruelty. Now she slept with this man she had seen only a few times. Knowing she should be horrified by her own actions, Noelle pondered her situation.

The Indian had terrified her with his touch, his kiss. John's kiss had elicited no response at all. This man's kisses tortured her memories, and his touch warmed her beyond her comprehension.

"Are you awake, little hellion?" His cheek touched the top of her head.

Had his lips brushed her hair, or had she imagined it? "Why do you call me that? My name is Noelle. I am extremely irritated that you choose to call me such an awful name." She scowled at him and then turned away as if by doing so she could eradicate his memory from her mind.

"Why? Because you are a hellion. Such a lovely name, Noelle. But your spirit is that of a hellion." Drake laughed.

Noelle tried not to giggle, but his laughter was infectious. "I'm sure I don't know what you're talking about. I'm a lady, not a . . . not a whatever you called me."

"Well, my dear lady, are you hungry?" Drake's tone of condescension enraged her.

"No. I'm going home. You may do as you wish. It's no longer necessary to protect me. I can saddle a horse and be home in twenty minutes." Noelle tried to rise.

The lead weight of Drake's arm held her fast against him.

"Hold on. I'm not going to let you run off alone. I'll escort you after we eat something."

He made no move to allow Noelle the freedom to get up. "If you'll move, I'll be ready to go in no time."

Drake studied the deep blue eyes that peeked from beneath the rough wool. The fire in her eyes was equaled only by that of his manhood. He desired her. This delicate golden blossom with the sapphire eyes stirred in him a passion he hadn't felt in some time. Noelle was different from the other women he'd known. She was unspoiled by the ravages of time and city life. The fresh quality of her gently bred manners excited him. She wasn't husband hunting, nor was she a teasing flirt. By God, he wanted her—and yet he was troubled by her revelation that she had been engaged to his uncle, a man almost thirty years older than she. Why would an intelligent, beautiful woman agree to such a marriage?

Drake sensed that she was relatively inexperienced sexually, if not virginal. She genuinely seemed to be unaware of her effect on men—or else she knew well what she was about and used her innocent appearance as a ploy.

The flutter of spun gold surrounding the deep blue of her eyes aroused him as did her clean, feminine scent. Without a thought for the consequences of his actions, his lips closed on hers with a tenderness and longing he thought he lacked. Her lips were drawn together in a hard line of defiance, and her body grew rigid against his. Gently his tongue teased her lips until they relaxed and melted with his into a searing kiss.

Noelle lay still, trying to discourage his advances but failing miserably. His kiss deepened, taking her breath away. Then she moved, deeper into his embrace of steel. Her lips parted with little resistance to his, although she had fought the Indian like a wildcat. The steady cadence of her heartbeat raged into such a wild drumming that she thought Drake would certainly hear it. She wanted to press against him, to allow him to continue to evoke this wonderfully burning feeling that spread through her body. But when the idea came to her that anything this pleasurable must be sinful, she wrenched away. "No. No! You mustn't."

Shocked, Drake studied her for a moment, his eyes penetrating hers. "And why not? You were enjoying it as much as I."

"It's sinful. We can't. Kissing is the devil's work. For all I know, you *are* the devil." Terror seized her at the thought, irrational though it was. Drake Hastings might not be the devil, but he certainly ignited the fires of hell in her body.

Drake clung to her and laughed. "What a ridiculous thing to say. I—the devil? You are very naive."

Noelle refused to answer his taunt. While she knew that Drake really wasn't the devil, she couldn't hold back her words. "How am I to know? Does not the devil come in numerous shapes to tempt innocent young women?"

"You're right, I suppose. Devil or not, I had no right to kiss you." Drake laughed and looked down at Noelle. His heart raged with desire for her, as was obvious by his physical condition. She seemed not to notice as she lay on the bed of hay.

Taking a deep breath, she drew the blanket across her bosom and propped herself up on one elbow. "I accept your most gracious apology."

He lifted his left eyebrow in a rakish expression. "Miss Arledge, I assure you that was no apology."

"Then what was it, you rogue?" she asked.

"Merely a defense of my identity." He smiled and glanced around the barn. They were alone, painfully alone, and the discomfort in his groin mocked him as he shifted to keep her from noticing.

"Were you assuring me or yourself?" Noelle picked a piece of straw from her hair and longed for the silver hairbrush that always lay on her dressing table. "Perhaps you should make a sign with your name on it and display it prominently on your chest. That way, when you failed to remember who you were, you could always look down and read your name."

"A first-rate idea," he retorted, enjoying the light banter that removed the war from directly between them and allowed them to see each other as people instead of enemies. "But I have a much better notion."

"And what, pray, might that be?" Noelle curled her arm beneath her head and rested more easily. Despite her hatred of the British in general, she found that she genuinely liked this particular officer.

"Well, here is how I see the situation," he began and, feeling the cold air whistling through the unchinked walls of the barn, snuggled closer to her. When Noelle shifted farther away in the hay, he ignored her obvious attempt to make sure his body didn't touch hers. "If I hang the sign on my chest, I shall have difficulty reading it."

"Do you mean because you can't read?" Noelle teased, unable to resist returning his earlier barb. Warmth from his body beckoned her, but she resisted, instinctively knowing that if she ever succumbed, she would be forever ensnared by the sheer magnetism of his presence.

"No," he whispered against her tawny curls and kissed the soft indentation behind her ear. "Because it would be much more interesting to see my name emblazoned on *your* chest."

"On my . . ." Her voice faded away as her gaze met his. His eyes, a dark, rich brown, were deep set and as warm as toasted chestnuts on a midwinter night. Alarm bells clanged furiously inside her head, but she felt helpless to protest even though she knew she should leap to her feet immediately and put as much distance between the two of them as possible. Her mind faltered, diffusing her thoughts like the scattered seeds of a dandelion.

For a moment he gazed deep into her eyes. How could eyes be so vibrantly blue that they sparkled even in the dim light of the barn? he wondered. The distance between them seemed to melt away like butter in a skillet, and his mouth met hers as he drew her slender body beneath him.

Her lips parted to invite a deeper kiss. Drake plunged his

tongue hungrily through her open mouth and sought the sweetness of its soft inner recesses. Vaguely aware of the groan that escaped his throat, he allowed his fingers to glide along her shoulder and arm. When her hands moved slowly up his chest to encircle his neck, he clasped her more firmly against the length of his body.

Noelle's body sang beneath the light touch of Drake's fingers as they stroked the thin fabric of her nightgown, sending ripples of pleasure through her. When his hand brushed her breast, a symphony of desire played harmoniously between them. Underneath his caress, her nipple hardened into a pebble-sized departure point for the sensations that stole her breath away.

Drake drew his fingers slowly from her breast and down her stomach, cherishing the passionate response his caress evoked. "I want you," he whispered and began to raise the hem of her gown toward her waist.

When the sound of his voice reached her ears, Noelle regained her composure and burned with humiliation. "Stop! Please stop," she cried.

Astonished by her outcry, Drake froze and stared at her. What was he doing? Confused, he pushed away from her and jumped to his feet.

The filmy gown she wore was hiked up to her thighs. He had never witnessed a sight more inviting. Turning to blot the vision of her loveliness from his sight, he stood up and rushed outside. He was fighting with himself to keep from ravishing her on the spot, despite her halfhearted protestations.

Needing to separate himself from the situation, he strode toward his uncle's house. He surveyed the damage and found the house a charred ruin. Nothing of his heritage remained to salvage, except the bodies of his aunt and uncle. Drake buried them in silence. As the shovel bit into the rain-softened dirt, he wondered how much his own part in the war had played in the deaths of John and Irene. He slowly made his way back to the charred remains of Ash Meadow.

Feeling the weight of grief settle on his shoulders, he dropped down on the stone steps that had led to the veranda. Confusion swept him away from the present, and he longed for the simpler days of his youth. Nothing seemed easy and fun anymore. Gone were the carefree days of hunting and playing the games of boys. In their place loomed the grown-up man's game of war and destruction. The concepts of right and wrong had never seemed hazier than right now.

Noelle had discovered the benefit of action. She rose and shook the creases from her nightgown as best she could. Her experience with Drake painted a scarlet flush in her cheeks that threatened never to dissipate. Why had she stopped him? It hadn't really been so bad, and nobody would ever know.

A smile teased at the corners of her mouth but never fully developed as she recalled her earlier accusation. No, he certainly wasn't the devil. He was far too handsome and perhaps too honest. The sincere glint of his eyes on hers had melted her resolve to hate him. She studied the silhouette of the first man ever to kiss her as he rose from the steps and moved to the dark barn. Maybe he would kiss her again, she thought, almost willing him to do so. But she had been the one to stop him, causing him to unhand her and rush away.

"Come, Noelle," he called resolutely now. "I'll take you wherever you wish to go. I can find none of the servants."

His disclosure cut through Noelle's reserve, and she fought gallantly to hold back the tears that threatened to flow. Her last contact with any semblance of home was gone. Her family Bible, her clothes, her few pieces of jewelry—nothing of value remained except Irene's pearls. Along with the Brookses' servants, Mandy had apparently been carried off. More likely, she lay dead in the ruins of the house.

In spite of his sympathetic expression, Noelle refused to

allow Drake to see her cry. Her grief was too private to share, even though he, too, had lost family.

Drake saddled Nightmare and beckoned Noelle toward him. "We'll have to ride double again. Soaring Eagle's men must have taken all the horses."

He watched her silently for a moment, studied the brave tilt of her chin, and knew her courage in those few seconds. Instead of collapsing in a feminine faint or succumbing to the caterwauling so common among other women in similar situations, she raised her eyes and met his gaze defiantly, as if challenging him to comfort her or even mention their kisses.

Inwardly warring with her emotions, Noelle snuggled closer into his coat and ran the short distance to him. He lifted her easily into the saddle and then swung up behind her. She leaned against his hard body, glad for the warmth, privately relishing the comfort he provided—and sad for the distance that truly separated them.

Though it was only October, the morning was exceptionally cold, and when they spoke, their words came with clouds of vapor. With only a murmur here and there to break the silence, Noelle remained quiet. Her hope was that some of her servants would return, or had returned already. Mandy was undoubtedly dead after the attack last night. Acknowledging that fact took a great deal of energy from Noelle, and she sagged against Drake.

Facing life alone right now was something she didn't want to think about. As they neared her land, she was cheered by the sight of smoke from the kitchen.

Smoke meant that someone must be cooking. Maybe Mandy *had* escaped the Indian raiders. The burden on her heart lessened as she smelled the scent of streak-o'-lean cooking. The thought of the thick bacon sizzling on a skillet made her realize how hungry she was.

Drake called, "Whoa."

Noelle slid from the saddle and raced up the stone steps to the kitchen. She paused only a second at the door, thinking one of the Indians might be responsible for the homey fragrance in the air, before charging inside. Mandy stood before the fire, stunned by Noelle's sudden appearance.

"Lawd, chile, I thought you was dead. Them soldiers kilt everybody but me. I hid in the outhouse. Old Ardelia's dead, too." Tears swelled in the old woman's eyes and spilled down her cheeks in silvery trails.

Noelle rushed into the arms of the slave and buried her face in Mandy's bosom. Both of them had tears to shed. Both had lost more than could ever be recovered.

Drake closed the door against the cold. For a moment he surveyed the room. It would keep the women warm for the present, and the walls were lined with casks of flour, sugar, and rice, and the smokehouse was well stocked. He could leave Noelle here, at least temporarily.

"My, that smells good. Any chance I could have some?" he asked.

The scorn in Mandy's eyes was thick enough to cut with the sword Drake wore so elegantly at his side. Once she recognized the problem, Noelle didn't hesitate. "Mandy, he saved my life. More than once."

Mandy read the truth in Noelle's eyes, and she grunted once before returning to her cooking. Noelle turned to Drake and once again became the gracious hostess. "While I set the table, you can wash up."

Mandy stirred the mixture in a large iron kettle without speaking. She laid a slab of streak-o'-lean on the griddle for Noelle and Drake. "Missy, I hope you don't be angry with me for comin' home. I knowed the kitchen wasn't hurt."

"Of course I'm not angry, Mandy. We'll take care of each other. Don't you worry. We'll be fine." In her attempt to soothe Mandy, Noelle reassured herself. Yes, they would be fine. It wouldn't be easy, but they could manage. At least Noelle wasn't alone as she had begun to fear she might be.

"That's right. We going to be fine. Ole Mandy take real good care of you. You just a little thing, hardly growed up.

You just let me take care of you, yes, ma'am. We going to be fine. Me and my missy." Mandy turned the meat. "I made a corn pone to go with this. We going to have a feast. Them soldiers and Injuns is gone, and we fine."

Noelle left Mandy to her cooking and put plates on the table. In the house, they'd have used the good plates as Father called them, but here they'd have to make do with these thick stoneware plates. Soon Mandy put a platter of steaming meat on the table and then a plate of cornmeal pancakes.

Drake and Noelle ate with gusto. Their appetites had been enhanced by their early morning ride. Food had never tasted so good to Noelle. Her senses were heightened by some strange phenomenon. The scents of breakfast, of the cedar firewood, were more noticeable to her. The rattle of the wind in the skeletal branches of the crepe myrtle outside the window sounded louder, more restless. Her skin reacted to the slightest touch. Was it because of her close call with death? Regardless, Noelle had never felt so alive.

While Mandy cleared the table, Noelle and Drake rested on cane-seated chairs before the fire.

Drake studied her. Despite her recent losses, she had taken the harrowing episodes well. He felt confident that Noelle would assume responsibility for Mandy and in the next few days would resume control of her plantation. He gazed at her for a long moment. "Noelle, I must leave you. I have messages to carry and must get back to my men."

Noelle was astonished. Though she had expected him to return to his troops, she hadn't thought he would leave so soon. "Will . . . will you come back?" Her voice trembled as the words tumbled out. For the first time she admitted to herself that she enjoyed his company. Why couldn't he stay a little longer?

"I don't know. I must do as I'm commanded." Drake stood up and looked into her eyes, knowing he'd never forget them or the sweet face to which they belonged. When he spoke again, his words reflected his new resolve. "I'll come back."

Noelle fought to keep her tears from falling. "I suppose I must keep in mind that you're British. Go on. Leave us in peace." She turned quickly away, refusing to give in to tears over his departure, even though she no longer considered him her enemy.

Drake grasped her shoulders and turned her to face him. "I'm not your enemy. Never will I be your enemy. I'll be back, Noelle, unless I'm killed." Her glittering eyes touched him more than he wanted to admit, and he realized what an effort she was making to hide her true feelings.

"Just go," she whispered as she slumped back into her chair. "Please go. And be safe."

CHAPTER
8

NOELLE WATCHED AS THE DOOR SLAMMED BEHIND DRAKE,
and a weight settled on her heart like an anvil. Her hatred
for the British soldiers did little to diminish the feeling of
emptiness she felt at Drake's departure.

Mandy snorted as she put away the plates they had used.
"Might have saved your life, but he still a Redcoat. Can't
nothing good come of him hanging around here. We be
fine, missy. You and me be real fine."

"Yes, Mandy, we're going to be fine. You have nothing
to worry about," Noelle comforted her servant. She had
known Mandy for years, but it was difficult to know exactly
what to say that would help her through this time of anxiety.
While Noelle's tragedy was deep and painful, so was
Mandy's. Just as Noelle had lost her family in the past few
days, so had Mandy. "Now we need to find something for
me to wear. Go down to the cabin next to the root cellar and
see if you can find one of Sissy's dresses for me. I can make
some moccasins if you bring some skins in. Oh, I'll be
cleaning a place for us to sleep."

"I be right back, missy. You don't have to do nothing.
Mandy take good care of you. I be back, don't you worry
none." Still muttering, Mandy waddled out the door.

Noelle climbed up the ladder to the loft. Dust flew as she
brushed past a chair with a broken leg. With difficulty she
dragged an old mattress to the entrance. When she heard
Mandy downstairs, Noelle called, "Help me with this,
Mandy. I'll hand it down to you."

The mattress ticking was dusty from lack of use, and as it dropped into Mandy's waiting arms, a cloud of stifling dust rose about her head. Both Noelle and Mandy coughed.

"This mattress going outside. I'll beat it right now. You can't sleep on this filthy thing. You just wait. Mandy clean it for you." She lugged the mattress out the door and draped it over a post.

Noelle watched through the window as Mandy beat the mattress with willow branches. When the dust clouds ceased to rise, Mandy ambled back inside. Noelle turned an inquisitive eye to the huffing and puffing servant.

"That thing needs airing. I'll bring it in after while." Mandy hobbled over to a bucket of water and took the gourd dipper from its nail. Sighing wistfully, she dipped it in the cool water and took a long drink.

Noelle looked around the room for ways to make it more comfortable for the two women. They would need some privacy, so she partitioned off a section of the kitchen for Mandy. Noelle would sleep upstairs. "Can you bring a mattress from Sissy's cabin? You can sleep down here, and I'll sleep in the loft."

"Missy, I'll sleep in Sissy's cabin. It ain't no use in dragging a mattress all the way up here. I'll wash this dress, and you can put it on." Mandy took a steaming kettle from the fireplace, poured boiling water along with a scoop of lye soap into a tub, and began stirring the dress with a wooden spoon. "It was the best one I could find."

"Thanks, Mandy, I'm sure it'll be fine," Noelle answered, thinking how Mandy had stepped in to fill the void. Noelle could never replace Mandy in a million years. Her kind spirit lent a cheerfulness to the unhappy circumstances.

"It ain't a fancy dress, but it ain't got no holes neither," Mandy muttered as she swatted at a fly buzzing around her head. "Them flies gettin' to be a strife for ole Mandy. They almost worse than my rheumatiz."

Noelle smiled. The flies were a nuisance. They sensed the coming of cold weather and sought the warmth of the kitchen. "The dress is perfect, really. Maybe we can wash the smell of smoke out of the few clothes I have left here. And you know the flies will be gone soon. Winter's on its way early, it seems."

"Dat's right. Them squirrels put up lots of acorns this summer," Mandy agreed as she wrung the soapy water from the dress. She placed the dress on the table and heaved the washpan into her arms to empty. She strode to the door, threw the dirty water out, and hesitated. "Missy, you think them Injuns will come back?"

Her question didn't really surprise Noelle, but it was one she didn't want to think about. "I can't answer that, Mandy. We just have to live each day as it comes." She looked at the old slave fondly, deciding to help as much as she could. Mandy's rheumatism seemed to be worse than ever. "We'll be fine. Why don't you finish washing the dress? We have a lot to do."

Mandy rinsed the dress and then sauntered outside to hang it on the clothesline. The normal activities of the day did little to relieve the apprehension that Noelle felt and Mandy voiced.

After a while Noelle walked to the yard and felt the hem of the dress. Though still damp, it was better than the flimsy nightgown she had worn since last night. She hurried into the house to put it on.

The dress was made of simple homespun in a deep coffee brown that would look good with Noelle's hair. Since it was the only clean dress she had right now, she was glad to get it. Perhaps later she and Mandy could make a dress if they found some fabric that hadn't burned. Noelle was certain that Louisa, the plantation's dressmaker, had kept some fabric in her cabin. Noelle dared not hope for Louisa's return. The slaves were probably still running and wouldn't stop until they reached Charleston.

Noelle and Mandy settled into a routine. Noelle sauntered through the garden, gathering a few onions, cabbages, and greens from the frostbitten plot. Mandy cooked the vegetables and served them with rice. Together they ate quietly as both women pondered their situation.

Afterward, they cleaned several rooms and spent some time retrieving items from the big house that would be useful in her temporary home—the kitchen. At first Noelle was afraid to sleep in the kitchen alone, but she overcame her fear quickly when she collapsed onto her bed, trembling with exhaustion. After all, she wondered as her tired muscles gradually uncramped, what else could go wrong?

Chores consumed most of Noelle's days, and at night she fell asleep fatigued and numb. When she was alone and quiet, the memory of Drake's kiss slipped in to distract her. No matter what she did, his face refused to be erased from her mind, and her fear for him was compounded with each day he was gone.

One evening as rain fell steadily outside and Noelle sat peacefully in front of the fire, a creaking board on the porch startled her. Mandy had long since gone to her cabin for the night, and Noelle doubted that the old woman would return in this weather.

In two steps, she reached the door and curled her fingers around the handle. She froze before she disengaged the latch. Whoever was outside knew the cabin was occupied. The roaring fire kept away the cold, but it also advertised her presence. Maybe she could peek out the window and see who'd made the noise. Noelle sneaked to the window beside the door and knelt down. Edging closer, she raised up and peered out at the corner of the lower pane.

A dark shadowy face stared back at her. Stunned, Noelle fell back on her derriere. "Oh," she whispered and crawled back out of sight. She didn't know what to do.

A light tapping on the door startled her so badly that she almost fell into the fireplace.

"Missy?"

Noelle's eyebrows knitted as she tried to identify the

familiar masculine voice. This was someone she knew—perhaps one of the servants. Feeling a flood of relief, she hurried to the door and flung it open. When she saw Lard standing there, she instantly recalled the deep, resonant voice she had of course heard so many times before.

"Oh, Lard," she cried, breaking into laughter. "You scared the life out of me. I'm so glad to see you."

"I'se glad to see you, too," he said and smiled.

"Come in." Noelle stood back and motioned for him to enter the kitchen. "Hurry. The wind is blowing rain in all over the floor, and it's cold out there."

"I know that's right. I been hidin' in the woods ever since them Injuns come to the Brooks place." He removed his floppy hat and looked longingly at the fireplace.

Noelle noticed and pulled another chair over to the fire. "Come over here and tell me everything."

"Well, Missy," he began and glanced at the table.

"Have you had anything to eat?" Noelle asked. "Let me cut you some bread."

"I ain't had nothin' much since that night. Nothin' 'ceptin berries, and I stole a fish out the basket." He ran his tongue across his lips as Noelle sliced the bread and spread it with butter.

"Here. Eat this while I pour some milk." Noelle felt like a giddy child. The first of her servants had returned! If he was alive, perhaps others were, too. "Tell me, have you seen anyone else?"

"I ain't seed hide nor hair of nobody else." He took a big bite of bread and gulped down a swallow of milk. "I'se afraid to come up to the kitchen at first. I seed a stranger come in here this mornin'."

Noelle nodded. "That was the man who saved my life, a British officer. When Soaring Eagle tried to . . . to hurt me, Drake stopped him."

"I thanks the Lawd for that, but he's still a Redcoat." Lard poked the last of the bread into his mouth and rubbed his stomach. "I think that's the finest meal I ever ate."

A noise outside on the porch startled both of them, and Noelle closed her eyes briefly and said a silent prayer. When would all this fear end? she wondered.

Lard's eyes opened wide, and Noelle knew he was imagining all sorts of horrors. She put her fingers to her lips and then tiptoed to the door to listen. She heard someone shuffle about on the porch, but the rain kept her from hearing enough to determine the origin of the sound.

Creeping slowly across the room, Lard joined her at the door and lay his head against the wood to listen. After a moment, the door flew open, banging him soundly on the forehead and knocking Noelle to the floor. Unconscious, Lard fell backwards on top of her.

Peering over his unmoving body, she saw Mandy standing over them both with an ax.

"No!" Noelle screamed, scrambling to get out from under Lard. "It's Lard. Don't hurt him."

Until Mandy slowly lowered the ax, Noelle didn't breathe, and then air whooshed out of her lungs. Tension flowed from her prostrate body. "Help me get him off."

Mandy bent over and took Lard's arm. She began to pull. "He sho' is a big un. Bigger'n I recollect."

Noelle laughed and agreed. "I'm glad. He'll be a great help to us."

"If'n I coulda got here 'fore he got in, he'd a been dead as them fish we et." Mandy had put down the ax, but that did little to relax her vigilance. "Missy, how you know this ain't a trick? He been gone a long time."

Lard sat up, rubbing his forehead, and glared at Mandy. "Doan you say nothing like that 'bout me. You know me a sight better than that."

Noelle laughed and rolled her eyes at the outrageous suggestion. Lard had been a loyal and hard-working overseer for too many years. He'd been rewarded well for his good record, even though he was a slave. Noelle's father had built Lard a large cabin with three comfortable rooms, had given him a small plot for a garden of his own, and had required him to work reasonable hours. At one time she suspected that Lard and Mandy were in love. Now, looking at the two of them, she wasn't sure.

Charles Arledge had never owned more than nine slaves, and they all seemed like members of the family. Noelle had spent many hours sitting at Lard's hearth and listening to the yarns he spun.

"Mandy, I'm as sure of him as I am of myself. You should be, too." Already considering the possibilities for renovating her home, Noelle walked back to her rocker. "Lard, sit back down. You, too, Mandy. We're going to have a long talk about the future of Tyger Rest."

They talked long into the night, and when Noelle finally climbed the stairs to the loft, she was hopeful that things could now return to normal. Lard was home again. Together, the three of them could make Tyger Rest seem like home now.

Noelle awoke to the sound of hammering. She sprang from her mattress to peer out the tiny loft window. From her high vantage point she could see Lard straddling the peak of the roof and nailing boards unevenly across the huge charred gap left by Soaring Eagle's fire.

Pausing long enough to don her petticoat and dress, Noelle could hardly wait to see the result of Lard's work. Tying a kerchief around her shoulders, she ran out the front door of the kitchen and into the back door of the house. Striding as quickly as her bare feet would carry her, she raced up the stairs, skipping two at a time until she reached the second story. She hesitated a few seconds to inhale deeply before she entered the dormitory room.

By this time, Lard had almost covered the opening in the roof. He grinned down at her and then laid the last roughly hewn board into place. In the dim light, she once again inspected the room. Ashes covered everything, and sparks had burned tiny holes in the floor and furniture. The acrid smell of smoke still lingered and nearly choked her. The bearskin that covered the center of the floor had large blackened areas and would have to be discarded.

The sound of hammering stopped, and Noelle started back down the stairs. Her feet were freezing, and she wanted to find her shoes before she did anything else.

When she entered the kitchen, Mandy stood before the fire stirring the venison stew from the day before. "I'se be fixin' somethin' to eat in a minute. I wants to simmer this stew a bit longer. Seems to me that meat awful tough."

Noelle grimaced at the reminder of how she had almost choked. "No hurry. Maybe some hominy today?"

"Hominy sound good." Mandy picked up the broom and swept some ashes back into the fireplace. "This place a mess. Look like heathens live here."

"Don't worry about that." Noelle took the broom from Mandy's hand. "I'll sweep. You cook. I imagine Lard will be starved by the time he gets off the roof."

"Harrumph," Mandy snorted. "That man always starved."

"Well, he works hard around here," Noelle said in his defense and then suddenly remembered how cold her feet were. She propped the broom against the wall and found her shoes and a pair of stockings. Sitting on the rocker as she put them on reminded her of the times she'd sat there in Drake's lap. Instead of dwelling on him, she continued her conversation with Mandy. "Lard earns everything he eats and more. I wish you'd stop picking on him."

"I never seed a man so full of hisself." Mandy stirred the hominy vigorously. "You want some bacon this mornin' or what?"

"Bacon's good." Noelle pulled on the second shoe and held her feet toward the fire. "My, but that feels good. I was so excited about getting the roof patched that I ran out without my shoes!"

"I know you didn't learn none of that from ole Mandy. I done taught you how to be a fine lady, not some hoyden with manners like a field hand," Mandy scolded as she poured the hominy in a bowl. "If'n yo' Pa could see you now, he'd beat yo' behind 'til it come up with blisters. If'n I wasn't so old, I'd do it mysef."

Noelle stared at Mandy for a minute. She meant well, and if it cheered her up to remember better days, Noelle would never interrupt. But times were different now, and she had to react in a manner consistent with survival—not some set of proper manners designed for a lady who never ventured out of a parlor.

"I ain't seed that Redcoat in a week." Mandy placed the bowl on the table and returned to the fireplace to remove the bacon and toasted bread. "I reckon we's rid of him."

Catching Mandy's eye momentarily, Noelle felt the color touch her cheeks. Drake had been gone for eight days, and she hadn't heard anything from or about him. For the past few nights, she'd lain awake until the early hours of morning, wondering about his safety, where he was, who he was with, and what damage he was doing to the Patriots' efforts. At times, she grew angry thinking about him. At others, her thoughts were soft and romantic, filled with hunger and longing. Her heart and head still warred over the dilemma.

During the day, she moped about, hardly attending her chores, noncommittally answering any questions Lard or Mandy asked. Noelle's moods swung from elation, knowing she was rid of him, to deep depression when she thought he might lie dead on some battlefield. She refused to dwell on that thought. Somehow, he was alive and would return when he could.

The days grew shorter, and soon two weeks had passed. It was now mid-October. Noelle tired of salted meat, and in her desire for something different, she set the fish trap in the Tyger River and left it overnight, hoping to catch enough fish for herself, Mandy and Lard.

Early the next morning, Noelle ran down to the river without even taking the time to braid her hair. She pulled up the wicker fish trap and found it filled with bream, sunfish, and trout. Gingerly she stuck her hand into the basket, pulled out more than enough fish for their meal, and placed them in a wooden bucket. She dropped the wicker trap back into the river. The remaining fish would live until she needed them. Proud of her accomplishment, Noelle, her long golden curls flying free behind her, rushed up the bank with her catch.

As she scrambled up the hill, she bumped into a Redcoat, and her bucket of fish tumbled over, spilling her catch. "Oh," she cried and scrambled to keep from sliding down the bank into the river.

Noelle fell into a heap beside the madly flapping fish and cringed with fear that she might come face to face with Cornwallis's men. Her gaze rose slowly from the highly polished boots seemingly rooted in the slope above her head to the legs and body, before coming to rest on Drake's face. "Drake! I'm so glad to see you!"

Laughing, he sat down beside her and pulled her into his arms. "And I'm happy to see you, Noelle. I've missed you," he whispered into her hair.

"Oh, I've missed you also. Every day I wondered if you'd come back." She hugged him gleefully, then realized what she was doing. Blushing, she took her arms from his neck and tried to rise but slipped on the wet leaves. She'd never intended for him to know how much she missed him and worried about him.

"I like you better when you don't think about what you're doing. Are you really glad to see me?" Drake tossed the fish into the bucket and turned to Noelle. "Anyway, I'm glad to see you again."

"Where have you been? You've been gone nearly two weeks." Her heart thundering in her chest, Noelle gazed at him.

Unable to look away, Drake stared hungrily down at her and felt the tension in his groin. He'd missed her more than he'd allowed himself to admit. This feisty pioneer girl had insinuated herself into his life, and he knew she hadn't done it intentionally.

When he looked into her deep blue eyes, Drake wanted to forget everything—the war, England, everything—and concentrate on making her happy. His voice low and raspy, he ignored her question and whispered, "I've missed you terribly."

Beneath his penetrating gaze, Noelle found it difficult to speak. She, too, had missed him. Not a day, nor an hour, had passed without something reminding her of him. One day it was the blacksmith barn when she recalled their first night together. Another time it was the smell of Mandy's cooking stirring her memories. The nightgown she wore each night reminded her of him, of the time they'd spent in John's barn. Even the bridge brought his face to mind as she thought of the time they'd sought shelter there from the storm, when he'd first kissed her, really kissed her. A crimson flush crept up her neck and tinged her cheeks with pink as she looked at him, wishing he would kiss her again.

What was she thinking? Drake wondered and found himself wanting desperately to kiss her. She'd flung herself into his arms freely moments ago, but now she seemed distant. Like a blossoming flower, her rose-colored lips parted slightly, and he could hold back no longer. "Noelle," he whispered against her cheek before claiming her mouth with his.

For a second she hardly moved. Then she melted into his embrace as if she had always belonged there. Drake was so stunned he could hardly breathe. Her luscious breasts, full and taut, pressed against his chest as he pressed her back against a bed of moss.

Noelle's breath came in short gasps when Drake pulled away. Cold air surged between them as he gazed down at her, as if questioning her. There was no way she could have answered him, even if he'd asked a question. She could only return his stare and revel in the warmth that exuded from his touch.

All thought of conversation abandoned her as he kissed her again, cradling her head in the crook of his arm. His tongue gently searched the inner recesses of her mouth, and she timidly met his caress with her own. Noelle's arms slid around his neck, and a soft moan escaped from her lips.

Drake drew away again and continued to stare down at her. The reality of war seemed distant when he held her in his arms. He wanted nothing more than to hold and protect her, but he doubted that she'd ever allow that to happen. In times like these, moments when he'd been away or when she was scared, she didn't seem to mind his company, even his caresses. But after the initial shock of seeing him wore off, she would revert to her cool demeanor.

"There must be a way."

Noelle studied him closely. "What?"

Drake stared at her. He didn't realize he'd spoken aloud and now he had to explain his thoughts to her. "Uh, I was just thinking about . . . never mind. Tell me what you've been doing."

Puzzled, Noelle allowed him to pull her into a sitting position and snuggled more closely into his embrace. "Not much, really. I've tried to relieve some of Mandy's burden, you know, gardening, milking the cows, cooking."

"You're doing all that?" he asked, surprised.

"Of course. Even though we have servants, the mistress of a plantation must know everything about running a household. I can do almost anything," she admitted proudly. At the time she'd been learning all the tasks Papa insisted upon, she'd thought he was cruel to force her to do such work. Now that all her servants were gone except Mandy, Noelle silently thanked him.

"Maybe one of these days you can cook me another good meal." Drake hugged her close and inhaled the sweet fragrance of lavender water. He glanced around at the serenity of the woods. The land around seemed to welcome him. The soft breezes that cooled the days, the fertile soil, the brilliant southern sun—all were a part of him even though he'd lived in England for more than twenty years. When he'd returned to upstate South Carolina, he knew he'd come home.

"How about fish?" she asked, watching him as he gazed all around them. She supposed he was looking out for Indians or the militia.

"Fish?" Wondering where he'd lost the conversation, he turned to look at her. Once again he was struck by her beauty and her naïveté. She didn't realize how she affected him.

Noelle shook her head and pursed her lips. He hadn't been paying attention to her at all. He'd forgotten that he'd asked her to cook a meal for him. "For dinner. Fish to eat. Remember the fish in the bucket?"

"Oh, fish!" he exclaimed. He felt like a fool, like a doddering old man. "Sounds wonderful. I'll clean them for you."

"Would you?" Noelle sighed with relief. Although she knew how to clean fish, she hated the slimy task and avoided it whenever possible. "We have a few potatoes. I'll put some in the fireplace to roast while you do that."

Drake stood and extended his hands to Noelle to help her up. He watched with interest as she peered over her shoulders and tried to brush away the leaves clinging to her back and skirt. After a moment he took over and completed the job. "It's a deal."

A little embarrassed by his personal touch, Noelle led the way back to the cabin, and they chatted amiably about uncontroversial issues. Drake carried the bucket, and they held hands. She told herself that the dead leaves were slippery after the night's rain and that she allowed him to hold her hand to keep her from falling, but she couldn't deny the tingles that the contact sent through her body.

"Where have you been all this time?" she asked once more, trying to keep the quaver from her voice. A part of her wanted to run and sing, to whirl and dance with joy that he was safe, but another part of her wanted to know if he'd been actively warring with her friends.

"That's a military secret. But to keep you from being jealous, I can tell you I haven't been with anyone as pretty as you." The laughter lines around his eyes and mouth became more pronounced as the smile spread into a warming beam.

"Of all the ridiculous notions. Why should I be jealous of you?" she asked, as if the idea seemed alien to her. Yet she *was* jealous. He hadn't said he wasn't with another woman, only nobody as pretty as she. Noelle scolded herself. Why should she care? But she did. Angrily she dropped his hand, crossed her arms over her breasts, and said nothing more.

He grinned at her. When she was angry, her eyes glinted with such a vivid violet that he was reminded of spring in his mother's garden. This time Drake did not restrain himself. He slid one arm behind her and pulled her back to the ground with the other and leaned across to kiss her. His kiss wasn't gentle, for he meant for her to know that she had been kissed by someone who knew what he was doing.

Noelle gasped for breath. She hadn't expected his kiss. Drake's lips branded hers, and she felt like they would belong to him forever, no matter what happened. A quiver raced through her body to be followed quickly by a second and third, like the small tremors after an earthquake.

Cradled in his arms, Noelle wanted the moment to last forever. This time, she didn't know if she possessed the willpower to stop him.

"Missy!" Lard's deep voice rang through the trees. "Missy! Where are you?"

Drake's face flamed with anger as he drew away and listened to the sound of someone crashing through the bushes. The intrusion was unforgivable. He gazed into Noelle's eyes and detected a faraway look, one that led him to believe she felt as he did, and that without interruption, they would have—

"Miss Noelle!" Lard called. "You answer me right now afore I has a fit."

The strained voice finally penetrated the fog surrounding Noelle, and she inhaled deeply. "Here I am, Lard."

Drake scrambled to his feet and nearly dragged Noelle to the boulder nearest them.

Above their heads, a huge black man appeared carrying an ax. "Great Lawd a mercy. Hit's that Redcoat done kidnapped my Missy."

Lard swung the ax over his head, and Noelle screamed. "No! No, Lard, don't do it!"

With the ax perpendicular to the ground and above his head, Lard looked like some mythical Titan. Drake didn't doubt for a second that the man would use the tool to chop his victim to bits.

Lard gazed at Noelle as if he wondered why she stopped him. "Missy, you step away and I takes care of dis Redcoat afore the next acorn fall."

"No, Lard. Put down the ax." Protectively, Noelle moved closer to Drake to convince Lard that Drake was not the enemy.

"Missy, that scoundrel already be a dead man if'n he laid a hand on you. You jus' give me the word." Lard wiggled the ax menacingly. "He one less Redcoat we has to worry about."

"Lard, Drake is a friend." Noelle glanced at Drake and smiled. His face was blanched and pained. For once, he'd met his match. Maybe she should let him stew for a few minutes before she stopped Lard. But that wasn't fair, and Lard was serious. He'd kill Drake without thinking about it if he thought Drake had trifled with her. "Captain Drake Hastings, allow me to present my servant . . . and body-guard, Lard. He was my father's overseer. Lard, Captain Hastings."

Drake broke into a grin. He didn't know what else to do. If he could reach his gun without that ax thudding into his skull, he'd have the upper hand. But the Negro never relaxed as he nodded. "I'm pleased to make your acquaintance, Lard."

"Lard, Drake saved my life," Noelle explained, hoping that Lard would see that she wasn't hiding something. "Twice."

"Three times actually," Drake injected.

Noelle glared at him.

"If my Missy say two, then two it is, and don't you be contrary to her," Lard stated forcefully.

"Lard, put down the ax." Noelle watched as he relaxed his stance a bit. "Put it down. Drake is correct. He saved me from the Cherokee twice and from myself once."

"Thank you," Drake whispered. "Say, Lard, how are you at carpentry? I hoped to repair the roof of the house enough to keep out the cold air and rain."

"I done did that." Lard rested the ax on the ground but didn't loosen his grip on the handle.

The wind shifted, and leaves fluttered all around them. Noelle shivered. She'd forgotten that she was poorly dressed against the chill morning air. She quivered again. "I'm cold. Let's go back to the house and talk."

Drake agreed and took her elbow to assist her up the bank. Lard watched his every move. From the grimace on his face, he still didn't trust the soldier, and Noelle smiled to reassure him.

When they reached the kitchen, Mandy stood at the fireplace stirring soup. "Y'all c'mon in. I'se fixin' to put the soup on the table."

Lard, eyeing Drake suspiciously, nodded and returned to the yard to wash his hands at the well. Drake followed. For a moment, Noelle started to accompany them to keep the peace, but decided that the two men must learn to trust each other, and nothing she could do or say would help.

She climbed the ladder to her little room and found her brush. After removing the leaves and twigs from her hair, she hurried back to the kitchen. The men were still outside, so she washed her hands at the pitcher stand and waited.

"They'll git along," Mandy muttered as if to herself. "Them's two good men. They'll do all right."

Noelle sighed with relief, trusting Mandy's assessment of the situation instinctively. Before she could comment, Drake and Lard returned to the kitchen.

Watching to see how they got along, she found nothing to satisfy her curiosity. Neither of them spoke much during dinner, and when the chairs were pushed back at the end of the meal, Lard left. Soon afterwards, Drake followed.

"Mandy, do you really think they'll be all right?" Noelle asked, peering through the window above the table. She saw them talking in the yard, and Lard gestured toward the house, but she could hear nothing. At least they weren't yelling.

Turning to face Noelle, Mandy stopped clearing the table. "Honey chile, only the Lawd knows what's in a man's heart."

Mandy glanced around and mumbled something. Noelle followed her onto the porch and watched her friend disappear down the path toward her cabin. When Noelle turned around, Drake was walking toward her. Feeling happier than she had in some time, she smiled as he approached and placed her hands on his shoulders. From this vantage point she could almost gaze directly into his warm coffee-colored eyes and felt the flush creep up her cheeks. "How long can you stay?"

"Not long enough, I'm afraid. I must rejoin my regiment tomorrow." He held the door for Noelle to enter and watched as her hips swished back and forth in the homespun dress. "Too bad you found a dress. I rather liked you in the nightgown."

"What an impertinent thing to say! I should throw you out without dinner." Noelle wasn't really angered by his remark. In fact, she was secretly flattered that he had noticed her appearance, and she blushed yet again. "If you can keep a civil tongue, you're welcome to eat with us."

"Thank you. I hoped you would ask. I tire easily of the

salt meat we have in camp." Drake placed the bucket on the table and looked around. "Where is Mandy?"

"She's probably down at her cabin puttering around. We don't keep very regular hours, I'm afraid. She should be here shortly. Do you prefer her company to mine?" Noelle teased, wondering why she vacillated between anger and amusement with him. But she felt much better when she wasn't angry. Their lighthearted banter allowed her to forget the troubled times for a little while.

"Hardly, wench." Drake swept her into his arms and kissed her like a man deprived of food for too many days.

Noelle relaxed against him and relished the warmth of his body against hers as all anger deserted her quicker than it had come upon her. Her lips parted slightly, and Drake plunged his tongue deep into her mouth. A moan escaped her throat, as if to tell him she was as hungry for his touch as he for hers. The fire that sped through her veins inflamed every inch of her, and she swayed against him, wanting the moment never to end. The sound of Mandy singing at the top of her voice startled Noelle, and she jerked away from him. She avoided Mandy's eyes and the shocked expression the slave would be wearing.

"Mr. Hastings, when did you come? What you doing in this cabin with my baby? Don't you know she can't receive male callers without a chaperon? You ought to be ashamed of yourself. I don't know anything about them hussies in England, but my missy ain't like them." Mandy scolded Drake soundly. "An' another thing, it ain't fittin' for—"

"You're right, Mandy," he interrupted, hoping to stem the flow of her angry words. "I'll try to avoid being alone with Noelle in the future." Drake gave in easily. "Now how about something to eat? Are you too angry to feed a starving soldier?"

"If you hadn't saved her life, you'd have to kill me to eat in this cabin. But seeing as how you did, I reckon I'll feed you." Mandy removed the fish from the bucket as she talked.

"Here, give me a knife and I'll clean those for you," Drake offered, wondering if she'd allow him to perform even that small task for her.

"You just rest your Redcoat self while I do it," she scolded and dressed the fish as she spoke. "I ain't sunk so low as to need the help of a British devil."

"Mandy!" Noelle exclaimed, jumping to Drake's defense. "After all he's done for me . . . for us, I should think you'd be more civil than that. I'm surprised at you."

Drake laughed. "Don't fuss, Noelle. She has every right to her opinion. After all, she didn't lose a bet with me. Do you think I should make some sort of wager with her?"

Before Noelle could respond, Mandy whirled around and glared at Drake. "I ain't a bettin' woman, and neither is my baby. You can jus' take your devil's ways and scat. If'n you gonna tempt my baby to do wrong, you ain't welcome here."

Drake smiled understandingly. "All right, all right. You win. I'll behave myself. While you're cooking, we'll go pick some apples in the orchard I saw the other day."

Mandy eyed him suspiciously. "Well, if'n you promise to behave like a gentleman."

"I promise, ma'am." Drake grinned at the old slave. "I'll pick enough for a pie."

As they walked out the door, Noelle picked up a reed basket and hung it over her arm. "I hope you'll pick a few extras. I can't reach too many without climbing the trees and I'm afraid I'll break the limbs."

Drake studied her a moment. He knew she wouldn't break the limbs even if she climbed very high, but she might fall and hurt herself. "Wait a minute."

He ran back up the steps and into the cabin. When he returned, he was carrying several baskets. "We'll pick as many as we can."

They hurried past the towering magnolia trees and through the pecan grove. Before long, they reached the apple orchard. Noelle looked up. "See what I mean?"

Drake nodded. He spotted a rickety ladder and carried it to the first tree. Minutes later, with him picking apples and handing them down to Noelle, they'd filled the first basket and moved on to the second tree. When they'd heaped the baskets full, he climbed down from the ladder for the last time. He picked up the first basket and turned to Noelle. "I can carry . . ."

Noelle glanced up at him and found him staring at her, his mouth open. Puzzled by his expression, she prodded, "Yes?"

For a few seconds, Drake did nothing and said nothing. Then he placed the basket on the ground and laid his hands on her shoulders. After waiting for her reaction, he pulled her closer and whispered, "Noelle, you don't hate me, do you?"

"Hate you?" she repeated, stalling for time. No, she didn't hate him, but she couldn't remember when she'd stopped, when her feelings had changed.

"I . . . I don't want you to hate me," he began and clung to her, nestling his face in her hair. "Noelle, I hate this war as much as you do. These moments when I steal away to see you keep me sane."

At times like these Noelle knew why she couldn't hate him. He expressed her own feelings as well as his own. "Drake, what's happening? Are the . . . are you winning the war? I hear so little being isolated like this."

"It's hard to tell who's winning. The Patriots win some battles, and we win some." Drake held her close and closed his eyes. With her he could almost forget the war and its atrocities. Breathing deeply of her sweet scent, he raked his fingers through her curls and smiled. "Why do you bother to braid your hair or pin it up? It's so lovely when it falls free around your face."

Noelle blushed at the compliment. This was the first time he'd said anything about her appearance. She decided to comment on his reference to her hair rather than on their relationship. He'd changed the subject, but that was all right with her. She heard enough talk about the war from everybody else. "All ladies must wear their hair in braids or buns. Didn't you know?"

"I believe women do it to make themselves appear more untouchable." His hands caressed her back, and he regretted that she had to change from the sheer nightgown into the more proper thicker homespun, even though the color seemed to enhance her beauty.

Smiling, Noelle raised her eyebrows pensively. "It doesn't appear to have worked with you, sir," she teased.

Drake laughed at her haughty demeanor, seeing it for a ruse. His sense of humor was as acute as hers, and he shot back, "Perhaps it would if you were as similar in appearance to a scarecrow as others."

"And do your eyes rove to appraise all women you meet?" she asked, fluttering her eyelids coquettishly at him. She could play the game as well as he. "Or is it only the comely miss who attracts your eye?"

"I say nay to your accusation, miss," he protested, trying not to smile. " 'Tis only to your beauty that my eye roves."

"Ah, methinks thou dost tell a fib, dear sir," she countered. "I recall the mention earlier that you have not been with a maid as pretty as I, but you did not say you had been with no maid at all."

"Alas, I am caught in my deception." He hung his head repentantly and sighed. "I confess that I have been with a lady recently."

"I knew as much," she said triumphantly, but somehow didn't feel as joyful at his confession as she thought she would when she bested him. "And who is this maiden who is my rival for your attention?"

By this time Drake could no longer keep from laughing. "I confess. I have an appointment with her this very day. I had promised luncheon with her."

"But you can't," Noelle wailed, aghast that he even contemplated leaving before dinner. "You've already told Mandy that you're staying to eat fish."

"And it is that lady with whom I have my appointment," he teased and ducked to escape the slap he saw coming from his captive miss. "Are you jealous, my dear Noelle?"

"Jealous? How ridiculous." Noelle bristled as he caught her hand and kept her from striking his insolent face. "I'd sooner be jealous of the sow and her corncobs. Why, I—"

Drake kissed her to silence her ranting. In her anger, her eyes glimmered with a sapphire that bordered on violet. His lips found hers willing, and the kiss soon became as passionate as any they'd shared.

As he drew away, Drake knew that one day soon they would have to part. His regiment would be called to march north, and he would have no choice. For now he enjoyed these moments with Noelle and treasured every second of them. In fact, quite often when he lay on his blanket at night, the cold air frosting his breath, he closed his eyes and savored his memories of her. The warmth he gained from seeing her in his mind often caused a discomfort that he found a nuisance, but he refused to stop thinking about her, couldn't stop thinking about her.

"Maybe we'd better take these apples to Mandy before she comes looking for us," Drake suggested and hugged her close once more.

"Oh, yes. I'd quite forgotten her." Noelle took the baskets he proffered and strode briskly down the path.

She couldn't trust herself to look at him as they walked in silence back to the cabin. Once in sight of the wooden structure, she hurried along until she thought she might stumble. Hunger pangs teased her stomach as she smelled the aroma of dinner cooking. With Drake lagging along behind, she raced up the steps and inside.

Fresh fish, dipped in cornmeal and frying in a black skillet, tempted Noelle. "Please hurry, Mandy. I'm starving."

Mandy placed plates of fired fish on the table, along with corn from the garden and corn cakes. Both Drake, Noelle, and Lard hastily filled their plates. Conversation was kept at a minimum as they ate ravenously. Mandy puttered about the kitchen humming softly while she peeled the apples and then cooked them.

"Come, sit with us, Mandy," Drake suggested. "I promise not to bite you."

"Huh. I bet your bite is worse than a mad dog's." Mandy continued working and refused to sit with them.

When dinner was finished, Noelle stacked the pewter plates and wiped off the table. "Those apples smell good. When will they be ready?"

"Jus' a minute," Mandy answered and never looked around. "You sit still."

"Here, I'll pour you some more milk." Noelle went to the earthenware jar of milk, removed the soft cloth that covered the jar, and dipped into the cool liquid.

By the time she returned to the table, Mandy had placed a bowl of spicy fried apples in the middle of the table. Noelle found two bowls and spoons and served Drake.

"Those are the best fried apples I ever ate." Drake wiped his mouth on a napkin and grinned. "I bet you're the best cook in the Colonies, Mandy."

Mandy couldn't hide her grin of delight. "You're jus' sayin' that to tease me."

"No. No, I'm not. They're wonderful." Drake finished the last of his apples and looked longingly at the bowl. "Do you mind if I help myself to some more?"

"No, sir, they's plenty where them come from," Mandy said and chuckled as she turned away, mumbling under her breath. "We ain't got nothing to be afeared of if the Tories don't feed they men any better than that. That boy fair starvin' to death."

CHAPTER
9

NOELLE WATCHED AS DRAKE WASHED HIS HANDS AND FACE at the washstand. Without his thick woolen cloak his muscles rippled and danced beneath the worn linen of his shirt. His narrow hips and muscular legs appeared to be well exercised. When he turned around, water dripping from his face, he caught her staring and smiled.

"Is something wrong?" he asked innocently, his expression perfectly serious, although he knew she'd been watching him. His sense of humor threatened to give him away.

"Wrong?" she stammered, hating herself for the flush that rose so quickly to stain her cheeks. During the morning, she'd felt like a school miss, sneaking looks at the boys dawdling on the street outside the schoolhouse. For some reason she couldn't keep from staring at Drake. "No. Why do you ask that?"

"No reason, really. You were looking at me as if I had three heads." Drake tried to maintain his dignity and lifted an eyebrow questioningly.

Noelle laughed nervously. "What a ridiculous thing to say."

"Well, then, what is it?" Drake moved to stand closer to her. "Have you never seen a man wash before?"

Glaring at him did little to relieve her embarrassment. How dare he ask such a question? "No. No, I haven't," she retorted and sprang from her chair to stare out the window.

"It's all right, Noelle, you don't have to be afraid of me," he added thoughtfully, as if studying the situation for further implications. "Perhaps I have butter remaining on my chin? Or have I popped the buttons off my pants?" He glanced down as if in dismay and faced her once again, noting the crimson of her cheeks.

"I assure you, it's nothing," she stated adamantly, wishing he'd change the subject. "I apologize if I offended you."

"Oh, to be sure, you didn't offend me." Drake strode to her side and placed his arm about her shoulders. "I just thought you were expressing interest, and I am never offended by that."

An impertinent remark forming in her mind, Noelle looked up at him and opened her mouth to speak. "I assure you—"

No longer able to keep the ruse, Drake drew her into his arms and kissed her more passionately than ever before. Her body rested against the large table beneath the window, and she could never have escaped—even if she'd wanted to.

Noelle gasped for breath as he placed tiny butterfly kisses on her lips, eyelids, temples, and behind her ears. She heard a low moan and recognized her own voice. Once again color sprang to her cheeks, but this time she didn't care. She didn't want Drake to stop, and she clung to him, relishing the feeling of his hard body and inhaling the soft clean fragrance that clung to his skin after washing. The pressure of his body against hers excited her more than she ever thought possible. When he lifted her into his arms and crossed the room to the cane-seated rocking chair, her head hung limply against his shoulder, and she breathed as if she'd run all the way home.

He sat down and began to rock, holding her close all the while. They remained in the rocker for several minutes, not speaking, not moving except for the steady motion of the chair. Nothing interrupted them other than the occasional crackling and popping of the fire.

Drake finally broke the silence, whispering, "Noelle, my darling, I have to go."

Noelle felt as if he'd stabbed her with a rusty knife blade and then twisted it. "Now?"

"Yes," he murmured against her hair. Her silence indicated to him that she would truly be sorry to see him go—even if her response to his kisses hadn't already convinced him.

Damn, but he hated to leave her here all alone. Mandy would be no help against any sort of attack, no matter how weak or ill planned. Drake knew that Soaring Eagle would honor his word only as long as it suited him.

After a long silence Noelle finally found her voice. "How . . . how long will you be gone this time?" She gulped, uttered a silent prayer, and continued. "You will come back, won't you?"

Drake closed his eyes and savored the feeling of Noelle in his arms. It might be a long time indeed before he could return, but he couldn't tell her any details. "I believe I can return. I just don't know when. But I promise I'll be back as soon as possible if—"

"No," she interrupted, clapping her hand over his mouth for a moment. "Don't say anything about . . . anything bad."

"But, Noelle, we have to face—"

"No. Don't say it. Both of us know . . ." Her voice trailed off as she tried to think of a way to make her point without actually saying the words. "Both of us know that . . . war is unpredictable. We have to pray for the best."

Drake realized that she was telling him she knew the risks of war and accepted them. Also, he figured she was superstitious about some things, and this appeared to be one of them. She seemed to believe that saying something aloud could make it happen "I'll be back."

In the distance, thunder rumbled, and Noelle shivered. "Must you leave now?"

"I should. Let's go out and see what the weather is like." Drake waited for Noelle to stand, and when she didn't, he cupped her chin in his hand and turned her face to meet his. This time, his kiss was tender, silently expressing a knowledge that they shared and making a promise for the future.

Noelle's composure almost crumbled when he kissed her this time. When he finally drew away, she lay against him for a few seconds before standing. She found that her legs were reluctant to hold her erect and she almost fell back into his lap. Then, biting her lower lip, she sauntered across the kitchen as if their intimacy meant nothing.

Watching her with a tenderness he'd never felt before, Drake smiled and shook his head gently. One day perhaps they could fully express the feelings that lay between them, but that day seemed to be a long way off. He rose, uncomfortably aware that his desire for her showed so obviously. Stooping slightly to hide his embarrassment, he walked to her side.

Her eyes narrowed as she watched him come toward her. "Is something wrong? Have you injured your back?"

Cursing his condition, he felt his cheeks warm. Damn her for being so observant. She noticed everything. "No. Just a little catch."

"Oh, it's my fault," she cried, hurrying to his back and massaging his taut muscles. "You did this when you carried me. I'm too heavy."

"Nonsense," Drake protested, wishing she'd stop. Her tender ministrations made his condition worse instead of better. He straightened slightly, to convince her that his back felt better and grabbed his coat. "You're as light as down."

Noelle noted that he stood straighter and smiled with satisfaction. Her massage seemed to have helped. "I'll get my shawl."

She strode to the hook where her shawl hung and took it down. With a quick motion she flung it over her head, with the triangular tip pointed down, and knotted the other two ends across her breast. He opened the door, and she walked onto the porch.

Drake looked across the fields at the approaching storm. Already he could see the curtain of rain as it crossed the fallow land and came closer. "It may pass over quickly. I'll wait."

They returned to the sanctuary of the kitchen, and Noelle busied herself preparing a snack for Drake to carry with him. After wrapping several items in thick paper, she took a set of pockets and placed several apples, johnnycakes, cheese, and thick slices of buttered bread inside.

"There. That should keep you from starving to death for a while." She folded the pockets so that the waist tapes held them securely and laid them on the table.

Drake smiled. He knew she was finding ways to keep busy to prevent her from thinking of his departure. "Thank you. I know I'll really appreciate that on the trail. Now come over here and sit with me until I have to leave."

Noelle felt the tension rise in her. She had to stay busy. If she didn't, she'd end up begging him to remain with her instead of leaving to face the war. "I'm going to fix some supper. You'll need—"

"I need you to . . . sit with me," he interrupted. "I can find food on the road. Your company means . . ."

His voice dwindled off as he walked across the room and took the spoon from her hand. "I don't want food. I want to be with you."

Noelle nodded and allowed him to lead her back to the rocker. Rain pelted the roof as she rested her head against his broad shoulder. Closing her eyes, she wished that this moment could last forever, but knew in her heart that it would end all too quickly. Thunder and lightning raged overhead like her own emotions, and she timorously snaked her arms around him as far as she could reach.

Suddenly she sat up and gazed around. "What if Mandy comes in? She can't see us like this. She'll—"

"Mandy is probably hiding beneath her bed and will

remain there until the storm passes," Drake informed her and turned her face to his. "We're alone and shall be for the duration of the storm."

"But how do you know?" Noelle persisted, gazing into the depths of his warm brown eyes. The room had grown dark, except for the light from the fire and the flashes of lightning. In the dim light, she studied his face and found herself turning up her lips to kiss him.

Mandy no longer mattered. Their lips met hungrily, and Noelle found herself locked in a steel embrace that took her breath away. With her eyes closed, she imagined that this moment could last forever.

Drake felt swept away from the passage of time, from war, from reality, but he knew that all of those horrible factors remained. Foremost in his mind was Noelle's safety, and he could not put off raising the subject for much longer, he realized as he deepened his kiss. Her reaction to what he must say would destroy their intimacy, but Drake never shrank from duty.

After a few minutes he pulled away. "Noelle, we must talk about your future. You know you can't remain here alone."

"I won't be alone," she replied, slowly opening her eyes. How could he think of that at a time like this? Gazing at him in wonder, she tried to think, but her thoughts were scattered, and she felt vulnerable. "I have Mandy and Lard. And some of the other servants may return."

"They're no protection," he said once again. Their discussion of this subject remained the same. "And if the other servants could return, or wanted to return, they would have already."

"Not necessarily," she shouted and jumped up. "You can't just kiss me and think you control my life. I'm a grown woman and I won't be ordered about like a child by you or anyone else." She couldn't tell him that Tyger Rest was her anchor. It was all she had left and she couldn't leave it.

Drake grabbed her hand and jerked her down into his lap again. "If you persist in acting like a child, I shall have to treat you like a child. Tell me where your relatives live, and I shall take you there tomorrow."

"I refuse," she stated adamantly and crossed her arms in anger. "And you can't make me go. You're not my father or my husband. You're not even my intended. You're the enemy and you're going to be killed, and I'll be all alone, so just go."

Once the words were out they couldn't be retracted, nor could she hope that he hadn't heard. Mandy had probably heard the shouts all the way down to her cabin.

Drake winced at the words. They pointed out an idea that he'd been toying with. He did feel responsible for her, not as her father would, but as her suitor. He'd even allowed himself to think of her as his wife. During the long nights alone in the woods, it comforted him to fantasize about coming home to Noelle—his wife. He'd never thought of another woman in that regard, and had in fact worked very hard to prevent that from happening. Now fantasy blurred with reality, and he found that he did want to come home to her every night.

A sound nagged at his mind as he looked down at Noelle's scowling face. Singing as she walked, Mandy was coming up the path from her cabin.

At almost the same instant, Noelle heard the melodious voice, too, and jumped up again. Glad for the interruption, she hurried to the fireplace and picked up a bowl. "Would you like some stew? Mandy just made it from a rabbit she caught."

Drake made a face at her and picked up a candle. After lighting it from the fire, he proceeded to light the other candles in the kitchen. "You aren't completely free from this discussion. I assure you that—"

The door swung open, interrupting him in mid-sentence. Mandy lumbered in and shook the raindrops off her skirt.

"It rainin' powerful hard. If'n I wasn't so hungry, I'da jus' gone to bed."

She looked at Noelle and followed her gaze to Drake. "You still here? I thought you left a long time ago." Her eyes narrowed, and the glittering black pupils could hardly be seen. "You ain't been up to nothin' has you?"

Drake laughed and sat down. "Afraid not, Mandy."

Mandy frowned and glanced at Noelle. "Her face seem mighty red for to have nothin' goin' on."

Noelle bit her lower lip and thought quickly. What could she say that would explain her blush—without telling the truth? "Cooking. I'm cooking. The fire's hot."

"Right," Drake agreed, smiling at Noelle's quick mind. "She's about to serve stew. We thought you'd be tucked in sound as can be."

"I'm powerful hungry." Mandy went over to the kettle. "You jus' get out of old Mandy's way. I be fixin' the vittles. You pour some milk."

"Yes, ma'am," Noelle replied obediently and strode to the milk jar. "Milk for you, Drake?"

"Yes, please," he answered and busied himself arranging chairs around the rough pine table. "May I help you with something, Mandy? That smells wonderful."

Mandy grinned and shook her head. "Jus' set down. A man ain't got no business messin' with fixin' supper. How come you still here?"

"The storm kept me from leaving." Drake sat down at what had come to be his regular place at the table and leaned back in the chair to watch the two ladies.

"You are leavin' today, ain't you?" Mandy continued to probe. She placed a steaming bowl of rabbit stew on the table and propped her hands on her hips to hear his answer.

From her stern questioning, Drake knew that she left him no real choice, not that he had a choice anyway. His orders were to rejoin his regiment by the day after tomorrow, and he would have to leave soon to make it. "I'm sorry to disappoint you, but I do have to leave today," he teased and continued before she could protest that he had misunderstood the intent of her question. "But don't you worry your pretty self. I'll be back as soon as possible."

Mandy beamed at his compliment but recovered her dignity. "I wasn't askin' you to stay."

Drake did his best to look astonished without laughing. "You weren't? I would have wagered King George's crown that you wanted me to stay on."

"And you'd be settin' in jail now, too, cause you'da lost. And ole King George would stretch your neck tomorrow," Mandy predicted and laughed. "An' you tall enough as it is."

"I'm crushed," he replied and hung his head. "I thought you were beginning to like me."

"Harrumph. The day I likes a Redcoat soldier, I hope the Lord jus' take me to heaven, 'cause I'll be ready for the Promised Land." Mandy ladled out another bowlful of stew from the kettle and placed it on the table. "Set down here and eat, chile. Mandy'll do that."

Trying to hide her mirth, Noelle obeyed. Mandy moved to the spoon bread and put a large helping on each plate. "Now jus' hush and eat. I wants to be back in my cabin 'fore it gits too dark. An' you gonna be gone 'fore me."

"Yes, ma'am," Drake replied contritely and ate his stew like a reprimanded child. After a while he glanced at Noelle, winked, and then looked at Mandy. "You know, I'd almost marry a woman who could cook this good, and I've been avoiding marriage all my life."

Mandy smiled broadly and then laughed. "Soldier, I b'lieve they'd hang us both for that. You jus' go on avoidin' marriage, and I'll go on cookin' stew."

When Noelle smiled, it was a hollow smile. Mandy had told her how difficult it was to catch a good husband, but Noelle had never really believed the old woman. Now Drake confirmed what Mandy had said. Noelle felt confused and somehow violated. She'd trusted him, had allowed him to kiss her, and had kissed him back. She hadn't really thought of marriage, but she never considered that he was merely dallying with her.

Mandy had warned her about that kind, too, the kind of men who were all sweetness and caresses until it was time to stand before a preacher. Men who were honest and upstanding were few. Was Drake Hastings one of these men?

No, he couldn't be—or could he? How could she tell? If he was bad, would he have ridden all that distance just to see her? But he was a British soldier.

Noelle had fallen into his trap. No, she had leapt into it voluntarily. She vowed that she would never be so gullible again.

Still confused, she scooped up a spoonful of stew, gulped it down almost without tasting it, and choked on a large piece of meat. Racked with coughs, Noelle gasped for breath.

Drake's eyes lost their mirth when he realized that she was suddenly turning blue. He jumped up from his chair, overturning it, and grabbed Noelle by the waist, yanking her from her seat, and pounding on her back with one hand until the offending meat burst from her esophagus.

For a moment he thought he had reacted too late. She collapsed in his arms, and he could hardly hold her up. Like water through a sieve, she slithered almost to the floor before he could catch her. "Noelle, are you all right?"

Mandy ran across the kitchen and helped him lay Noelle on the floor. "No, not my baby. Lawd, don't take my baby. I ain't got nobody else."

"Hush, Mandy, she's going to be all right. Look, her eyes are opening." Drake said a silent prayer when the sapphire eyes, glittering with tears, caught his gaze. "Noelle, can you talk?"

Noelle tried to speak, but her throat ached when she did, so she shook her head. She glanced at Mandy's face, wet with tears, and tried to smile, to reassure her servant and friend.

"Put your arm around my neck," Drake directed as he picked her up. When she complied, he walked to the rocker and sat down with her in his lap. At the moment he didn't care what Mandy said. He'd come too close to losing Noelle to bother with an old woman's concern with appearance and manners.

Hugging her close, he rocked and tried to keep from crying himself. Drake never realized that he'd come to . . . to like her so much. Expecting to get a scathing tongue-lashing from Mandy, he glanced at the old servant.

She mopped her eyes with the hem of her white apron and then looked at him. Instead of berating him, she let her lips curve slightly upward into a hint of a smile. Mandy didn't speak for a minute, but watched the two of them carefully. After she recovered her composure, she arranged her features into a scowl and shook her finger at him. "I 'preciate you savin' my baby, but this ain't no time to be forgettin' who you is and who we is. You just set her down in her chair and stop grinnin' 'cause you ain't nowhere good enough for my baby."

Grinning broadly, from the relief he felt deep inside and from the return of his good humor when Mandy recovered her good sense, he rose and placed Noelle in her chair. "I apologize for taking advantage of an unfortunate accident."

"Don't be sweet-talking my baby," Mandy continued to scold. "She ain't got no ears for honey-drippin' words said by a Redcoat."

Though it hurt, Noelle giggled. The situation, since the catastrophe had been averted, seemed rather silly. Drake's face had turned white when she began to choke, and Noelle knew that he cared about her even if he didn't intend to marry her.

Even though she remained angry with Drake, she felt better. With lifted spirits she smiled warmly at Mandy and hoped to alleviate some of the old slave's concern. To her surprise, Mandy seemed more cheerful then Noelle expected her to be, and she sensed a change in the atmosphere of the room.

Drake stood and donned his coat. "I'm afraid I must leave you ladies."

"So soon?" Noelle found her voice hardly more than a rasp. "It's getting dark."

"Missy, you ain't gonna keep this man from doin' what he gotta do," Mandy chastised and wiped her hands on her apron. "He needs daylight to git where he goin' and you wastin' it."

Smiling, Drake strode toward the door. "I'll see you when I can."

Speechless once again, Noelle raised her hands in a futile gesture to stop him from leaving, but dropped them when she realized that this time he had to go. Glancing quickly at Mandy, she turned back to Drake and said, "I'll walk a ways with you."

"Oh, no you won't. It's too dark and cold for you to be out." Mandy started across the room toward Noelle. "You'll catch your death of cold. When I git to Glory, I don't want the Lawd to turn me away 'cause I didn't do my duty."

Almost wild-eyed with fear that Mandy would catch up before Noelle could scramble out of reach, she snatched a shawl from the hook by the door and dashed out past Drake. "I won't be long."

"Missy? You ain't got no raisin' at all. I know old Mandy did better . . ."

Noelle scurried out of hearing distance toward the barn with Drake on her heels. Both of them were laughing by the time they reached his horse.

Taking only the time necessary to saddle the tall animal, Drake whispered, "I thought she'd follow us."

Noelle peered out of the barn and then around the yard to see if he was right. She couldn't see Mandy anywhere. "Go quietly," she whispered as they led the horse from the barn.

When they passed the kitchen, Mandy stepped onto the

porch and looked at Drake. She leaned against the post supporting the roof of the porch and closed her eyes a moment. When she opened them, she stared directly at Drake and muttered something.

"What did she say?" Noelle asked as they walked between the crepe myrtles lining the broad lane that led to the house.

"I can't be sure," he admitted. "But it sounded like 'take care of yourself.' "

"Goodness, that's a reversal." Noelle considered the change for a minute. "Why, just the other day she said . . . never mind. You must have done something to make her change her opinion of you."

Drake nodded and moved to the same side of the horse as Noelle. "I noticed that, too. Must have been after you choked."

Noelle flushed with embarrassment. No lady should ever swallow a piece of food large enough to make her choke. What's more, he'd had to save her life because she could never have dislodged the meat herself.

A feeling of fear touched Drake as he looked down at Noelle, and he took her hand as if to comfort her. She seemed so rigid, as if he'd mentioned a sensitive subject. He admired her a great deal for her courage, but found her defiance over going to stay with relatives bordering on stubbornness. They reached the end of the lane, and he stopped to tether his horse to a limb of crepe myrtle. He glanced around and found a grassy spot beneath the over-hanging trees. "Let's sit for a moment."

He studied Noelle as she followed the direction of his outstretched hand and thought she would balk. Lifting her chin, she strode past him onto the soggy ground and waited while he placed his coat on the ground for her to sit on. When she seated herself, he chose a spot close to her. Pulling a slip of new growth from the grass, he gazed at her, knowing that he might not see her again for a long time. He memorized every part of her face. Her turned-up nose, her widow's peak, the soft peach of her cheeks, and the cherry tint of her lips were emblazoned on the back of his eyelids before he spoke.

"Noelle," he began and twirled the grass nervously between his fingers. It was imperative that he find a way to persuade her to go to safety. "I don't know what else to say to you. I've used every argument—"

"Then don't say anything else," she interrupted and started to rise.

He caught her wrist and pulled her back down beside him. When she sat back down, she lost her balance and ended up almost lying in his arms. Imprisoning her with his embrace, Drake shook his head slightly and sighed. She didn't intend to give in easily. "It's dangerous here. Even for men. I can't depend on Soaring Eagle keeping his word. British troops, renegades, Tories . . . hell, anybody could come through here and . . ." His voice slowly became silent.

Gazing up into eyes almost as dark as the midnight sky, Noelle felt the growing warmth in her body that always resulted from contact with Drake. She wanted to bolt away, but part of her refused, and she did nothing. "Drake, I can't go. I have to stay here."

"But, Noelle," he broke in, sensing her uncompromising position once again, but knowing he must confront it.

"No, wait," she continued before he could say anything else. "Let me finish. If I go away, I don't know when I'll be able to see you. You're so unpredictable. If I go, I may never . . . I just can't go, and I won't discuss it."

Drake smiled inwardly, but soon his delight abandoned him. A part of the reason she refused to go was her bond with him. "If something happens to you as a result—"

"Don't say it!" she commanded. "Don't even think it. I'm going to be fine. Besides," she lied, "I don't have anywhere to go."

"You must have someone." Drake eyed her suspiciously. He didn't doubt that she would like to end the conversation. For now he let the subject drop, but when he returned, he would question Mandy about Noelle's family. "All right. I give up."

Noelle's smile brightened considerably. She'd won, at least for the present. The subject would be discussed again, she knew, but for now she didn't have to deal with it.

More reluctant than ever to leave, Drake continued to gaze down at her. She appeared so innocent, so fragile, that he hated to leave her in Mandy's care, but there was nothing else to say.

Suddenly she knew he was going to kiss her, and she wondered why she didn't scamper away from him like a squirrel. Still a little angry for the revelation he'd somehow let slip when he was talking to Mandy, Noelle quelled the growing urge to reach up and touch his face, to make one more memory to keep her warm at night while he was away. She didn't move away at all. If anything, she met him halfway.

Their lips fused in a passionate kiss, hungry for the present but acknowledging the famine to come. Noelle rested her head in the crook of his arm and allowed him to deepen the kiss until she thought her insides would burst.

Her spirit seemed to leave her body and soar like a hawk above a cornfield, swooping down, catching an updraft, and gliding like silk on the wind. When he drew away, the wind became icy, and she tumbled back to reality like an injured bird tumbling to earth. Gradually her eyes opened, and she stared pensively at him.

"Noelle, I don't know how to . . . I want you to know that I . . ." Deep inside, Drake wanted to kiss her again, never-endingly, to know that she desired him as much as he wanted her. He, too, felt the unfettered freedom of their experience and wished that reality would stay beyond the boundaries of Tyger Rest.

Reality. His reality at the moment was war, and Noelle could have no place there until its conclusion.

Agonizing over the distance he had to place between them, he got to his knees and looked down at her. The memory would have to last much longer than he would have chosen, but he had no say in the matter.

Cold dampness seeped through Drake's cloak until Noelle felt uncomfortable. After a moment's consideration, she realized that the discomfort had been there ever since she sat down, but his kiss blotted out all other feeling. She sat up and tried to project a confidence she didn't feel. Beneath Drake's piercing gaze, she felt giddy and angry and lonely and comforted and . . . Too many emotions flooded over her. She wanted him to go away; she wanted him to stay.

"Trust me, Noelle," he murmured close to her earlobe as he embraced her once again. "I'll be back."

Noelle watched him pull on his coat once again and turn to face her. He touched her lips with a brief, tender kiss and turned to walk away. She felt her eyes glisten and knew she was on the verge of bursting into tears or calling him back.

She could do neither. Noelle refused to add to his burden by crying and clinging like a petulant child who couldn't get her way. Pulling her shawl closer about her shoulders, she studied him as he climbed into his saddle and glanced back at her one last time.

Then they both heard the clatter of horses' hooves and an approaching wagon. Seeing that Noelle was about to run toward the sound of the wagon on the road, he jumped from his horse, grabbed her arm and pulled her back. "Don't be silly. You could be in danger!"

"They must be friendly," she said. "No enemy would approach a house making that much noise! That would be foolish."

"Yes, but it's just as foolish of you to assume that." Drake held her close against him and refused to let her go.

A horse came into view at the end of the boxwood-lined drive. Noelle recognized her friend Kathleen immediately and broke free of Drake's grasp. "Kathleen!" she called, running toward the wagon.

"Oh, Noelle!" Kathleen Foster cried. "Stop the wagon, Joe."

The driver pulled back on the reins, and the wagon stopped. Kathleen didn't wait to be helped, but jumped down to her friend.

"Oh, Noelle, I thought you were dead. We just came from . . . from John Brooks's place. It's burned to the ground."

Noelle closed her eyes a moment to steady her nerves. Two people had died there, two people she loved. "I was there when it happened."

"Tell me all about it," Kathleen demanded and tugged on the ribbons of her bonnet. "Let's go inside."

"How inhospitable of me. Come in." Noelle opened the door of the house and let Kathleen enter the parlor.

It still smelled strongly of smoke, and it looked little better than it had on the evening of Soaring Eagle's attack. Noelle had been working hard, but everything had to be washed before she could eradicate the odor. "Come in and be seated. I'm sorry about the horrible smell, but there's little I can do without a thorough cleaning."

"Think nothing of it." Kathleen seated herself on the sofa and removed her bonnet. "I've come to say good-bye."

"Good-bye?" Noelle dropped onto the sofa beside her friend. "Where are you going?"

Before Kathleen could answer, Drake strode into the room. He smiled and bowed to the visitor and Noelle. Gratefully, Noelle noticed that he had removed his red coat and rolled up his shirtsleeves. He had obviously decided not to leave yet. "Kathleen Foster, allow me to introduce my friend, Drake Hastings."

Drake bowed again from the waist. "My pleasure to make your acquaintance, Miss Foster."

"The pleasure is mine, sir." Kathleen glanced at Noelle and then at Drake. "I don't recall seeing you around here before."

"I . . . I'm new in the area," Drake answered, staring at Noelle to silence her. "John Brooks was my uncle."

"Oh, yes," Noelle interrupted. "John and Irene's sister is Drake's . . . Mr. Hastings's mother."

"Do tell," Kathleen said, smiling prettily at the handsome stranger.

"Miss Foster, did I overhear you say that you'd come to say good-bye?" he asked and seated himself across from the ladies.

"Yes, I fear you did," Kathleen acknowledged and patted Noelle's hand. "Mother insists on going to live with her uncle Paul over in Ninety Six. She's too afraid to remain here."

"Perfectly sensible thing to do," Drake replied as if she'd spoken to him instead of to Noelle. If anyone knew of Noelle's kin, Kathleen probably did, so he continued, "If Miss Arledge had any relatives, I'd whisk her off to live with them in a second."

"Oh, but she does. In Charleston," Kathleen began and looked at Noelle curiously.

Noelle glared at her friend and rolled her eyes. Drake would never let the question lie until he knew the truth. If he knew the truth, Noelle was as good as gone to Charleston.

"She has a lovely aunt and cousin. Two cousins, in fact. Why, just the other day—"

"Kathleen, will you hush up?" Noelle jumped to her feet and strode across the room. She turned and glanced around. She loved every piece of furniture, every stick of wood, every book and candle in this house. Kathleen had ensured that Noelle would leave almost immediately without ever knowing what she'd done.

"How interesting," Drake replied and smiled at Noelle. "Miss Foster, how long can you remain with us?"

Kathleen looked from Drake to Noelle and stood. "I really must be going. I promised Mother I'd be gone no more than an hour, and that time has almost expired. We were unaware that Ash Meadow . . . well, you know."

"How well I do," Noelle answered and sighed. "Please stay awhile. I can't bear for you to leave without gossiping just a bit." She glowered at Drake, who stood and stretched.

"I'm sorry I can't remain here and while away the day." Drake reached for Kathleen's hand and kissed it tenderly. "I have many things to do before I rejoin my regiment."

"Oh, you're a soldier?" Kathleen gushed and colored with excitement. "Please do take ever such good care of yourself. We'd be heartbroken if something happened to you."

Drake smiled and closed his eyes briefly as if memorizing her words. "Miss Foster, you've made a happy man of me, knowing that somewhere a lovely young woman cares that much. Why, it's almost more than a body can bear. Until we meet again."

"Oh, Mr. Hastings, you may want to hear this," Kathleen called as he strode toward the door. "I heard just this morning that some weeks ago at Kings Mountain, Major Patrick Ferguson, leading a band of Tories, was killed in the battle. Many of his men were killed or injured. The overhills men heard that he intended to kill all Patriot officers and burn their homes. They came prepared to fight. Not a single Tory or Provincial escaped. They were all killed, injured, or captured."

Noelle glanced at Drake to gauge his reaction and said, "Do you think the accounts were exaggerated?"

"Oh, no. I heard it from a man who was there." Kathleen smiled and nodded. "I'm sure every word is truth."

Drake's face looked strained as he watched Noelle's response to the news. He saw her gaze at him and knew she felt compassion. In fact, Drake had already heard the news and had sent word on by messenger to Clinton in Charleston. "An outstanding victory, ladies."

He kissed her hand once more and strode out the door as

quickly as he'd come in. Noelle watched him go with her mouth open.

Kathleen, too, watched Drake leave the room, and when she heard the back door shut, she turned to Noelle. "Where has that handsome man been hiding?"

"Oh, Kathleen, you're such a twit. He's . . ." Noelle's voice tapered off as she saw shock register on Kathleen's face. "I'm sorry Katie, sweet, but he makes me very angry."

"You're forgiven." Her attention turned in full to Noelle who settled back on the sofa. "Tell me everything about him."

There was nothing to do but tell. Noelle didn't divulge Drake's affiliation with the British army at first, but Kathleen guessed: "He's the man who saved you. The one you saw the evening of your party at Ash Meadow. Is he really the Brookses' nephew?"

"Yes." Noelle began to worry. If Kathleen knew who Drake really was, his life was in danger. "Please don't tell anyone. He's really been a friend to me. He saved my life twice."

"Three times."

Noelle jumped to her feet again. "Why, you rotten scoundrel. Even the servants know better than to eavesdrop. You're nothing but a—"

"Nothing but a scoundrel of a British soldier who saved your life thrice," he finished for her. "Like it or not, that's who I am."

"A real British soldier?" Kathleen stared at Drake as if he were an apparition. "Are you going to kill us?"

Drake shook his head gently. "No, Miss Foster. I mean you no harm."

"Really, Kathleen, do you think I'd allow him to come here if he were as bad as all those others?" Noelle asked impatiently. "He's been more than a friend. As he said, he saved my life three times. He's helped considerably around here. I don't do very well at chopping wood and killing game. He's kept food on the table."

"What about your servants?" Kathleen sank to the sofa beside Noelle.

"I'm afraid all of them are dead, or have run off, except Mandy and Lard." Noelle closed her eyes briefly before she could continue. "Lard returned just recently."

"Which brings us to the present," Drake said, looking from Kathleen to Noelle. "We're about to put in some onions and collards if you want them. Lard thinks there's still time for the greens to mature before winter."

"Do whatever you think best." Noelle studied him. Drake hadn't intended to eavesdrop. He'd returned to ask a legitimate question, and she'd berated him for it. "I apologize for acting so silly. I . . . I don't really think you're a scoundrel."

Drake broke into a wide grin. "Thank you, Miss Arledge, for your vote of confidence. It's been delightful here, but it's time to go to work."

Color sprang to Noelle's cheeks, and she picked up a book. She flung it at him as hard as she could, barely missing him as he ducked. "Oooh, you are a scoundrel."

Laughing, Drake retrieved the book and placed it on the tea table. "Perhaps you're right. Only you would know."

Noelle glared at him as he turned and stalked away. "That is the most infuriating man I ever met."

Kathleen had leaned back to protect herself from Noelle's tirade. "My, my. That's the angriest I ever saw you. In front of a gentleman, too. Tsk, tsk."

"Gentleman?" Noelle leapt to her feet and scowled at Kathleen. She strode across the room, then began to pace back and forth. "That man is no gentleman. A gentleman would never say anything to embarrass a lady."

"And what did he say to embarrass you?" Wide-eyed with curiosity, Kathleen edged forward on the sofa. "Tell me. Don't you dare try to keep a secret from me, Noelle Arledge."

Noelle stopped pacing. She'd said too much already. No matter how angry she was with Drake, he didn't deserve to lose his life for helping her. She gripped Kathleen's hands as hard as she could. "Please, Kathleen, promise me you won't tell anyone about this. You've got to promise."

"I'll promise, if you tell me everything." Her face lit up as if she had made a sudden discovery. "You're in love with him!"

Noelle colored again. "What a ridiculous thing to say. You know me well enough to know that I'd never fall in love with the enemy."

"Nevertheless, you love that man." Kathleen grinned and smoothed the skirt of her calico gown.

Kathleen's smug demeanor caused Noelle to sigh with frustration. Having little choice, she sat down again and began to talk about her relationship with Drake. She left out very little, knowing that Kathleen would guess the truth—or something more fantastic than the truth—if Noelle wasn't honest.

Listening intently, Kathleen nodded occasionally and smiled. Noelle could see the path her friend's romantic and devious mind had taken. "Kathleen, stop your daydreaming and listen. I'm trying to tell you—"

"You've mentioned nothing about love," Kathleen said. "When I said I wanted to hear everything, I meant every little detail."

"You goose. I don't love that man." Noelle cast about for a way to convince Kathleen of her honesty. "You're a twit to believe I do."

"Twit or no, I know when you're lying." Kathleen put on her bonnet. "Well, since you can't seem to trust me enough to tell me the truth, I'll leave."

"No, please don't go," Noelle pleaded, raking her fingers through her hair. "I'll tell you everything. But I don't love him."

"Oh, yes, you do," Kathleen countered. "You may not realize it yet, but you do."

Exasperated, Noelle nodded. "Have it your way. Now, do you want to listen or not? I must secure your promise to remain silent."

For now her anger with Drake came second. Her fear for his life came first. Noelle had revealed information that might snuff out his life if she couldn't find a way to stop Kathleen from talking.

CHAPTER
10

NOELLE WATCHED KATHLEEN'S WAGON UNTIL IT DISAPPEARED down the drive. She felt almost confident that Kathleen wouldn't divulge Drake's whereabouts or habits to anyone.

She'd had to lie to keep Kathleen from spreading the word about him. Returning to the sitting room, Noelle sat down and cradled her forehead in her palms. "What in the world made Kathleen think I love that—"

"That scoundrel?" Drake finished for her. "That's an interesting question."

Noelle raised her head and stared at him. "Don't you believe in making your presence known when you enter a room?"

"I used to, but I've found that one can learn some interesting things by remaining silent," Drake teased, "and today I've gleaned a wealth of information."

"Today you made me almost angry enough to kill you myself." Noelle leaned back on the sofa and watched him cross the room. "Then there'd be one less British soldier to worry about."

"So I've heard." Drake dropped onto the sofa beside her and mopped his perspiring face with his handkerchief. "Your friend is gone?"

"Yes, she's gone. Kathleen and her mother are leaving in the morning." Noelle studied him. With his sleeves rolled up, his muscles showed like thick cords in his arms. Noelle wondered briefly what he'd look like with all of his clothes off. Blushing, she averted her eyes.

"Thinking of me, I hope?" he asked and moved closer. Tucking his arm behind her, he pulled her into his embrace.

Noelle leaned away, but couldn't move out of his reach. "No. Of course not. I was thinking of . . . of the garden. Did you finish planting the onions and collards?"

"Thinking of collards makes you blush?" Drake laughed and kissed her. "What a naive miss you are."

"Stop that," she said. "What if Mandy should come in? Or Lard?"

"Lard's finishing in the garden, and Mandy's down at her cabin." Drake kissed her again. All afternoon he'd thought of nothing but her. Kathleen seemed like a shadow compared to Noelle's vibrancy.

"They won't be there much longer." Noelle tried to rise, but Drake blocked her.

"I want to talk to you."

"Talk? About what?" Noelle felt herself go limp. She knew what he wanted to talk about as well as she knew her own name. "I need to go back to work."

"Not until we're finished with our discussion." Drake locked his hands, effectively imprisoning her. "Now, I want to know about those two cousins Miss Foster mentioned."

"Kathleen's a twit. You should never listen to her." Noelle wriggled to free herself but found his arms tightening with her every move. "You're hurting me."

"I don't want to hurt you, but we're going to discuss this here and now if I have to sit on you."

Noelle's eyes widened. "You wouldn't dare."

"Wouldn't I?" Drake hoped she wouldn't call his bluff. He could never harm her, no matter what the circumstances. "Now, talk."

"I have one aunt and two uncles." Noelle sighed and closed her eyes. Already she could envision her trip to Charleston. Leaving Tyger Rest was almost more than she could bear, but she knew Drake was right. "The aunt is my mother's sister. My father's brother also lives there."

"We leave tomorrow," Drake announced. "One of them is bound to take you in."

"Drake, please listen. I belong here." How could she make him understand her feelings? Did she know her own feelings well enough to convey them to him? "I can't go to Charleston. I can't leave Tyger Rest."

For a moment Drake thought she would admit that she didn't want to leave him. He'd seen the look on her face when Kathleen announced that she thought Noelle loved him. The astonishment he recognized was an honest emotion, but the dawning of understanding told him more. Maybe she hadn't accepted it yet, but Noelle Arledge loved him.

"Noelle," he began softly. "Nothing will change. Tyger Rest will be here when the war is over. Mandy and Lard can look after it. I'll come by and check on it occasionally."

"It isn't the same. I need to be here." Noelle stubbornly refused to give in. Charleston was so far away. She had to be here where she could get information about Drake.

Drake gazed down into her ever-changing eyes. Once again they'd gone from sapphire to violet. Framed by thick lashes, her eyes were entrancing, and Drake found himself drowning in their violet passion. "I'll visit you in Charleston," he whispered and closed the distance between them. "Don't worry, I'll see you again."

Noelle's eyes closed as Drake's lips descended on hers. All her anger converted itself to passion, and she met his kiss eagerly. His grip of iron relaxed a little, and she clung to him now as firmly as he clung to her. This moment of passion would be short-lived, she knew, and Noelle took advantage of it. She memorized every little tingle, every touch, every sensation that radiated from Drake's contact.

With her response to Drake's kiss, Noelle lost her will to fight even though she hadn't agreed to go with him to Charleston. She knew the moment she would give in was near.

Drake drew away and studied her for a long moment. "We'll leave tonight."

Noelle bolted out of his arms and turned to glare back at him. The scent of smoke tainted the air as surely as his words tainted her heart, as surely as the war tainted the landscape. Rage poured into her mouth, and fury made her spit out words she wouldn't otherwise have dreamed of saying to him. "How dare you presume to tell me when I will leave my plantation? How dare you come in here and take advantage of me when you know I'm weak? You self-righteous bully, you can take your carcass and remove it from my sofa and from my sight. I never want to see you again."

Drake physically drew back from her verbal assault. He'd never seen a woman as angry as Noelle and hoped never to see another one. If her words didn't inflict enough pain and damage, the candlestick she threw did. Caught off guard, Drake felt the base of the silver candelabrum bite into his forehead.

Before he could lift his hand to wipe away the blood, everything became fuzzy and faded. He tumbled forward from the sofa to the floor and lay still.

"You can just stop feigning injury," Noelle demanded, acting braver than she felt. She waited a few seconds, but when he still hadn't moved, she edged toward him. "Drake? Don't tease me."

Noelle watched him closely and waited almost a minute. Biting her lip, she moved next to stand over him. She could see blood pouring from a gash on his forehead. "Oh, God, what have I done?"

Dropping to her knees, Noelle turned him slightly to see the injury clearly. A cut about two inches long, shaped like a crescent, stretched from his eyebrow almost to his hairline. "Thunderation!"

She pulled a tatted doily from the arm of the sofa and pressed it to the cut. Knowing that she should apply pressure and that she needed help, she folded the doily in quarters and propped the Bible against it.

Running for her life, she rushed to the back door. Her hip thudded against the doorjamb, but she didn't even pause to wince. Drake was more important at the moment. She flung the back door open and screamed, "Lard! Mandy! Come quickly!"

Retracing her steps, she scurried back to Drake's side and fell to her knees. "Drake, Drake, please wake up."

She slid her knees under his head and cradled him on her lap. What if he dies? she thought. Oh, I'll never disagree with him again. "Drake Hastings, don't you die on me, you scoundrel. When I start an argument, I mean to finish it, and you won't get off that easily."

Noelle knew she made no sense, but she chattered on. "You can't just dance into my life like this and die. You're not going to do that to me. I've invested too much concern in you already."

"Missy?" Mandy flew through the door as quickly as her ambling frame could carry her. "Is you hurt? What's the matter with you?"

Lard burst through the front door and saw her on the floor with Drake's head in her lap. "Did that Redcoat hurt you? I'll kill that—"

"Lard," Noelle interrupted, raising a hand to silence him. "I may have killed Drake. He's bleeding."

Lard and Mandy leaned over to peek at Drake. Edging closer, Lard whistled and said, "That's a powerful lot a blood. Is he dead?"

Noelle cringed at the words, feeling a chill creep down her spine. She gazed at Drake and saw that his face was pale except for the bloodstains on his forehead and temple. All around the crescent-shaped cut, the tissues swelled, and a large lump arose.

"Help me get him to Papa's bed," she instructed Lard. "Mandy, you go turn down the sheets."

"You ain't puttin' that bleedin' Redcoat in Mr. Charles's bed," Lard stated and crossed his arms.

"Lard, if you don't help me, I'll . . ." Noelle's voice faded as she wondered what kind of threat would induce her servant to obey her. Force had never been used at Tyger Rest, and she didn't want to begin now, but Drake was seriously wounded. "I'll . . . I'll carry him myself."

"No'm, you won't. I'll tote him down to the slave cabins, but he ain't layin' in Mr. Charles's bed while I've got breath."

Lard moved to pick up Drake.

"Lard, if you won't obey me, get off my land. I don't have any use for someone who won't help an injured man, be he British or Patriot, black, white, or Cherokee. He doesn't deserve this kind of treatment after all he's done for us." The words poured from Noelle's mouth as she slid from under Drake's head. She would drag him to her father's bed herself and then chase Lard away if he didn't help.

Lard's eyes widened until she could see only two white orbs in his black face. "Missy, you wouldn't run ole Lard off, would you?"

"Just as soon as I get him to bed, you can depend on my word. I refuse to sink to the level of the British and Indians." Noelle lifted Drake's shoulders and started to drag him toward the bedroom.

Mandy hurried ahead and threw the covers down so they could put Drake to bed, if Noelle could drag him that far. Heaving, she pulled as hard as she could, but he moved only an inch or so.

"Jus' git out the way," Lard said, elbowing Noelle aside. He slid his arms beneath Drake's supine figure, lifted him easily, and deposited him between the clean sheets of Charles Arledge's bed.

"Thank you, Lard. I knew you couldn't let an injured man die that way." Noelle turned to Mandy. "Get me some hot water and soap. I want to wash that wound and bandage it."

"You don't have to tell me. I knows what to do." Mandy was already on her way to the kitchen. "Mr. Drake need Mandy and Mandy gonna help take care of him."

Smiling, Noelle lifted the blood-soaked doily and handed it to Lard. "Throw this away. I don't ever want to see it again, even if we could get all the blood out of that tatting."

Before Mandy returned, Drake opened his eyes. He saw Noelle's worried face and felt warm all over. She did care. Her hands kneaded his, and tears rimmed the corners of her eyes. His head ached as though he'd been struck by a musket ball at close range, but he would have gone through it again just to see her looking at him like that. "What happened?"

Noelle jerked her hands away from his. "Drake! Oh, Drake, I was so worried. I'm so sorry. My temper just—"

"Oh, it's all coming back to me now. You tried to kill me," he teased without smiling. He knew his barbs would draw a fresh onslaught of abuse,. but he couldn't resist.

"Oooh, you're impossible." Noelle jumped up and paced back and forth in front of the cold fireplace. "I was so worried, and all you can do is be mean."

"You threw a candlestick at me." Drake raised his hand to his forehead to emphasize his remarks. "Am I wrong? Was that a love tap?"

"Love tap?" Noelle spun on her heels and glared at him. Even half dead he was impossible to reason with. "You're the most pigheaded dolt I ever encountered. I wish I'd let Lard drag you down to the slave quarters. You don't deserve to be attended by a lady."

"Lady?" he asked and tried to raise himself up on one elbow to see her better. The pain increased in his forehead and temple, and he lowered his head slowly. "I thought I'd been attacked by a shrew."

"Shrew!" Noelle exclaimed and rushed to the side of the

bed. "Why, you no good, rotten, pigheaded scoundrel, I'll—"

Aching head or not, Drake reached out and pulled Noelle down beside him. His lips found hers open, and his tongue plundered the sweet inner recesses of her mouth. When he released her, she moved quickly to the side of the bed and stood up, pressing her curls back into a semblance of order.

Noelle knew her face was as crimson as the blood that had poured from Drake's cut. Her anger with him had diminished, but she was furious with herself. With a single kiss, he'd effectively silenced her tirade and released all the pent-up frustration that caused her anger.

"I'm back, missy." Sporting a peculiar smile, Mandy plodded into the room and placed a teakettle of steaming water on the washstand. "I see you're working hard to keep him breathin' and alive."

If possible, the color in Noelle's cheeks heightened. It was quite obvious that Mandy had witnessed the intimate moment and that she intended to make the most of it. Always one with a sense of humor, she refused to let Noelle's embarrassment die. "I never seen nobody nurse a dyin' man thataway. Must be powerful medicine, though, 'cause it done stanched the flow of blood to his head and stuck his right color in his face. Mighty peaked lookin' he was when I left, and now his cheeks the color of a ripe pomegranate."

Noelle turned her back on the smiling Drake and the prattling Mandy. Both of them were laughing at her, and she had no choice but to remain silent. Anything she said would undoubtedly bring on gales of laughter from the two.

She composed herself and turned to face them with a smile. "Well, since the two of you appear to have everything well in hand, I'll be about my business."

Without awaiting their answers, she strode into the sitting room and hunted for the candlestick that had caused the damage. She found it lying behind the sofa and stooped to pick it up. Carrying it gingerly, she placed it on the mantel and began to look for the candle. Fall was candle-making time, and they were getting low, so she couldn't afford to lose one.

Running her hand under the sofa, she found the tallow and pulled it out. It was broken, but not too badly. For now it would have to do.

As she walked past the door to her father's bedroom, she glanced at Drake lying quietly. Mandy muttered all the time she worked, so he had little to do but listen. Noting that Mandy was almost finished, Noelle hurried to the back of the house.

She needed some time alone. Drake would most certainly press the issue of going to her relatives in Charleston. Several years had passed since Noelle had visited her aunt, uncles, and cousins. She wondered absently what her cousins looked like, what they were doing, if they were married, or if they were still alive.

Charleston had been under siege since May, and life was difficult for Patriots living in the city. Sir Henry Clinton, the British commander in South Carolina, required all South Carolinians to sign a statement of loyalty to the king. For that reason alone, Noelle didn't want to go there.

She made her way to the riverbank and sat down. In many ways, she recognized that Drake was right. She needed to be with her family, with other people like her. Kathleen and her mother were going to Ninety Six because of the war, and others would soon follow. Noelle would be left virtually alone out here at the end of civilization with two servants.

Tyger Rest meant a great deal to her. Ever since she was old enough to toddle, she had followed her father around the grounds as he gave orders for the day's work. The slaves had adored her as a spunky child with ever-changing blue eyes. She sang their songs with them, played with their children, and often ate at their tables. Her plantation wasn't vast by any means, nor did it generate wealth, but it lived in her and she in it.

How could she abandon it?

Noelle drew her knees up under her chin and rested uneasily. As soon as Drake recovered, he would demand that she make a decision, and he would not accept no as an answer.

"Ahem." Drake sat down beside her. "You were so deep in thought that you didn't hear my approach."

Her gaze flew immediately to the bandaged cut on his forehead and then to his eyes. The bruise extended beyond the bandage and looked painful and ugly. Remorse flooded over Noelle, and she lowered her eyes. "You shouldn't be up."

Drake studied her profile. Her nose turned up in an impish fashion that almost revealed her mischievous nature. In peacetime, Noelle must have been the delight of every party hostess. Her natural wit and charm probably kept everybody occupied and happy, removing the business of assuring that party guests were having a good time from the shoulders of the hostess. The tragedies of war seemed to have mellowed her a little, but the exuberance and fiery nature still broke through occasionally.

"Why aren't you still in bed?" Noelle demanded, gazing at the cut to see if it had reopened.

"I'm fine." Drake watched a leaf float down the river and then inhaled deeply. The time had come to discuss her trip to Charleston. Smiling, he looked behind her and all around before broaching the subject. "Noelle, we've got to settle something about your trip to Charleston. You know as well as I that with Kathleen's family leaving the area, you're vulnerable to all sorts of scoundrels. Not just me."

Noelle laughed at his attempt at humor, but she felt like crying. For the past half hour, she'd tried every way possible to convince herself that going to Charleston was the answer to her problems, but no matter what reasoning she used, she came up with one insurmountable problem: How could she see Drake or hear of his well-being?

"Drake, I've thought about this considerably and seriously," she began, trying to discover some last plea that would touch him enough for him to allow her to remain at Tyger Rest. "What would I do? You know the situation in Charleston."

"You would be safer there than here," he said softly, recognizing the pleading in her voice. He hated having to do this, but he felt he had no choice. Suddenly an idea came to his mind. "Noelle, suppose we agree beforehand that if the situation is too explosive, I'll bring you home again?"

Her eyes brightened, and a smile touched her lips. "Would you promise? I mean, could you take that much time? I know how busy you are doing whatever you do. If I don't like Charleston, you'll bring me straight back?"

Drake shifted his position. His head ached, and he didn't feel up to bargaining with her, but he simply couldn't leave her this far away from the protection of some female relative and the army. "I promise."

Closing her eyes briefly, Noelle thanked God for giving Drake the solution to their problem. She could go to Charleston, visit her relatives, and return to her home if living there became unbearable for her. "Thank you. When do we leave?"

Drake stood and held his hands down to help her up. "We start preparing immediately. We leave tonight."

"Tonight?" she asked, falling in step beside him. His long stride made it almost impossible for her to keep up when he had a purpose.

Noticing that she lagged behind, Drake slowed his pace a little and took her arm to keep her from falling as they practically ran through the woods. "Mandy and Lard can take care of everything here. There's plenty of food, and they know what to do."

"How do you know?" Noelle stopped and looked up at him.

"I talked to them before I came after you," he answered and urged her on. "Mandy's packing food for us now while Lard finds extra blankets and such."

"How dare you order my servants about?" Noelle wrenched her arm away. "You can't take over my life like this. I've agreed to go to Charleston against my better judgment, but I refuse to allow you to—"

"Noelle," Drake interrupted, swinging around to face her. Her face was screwed into a scowl that reminded him of her temper, and he touched his forehead involuntarily. "I meant no harm. Time is short, however, and we must stop this senseless bickering and plan efficiently. If you choose to while away the afternoon on the banks of the Tyger, then I have no choice but to assume that you're leaving the details of our journey to me. Now, if you wish to discuss this further, I see a stump just ahead and I'll be delighted to turn you over my knee and debate this issue as you deserve. My time is valuable, whether you like it or not. Now, shall we attend this matter as adults, or do you wish to converse about it while turned over my knee?"

Shock registered in Noelle's eyes as she gazed at him in disbelief. Never before had he done anything to indicate he had a temper—until now. The crimson rage in his face was accentuated by the white bandage across his forehead, and for once Noelle kept her counsel and bit back the retort that sprang to her lips. "I . . . I believe we can go on. I didn't realize . . . I mean, I'm sorry for delaying you. I know you have duties to attend."

Drake felt a little foolish. He'd bellowed like a bull, and guilt consumed him. Noelle didn't deserve such treatment, and to threaten violence against her was unconscionable. He'd achieved the desired results, however, and fought the desire to kiss her, to make up for his harsh treatment. "Well, that's better. Now, I assume you have a horse to ride."

"Oh, yes. Lard found Sunshine yesterday. She was out in the graveyard, scared to death." Noelle found that discussing the details of their trip allowed both of them to forget their caustic remarks and be friends again. She liked it much better that way.

"Is Sunshine agile enough to travel at night?" Drake glanced around, surveying their surroundings automatically, a reflex from his scouting missions for the British.

"Must we ride in the dark?" Noelle had begun to look forward to the journey but didn't relish the idea of traveling at night. "Is it that dangerous here?"

Drake didn't want to lie to her, but didn't want to frighten her for no reason either. For a few seconds he considered agreeing to ride during the day even though he would feel safer at night. "Noelle, we don't know who will be about during the day. You are a Patriot. I am a British officer. If we encounter a band of Whigs, then I'm in trouble. If we happen upon a group of Tories or British, I'd have a difficult time explaining you. We might make the journey during the day without incident, but I prefer to ride at night just to be sure."

Noelle nodded. His reasoning was sound. "Sunshine will be fine at night, as will I."

"Good. Now, Mandy is making johnnycakes. She's fried some meat and boiled some rice. We can eat a good dinner tonight and leave immediately afterward, unless you know of some reason we cannot." Drake felt it imperative to allow her some part in the decision-making, even though he might have to countermand her will.

"I believe you've made the right decision. I'll be ready, and I won't be a burden on the trip." Noelle felt as though a weight had been lifted from her shoulders. She didn't want him to boss her around, but it was easier to accede to his will if he gave her a choice. "Have you enough warm clothing?"

"I have." Drake looked down at her. "Do you? The nights will be quite cold."

"Most of my cloaks and capes are still here."

"Good. I'd like you to be as comfortable as possible.

When we stop to sleep, we'll have little shelter unless we find a vacant cabin."

Noelle followed him dumbly. Within hours, she would leave her home, perhaps forever. Fighting tears, she vowed not to cry, but she had to bite her lip. Drake, she realized, would do everything within his power to make the trip as safe and as comfortable as possible. But no matter what he did, he couldn't soften the upheaval of leaving her home.

CHAPTER
11

NOELLE RODE SILENTLY BESIDE DRAKE AS THEY PASSED through the bower of crepe myrtles for the last time. Wind rustled the branches like ghostly bones all around her, reminding her that death could very likely await them on this journey.

They cantered southeast at a leisurely pace and talked little. The lump in her throat prevented much conversation, and she didn't really feel like talking.

After packing everything she couldn't bear to leave, Noelle had taken a short nap. Drake had worked steadily, loading their horses and the packhorse carefully to ensure that nothing would be lost.

Dinner had been a sad affair. Mandy and Lard were both somber, although Noelle sensed a growing affection between them. Watching as they worked side by side, she noticed little touches and smiles that they thought were known only to them. That, if nothing else, teased her face into a smile.

Knowing that they would do everything possible to keep Tyger Rest functioning, she left in peace. She sensed that when she returned to the plantation, they would have become husband and wife. She'd told them to sleep inside the main house, but both of them bluntly refused.

Noelle and Drake left the rattling crepe myrtles and their bleached branches behind and moved onto Blackstock Road. Her eyes had long ago adjusted to the darkness, and she could see fairly well.

Trees towered above the road, and the moon rode high on a silver-edged cloud, darting behind it occasionally to tease the riders. Owls hooted, and catamounts cried out as they passed, and Noelle scanned the road ahead and behind to make sure none of the night creatures came seeking her and Drake.

Drake rode beside her, his eyes alert to every movement. Every time a rabbit scurried across their path, his hand went to his rifle. "Riding at night makes the journey seem much longer. During the day, there is so much to see."

Noelle nodded and then realized that he probably hadn't seen her. He had little time to devote to watching her. "I hope there's not much to see at night," she answered as a catamount screeched not far away.

Drake laughed and turned to look at her. "Not scared, are you?"

Noelle considered his question. "No. Not really, although I don't like to hear a hungry mountain lion that close. Fortunately there's probably plenty of food for him without his looking hungrily at us."

"I hope so." Drake rode on, ever vigilant, but deep in thought. Now that he stopped to think, Noelle exhibited more courage than any woman he'd ever known. She'd fought long and hard against making this trip, but her reason had never been fear for her own safety. Most of her objections were related to the plantation and her servants in some way. Her own welfare came far down on the list of priorities. He stole a glance at her, once again noting the turned-up nose and the soft curve of her high cheekbones. He'd never met anyone quite like her.

Her feminine ways left him no doubt about her upbringing. She could hold her own in any parlor in London against any of the crones who were likely to attempt to upset her. The Charleston society women would not intimidate her, either. Drake felt sure she could walk into any home in Charleston and play the social games as well as any matron who'd lived there all her life. Being raised on the edge of civilization had affected her little, except to provide her with more raw courage than he saw in most soldiers.

A small sigh caught Noelle's attention. "Is something wrong?"

Drake cast a glance at her and then shook his head. "No, just daydreaming."

"Daydreaming?"

"Seems silly, doesn't it?" Drake agreed and quickly changed the subject. "Tell me about your parents. What was your mother like? And your father?"

Noelle tried to look at him but found that the trees blocked out too much of the moonlight. She wondered why he asked such questions after all this time. "There's not much to tell, really. My father died several weeks ago. His heart was bad."

"I'm sorry." Drake pulled back on the reins to slow Nightmare's trot. From his travels during the past few weeks, he knew that several farms lay just ahead, and he wanted to pass as quietly as possible. "Go on."

"He was a kind man. He loved Tyger Rest more than just about anything I know," Noelle admitted and shook her head. "He was gentle and peaceable. He hated this war, even though he knew it was necessary."

"Most good citizens do." Drake realized that what he said might upset Noelle, so he continued, "Both sides hate it, but both sides feel equally right."

She'd been about to lambaste him for his remark when he completed what he had to say. There was no reason to quibble about his point. Both sides did hate the war, and both sides thought they were right. In a way, she felt like King George. What had been his for a very long time was being taken away from him; Tyger Rest had been hers since birth and was now being taken away, if only briefly.

"There are some small farms close to the road ahead, so perhaps we'd better ride as silently as possible for a while," Drake whispered as they rode past a narrow dirt lane leading form Blackstock Road.

Noelle knew he could see her now, so she nodded. An excellent horsewoman, she rode without complaining. Long after midnight, she began to feel tired and sleepy. Her bones had been jarred and her small frame jostled about for longer than she'd ever ridden in her life, but she didn't complain. This trip needed to be made as hastily as possible.

The moon sank behind the horizon. The sun would be peeking out soon, and they needed to begin looking for a place to spend the day. In the complete darkness that preceded dawn, Noelle felt the cold biting through her cloak and pulled it closer about her until only her eyes were visible.

After riding for miles, Drake held out his hand and stopped her. "I believe it's time to rest."

Thank the gods, she thought, but didn't speak.

They rode a little farther while Drake searched the edge of the forest for a path that looked ill-traveled. When he stopped her again, he dismounted and helped her down. "Look here. Can you walk along this path for a short distance into the woods? We can't build a fire here, but we can at least have the shelter of the trees and shrubs."

"Lead the way," she answered and took Sunshine's reins. She followed him for a long distance into the woods. His reckoning of distance was nowhere near her own, but she didn't complain.

Finally he stopped in a small clearing. From there he searched in every direction to see if he could see any signs of life. The air smelled of autumn, but he could detect no hint of smoke in the air. He listened intently for the sound of cattle or sheep but heard nothing other than an owl screeching high above them. "I think this is safe enough."

Drake let the horses drink from a creek that edged the clearing before he unsaddled and fed them. Noelle took out bread and cheese and unwrapped it, and began to prepare their small meal.

When Drake returned, he said, "Ah, that looks great. I'm starving."

Noelle handed him a portion of the food and settled on her blanket. The ground was cold, but she didn't care. It felt good to sit on something that didn't wriggle and shift beneath her.

The eastern sky changed from black to gray while they ate, and soon clouds gathered on the horizon and glowed with the deep purples and mauves of daybreak.

In the semidarkness, Drake glanced around them. This clearing appeared to be safe for the day, but he wanted to scout the immediate area once again to be sure. "Noelle, I want to look around a bit to make sure we'll be safe here. Do you mind staying alone?"

Noelle bit her lip. She didn't want to sit here alone, but she knew Drake was right. If he didn't scout the area, they were vulnerable to an attack. "I'll be fine. You do what you have to do while I wash these plates."

Drake smiled and strode out of the clearing. Noelle picked up their plates and walked to the stream. Bending close to the ground, she scrubbed the dishes with sand and then rinsed them thoroughly.

By the time Drake returned, the sun had risen and a mist had formed all around them. "We'll be fine here. Do you think you can sleep?"

"I could sleep sitting in a tree." Noelle pulled another blanket from her pack and doubled it on the ground. Her cape would serve as a part of her coverings, but she found a quilt, too.

Drake watched as she spread the bed on the ground and smiled. "Do you plan on taking all the blankets yourself?"

Noelle looked back at the packhorse. There were no more blankets to be had. "Don't you have some?"

"No. All my belongings are packed with yours. The only thing in my saddlebags is a change of clothes." Drake looked at the narrow bed made so neatly on the ground. "Do you think we could share?"

"Of all the impertinent—"

"Only a suggestion," he interrupted, holding up his hands submissively. "I'll take one blanket and roll up in it. You can have everything else."

Noelle handed him the extra blanket she'd put between her and the ground. Although she knew the chill would seep through, she could hardly ask him to sleep without the benefit of at least one blanket. "Let me give you another. I have my cloaks to cover me."

Drake shook his head as she started to remove the second blanket. "Don't. I'm used to sleeping with little over me."

"You're very kind." Noelle settled herself between the blanket, her cloaks, and the quilt. Sleep came to her with little effort.

Watching her, Drake smiled. In sleep, her face appeared as innocent as an angel's. In reality, he'd seen the tirade that had resulted in the cut on his head. But despite her temper, she was innocent. Without guile she'd lain down and nodded off to sleep, trusting him to watch over her as he'd promised.

Drake felt that Noelle gave her trust far too easily. He drew the quilt she'd knocked off back across her sleeping form. One of these days he feared she would get hurt.

Noelle shifted in her sleep and caught his attention once again. A streak of sunlight surrounded her face like a halo, emphasizing her innocence. Drake wondered how long it would take this war to rob her of her naïveté, and hoped that would never happen.

He wanted to cradle her in his arms, to coo sweet words into her ear, and protect her from the world, but he knew that wasn't possible. Being here for her meant a lot to him, and he intended to be around as much as possible.

Drake awoke with a start. A noise had disturbed his sleep, and he lay motionless until he could determine its origin. Then he saw that Noelle was gone.

He sprang to his feet. No matter who or what had sneaked into their camp, he intended to save Noelle.

Spinning around, he noticed her moving noiselessly toward him. "Where have you been?" he asked gruffly.

"Down to the creek for some water." Noelle glowered at him, wondering why he'd awakened in such a sour mood. Color rose in her cheeks to give the lie to her explanation, but she couldn't tell him what she'd been doing. Some things a lady never discussed with a man, and this was one of them. "Did you sleep on a rock?"

"Rock? Why would you ask that?" Drake glanced around once more to assure himself that nobody else had stumbled into their camp.

"You're in such a foul mood, I thought perhaps you'd slept badly." Noelle hurried across the clearing to get their bowls. She knew that he'd be ready to leave immediately after their meal. "I'm afraid all we have is cold soup and johnnycakes, unless you feel it's safe to light a fire."

"Uh, no fire. We must eat quickly and pack up." Drake scanned the area and noted that the sun was setting. He wanted to be back on the main road as soon as possible. "Sorry."

"Don't worry about it. Cold food will be fine," Noelle lied as she ladled soup into his bowl. The soup would be greasy, but filling. She couldn't complain about something as silly as that when a war raged all about them. "Here."

Drake took the bowl and sipped his soup. He wished he hadn't so hastily denied her the comfort of a fire. There was no reason to suspect that anyone would see the smoke, and eating cold food would save time, but hot soup tasted much better than cold.

They ate quickly and quietly, but whether that was due to the cold soup, the cool weather, or Drake's foul mood, Noelle couldn't tell. When she finished, she scrubbed the plates again in the creek and packed them. By the time she completed her housekeeping tasks, Drake had packed away their blankets and saddled the horses.

"Are you ready to leave?" he asked and led Sunshine toward Noelle.

"Yes, thank you. I'm quite rested." Noelle flashed a smile she suspected he couldn't see because of the darkness, but it made her feel better to think there was something to smile about.

They walked the horses out of the woods, stopped near the road, and listened. Drake peered up and down the road and waited. He heard nothing that alarmed him, so he motioned for Noelle to follow.

When they reached the main road, Drake lifted her into the saddle, and they were on their way. Eventually, they would take a little traveled route that paralleled the Indian Road, but for now it was safe for them to ride along the easiest path.

The sun set, and a mist rose from the damp foliage and the ground. Crickets sang as Noelle and Drake intruded into the peace and quiet of the forest. Shadowy clouds drifted across the moon, making their path dark and difficult.

After about three hours, Drake stopped. "Into the woods," he whispered urgently. He dismounted and helped Noelle down.

Noelle grabbed Sunshine's reins and led her through the dense undergrowth for about two hundred yards before Drake motioned for her to lead the horse behind a thicket of shrubs.

"What is it?" she asked, her voice barely audible.

"Riders. Several." Drake's voice was low and clipped as they crouched behind the bushes.

An eternity seemed to pass before Noelle heard horses on the road. Fear snatched at her heart, clutching it firmly and causing sharp pains in her chest. After a few seconds she realized she'd stopped breathing. Inhaling deeply, she prayed silently that whoever was on the road would pass them by without noticing the tracks.

Overhead the moon burned as brightly as the noonday sun, or it seemed so to Noelle. Looking up, she saw a clear patch of sky cluttered with a million stars. Why didn't it cloud up and rain? She'd rather ride in rain if they could ride safely.

Thinking about the dangers they faced, she shivered. Drake looked down at her and edged closer.

"Are you cold?" he asked and draped his arm around her shoulders.

"Just a bit," she lied, unwilling to admit her fear. His embrace tightened, and she leaned against him for the warmth and companionship. Since they'd left home, he'd been no closer to her than the distance it took to reach his bowl at dinner.

Drake wondered why the riders were taking so long to reach them. If their tracks had been spotted, he wanted to know in time to escape if possible. "Stay here, Noelle. I'm going to have a look. Hold the horses."

"All right," she whispered and took the reins of Nightmare and the packhorse. "Please be careful."

"Don't worry." He moved toward the road and paused. "Try to keep the horses quiet if you can."

He took two steps and disappeared into the darkness. Noelle strained to see what was going on, but observed nothing other than the bushes in front of her swaying in the wind.

Nightmare stamped his foot and pawed the ground. She prayed that he wouldn't neigh or whinny. In the silence of the forest, a sound like that carried for miles.

Hours seemed to pass while Noelle waited for Drake to return. What if something had happened to him? she wondered. What if he'd been spotted and killed? Noelle tried to calm herself by remembering how capably Drake handled people, how easily he had persuaded Soaring Eagle to release her, but her efforts did little good. The more time passed, the more worried she became.

Noelle finally decided to go after him. What if he was lying somewhere injured? she reasoned and resolved to move.

A twig snapped to her left, and she glanced past Nightmare to see who or what approached them. The tall horse seemed restless, pawing and whickering. "Shhh!" Noelle whispered. "It's all right, boy," she cooed, hoping to soothe the animal enough to prevent other noises.

Another twig popped, and a pair of pheasants fluttered free of some shrubs close to her. They squawked and flew high and out of sight. Noelle clutched the reins to her breast and stared at the origin of the sound, but heard nothing. A few seconds later, she heard a noise to her right. She turned to stare in that direction, realizing now that it couldn't be Drake coming from two directions at once. Terror stalked her like never before.

CHAPTER
12

"NOELLE," CAME A VOICE NEARBY. "IT'S ME. DRAKE."

Noelle relaxed and turned slightly. She was so happy to hear his voice after listening to night sounds and imagining any number of horrors. "Drake?"

"Yes, it's me."

"I'm thrilled to hear that." Noelle felt her heart pounding and attributed it to her scare. "I let my imagination get the better of me—I was worried about you!"

"Quiet. Those men are still out there," he cautioned.

Drake smiled. Noelle had been frightened, but she hadn't panicked. He'd never met a woman so unafraid and willing to face danger.

Noelle peered through the darkness toward the road. "What can we do?"

Drake considered her question for a few seconds. "We can either remain here until they leave or try to sneak away."

"How can we sneak away?" Noelle felt much warmer with Drake's arms around her, and she hoped he'd stay put for a while. "Wouldn't it be safer to stay?"

"I don't think so. That's a band of renegade Loyalists. Bloody Bill Cunningham's gang. They won't care which side we're on," he explained. "I'd heard there were several such groups around, but I never dreamed they were this far north and west. I believe we'll be better off if we sneak away."

"Which direction are they going?" Noelle already felt the

warmth drain from her. "How do we know they won't hear us and follow?"

"They're headed west. The only way to escape without alarming them is to move the horses one at a time through the woods." Drake hated to ask her to sit here on the cold ground for any longer than he had to, but he couldn't think of another option. "Look, take these blankets and wrap up. I'll lead Nightmare first. He'll recognize my scent and won't make any noise when we approach later."

"Don't worry about me." Noelle folded a blanket in fourths to sit on and wrapped herself in the other blanket. "I'll be fine."

Drake looked at her closely. "I didn't plan on putting you through all this when we set out, but we have to take precautions. I won't leave you alone a minute longer than I have to."

"I said I'll be fine!" Noelle retorted, feeling her hackles rise. Why did he cause her feelings to change every few minutes? First she desperately needed him, and now she wanted to prove she was brave.

"Hold it. That was a compliment," Drake teased, trying to cool her temper before it warmed up.

"I'm sorry for snapping at you." Drake had every right to give her instructions and leave her to check their surroundings!

"I'll be back when I've taken Nightmare a safe distance. Try to sleep if you can," he told her.

Noelle watched as the big horse and its owner disappeared into the darkness. She knew that this little adventure would lengthen the time of their trip considerably. Moving around a little, she opened the blanket to lie down and covered up with her cloak and the other blanket. She dared not go to sleep, but she could rest better this way.

Before long, Drake stepped into her little camp. "Noelle," he whispered.

She sat up and looked at him. The moon rode high and cast a soft glow on them. "I'm glad you're safe," she told him in a deceptively calm voice. She wouldn't be able to stand the inactivity much longer.

"I'm glad to hear that you worry about me." Drake sat down. "I went back to the road to see if the brigands were still there. It looks as if they've decided to camp in the woods just across the way."

"What will we do next?" Noelle bit her lip. If these men were as desperate and depraved as Drake intimated, she didn't want to meet them.

"We're going to move on as quickly as possible, as planned. I think if you lead Sunshine, I can lead the packhorse without any problem." Drake wrapped his arms around her and nestled his face in her hair. She was so warm, he almost decided to wait here, but he knew to do so would be folly. Bloody Bill had a sixth sense and would find them for sure.

"Consider the job done." Noelle snuggled against him and sighed. Despite the tension, this trip had proved to be exciting so far.

Drake stood. "I'll go first. Leave a little distance between you and the packhorse in case I have to stop quickly. I don't want you running into the back of that animal. He may kick."

"I'll be careful and watch closely." Noelle accepted his hand and allowed him to pull her up.

Before moving on, he kissed her forehead and hugged her briefly. "Let's go."

Noelle waited as he led the packhorse away. When the horse was about ten feet ahead of her, she followed. Realizing that she wouldn't be able to see that far, she closed the gap a little and felt better.

The horses plodded quietly on. Noelle cooed to Sunshine and rubbed her velvety nose occasionally to reassure her, but never stopped. The trail was too dark to fall behind.

Drake moved silently forward. The packhorse lacked Nightmare's grace but managed to follow fairly well. Every now and then, Drake glanced back to see if he could spot

Noelle. Her petite figure bobbed up and down with the uneven terrain, but she kept up.

Drake's head ached slightly, and he reached up to feel the bandage. He would remove it tomorrow. Grinning, he recalled her temper. What a woman. What a feisty, courageous woman, Drake thought.

Slowing down, he eased forward. The clump of bushes just ahead looked familiar, and he knew they'd reached the spot where he'd left Nightmare. Looking back, he saw Noelle stop. Good, she was watching closely.

He trod easily ahead, careful to avoid startling Nightmare. When he could see the animal, he called to him softly and led the packhorse closer.

Turning, he watched Noelle move forward with Sunshine. He tethered the packhorse to a bush and motioned for Noelle to join him. He removed a blanket and laid it on the ground with just enough room for them to sit close together.

"Sit down here." He pointed to the blanket. "I want to rest a minute before I go back."

"Go back? What do you mean?" Astonishment creased Noelle's forehead as she obeyed. "For what?"

Drake dropped to the ground beside her. "I want to make sure those men didn't hear us. If they're still sleeping, we can ride on."

"I see," Noelle answered in a quiet whisper. "I'll just wait here, I suppose."

"Can you sleep? I know this is a tiring journey. Sitting in a saddle all night and then sleeping on the cold ground during the day isn't much fun." Drake tucked her in the crook of his arm and held her close. "I don't want you to be frightened, though."

How could she keep from being frightened? Noelle never was one to admit fear, so she smiled. "Don't worry about me. I'm fine." She seemed to have been telling him this fact all night!

Drake chuckled softly and nuzzled her hair, dropping a light kiss on her forehead. "I know you are."

When he rose and left, the frigid air swept across Noelle like a tide and sent a shiver up her spine. She snuggled under the blanket and lay down. Until Drake returned, she couldn't sleep, but sitting up was much colder than lying down.

At first she thought she imagined that the wind grew colder, but after a while, she realized that it actually had. She pulled the blanket close around her neck and covered her face. The time passed slowly, but she didn't move.

She heard Drake's footsteps and sighed with relief. As he got closer, she sat up and waited.

Without speaking he dropped down beside her and did his best to wrap the blanket around both of them. Lying on the ground while he watched Cunningham's camp, he'd gotten a chill that he couldn't shake off. "Aren't you cold? You must be freezing."

Noelle felt his shiver and rose. "Sit still. I'll get the quilt."

She pulled the quilt out of the saddlebag and returned to Drake. Draping the thick covering about his shoulders, she marveled at how wide they were. Noelle sat beside him and wriggled into his arms for warmth.

"That's much better," Drake whispered and drew her into his arms.

Together they sat in silence long enough for him to stop shivering. When Noelle could contain her curiosity no longer, she looked up at him. "What did you discover?"

Drake blew on his fingers and curled his arms around her again. "I believe they're all drunk and sleeping. Their guard fell asleep and snored while I watched."

"Good. Does that mean we can move on?" Noelle wanted to reach Charleston as soon as possible.

"I think so. The wind's rising, and clouds are rolling in. Rain will be hard to travel in, as cold as it is." Drake hugged her close. "If it's going to rain, I hope we can find some sort of shelter."

Noelle merely nodded.

"Well, let's go." Drake sniffed the sweet scent of her once more before they stood. "You always smell like lilacs."

Noelle's clothes had been washed and then rinsed in lilac water. "Thank you."

Drake lifted her into the saddle and hurried to mount Nightmare. Silently they moved on.

Assuming he would head for the road, Noelle was surprised when he kept to the woods for a great distance farther. Just before dawn, rain began to fall. She said nothing but pulled the hood of her cape over her head. It would offer little protection when it got soaked, but for now it kept her dry.

When Drake stopped, she was glad. She didn't know where they would make camp, but she wanted to find a dry spot as soon as possible. While she watched him, rain drizzled down her face and into her eyes. Noelle wiped her eyes and lowered her head. Traveling in cold rain was a miserable way to go.

"Wait here." Drake rode ahead about one hundred yards and paused. After a short wait, he motioned for her to catch up.

Sighing with regret that they weren't stopping for the day, Noelle followed wordlessly. They came to a narrow trail that had been a road at one time. Drake looked in both directions and then at her.

She tried to smile but felt she did a poor job of it. Drake grimaced and rode back beside her. "Noelle, go back into the woods about a hundred yards and wait. I think the brush is heavy enough to hide you and the two horses. I'm going to follow this road for a short distance and see if I can find a sheltered place to stop."

Noelle nodded and led the packhorse into the woods. She reached a place where she could no longer see Drake and dismounted under a tall tulip tree. The wide leaves gave her some protection from the elements. She tethered both horses and settled beneath the tree to wait.

Drake returned fairly quickly. He seemed in a hurry as he rode toward her. Fearing that they'd been seen, Noelle untied both horses and mounted Sunshine, ready to hightail it if need be.

Drake smiled and waved, motioning for her to join him. Noelle realized he wasn't running from an enemy and flicked her reins. Sunshine broke into a trot, and the packhorse followed suit.

"I've found a vacant cabin," Drake announced as she reached him.

"Is it all right to stay there? I mean, will we be safe?" Noelle shivered as she thought of Bloody Bill Cunningham.

"I think so. It's pretty far off the main road. The lane leading to it is overgrown in places, so nobody else will find it." Drake turned Nightmare and led the way. "Don't get too excited. It's not much."

"Anything is better than sitting under a tree in a rainstorm." Noelle refused to let him dampen her high spirits. A real cabin to sleep in seemed like a dream after sleeping on the hard ground. "Does it have a bed?"

Drake glanced back and laughed. "Yes, it does, but it's pretty bad."

Noelle didn't care. She rode with her chin higher and her back straighter as they cantered into the yard of the shanty Drake had graciously labeled a cabin. For a moment she didn't move. Even though he'd tried to prepare her for the run-down condition of the cabin, he'd failed. On one side the roof gaped open, and rain blew in. Biting her lip to keep from crying, she closed her eyes and said a prayer of thanks that it still had part of a roof.

Smiling brightly, Noelle slid off her horse into Drake's arms. "This will be fine."

Laughing, Drake took her reins and led the horses to the sheltered side of the house. The barn had long since collapsed and would be of no use. When he returned, he found Noelle standing in the middle of the one-room cabin.

"Pretty bad, eh?" Drake said almost apologetically. "We'll make do."

Noelle watched Drake drop a saddle on the floor and leave again. She turned slowly and took in the entire room. Aside from the hole in the roof, the cabin wasn't in too bad a condition. Shivering, she strode to the fireplace. It was dry and would serve them well. On a shelf beside the fireplace, she found a stack of wooden plates and two forks. Bedclothes were still on the bed, and she wondered who had left in such a hurry without packing anything.

Except for the dust and debris that had blown through the hole in the roof and through the glassless windows, the room was fairly clean. She looked more closely and found a little sewing kit, some utensils, two dresses, and several blankets.

Drake entered with another saddle and dropped it by the first. Noelle was standing with her back to him and didn't turn around. He thought she must be upset and hurried over to console her. Maybe it had been a mistake to mention the cabin before she saw it for herself. He pulled her into the circle of his arms. "I'll get a fire going, and we'll sleep warmly today."

Her smile was halfhearted, and she shivered again. "Don't worry about me. Can I help bring in something before it gets doused?"

"No. I've got to make one more trip." Drake hugged her close and then left again. The horses were protected by the house and had plenty of grass to eat, so he secured them as well as possible and took the last saddle in.

When he entered the cabin again, he found the shutters closed and Noelle sweeping the floor with a broom of rushes. She moved a rocking chair and swept where it had been and then replaced it. Moving systematically about the room, she finished at the cabin door and picked up the larger pieces of twigs and leaves that had blown in. "These are dry. Maybe we can use them for kindling. Whoever lived here left in a hurry and didn't bother to pack."

Drake searched his saddlebag until he found a flint and steel to start a fire. Within a few minutes he had succeeded in lighting the leaves and twigs. "I'll find something else to burn. I don't think that woodpile will last long."

Noelle glanced at the logs piled by the fireplace and agreed. If they didn't find more dry wood, the fire would be out before she could cook a meal and get to sleep. She watched Drake throw a large log on the crackling fire but decided fruit and cheese would suffice.

Drake glanced at the room and noticed that it looked much better now that she'd swept.

She turned to her stores and found apples and cheese. Silently thanking Mandy, she sliced two pieces of bread and buttered them. Supper would be a delight, meager as it was.

She smiled. Supper for breakfast. The sun rose behind dark clouds and did little to dispel the gray of dawn. But since they were going to eat and then sleep, she called the meal supper. By the time Drake returned, she was scurrying about and dusting the few odds and ends of furniture left for them.

"I wonder who lived here, and why did they leave?" she asked, glancing at Drake as he added logs to the woodpile. "Where did you find that?"

"It used to be the barn," Drake answered and looked around at the room that grew neater each time he entered. "Looks great. I don't know who lived here, but I know why they left."

"Why?"

"The house was falling in. Probably a widow or something. Must have moved back to civilization." Drake didn't look at Noelle. He'd found a body in the collapsed barn. From the looks of it, the woman was recently dead. Maybe while he was here he could find the time to bury her properly. For the moment he didn't want Noelle to know about the body.

"Do you drink tea?" Drake asked and held up a tin of tea. Turning quickly, Noelle realized he was teasing her, but hot tea sounded much better than water. "As of this moment, I am again a tea drinker."

"I guard this with my life," he remarked and handed the tin to her. "I'm not quite accustomed to the taste of coffee."

"Well, I confess to liking tea better, but I can tolerate coffee." Noelle looked around. "Did you see a well outside?"

"I did. Do you see a bucket?" Drake scanned the room. "Aha! There it is."

Noelle smiled as he took the bucket and hurried outside. He was much more eager than she to brave the elements. By the time he returned, she'd found a teakettle. She rinsed it out, filled it, and hung it over the fire.

"This is certainly cozy. Maybe I can patch the roof before we eat." Drake headed toward the door.

"Oh, Drake, don't be long. I'm starving." Noelle frowned, hoping he wouldn't linger. He'd probably move from one task to another without considering the time.

"I'll be back before the water boils." Drake strode out the door and closed it behind him.

He hurried to the pile of wood that had once been a barn and picked up one of the doors. It would serve as a patch for the roof.

When he reached the cabin, he looked first at the roof above his head and then at the heavy door. Without Noelle's help, he'd never be able to pull it onto the roof. He went to the cabin door and called, "Noelle, can you help me for a minute?"

"If it doesn't take too long."

"We won't be a minute." Drake led her to the corner of the house and explained the problem. "If you can help, I can pull the door over that hole."

Noelle waited while he climbed onto the roof. "Be careful. The whole thing may collapse."

"Don't worry." Drake slid to the edge and reached down to the door. "Now, when I lift, you help. But be careful of splinters."

Noelle nodded and lifted. As Drake drew the door up, she felt a splinter bite into her palm. "Ow," she cried, but continued to hold the door to keep it from falling.

Drake pulled it over the opening and glanced down. "What's wrong?"

"Splinter." Noelle watched him jump down beside her and look at her palm. She could see the dark sliver beneath the skin.

"Let me see." Drake took her hand and gazed at it. A red spot highlighted the black fragment of wood, and he groaned. "We don't have a needle to remove it."

Noelle remembered the sewing kit. "Yes, we do. The lady of the house had a sewing kit. I'm sure there's a needle in there, but let's eat first."

Drake agreed, and they went into the cabin together. "Sure looks wonderful. I'm hungry."

"Me, too." Noelle handed his fruit and cheese and a slice of buttered bread to him.

Drake started to eat and then said, "This is delicious. Mandy is an angel."

"You're right about that." Noelle sat down and took a sip of tea. "Maybe we should have brought her with us."

"Did you want to leave the plantation unattended?" Drake asked, also taking a drink of tea. "You make good tea for a Patriot."

"Don't start that. Let's just eat our meal in peace." Noelle glared at him for a moment before she realized he was teasing her again. "And I didn't want to leave the plantation unoccupied, but I think Mandy would have been safer with us."

"True, but she's an old woman who might not have withstood the journey." Drake finished his supper and pushed back from the table. "When you've eaten, I'll remove that splinter."

Noelle nodded and cleaned off the table. She washed the dishes in the bucket and stood them on the mantel to dry. "I can't imagine why anyone would leave all these things. It looks as if the owner was suddenly taken ill and died."

Her gaze flew to Drake. "You don't think . . . I mean, did Cunningham and his band . . . Oh, Drake, we've got to look around. Maybe some poor wretch is lying—"

"Noelle, stop it," Drake interrupted and gripped her shoulders. Her eyes were wild with fear and apprehension, but he couldn't bear to lie to her again. "I found a body earlier."

"The owner is dead!" she exclaimed and felt her knees weaken. She'd used the woman's plates and table, intended to use her bed. "Oh, Drake. This is awful. Is there anything we can do?"

Drake pulled her into the circle of his arms and held her as close as he dared. Absently rubbing her back, he pressed his face against her hair. "She's dead, Noelle. There's nothing we can do except bury her when it stops raining."

"Do you think that . . . that Cunningham killed her?" Noelle finally asked, burying her face in Drake's chest. "I hate this war."

"I hate it, too. I have no way of knowing whether Cunningham is responsible." Drake continued to rub her back and to smooth her hair. "There's nothing we can do now. She's beyond pain."

Noelle nodded gently and looked up through glittering eyes. "I'll be all right."

"Let me look at that splinter." Drake moved into the light of the fire.

Returning to the shelf where the sewing kit lay, Noelle sighed. Her palm didn't hurt yet, but it would soon. Drake was right to want to pull the sliver out now. "Here you go."

Noelle handed a needle to him. Drake held her hand and looked at the splinter. "It's not too deep."

Waiting for the prick to follow, Noelle watched uneasily. Mandy could have removed the sliver in seconds. Drake might be clumsy and the removal painful.

Drake held her hand closer to the light. He didn't want to

hurt her. With a gentleness he didn't realize he possessed, he probed the spot and withdrew the offending fragment. "There."

Grimacing, Noelle took the needle from him and put it away. "Thank you."

"I want to check on the horses. I need to make sure they have water and are secured." Drake patted her shoulders and smiled. "I'll be back in a minute. We don't want to go outside when the rain stops and find that our horses have disappeared."

"No, we don't. You go on." Noelle turned and continued straightening up the room.

Since she had a bed, she decided to slip on the only nightgown she'd brought with her. She dug through her saddlebag and pulled the soft batiste garment out. Looking around, she decided to peek out at Drake to make sure he wasn't headed back inside. Noelle opened the door a bit and peered outside. He was nowhere to be seen at first, but then she saw him out by the well drawing water for the horses.

Stripping quickly, she dropped her clothes at her feet and pulled on the nightgown. She spun around, searching for a place to hang her dress and petticoats to dry. She hoped all the moisture would be gone by the time she and Drake left.

When Drake entered the cabin, Noelle was sitting in the rocking chair before the fire. A candle was lit on the table where they'd eaten, and Noelle had laid their extra clothes over the back of the two other chairs to dry. A strange peace settled over him as he watched her brush her hair. Because of the cascade of her golden hair, he could hardly see her face, but the light of the fire silhouetted her body in great detail through the thin fabric.

He felt a stirring in his loins as he watched her perform the simple task. They belonged together, and he knew it. Fate had brought them together and then had bound them together on this journey. She had removed every obstacle from their relationship, except the war. Drake trusted that the war would not stand between them permanently. He refused to allow that to happen.

Noelle knew he was watching, but she didn't understand why he had stepped inside the door and continued to stand there. She glanced at him with a questioning look on her face. "Is something wrong?"

"Wrong?" Drake rasped, hating himself for staring at her when he should look the other way. In her innocence, she didn't know how she affected him, and more than likely didn't realize that he could see her breasts almost as clearly as if she'd removed the nightgown. "Nothing is wrong. Don't you think you'd better go to sleep?"

Sighing, Noelle rose. He was right, of course. She'd been sitting there in front of the fire, daydreaming about Drake, about how things would be if the war didn't exist.

Drake knew that if she stood there much longer, he would whisk her off to bed and make love to her. "Good night. Or good day, I suppose."

Noelle let out a groan. Drake fought the impulse to rush across the room and take her in his arms, but he couldn't stand much more of this exquisite torture. He turned on his heel and strode back out the door.

Staring blankly at the spot where he'd stood, Noelle wondered if she'd offended him. She shrugged and walked over to the bed. After throwing back the covers, she held the candle over the bedclothes to make sure there were no strange creatures lurking between the blankets. Satisfied that she would have the bed to herself, she sat down on the straw-stuffed mattress and slipped into the bed. Then she realized that the ropes beneath the mattress had loosened due to the rain. She got up to look for the key and found it hanging close to the bed. She inserted it into each of the slots on the bed frame and turned until the ropes tightened and the mattress rose enough to make sleeping comfortable. With a sigh, she climbed back into the bed, wishing that she'd brought a bed warmer with her.

When Drake returned some time later, she pretended to

be asleep. He stood above her for a few minutes and then walked over to the rocker, where he would spend the night. He lifted her hairbrush from the table and held it for a moment before putting it down. With a glance over his shoulder, he took his place in the chair.

Noelle watched him surreptitiously for a while and then closed her eyes completely. Before long they would be on the trail again, and she would be scolding herself for not sleeping in a bed when she had the chance. Did he mind giving up the bed?

Drake gazed into the fire, and Noelle's face danced before his eyes. A knot in the firewood popped, and he jumped, at first not knowing where he was. He glanced at Noelle to make sure the noise hadn't awakened her and then settled comfortably in the chair. Outside, the rain continued, at times a deluge and at others a mere sprinkle.

He heard a dripping noise and looked to the corner where he'd crudely patched the roof with the barn door. Without nails to hold the door down securely, the rain blew under the panel and caused a steady dripping sound. He got up and placed the empty bucket under the leak. This was a dirt floor, and if it rained hard enough, they would be walking in mud.

Drake went over to Noelle. She seemed to be sleeping soundly. He pulled the quilt over her and drew a lock of hair out of her face.

Tiptoeing back to his rocker, he resumed his position and began daydreaming again. With Noelle so close, smelling so good, he knew he would have a tough time going to sleep.

He realized he wanted Noelle more than he'd ever wanted another woman, and more astonishing to him was the fact that he hadn't pressed his advantage.

The room cooled off quickly under the influence of the raging storm. The steady plunk of rain dripping into the wooden bucket annoyed him, and the cracking knots of firewood were enough to send him into a rage. Drake jumped up and began to pace. Noelle's innocent presence caused all of his frustration.

If he hadn't loved her, he'd have thrown the bedclothes off her and kissed her into submission. He stood and watched her sleep. Was he strong enough to leave her alone?

CHAPTER
13

NOELLE AWOKE AND GAVE DRAKE A SIDELONG GLANCE AS HE
stood silhouetted before the fireplace, looking directly at
her. He hadn't moved for several minutes, but in the dim
light she could see his jaw working, as if he was angry or
talking silently to himself.

She peered at him a little more closely, trying to decide
what he was doing. He seemed to be at odds with himself
about something. She studied him. His dark hair framed a
face bronzed by the sun, and deep-set brown eyes danced
with fire when he was angry. Now they seemed to have
mellowed to a warmer color like brandy. His high cheekbones were accentuated by the planes of his face and formed
a square with his forehead and chin. Drake Hastings had a
strong face with readable expressions she would be slow to
disobey.

Wondering what she should do, Noelle realized that
Drake probably hadn't slept at all. Every time she'd opened
her eyes, he was either pacing or rocking. She saw the light
filtering in through the chinks in the walls and knew that the
sun was still up, even though it was behind the clouds that
deluged them with rain. She smiled at the steady plop of
water in the bucket he'd placed under the leak. Somehow
the whole scene was comforting, as if they belonged here in
this rough-hewn cabin.

Noelle didn't understand her feelings. Hate should be the
only emotion she felt for the tall soldier, but it was the only
one she didn't feel. She'd never been in love, but Kathleen

211

said Noelle loved Drake. Considering it for a moment, she wondered if it could be true. How could she know? When would she know?

Life confused her. Even though she was an adult, Noelle wasn't prepared to deal with the strong emotions of adulthood. She loved her father; she loved Mandy; she loved Irene. Her feelings for Drake were different. Each touch sent little flickers of fire through her, like millions of tiny suns dawning in her body.

When Drake held her, a warmth crept into even the coldest places. Now, as she lay in this large bed alone, a chill slithered through her like ice on the river in winter. Noelle remembered the fierce heat of his kisses and wanted him to kiss her again and again. Beyond kisses there awaited another event, one that remained mysterious to her, mysterious and intriguing.

Drake stared at her, entranced by the fan of golden curls that surrounded her face like a halo. He longed to wrap those locks around his hands and draw her to him, imprisoning her within the confines of his embrace. Noelle was as forbidden to him as the apple to Eve, not because of a stranger's rule, but because of his own love for her.

With each passing day, he respected her more. He admired her courage and honor, her generosity and honesty. To obtain this prize, he had to earn it. To take something not freely given would annihilate any chance of ever capturing it. He wouldn't risk eternity with Noelle for a fleeting moment's pleasure, no matter how great he imagined that might be.

Sighing, he started to turn away, but saw Noelle move. Her eyes were open, dusky blue in the dim light of the cabin. "Did I awaken you? I apologize."

A shiver racked Noelle's slender frame. Her decision had been made. Drake Hastings was a soldier. Any moment of his career could be his last. She knew without doubt that she wanted Drake to introduce her to that special relationship between a man and a woman.

She slid her feet to the floor and stood beside the bed. Without speaking, she strode across the room to him. She slipped her arms around his waist and closed the distance between his body and hers. For a moment she thought he would rebuff her, but he dipped his head toward hers and captured her lips in the agonizing ecstasy of mutual hunger and desire.

When he drew away, Drake fought to control himself. "Noelle, please, you don't realize what you're doing."

Drake was right; she didn't know what she was doing—exactly. But she did know that in his arms nothing could harm her, nothing worldly could touch her, that everything wonderful filled her body with aching for more than he had already given. Her voice deserted her. She couldn't answer him with words.

Noelle stood on tiptoe and touched his lips with hers. He rewarded her with a second breathtaking kiss that lasted much longer and turned her legs to jelly.

Once again Drake pushed her away. "Go back to bed, Noelle darling. If this continues, I . . . you mustn't do this. Men and women are different. You don't understand what you're doing."

In that moment she realized she would have to tell him her actions were planned, that what he withheld from her was what she wanted. Gulping back her fear, Noelle forged ahead. "Drake, I—"

"Noelle, look, this is dangerous. I'm a man and—"

"Sit down," she commanded and watched as he dropped back into the rocker. Without hesitation she settled into his lap and looped her arms around his neck. Stretching as she pulled his head down, she kissed him again and almost squealed with glee when he groaned and plunged his tongue deep in her mouth.

After a long, plundering kiss, Drake reached up and captured her hands, pulling them from his neck. He gazed deeply into her eyes and shook his head slightly. "Noelle, why are you doing this?"

How could she tell him what she wanted? Noelle didn't even know the words to say. "Love me, Drake."

Drake released her arms and stood. He carried her to the bed. She needed say no more. What he'd assumed was innocence had been merely a veil of illusion, a flirtation. That explained her relationship with his uncle.

Needing no further prodding, Drake laid her on the bed and drew the covers over her. He removed his clothing as quickly as possible. With nothing left to cover his body, he gazed down at her for a moment, realizing that the dream that had tormented him for the past few weeks was about to come true.

Noelle's eyes widened as he stripped. Though the light was too dim on this side of the room to see clearly, she viewed the naked figure of a man for the first time. His proud, broad chest narrowed to a slim waistline, and her eyes were then drawn down to the dark area at the joining of his long, muscular legs.

Before she could catch her breath, Drake slid between the covers with her and caught her in his arms. The length of hard muscle pressed against her, and she felt the warmth of his skin through her gown. His kisses catapulted her into a netherworld that seemed fuzzy around the edges.

As his mouth deposited tiny, feathery kisses over her face and neck, Noelle trembled and strained to be closer to him. The realization that in a few moments she would truly become a woman lifted her higher than a circling hawk as Drake's lips danced over her skin.

"Drake," she whispered, and savored the taste of his lips as they found hers again. The sound of his name enhanced her feeling of flying, and she closed her eyes to soar with the hawk as his wings lifted her higher.

Her nipples tightened into little buds as Drake's hand cupped her breast. Noelle moaned and was surprised to hear her involuntary response. Drake's kiss deepened, and she felt that she would be swept away by the ferocious air currents that held her aloft as her body began to react instinctively.

Drake held her in a captive embrace that melded their bodies together. His hunger for her seemed insatiable, but he didn't want to hurry. He knew that the beauty of the moment was best savored as it approached, rather than in retrospect.

Her gown became a scourge as he tried to slip it off her writhing body, and he fought the desire to rip it to shreds and seek the luscious gifts beneath. With a concerted effort Drake drew the gown over her head and threw it aside.

Body against body, flesh against flesh, Drake molded her to him, feeling a surge of desire flood over him anew with the direct contact. Tracing a slender trail of kisses down her neck, he finally captured a taut nipple in his mouth.

Noelle gasped. The intimacy of his action took her breath away, and she quivered in his arms. Her body and mind soared with passion, and Noelle never wanted the experience to end. As Drake caressed her, she knew not what to do except enjoy his ministrations. Perhaps one day she would learn how to arouse in him the same exquisite feelings he drew from her, but for now she cherished the pleasure he gave her.

Drake found Noelle a responsive lover. With every touch, every kiss, she writhed and moaned, urging him on without ever speaking a word. Her sweet taste inspired him, cajoled him to make every moment count, and he did. Loving her slowly, he lifted himself over her and slid between her legs.

From her frenzied animation, he realized that she wanted him as badly as he wanted her. The time for their joining was upon them. Carefully, Drake slid into her, passing the negligible opposition quickly.

Noelle gasped as a sharp pain skittered through her and dissolved into an ache that soon faded. She sensed his pause and opened her eyes. Had she done something wrong?

Drake gazed down into her eyes. At once he knew he'd been mistaken. Why had she seduced him? he wondered. "Seduce" was the only accurate word to describe her actions. He now realized she had no knowledge of men. Had she been innocent in her seduction, or had it been intentional?

The deed was done, and Drake couldn't take back his part in the violation of her innocence. Her gasp indicated pain instead of pleasure, and Drake slowed to accommodate her acceptance of him inside her. When he felt her relax again, he proceeded to love her as gently as he could.

Noelle flew again with the hawk. The tumbling from her cloud had been brief, and now she rode high with the beautiful bird as it caught the wind in its feathers and climbed. Sensations of currents flew through her body as the bird within her fluttered and pulsed, spurring her emotions to new heights. Noelle lost the sense of her body and became a writhing unit of pleasure that enveloped the entire sky.

She heard herself moan against his lips as she quivered in ecstasy, a moment of rapture so unadulterated and pure that she felt she would never experience it again. Clinging desperately to Drake, she matched his rhythm for a time and then gasped for breath.

Drake withheld his pleasure until he saw the elation in Noelle's face and felt it in her quivering body. Freed at last to seek his own fulfillment, he increased his pace until a shudder racked his body and he collapsed beside her.

For a few seconds he was stunned at what had happened between them. Noelle had given her virginity to him for a reason he couldn't fathom. Her taut body relaxed again in his arms, and for several minutes, he kissed her and caressed her like the treasure she was to him.

After a silent period when he expected her to explain her actions, Drake realized she didn't intend to do so. "Noelle," he said, continuing to cuddle her in his arms, "why would you do such a thing?"

Noelle opened her eyes. What could he mean? "I . . . I'm sorry. I thought you would want . . . You see, I never dreamed that . . . Oh, dear."

Drake listened, trying to understand her stuttered explanation. It still made no sense. "Do you realize what you've done?"

Gazing into his deep brown eyes, Noelle thought for a minute. "I'm not sure."

"By all that's sacred, Noelle, what we've done is reserved for people who love each other, husband and wife. We—" Drake paused and studied her. Did she love him? Could she possibly have come to love an enemy in so short a period of time? He decided she didn't know yet how she felt. "I wouldn't have done that if I'd known."

"Known what?" This wasn't turning out the way Noelle had planned at all. Instead of being overjoyed at their union, he seemed reserved, maybe even angry. She was the one who would be most harmed if word of her indiscretion got out. No respectable family would receive her ever again. Noelle had weighed the risk against her possible loss and chose to gamble.

"I wouldn't have taken your virginity," Drake answered flatly. How could he discuss this with her? She was too innocent to know the consequences of their act.

Noelle's chin jutted out in anger. "You didn't take it. I gave it."

"I realize that, but why?" Drake watched her eyes glimmer in the soft light and understood that she couldn't really talk about what they'd done. "Noelle, what can I say?"

Swallowing hard, she stared at him. What could *she* say? How could she explain that she'd given herself to him because she was afraid he might die before she could marry him? He hadn't said he loved her. He hadn't indicated that he wanted to spend any more time with her. He was taking her to Charleston to dump her at her aunt's house, to be rid of her. "Say nothing."

Drake knew that the honorable thing to do would be to find a preacher and marry Noelle as soon as possible. What if she was pregnant? What if she regretted her action?

He couldn't burden her further. If she was pregnant, he'd marry her. If not, he would wait until the war ended. She'd been through so much already that he couldn't force upon her the agony of waiting for a husband to return. "Noelle, you've given me the greatest gift a woman can give a man. I'm not worthy of your graciousness, but I cherish it no less. I wish I could . . . I mean, if it weren't for the war . . ."

If they weren't enemies, perhaps he'd care for her. Was that what he was trying to say? "You owe me nothing. I have given what I gave because it was mine to give. I chose you. Don't worry about me. I'll never speak a word of this to anyone. Your reputation won't be soiled."

"My reputation!" he exclaimed. "Noelle, what if you're with child?"

She smiled, and her face lit up with pleasure again. "Then I'll cherish it as you cherish the gift I've given you."

"It's not that simple. A child needs both parents." The idea of a child brought a feeling of pleasure that he'd never considered before. Noelle's child. It would be blond with blue eyes, a darling little girl. A replica of her mother. He suddenly wanted that child more than anything. "I'm a soldier."

How well she knew. It she carried a child of this union, Noelle would be proud. She'd lie and tell people her husband had been killed in the war, fighting proudly for his country. In her lie would reside the truth. At the moment of their union, in her mind, she and Drake became one, husband and wife. He fought proudly for his country. And he might die for it.

Her eyes glittered for a moment before the tears spilled over. They ran down her cheeks and onto Drake's shoulder.

"Noelle darling, don't cry." He had hurt her feelings. "Please, everything will turn out all right. Don't worry."

He could say don't worry. The person he loved didn't face enemy bullets every day. The person he loved didn't risk her life every day. The man Noelle loved was brave and did risk his life and would think himself less a man if he didn't do it.

Gradually her tears subsided. Drake continued to hold her until she fell asleep. He cuddled her against him, wanting the rain never to stop, for when it did, they would have to move on. His time was not his own, and he wanted Noelle safe above all things.

When Noelle awoke, Drake was gone. She darted out of bed, realized she was naked, and searched for her nightgown. Blushing furiously, she dug into the bed, threw the covers here and there before she found it.

On top of a little cabinet she found a pitcher and wash bowl. She picked up the pitcher, intending to fill it, but found it full. A clean cloth lay beside it. Drake had done this, she realized, and she washed quickly. She wanted to be completely dressed by the time he returned—if he returned.

Moaning inwardly, she remembered their conversation after their wonderful union. Why had he seemed so reserved, so distant? Did he hate her for what she'd done? Mandy had often told her that men never married women who allowed them even a little liberty. Had her desire destroyed the thin thread that bound them together?

"Good morning," Drake called from the doorway. He saw her standing in her nightgown and backed away. "I'll wait until you're dressed."

Noelle nodded. She put on her dress and petticoat as quickly as possible. She didn't want him to see her undressed again.

When he returned, she stood fully dressed in front of the fire, having tossed in a fresh log to rouse the flames enough to cook. Smiling timorously, she glanced at him and then turned to slice some apples. "Breakfast will be ready shortly."

He watched her work for a few minutes and realized how afraid of his reaction she must be. Their intimate act changed everything. Gone was the easy, teasing relationship that he'd enjoyed so much. Replacing it was a deeper love, an abiding admiration that he wanted to shout from the top of the highest tree. But those words would have to be saved until the war was over. "No hurry. I've checked on the horses. They're fine. It's still raining as if it will never quit."

She paused and looked over at him. "I hear it on the roof. Isn't it a nice sound?"

"Yes. Did you sleep well?" He scolded himself for asking the question the moment it was out. He shouldn't have reminded her of making love. And sleeping together was sure to come to her mind.

Color sprang to her cheeks, and Noelle nodded. "I . . . I did." She glanced at him to gauge his reaction. "And you? Did you sleep well?"

Drake wanted to shout that he hadn't slept at all, that her seduction left him with questions and recriminations that tormented him all the time he lay there. "Not very well. I had too many things on my mind."

Serves him right, she thought. "I'm sorry."

Noelle put the apples in a skillet and cut a slab of butter to go on top. While they were sizzling, she sprinkled them with sugar and cinnamon. "I'm afraid all we have is apples and ham."

"Sounds wonderful." Drake strode to the table and started to sit down, then hesitated. "Is there something I can do to help?"

"Pour the tea. You can sip it while I finish here." Noelle didn't watch him. His body intrigued her, and she decided to avoid looking at it. "Here we are."

She spooned most of the apples onto his plate and the remainder on hers. After putting ham on both plates she sat down. Eating silently, she watched him surreptitiously. It was hard to keep the smile from her face when she realized he was watching her, too. An uneasy truce.

"This is delicious," he said, finally breaking the silence. He knew they needed to discuss their lovemaking while the rain lasted because after they were on the road, they would talk little. But he couldn't broach the subject. He wasn't ready to reveal his emotions, his vulnerabilities.

"Thank you." Noelle scraped the last of the apples from her plate and ate them. Standing, she gathered their plates and then took them to the bucket of fresh water he'd brought in. "Do you think the rain will let up before dark?"

"I hate to say it, but I believe the rain will last through the night. It shows no signs of stopping." Drake swallowed the last of his tea and handed her the cup.

Noelle busied herself around the cabin, making it as neat and comfortable as possible while Drake brought in more firewood and water. The wood now was wet and needed considerable time to dry before it would be of any use to them. The pile of dry logs had dwindled considerably.

"Noelle," he began, trying to decide how to conserve their supply of wood. "We must think of some way to save wood. If we stay here much longer, we may run out."

Noelle looked at the dwindling pile. "Well, that's simple enough. We'll use only what we must for cooking."

"No, we've got to stay warm, too. We'll just have to sit closer to the fire. Maybe we could string the blankets up so that we have a smaller area to heat." He glanced around the cabin, looking for a place to tie a rope. His solution would help but would not keep them warm indefinitely.

Noelle found thick twine and handed it to Drake. "Will this do?"

"It should work well." Drake found a protruding nail and tied the string to it. "We need to keep the door outside of our protected area." He located a nail hanging from the ceiling and hammered it with his boot until it was bent enough to hold the twine. "Get some blankets."

The blankets left by the previous owners were in the lone cabinet. Noelle pulled them out and shook them well. "Here are all the extras."

Drake took them and draped them over the twine. It sagged in the middle but held. When he'd finished, they had a much smaller room. He wondered why he hadn't done this earlier. It might have prevented him from taking Noelle's virginity earlier.

Noelle dragged the rocker into the circle of blankets. "Now we'll be warm and cozy."

Drake spun around and gazed at his handiwork. For a while his arrangement would work very well, but at bedtime they would have a problem. The bed was outside the circle he'd created, and there was no room to drag it inside. They would just have to share it.

With his task done, Drake went to check on the horses. He hated to leave them outside in this cold weather. Maybe he could take part of the barn and make a lean-to of sorts.

With Drake gone, Noelle had nothing to do except sit by the fire and keep warm. The steady drizzle beat on the roof and almost put her to sleep. The rhythmic sound of the rocker calmed her down a little and eased her pain at what she considered Drake's rejection of her. But the memory of their shared bed brought a smile to her lips and a flicker of renewed desire to her body.

"Noelle," Drake called.

The sound of his voice broke through her reverie. "Yes, Drake?"

"Are you busy?" he asked from outside the wall of blankets.

"No, I'm sitting in front of the fire rocking," she explained and rose. She strode to the blankets to peek through and met Drake face to face. After a few seconds' confusion she laughed. "What do you need?"

"I think I've found a way to protect the horses. Do you think you can help?"

"Yes. I'll be glad to help." Noelle started to take her cape from the nail it hung on but then decided not to get it wet. If they had to ride tonight, she didn't relish the idea of riding in a wet cloak.

"Won't you be cold?" Drake asked and held the door open for her.

"Probably, but I don't want to get my cape wet," she explained.

"I see. Well, come on. This isn't going to be easy, and we may not succeed." Drake took her to the ruins of the barn. He had carefully removed the body of the woman so that Noelle wouldn't see it. From what he'd seen of her wounds, he was sure the woman had been murdered. "That wall is intact," he said. "If we can dig holes deep enough to plant some corner posts, we can build a lean-to for the horses."

Noelle looked at the pile of wood. The side of the barn had fallen in one piece, and several thick posts remained to make supports. "I think that's a wonderful plan."

They worked together in the drizzle for more than two hours. By the time they led the horses under the shelter, Drake and Noelle were nearly frozen.

"Get back in by the fire. I'll finish up here." Drake pushed her toward the door. "I'll feed and water the horses."

Noelle watched as he dragged a watering trough toward their new structure. "Let me help."

She bent over and picked up one end. Together they placed it in front of the horses. "You fill it with water. I saw some straw underneath the other wall of the barn. I'll get it."

Drake studied her as he drew the water from the well. Her hips swayed enticingly, although he knew she wasn't conscious of her motion. When she finished dragging the straw over to the shelter, she smiled. "How would you like some fresh greens?"

"Fresh?" he asked, his mouth watering at the thought of fresh vegetables. "Where will you get them?"

"There's a garden." Noelle turned and scampered away. She found a basket and hurried down the path behind the barn. After wading gingerly through the mud, she found onions, greens, turnips, and carrots. She glanced at the edge of the garden and saw some potato hills. Bending over, she stuck a finger into the mud at the base of the plants. "Ah, potatoes, too."

She filled the basket with an assortment of vegetables. Their fresh scent made her feel good as she hurried back toward the cabin. She could almost taste them already.

The sound of a twig snapping stopped her cold. "Drake," she called quietly. "Is that you?"

A strange man emerged from the woods and grinned at her. His lopsided smile showed a nearly toothless mouth, and tobacco juice dribbled down his chin. Noelle shivered. "Who are you?"

"I sure as hell ain't called Drake." He took another step toward her. "What's a purty lady like you doin' out here all by your lonesome?"

"I . . . I live here," she lied, hoping he'd understand that she wasn't alone. "What do you want?"

His leer answered her question before he opened his mouth again. "Funny you ask. I'm starvin' to death fer a little good food and company."

"Food I can give you. Company is out of the question." Wondering where Drake was, Noelle edged away from the stranger and tried to calculate whether she could beat him to the cabin. She thought of yelling for Drake, but decided that if the man wasn't traveling alone, she would alert his friends.

"Well, now, I've a mind to have a little of both." He stepped closer and held out his hand. "Want me to carry your basket?"

Protectively, Noelle pulled the basket closer and backed farther away. Rain fell a little harder and drizzled into her eyes. Where was Drake? she wondered. She looked down at herself. She looked like a poor farmer's wife. The man seemed to have decided they could be friends. "Look, I think you'd better wait for . . . for my husband. You stay right here."

Noelle turned and raced up the path toward the cabin. The stranger flew at her and seized her before she reached the barn. He caught her waist, and the two of them tumbled into the muddy garden.

CHAPTER
14

THE BASKET ROLLED OUT OF REACH, LEAVING NOELLE WITH no weapon. She beat at the man's chest and kicked as hard as she could from her inferior position beneath him.

He covered her mouth with his hand and twisted one of her arms until she gasped in pain. Not to be outdone, Noelle bit his hand with all her might.

"Hellfire and damnation, woman," he screeched. "What's the matter with you?"

Noelle ignored his question and kicked with all her might. Her knee landed between his legs. Falling off her with a howl of agony, he rolled over and over.

Scrambling to her feet, Noelle located the basket, picked it up, and replaced the scattered vegetables. "You get off my land, or I'll take a pitchfork to you."

"You coulda killed me. Don't never hit no man like that." He held himself between the legs and peered warily at her.

"I said get out of here now."

"Just hold on. All I wanted was some victuals." He sat up in the mud and glared at her. A lopsided smile creased his mouth, and he nodded. "Right spunky, ain't you?"

"Spunky enough to kill you where you sit if you don't get going." Noelle backed up and bumped into a wall of muscle. She spun around and found herself in Drake's arms. "Oh, Drake, I'm glad to see you."

The smile on Drake's face told her he'd seen everything. He gazed past her at the man.

"Say, you her old man?" the stranger asked. "That's the purtiest gal I ever seen." He tried to stand but slipped in the mud.

Drake smiled at the stranger and helped him out of the mud. "Yes, she's beautiful." He nodded as if to emphasize the fact. "Trouble is, she's a bit ornery. Fact is, she's about the meanest heifer I ever come across."

Noelle stared in disbelief as Drake talked to the man. Before she could defend herself, he continued. "See this bandage?"

"Yeah. What happened to you?" the stranger asked.

"Knife wound. Little hussy threwed a kitchen knife at me sure as I'm a standin' here." He hung his head.

"Do tell," the man said and looked again at Noelle.

"Before that, she bashed me in the head with a Bible box." Drake hung his head even lower, until his chin touched his chest. "She's a little touched, too. See the way she's starin' at us? Looks to me like she's about to have another one of her fits."

"Fits?" The man edged away from the two of them, even though he had to do it on his knees. "What kind of fits?"

"Like fits you ain't never seen before. Why, I brought home this friend from church, and she 'bout beat him to death." Drake nodded sadly while Noelle watched in astonishment.

The stranger's eyes widened, and the smile left his face. "Well, it was nice chattin' with you folks. I reckon I'll be headin' on."

Rain continued to fall, and the man slid again as he tried to rise. Drake helped him to his feet. "Say, why don't you come have dinner with us? We'd . . . I'd sure like some company."

"Me? No. I gotta move on. Headed down toward Charleston way myself. I got to . . . Well, anyhow, I'll be seein' you folks." He backed slowly away, never taking his eyes off Noelle. "Ma'am, you sure are purty to be so danged ornery."

Before Noelle could open her mouth, he scrambled away. Running at full speed, he was soon gone from sight. She turned to Drake. "Why did you tell him all those lies?"

"Because he's one of Cunningham's men." Drake put his arm around her, and they returned to the cabin. "I don't think they'll come back this way tonight. That man wasn't heading toward Charleston. I think he's a scout. This place is pretty far out of the way and not wealthy enough to attract that bunch of cutthroats."

"Are you sure?" she asked, stepping through the door to the cabin.

"Can't be sure, but I doubt it. They're probably holed up somewhere to keep the rain off." Drake stamped the mud off his boots.

Noelle sat down and removed hers. Mud caked them up past the buttons. "Why didn't you shoot him?"

"Because I don't know how far away Cunningham's band is. Stay here." Drake returned to the door. "I'm going to follow him."

"No!" Noelle shouted. "Please don't. They'll kill you if they think you know who they are."

"Don't worry. I'll keep out of sight." Drake disappeared through the door and then returned. "Noelle, you stay in this cabin. Bar the door and don't open it until I say my name."

"Please reconsider, Drake. I don't want you out there alone against all those men." Noelle could hardly keep back the tears. She stood up and put her hands on his chest. "Please don't go."

Drake looked down at her and recognized the fear in her eyes. It was as he suspected. She feared for his life. How bad would it be when he left her to rejoin his regiment? "Don't worry. I'll be back before long. Now remove those wet clothes and dry yourself off before you catch pneumonia."

Noelle nodded, feeling anxious about this journey. Drake

would be vulnerable all alone out there with all those nasty
men. She looked up and tried to smile.

Drake paused a moment. Her lips were pursed, and she
smelled sweetly of lilacs. He wanted to kiss her.

Drawing her into his embrace, he nuzzled her wet hair.
He hated to leave again, especially in these dangerous
circumstances. Cupping her chin in his hand, he lifted her
face to meet his lips. Tentatively he touched his lips to hers.
When she didn't bolt from his arms, he crushed her to him
and plunged his tongue into her mouth. Her eager response
was more than he'd hoped for. When he drew away, he
wasn't at all sure he wanted to go, but knew he must.

He turned and was gone. Noelle slid the thick board into
the two iron slots on either side of the door and moved into
the small space in front of the fire.

Removing her dress and petticoat, she shivered and
stepped as close as possible to the flames. It would take a
long time for her to get warm, especially since Drake was
gone. She hung the wet garments over the back of a chair
and pushed them as near the fire as she dared, spreading the
skirts out so they would dry more quickly.

Noelle found her spare dress and petticoat and put them
on. When Drake returned, he would probably be hungry, so
she peeled and diced the turnips and put them on to boil.
She found a pot and cooked some washed greens with water
and bacon drippings. Then she sliced some of the carrots
and boiled them with brown sugar and butter. Dinner would
be a feast.

She swept the floor again, then set the table for dinner.
Time passed slowly, and when her tasks were done, she had
nothing to do but rock in front of the fire and stir the food.

Drake moved silently through the undergrowth, tracking
his quarry easily in the rain-soaked earth. He'd spotted the
stranger soon after he left the cabin. As he suspected, the
brigand headed straight back to the outlaw's camp.

Before the straggler could reach Cunningham and report

on Noelle's presence, Drake accosted the man. If he reached the renegade Tories and described Noelle, the band would return to raid the cabin. In all likelihood, they would ambush Drake and ravish Noelle, probably taking her prisoner for their lustful needs as they rode.

Drake had heard of Cunningham, and the tales were of a brutal, unfeeling cutthroat who cared nothing for the decency and honor of the homesteaders. They killed the farmers they encountered, then raped and tortured their women. Drake refused to allow that to happen to Noelle.

Stumbling as though he'd been drinking heavily, Drake approached the man who'd experienced Noelle's wrath. Her vicious treatment of the brigand still brought a smile to Drake's lips, and he had to force himself to forget the look on the man's face in order to carry out his ruse.

"Hey, ain't you the fella I just talked to back there with that feisty bitch?" the robber asked, wiping the rainwater out of his eyes.

"Yes, sir, that was me. You got her pegged all right." Drake slurred his words and allowed his eyes to almost close. He recognized the glint in the enemy's eyes. "That's one hell of a . . . what'd you call her? Bitch?"

"Yeah, that's her. Bitch," the stranger agreed. "My name's Lester."

"Howdy do, Lester. M'name's Drake." Drake weaved back and forth as he talked and finally leaned against a tree. Somewhere in the distance, thunder rumbled and lightning lit the darkening sky, but he pretended not to notice. "That scuppernong wine sure is powerful stuff."

"You got some with you?" Lester asked. "I could use a snort about now. Say, where you headed?"

"I was lucky to get out with my life. After you left, that woman commenced to throwing things again. I ain't never seen no woman with a worser temper than her." He allowed his head to roll forward as if he were in a stupor.

Lester edged closer. He studied Drake carefully and

glanced around the clearing where they stood. "You by yourself?"

"Shore am."

Eyes keen with eagerness, Lester moved even closer. Drake noticed the handle of a knife sticking out of Lester's breeches and tried to remain alert to sudden movements. The storm was closer now, and the lightning streaked across the sky. Fighting during a thunderstorm made Drake wary. Too much could go wrong, but he knew he could overpower the man. He didn't want to kill the brigand without cause, but he couldn't afford to allow Lester to reach Cunningham.

Drake's head fell forward again and rolled to one side. He saw Lester finger the knife handle and steeled himself against the imminent attack. When Lester drew the knife and lunged at Drake, he was ready. The two men tumbled about in the puddles, weeds, and shrubs until Drake wrested the knife away and killed Lester. Blood poured from the dead man's throat and tinged the mud puddle he was lying in a rusty scarlet.

Hating what he'd had to do, Drake inhaled deeply and threw himself on the ground near Lester. After assuring himself that the man was dead, Drake rose and stumbled back toward the cabin. He stopped by the creek long enough to wash the blood from his hands, but he could do little about his shirt without removing it. Because of the fierce rainstorm, he planned to change clothes when he reached the cabin anyway, so he did his best to hide the blood.

Noelle paced the small space in front of the fireplace. Drake should have returned long ago. She expected him to be gone no more than twenty minutes or so, but he'd been gone at least an hour. The sun was setting already.

She could stand the wait no longer. Noelle strode over to one of the shuttered windows and unbarred it. Opening it a little, she peered out into the twilight. When she saw nothing moving, she closed the window, moved to another, and did the same thing.

Feeling melancholy, she closed the last window and sat down. Absently stirring the turnips, she remembered Drake's face when he made love to her. A blush stained her cheeks, but the expression on his face brought a feeling of desire to replace her sadness. Drake would be all right; he had to be.

A loud rapping on the door startled her, and she jumped from her rocking chair so fast it tilted over backwards and crashed to the floor. Glancing behind her, she raced over to the door and started to remove the bar until she remembered Drake's warning about opening the door to strangers. Should she ask who was there or wait for him to call out to her?

Biting her lower lip, she sighed and reached for the bar. Her fingers trembled as she touched the wood and brushed against the cold steel brace. Indecision nagged at her as she hesitated and then jutted out her chin.

"Noelle! It's me, Drake," came the shout from outside. "Open the door."

Relief washed over Noelle as she lifted the heavy board from its iron brackets. The door swung open, and Drake almost fell inside. "Goodness, I was worried about you," she said.

Shivering from the cold rain and brisk wind, Drake hurried to the fireplace and rubbed his hands together. "It's getting really cold out there. Do you have some tea made?"

"I do," Noelle confirmed and reached for the kettle. "Dinner's about ready, too. Drink a cup of this hot tea to warm you a bit and then change your clothes. You'll never get warm in all that wet wool." Noelle helped Drake remove his coat and turned away to hang it near the fire. "I'll finish dinner while you change clothes."

Drake disappeared behind the blankets to change. Noelle spooned turnips, greens, and carrots onto two plates. She'd made fresh johnnycakes to top off the meal, and she served them with plenty of butter.

When Drake sat down, he grinned. "It's been a long time since I've had anything to compare with this."

Noelle smiled. "I didn't prepare a meat. With all those vegetables, I didn't think we'd have room."

Downing a big mouthful, Drake shook his head and sighed. "You can't imagine how good this is. Especially since everything inside my body feels frozen."

Watching him eat made Noelle happy. He ate with such gusto that he finished almost before she started. "I made dessert, too. Can you eat some?"

"I wish you'd told me before I ate the third helping of all that other food." Drake rubbed his belly vigorously. "Maybe if I chop some wood, I could eat dessert."

Noelle lifted the clean cloth that covered the dessert. "They're fresh baked apple pies."

Drake reached for one and grinned. "I changed my mind. I'll make room for these."

Pouring him another cup of tea, Noelle watched his face. It revealed nothing about his foray into the woods. "Uh, did you find the man?"

What could he tell her? Drake put down the pie and smiled, trying to reassure her. "Oh, he's gone. We don't have to worry about him. He was just a wanderer."

"Are you sure? He seemed awfully . . . I mean, he did attack me." Noelle studied Drake carefully. She felt instinctively that he was trying to protect her by withholding the truth. "Drake, be honest with me. I'm not an infant who needs a sugar tit and pretty gewgaws to pacify her."

Cursing inwardly, Drake gazed back at her and realized that nothing less than the truth would satisfy her. She seemed to have an uncanny way of knowing when he was lying. "Noelle, you don't want to know. Just leave the subject be."

"You killed him." Noelle affirmed aloud what she'd already sensed. He didn't have to say another word for her to know the truth. His face was carved with the agony of that action and the memory of it. "I'm sorry."

"You're sorry? He would have come back here with all those ruffians and—"

"No, no, that's not what I meant," Noelle interrupted and hastened to add, "I meant I'm sorry for the way I know you must feel."

To Noelle Drake seemed aloof and withdrawn, as if he was angry. "Is something wrong?" she asked.

Watching the fire, he tossed a scrap from his plate into the flames. "Everything is wrong. I came here filled with purpose. I came to fight for my country's honor. Now I find dishonor everywhere I go."

Drake glanced at Noelle and rose suddenly. He opened his mouth to speak, changed his mind, and left the cabin. She watched silently as he closed the door behind him. In the past few weeks, she'd come to know him pretty well. There were times when he needed to be alone, and this was one of them.

Drake checked on the horses. He had had to get out of the room. Noelle was a paradox. She possessed an understanding far more mature than her years. After making sure the horses had food and water, Drake sat down on a stump beneath the lean-to and twirled a piece of straw between his fingers.

Too many changes were occurring. This war wasn't as simple as he'd been led to believe by his superiors. Lord Cornwallis knew little of the life of these Carolinians, of their integrity, their hard work, their honesty. Drake himself knew little, but his association with Noelle had given him new insights. The debate within him grew, and Drake wasn't sure he could resolve his feelings.

Noelle understood that Drake would return when he'd fought his demons. A man as sympathetic and gentle as he would have a difficult time justifying killing a man, even if that man was a criminal.

Yawning, Noelle slipped into her nightgown as she

waited for Drake. She dropped into the rocker and began brushing the tangles from her hair. With killing on his mind, he might remain outside for hours, and she didn't want to interrupt his thoughts.

As she watched the fire, Noelle allowed her memories to return to the amorous scene with Drake last night. How much she had changed over the past weeks, from a prim and proper girl to a passionate woman. If only Kathleen knew the truth about the relationship between a man and a woman.

Perhaps Kathleen of all people had taught Noelle something. When one fell in love, one didn't always recognize it. Sometimes it had to be pointed out by a friend who sensed the change. Noelle smiled at the thought. A warmth swept through her as she realized that she loved Drake.

She stopped rocking and leaned forward, propping her elbows on her knees. She wondered how and when she should tell Drake that she loved him. Should she wait for him to say something first or fling herself into his arms and announce it? Should she behave like a proper lady and conveniently forget all that had transpired in the last day?

Questions plagued Noelle. When Drake returned, he found her staring into the fire as if she'd been bewitched by the dancing orange flames.

Drake stepped inside the door. His feet were silent on the dirt floor of the cabin, and he stopped before pulling back the curtain. A narrow slit allowed him to see her, sitting as she had that morning, brushing her hair. Warmth flooded over him, despite the chill he'd gotten outside. In the firelight, the outline of her breasts was clearly visible beneath the wisp of gown she wore, and his desire for her grew. Every move she made was seductive, though he knew that she was still unaware of the effect of her actions.

Noelle pulled her long hair across her shoulder and continued to brush it. Feeling that she was being watched, she turned a questioning gaze to Drake. Thankful that he had returned, she smiled tentatively. "How long do you expect our trip to take?"

"I don't know. If we rode openly, we would reach the outskirts of Charleston in a little over a week. But I want to keep to the woods to avoid being spotted. I expect that to double our time." He moved into the circle formed by the blankets. "It's still raining. I suppose we'll be here another day at least."

"I'm sorry to be so much trouble. I know you have other, more pressing duties." She stopped brushing and looked directly at him. "Although I'm glad you aren't out killing my countrymen."

Drake poured the remaining tea from his cup and refilled it. "Noelle, they're my countrymen, too. I didn't start this war, but I feel obliged to serve my country. We shouldn't talk about this, or we'll end up arguing."

Noelle nodded. He seemed so sensitive to other people's feelings, to their wants and needs; she couldn't imagine an enemy with such admirable traits. "Well, I think I'll go to bed. It's late, and I'm sleepy."

Without further discussion, she rose and hurried through the blankets to the bed. Shivering with the cold, she wished she'd had the sense to pull the mattress into the little room Drake had made.

Sliding between the cold bedclothes, she thought of Drake. Would he follow her? Should she tell him that she wouldn't object? Loving relationships posed many questions that she couldn't answer yet, but she intended to discover the answers as soon as possible.

In the pervading silence, she occasionally heard Drake moving about. The screech of the arm over the fireplace as he pushed the kettle back over the fire jolted her from dozing.

A shard of light fell across the covers and Drake peeked through the blankets.

"Noelle? Are you asleep?" He moved to the edge of the bed and sat down. "I know how patriotic you are, but—"

"Drake, don't say anything else." Her mood was too

dreamy to think about politics. "We're on opposite sides, but we're people. I like you. I don't want to think about killing. I want to be your friend. I've tried to hate you, but I can't. Between us, there will never be any war."

Noelle gazed up at him, so close she felt his breath on her face, but she was unable to see him clearly. Moving only slightly, she touched her lips to his.

Her touch was all he needed. Drake crushed her to him, allowing the hunger of the strange day to manifest itself in one long, deep kiss.

Noelle responded passionately. She slipped her arms around his neck, unaware when he pushed her back against the bed. Her desire had grown all day until she could think of nothing but loving him.

Drake's kisses swept her along with a current as stiff as that of the Broad River. Hardly keeping her mind afloat, Noelle succumbed to his skillful lovemaking. Her body, sensing the coming passion, squirmed for his touch as he kissed her and removed his clothes.

With his lean body lying next to her, his hands awakening her to the myriad pleasures between a man and a woman, Noelle groaned and clung to him. Her kisses were butterflies across his face and chest, her fingers like silk as they traced minute patterns over his body, returning to him the fire that he ignited in her.

Drake fell back on the bed and let her explore. With her soft touch, she skimmed across his skin, pausing to caress the patch of dark hair that covered his chest. Teasing, frolicking, her nails were here and then there, her lips and teeth nibbling and driving him to new heights.

Her innocent investigation of his body sent shivers of pleasure through him until he could stand it no longer. With a long, deep kiss, Drake turned her on her back and found that softness he craved. As gently as possible, he thrust inside her and established a rhythm she could match. Her fingers played across his flesh like a shower of feathers, tickling and captivating him with their soft caress.

"Love me, Drake," she whispered and abandoned herself to his lovemaking.

Sensing her need, Drake urged her on with deeper kisses and caresses. They reached a whirlpool of emotion and sensation, whirling and sinking deeper into the vortex of rapture until he recognized her fervent animation. Her ecstasy jolted his own passion, and they merged for a moment into one flurry of gratification.

Noelle cupped her hands around his face and met his kisses with an ardor she hardly recognized. Drake did care about her. He'd proved it. Maybe now he would take her home so that he could visit freely. Her heart sang as she fell asleep in his arms for a second time.

Another day passed with Drake and Noelle pretending to be homesteaders while it rained outside. Their wood was fast disappearing, but Drake knew they could keep each other warm for a while. Settling into a routine with Noelle pleased him greatly. He didn't want to go on to Charleston; he didn't want to return to the war.

After a week the rain finally stopped. When the moon rose, Drake and Noelle packed their belongings. When Drake lifted her into the saddle, Noelle looked at the cabin once more and regretted leaving it, but they would find the same happiness together at Tyger Rest.

"Will we make it home by tomorrow?" she asked, settling herself into her saddle.

Drake spun and stared at her, wondering what she could mean. "Home? What are you talking about?"

"Home. Tyger Rest. Will we be home tomorrow?" she repeated. Wondering why he was looking at her so oddly, Noelle waited for his explanation.

Walking back to her side, Drake reached up and put his arm around her waist. "Noelle darling, we're going to Charleston. I can't leave you alone at Tyger Rest."

"Charleston?" she repeated dumbly, as if he'd struck her

in the face. "We're going on . . . after . . . I mean, I thought that we . . . Drake, why?"

Anguished at the pleading in her voice, Drake hung his head. How could he explain to her that she meant so much to him that he dared not leave her unprotected in the wilds of upstate South Carolina? At best the Ninety-Six district was dangerous. Now, with Bloody Bill Cunningham raiding the plantations along with Soaring Eagle, Drake refused to subject her to the peril. "Can't you see that after these few days, I can't leave you unprotected? I'd spend every moment wondering if you had been killed—or worse. Within a week, I'd be a useless wretch."

"But you could come and see me at Tyger Rest," she said, cupping his chin in her hand. The thought of being separated seemed worse than death itself.

How innocent she was. Her naïveté never allowed her to consider what Cunningham and his men would have done to her. The pleasure she'd gained from Drake's lovemaking didn't give her any clues as to the pain another might inflict with a few changes in technique. "Noelle, believe me when I tell you that I have no choice in this matter. I'll come for you as soon as possible. We'll . . ."

Drake stopped. What could he tell her? Could he ask her to wait for a soldier who might never return? His duty was more dangerous than most. A fighting soldier saw his enemy and tried to defend himself. Drake, a scout, seldom saw his adversary until it was too late. His opponents, unlike soldiers on a battlefield, were difficult to discern.

No, he could never subject Noelle to the torture of not knowing. Better to leave his feelings unexpressed than to cause her unnecessary worry. "Come, Noelle. We must go."

Noelle bit her lip. How wrong she'd been. Drake had enjoyed their tryst and now wanted to dispose of her. Flicking Sunshine's reins, Noelle followed where he led.

The next few days were uneventful and quiet. Noelle and Drake said little to each other. She answered his questions but posed none herself. Charleston grew closer.

CHAPTER
15

THE TRAIL THEY FOLLOWED WAS WELL TRAVELED. DRAKE seemed to know his way now, and they moved more quickly.

They arrived at a British encampment at the entrance to the city, and Drake dismounted. He moved to her side and helped her down. By this time Noelle felt as if her bottom had grown to the saddle, and while Drake talked quietly with a young Redcoat, she stretched and walked about.

Noelle knew they were discussing her. The young man was smartly dressed and stood as erect and stiff as Drake, but without his handsome features. When she saw them approaching her, she sighed and turned to await their arrival.

"Noelle, this is Lieutenant Barkley Long." Drake turned to Lieutenant Long and smiled. "Bark, this is Miss Noelle Arledge. As I mentioned, her relatives are dead, and I'm taking her to her aunt in Charleston."

"Quite pleased to meet you, Miss Arledge." Barkley Long took her hand and kissed the back of her knuckles. "You'll be safe with me until Captain Hastings returns for you."

Noelle smiled widely at the young lieutenant. He couldn't be more than a year or two older than she. "I'm delighted to remain in your company, sir. Captain Hastings has worn me out with an arduous journey. Is there someplace I may rest?"

"Of course. Come with me." He took her arm and led her

239

toward a cabin confiscated for his use. "Hastings, you can rest assured that she will be quite restored when you return. How long do you anticipate being in the city?"

"Long enough to locate her aunt." Drake watched Noelle. She turned her back on him and entered the cabin. The urge to call her back nearly overwhelmed him, but he knew that he was doing what was best for her. Bark Long saluted smartly and followed Noelle into the cabin, leaving Drake with nothing to do but go on with his plans.

Many buildings in Charleston lay in ruins. Drake rode down Meeting Street and looked for the intersection with Bay. Noelle had given him directions as she recalled them, but the city had changed considerably since her last visit.

He found South Bay and the house she had described to him. Tethering his horse, he hesitated before going in. Once inside, he could hardly change his mind. He considered returning to the encampment and taking Noelle back to Tyger Rest as she wished, but he knew she would be safer here away from the Indians and outlaws.

His choice had been made for him. Drake strode confidently along the walkway and up the steps. The wide veranda showed the marks of cannon fire. He turned and glanced over White Point Gardens. Her description had missed the mark entirely. Now equipped with fortifications, the area looked like a salvage yard.

Beyond the gardens, Drake saw the Ashley and Cooper rivers join and head for the open sea. Out in the harbor, Fort Moultrie guarded the city, but not well enough. Lord Charles Cornwallis and Sir Henry Clinton had organized the assault well, and though the battle had lasted for one month, from April into May, the city had finally come to its knees.

Drake turned and knocked at the door. As he waited for an answer, he knew instinctively that Noelle would be devastated when she saw the destruction. Fortunately, her relatives' house was still standing.

The door swung open, and a young black woman peered out at him. "Yes, sir?"

"I'm here to see Mr. Banning." Drake held his head erect and tried to look trustworthy. He knew the people of this house would probably have little reason to trust a British officer.

"Mr. Banning ain't seein' company. He took sick and ain't able." The black woman stated the facts quietly.

"Well, then, with whom may I speak regarding the welfare of Mr. Banning's niece, Miss Noelle Arledge?" Drake asked, wondering if he would obtain any satisfaction from this woman who glared at him so malevolently.

"Mrs. Banning ain't seein' nobody neither." The woman appeared to study the situation. "I reckon you can talk to Miss Erin. I'll ask her."

The woman closed the door. While he waited, Drake glanced at the surroundings. From where he stood, the fortifications looked strong enough to withstand almost anything. He suspected that the bombardment of the homes in the area had forced the surrender of the city.

"May I help you?" came a feminine voice behind him.

Drake spun around and found himself facing a lovely young woman. "Er, yes. I've come to speak with someone about the well-being of Miss Noelle Arledge."

"Noelle!" The door flew open, and the young woman stepped onto the porch. "Where is she? Is she hurt? Oh, my gracious. I've been so worried. What about her husband, that nice Mr. Brooks? Is he injured?"

"Well, perhaps, I'd better—"

"How rude of me. Please come in." Erin Banning held the door open and stood back for Drake to enter. She stepped into the parlor and sat down. "I'm Erin Banning, Noelle's cousin. Our mothers were sisters. Will you please take a seat?"

"Delighted to make your acquaintance," Drake said and smiled as he sat on a blue brocade chair. The room was elegant but comfortable. A large portrait of a woman resembling Miss Banning hung over the fireplace. The center of the room was dominated by a large carpet of a deep wine color. "I don't see much of a resemblance between you and Miss Arledge."

He motioned to her lovely auburn hair and striking green eyes. "Miss Arledge is fair-haired and has the most startling blue eyes I ever saw. Why, did you know that when she's angry or . . ." Drake realized he was chattering and stopped. "I apologize, Miss Banning. I've come about a rather urgent matter."

Erin smiled at the handsome young captain. She'd seen many British officers during the past few months, but none as nice as this one appeared to be. She suspected that he was quite taken with her cousin. "How may I help you?"

"Yes, well. Miss Arledge never married." Drake wondered if Miss Banning would ask about the circumstances. He didn't know much about Noelle's relationship with John Brooks except that she didn't love him and they hadn't become intimate. Perhaps one day she would trust him enough to tell him the entire story. "Miss Arledge's parents are both dead, and she is left with no one to care for her. I've brought her to Charleston in the hope that—"

"Here? Noelle's here?" Erin sprang to her feet. "Where is she?"

"I've left her at the British encampment." Drake wondered how he could explain his reason for that. "You see, I wanted to see the city, the circumstances of the occupation, before I brought her in."

Dropping back onto the sofa, Erin smiled wryly. "Yes, we're an occupied city. Beg your pardon, but that fiend Clinton is impossible to deal with."

Nodding sympathetically, Drake edged forward. "May I bring Noelle here? At least for the present? You can't imagine the danger she would face at Tyger Rest alone."

"Of course, bring her immediately." Erin stood and took his hand. "Noelle and I were quite good friends. It will be wonderful to be reunited with her."

* * *

Noelle stared at the little man who glared at her. She didn't know why he showed so much resentment toward her. She'd never met him before as far as she knew. Lieutenant Long had introduced the man as Sergeant Malcolm Niven. From the moment of the introduction, the sergeant had made her feel uncomfortable.

Bristling with anger, she rose and stalked out of the cabin to find Lieutenant Long. He, at least, was pleasant to her. Niven followed her into the yard.

"You needn't trouble yourself, Sergeant. I'm merely stretching my legs." Noelle tried to smile but didn't fully succeed.

"I'm assigned to see after you while the lieutenant is about his chores." He glowered at her and stepped outside, too.

Noelle rolled her eyes and walked farther into the yard. Silently calling Drake every nasty name she could remember, she strode to the fence and looked around. Lieutenant Long was nowhere to be seen.

"Why don't you take yourself back into the cabin? It's a might chilly out here." The sergeant shivered and crossed his arms. "If I have to watch you, I'd like to do it in comfort."

"I don't need you to watch me. I'm quite capable of taking care of myself." Noelle turned and walked away.

Sergeant Niven caught her by the arm. "I'm to look after you anyway. Damned rebel women ought to be put away."

Noelle spun around, fire flashing in her eyes. "What did you say?"

"You have no reason to be traveling during wartime. You should be jailed for leaving your house." Niven gripped her arm tighter. "I got more to do than watch you."

For a few seconds Noelle was too angry to reply. Words refused to form on her lips, but the fury showed in her violet eyes and in the scarlet color of her face. "I left my home not by choice but by an order from one of your soldiers because

the Cherokee burned the residence of my fiancé at the
request of your army. I have no intention of standing here to
be insulted by an ill-mannered dolt who assumes that the
color of his uniform deifies him. I didn't choose to sit here
this long with nothing to do."

She turned and stalked across the compound, muttering
all the way. When she glanced back, the sergeant glowered
at her and hesitated. Thinking that she was finally rid of his
unwanted presence, she sat in a chair on the porch.

"Listen here, missy, you are a prisoner here. You'll do
what I say or I'll force you," he commanded. "Now, return
to the cabin or else."

"Or else what?" Noelle asked, her voice calm and quiet.

"Or else I'll drag you back in." Sergeant Niven moved
steadily toward her with an odd gleam in his eyes. "Come
with me, missy."

"If you touch her, you'll be dead before you get to enjoy
it," Drake called from behind them. He glanced around.
Where in the bloody hell was Bark? He gazed at Noelle,
visually confirming that she was unharmed.

"I wasn't going to harm the little miss," Niven explained,
smiling broadly at Drake. "Sir, I was merely doing my
duty. The lieutenant told me to guard her. That's exactly—"

"Thank you. You're dismissed." Drake watched the man
salute weakly and slink away. The relief in Noelle's eyes
convinced him that Niven had been rude and abusive. "I
apologize for Sergeant Niven. He's forgotten his manners,
I'm sure."

Noelle felt her heart lift. Drake had returned much sooner
than she expected. "I'm not sure that he ever had any
manners. Did you find my aunt and my cousin?"

Drake smiled. Erin Banning would be wonderful for
Noelle. With the young Charlestonian, Noelle could be a
girl again, unfettered by adult problems. "I did. Miss
Banning is delightful, and I'm sure you'll get on well."

For a moment, jealousy tried to attain a hold on Noelle,

but she refused to allow it. Smiling, she nodded. "We always did. When can we go?"

"We can leave now." Drake picked up the small parcel of her belongings that he'd left with her and escorted her out the door. He glanced around the compound for Bark and spotted him arguing with Niven. "Bark! Come here a moment."

Lieutenant Long ran to join them. "I see you've returned," he said. "Did you find a place for Miss Arledge to stay?"

"Yes, thank you," Noelle answered for Drake. She didn't like being talked about as though she weren't there. "I appreciate your time this afternoon. I apologize for keeping you from your duties."

"The pleasure was mine, Miss Arledge. Where will you be staying? May I call on you?" he asked, taking her hand and kissing it gently.

Drake watched for a moment and then interrupted. "Miss Arledge will be with her maternal aunt, Mrs. Banning, and under strict supervision. I doubt seriously whether Mrs. Banning would approve of your visit. Good day, Bark."

Noelle smiled. It seemed that Drake was jealous of Bark. She said nothing and allowed Drake to lift her into her saddle. She nodded at the lieutenant as she rode silently away.

They passed another encampment and then entered the city. Noelle craned her neck to see everything. As they rode past the wharf, she was surprised by all the activity. While Charleston was under siege, it had never occurred to her that ships would be allowed in and out of the harbor.

Gazing about, Noelle spotted a young woman being escorted into a tearoom by a young British officer. She thought she recognized the girl but couldn't be sure. Her other cousin, Lilly Arledge, lived here with her father. Noelle disliked her father's brother a great deal. He always seemed to be finding ways to persuade people into giving him money, which he never repaid. Her father had given Jonathan Arledge money more than once.

Now the girl was gone. But Noelle would have felt foolish calling out to her only to find that she was someone else entirely.

Noelle looked ahead. They were coming to the street where Erin and her parents lived. "My, but this place has grown since I was here."

Drake nodded. "It's the largest city in the southern colonies. Noelle, there's something we need to talk about."

"What is that?" Noelle studied him. Something was troubling Drake. He'd succeeded in bringing her to Charleston as he wanted, so what could be his problem?

He breathed deeply as he turned onto Queen Street. What he had to say would send Noelle into a tirade. Drake wasn't sure he had the strength to force her to comply with Clinton's orders. "Noelle, before I take you to your aunt's, we must stop at Lieutenant Colonel Balfour's office."

"Balfour? Who is he?" she asked, beginning to sense his anxiety. "What has he to do with me?"

"Sir Henry Clinton has declared that all citizens of South Carolina must sign an agreement declaring allegiance to King George." Drake gauged her reaction and recognized the crimson splotches on her cheeks as her anger grew.

"Sign an oath of allegiance to King George? Never!" How could Drake imagine that she would sign such a document?

"Noelle, you have no choice. In order to live here, you must sign." Drake stopped in front of Balfour's office on Queen Street. He looked down at Noelle, wondering what would happen if he took her in and she refused to sign. The stubborn set of her jaw answered his question. She would die before signing. "Maybe we should come back later, after you're used to the way things are done now."

Glaring at him, Noelle didn't answer.

As they rode over to Meeting Street and turned south,

Drake said, "The wharf area along Bay Street is busy and smelly, but we'll have a nicer ride on Meeting Street."

Still seething, Noelle remained silent. She knew she shouldn't blame Drake, but he was British and he was the only one close by. British soldiers walked up and down Meeting Street, calling to the girls who stood on verandas and giggled. The girls seemed to enjoy the attention, and more than one spotted Noelle and Drake as they rode past.

Within the next few days, Noelle would meet those girls face to face. She lifted her chin and stared back at them. Noelle's clothes were dingy from her long journey and unfashionable at best. From their snickering, she could tell that the young women were making fun of her. What would they think when she told them she hated the British? She didn't hate Drake, but she hated the rest of them and the Colonial Tories who wore their green so proudly. Could Noelle find a niche in this city?

Charleston society allowed entrée to few who weren't born into their little group. More than once Charles Arledge had remarked on the closed little cluster of snobs.

The Bannings had been admitted to the fringes of this elite corps of planters. Their small plantation at Goose Creek gave credence to their claim to belong to the planter society, although it did not add wealth to the Bannings' pockets. Arlen Banning owned a business of some sort, although Noelle couldn't remember exactly what it was. She knew he owned a small wharf on the Cooper River.

Almost as if he could read her mind, Drake interrupted her thoughts. "Noelle, your uncle is ill. I don't know exactly what afflicts him, but I spoke with his daughter because neither he nor Mrs. Banning will see guests."

Noelle turned so quickly that she almost fell from the saddle. "Uncle Arlen is ill?"

"As I said, I know little of the matter." Drake slowed Nightmare and turned onto South Battery Street.

Pulling on Sunshine's reins, Noelle looked out across the fortifications. "Is that the ocean?"

"Not exactly. It's Charleston Harbor." Drake pointed to his left. "Can you see that little island over there?"

Noelle nodded. She could hardly believe what she saw. There were soldiers everywhere. "Yes, what is it?"

"That's the fort on Sullivans Island. Ahead is Fort Wilkins. Although it has sixteen guns, no shots were fired from here during the siege." Drake wondered why the Charlestonians had bothered to outfit the fort if they didn't intend to use it. "Most of the fighting occurred up at the neck of the Ashley River."

Looking across the harbor, Noelle watched a ship sail in slowly. A flock of birds flew behind it and occasionally plummeted to the water for fish. The scene was so tranquil and beautiful that she found it difficult to remember that Charleston was occupied by British soldiers.

"Noelle, take this." Drake handed her a small leather pouch.

Taking the heavy pouch, she gazed at him, puzzled by his actions. "What is it?"

Drake didn't want to talk about it. He'd have preferred to give the pouch to her after they arrived at the Banning house, but he couldn't figure out how to do it without raising the ire of Mrs. Banning. "It's money. Not much, but enough to buy you a few clothes and—"

"I don't need anything."

"Now, don't get excited. Uncle John said I was to care for you, and that's what I'm doing. Use the money to buy what you need. If you don't spend it, you can give it back to me after the war is over." Drake glanced around White Point.

"Drake, this is totally unacceptable. You know I can't take money from you." Noelle could tell by the weight of the bag that it contained a large sum of money.

"Consider it a loan, then. You're going to be here for some time and you'll need it. Come, Noelle." Drake flicked his reins as he spoke. He considered the matter of the money decided. "Your cousin is waiting for you."

Noelle hurried to catch up. She tucked the pouch into her pocket. She felt uneasy about seeing her relatives for the first time in several years. What if she didn't like them? What if they didn't like her? What if they were Tories?

She scolded herself for being silly. Of course she would like them. They couldn't be Tories.

Drake rode up to a large house with a veranda surrounding the sides she could see. A black servant stood there leaning on a broom. When she spotted Drake dismounting, she ran into the house and slammed the door. Some people in Charleston were apparently afraid of British officers.

Noelle waited for Drake to help her down and then strode confidently up the walk, her head held high. She was prepared for a reception similar to that of the girls she'd seen on Meeting Street.

Before they reached the top of the steps, the door flew open and a young woman hurried across the veranda to meet them. "Noelle, my dear Noelle. How delighted I am to see you again." Erin Banning threw her arms around her cousin and hugged her close. After a moment she remembered her manners and turned to Drake. "And you, Captain Hastings. How can I thank you for bringing our dear Noelle to us? Please, both of you, come in."

Feeling a little better about her cousin, Noelle followed Erin inside. "Here, let's sit in the small parlor. It's much cozier than the formal one."

Noelle and Drake followed her past a curving staircase and into a large room outfitted with rose-colored silk draperies, and their feet sank into a rich floral carpet bordered by the same color. Turning to look at her surroundings, she marveled at the luxury she found. Her own home was considered grand, but this place was opulent.

Noelle wanted to touch the rustling silk of Erin's dress but didn't dare. It was the loveliest shade of peach she'd ever seen with rows of lace on the elbow-length sleeves. The front opened over a pleated petticoat edged with the same lace. Noelle looked down at her own drab homespun and felt dowdy, but Erin hadn't seemed to notice. For that Noelle would love her cousin forever.

A fire burned cheerily in the fireplace, and Erin motioned her guests toward the circle of chairs close to the hearth. "Sit here. I'll call for some coffee."

When Erin left, Noelle examined the room more carefully. Along one wall was a cabinet she recognized. She walked to it and stroked the smooth wood.

When Erin returned, she found Noelle standing there. "Isn't that lovely? Thomas Elfe, a local cabinetmaker, made that for us. His work is really fine, don't you think?"

Noelle nodded and then returned to her seat. "My father's books are stored in a cabinet like that. It, too, was made by Mr. Elfe. It makes me sorry I left home."

"Oh, nonsense, Noelle. This is where you belong." Erin jumped up and hugged her cousin. "We're going to get on famously, just you wait and see. Ah, here's Cammie with our coffee." Erin pointed to a small table near her chair. "Just put it down there, Cammie. And take Miss Noelle's cloak."

The black woman nodded and placed the tray on the table, then waited while Noelle unbuttoned her cape.

"Erin, that smells wonderful. I'm so cold." Noelle removed her cloak and gloves, handed them to Cammie, and then rubbed her hands together.

"Well, after Captain Hastings leaves us, we'll make sure you get warmed up. I'll bet a nice hot bath sounds good." Erin poured the coffee and handed a cup to Drake. "I apologize, Captain, but we have no tea in this house."

"I understand completely." Drake took the cup and smiled at Erin. "And thank you for your hospitality."

"You're welcome here anytime, sir. Anyone who braves the trail from the wilds of the Ninety-Six District deserves our friendship, be he British or Patriot."

Noelle sighed with relief. Drake could come and go in Charleston as he chose. His welcome in this house was something she hadn't been sure of until now.

Erin looked at her cousin. Clearly some relationship

existed between the two. She would find out more after the handsome captain left. "Here, Noelle. Drink this. It'll go a long way toward warming you up."

"Thank you, Erin. I appreciate your taking me in like this, so suddenly." Noelle didn't know exactly what to say to her cousin.

"Oh, you goose. You've always been welcome here." Erin patted Noelle's hand. "Captain, we'll be having a small dinner party to welcome Noelle. Could you attend?"

Drake glanced at Noelle. Gratified by the light that shone in her eyes, he smiled. "I shall be delighted to attend if I am in Charleston at the time. When do you plan to have the party?"

Erin looked from Drake to Noelle and caught the gaze between them. Wriggling with anticipation of a romance, she answered, "During the last week in November, I think. I'm sure you can arrange to be in town until then."

"I will be in town for several weeks. I'd be delighted to come." Drake returned her smile and placed his cup on a table nearby. "Now I'm afraid I must run along."

Noelle jumped to her feet, feeling panic begin to rise in her. "So soon?" She turned to Erin. "I don't quite know how to ask this, but will Drake . . . Captain Hastings be the only British officer at the party?"

Erin laughed. "No. We'll have plenty of people the captain will know."

Drake said good-bye and left. Noelle watched as he strode back to his horse. Hers, as if by magic, had disappeared. "Where is my horse, Sunshine?"

"The groom has stabled her. You didn't want to leave her on the street, did you?" Erin linked her arm with Noelle's. "Come, we have a multitude of things to talk about."

They mounted the stairs, and Erin led her down a wide hall. "This is my room," she remarked as they passed. "Your room is just beyond. I've taken the liberty of having a fire laid and a bath prepared."

Noelle smiled with gratitude. "You can't imagine how badly I want and need a bath."

Erin smiled and hugged her. "Come on in. I'll sit with you and chat if you want me to."

Noelle nodded. Her vivacious cousin intrigued her. She'd invited Drake into her home without a second thought, yet proclaimed by her refusal to serve tea that the Banning household was Whig. And what of her aunt and uncle? She'd seen neither of them yet. Maybe they would be present at dinner.

Noelle gasped as they entered a lovely room. She couldn't resist touching the delicate blue print wallpaper by the door. A huge bed with sumptuous handworked draperies caught her attention. The large room also contained a lovely white and gold dressing table, a small divan, and a stuffed wing chair. "This is wonderful. I don't know what to say."

"Say nothing. This is your home." Erin sauntered to the bed and tugged the bellpull. "Mother and Father are not receiving guests. I suppose Captain Hastings mentioned that. Father is gravely ill."

"Oh, my, I'm so sorry." Noelle felt a genuine sorrow. She'd always liked Arlen Banning. "Is there anything I can do?"

Erin smiled and opened her mouth, but a knock at the door kept her from answering. "Come in," she called.

Cammie opened the door and stepped inside. "Yes'm?"

"Cammie, run along to the dressmaker on Tradd Street and ask her to come over immediately." Erin waited for Cammie to disappear. "I realize you weren't able to bring many of your clothes. My dressmaker does a lot of work for us. She'll whip up something for you in no time."

"Really, Erin. I—"

"Now, don't say you don't need gowns. A lady needs plenty of them in Charleston these days." Erin went to the door and looked out. After closing it, she came back and whispered, "The walls have ears."

"Whatever do you mean?" Noelle asked, remembering how intriguing her cousin was.

"Here, let me help." Erin began to help Noelle remove her clothes. "The bathwater will get cold."

For the first time, Noelle noticed the large copper tub in front of the fireplace. "My goodness. That's tremendous."

Erin laughed again. "It's wonderful. Nothing feels better than to settle back in that with a lot of hot water."

Without having sat in it, Noelle still agreed. The thought of a hot bath tantalized her more than anything. "Are you sure your dressmaker is necessary? I can remain hidden up here, and your guests will never know about me."

"I won't let you stay up here. You're going to help me entertain my guests." Erin dropped the last of Noelle's garments on the floor by the tub and spooned a few fragrance flakes into the bathwater. "I'll go get a dressing gown of mine. When Miss Hawkins arrives, she can measure you and do all those things that dressmakers have to do. Then we'll sit and have a long conversation, unless you'd rather sleep."

"Oh, no. I want to talk to you. Goodness, it's been several years since I was here last." Noelle stepped into the tub and sank down into the steaming water. Her bones were chilled from the trip, and the hot water seemed as though it might scald her. Within a few minutes, her skin glowed a rosy color.

Erin opened the door between the bedrooms. "Here. This will look lovely on you." She threw a dressing gown over the arm of a chair. In her other hand, she had a beautiful ice-blue silk gown. The petticoat, a white pleated one similar to the one Erin wore, had little sprigs of artificial flowers tied with dainty ribbons on the ruffle. "You can wear this to dinner tonight."

Noelle could hardly wait to get out of the tub and put the gown on, but she shook her head. "I can't wear your clothes. I wouldn't feel right."

"Stuff and nonsense. This will look wonderful with your

coloring." Erin dropped it on the bed. She left the room and
returned quickly with a shift of gauze. "I forgot this."

While Noelle bathed, she listened to Erin talk about
Charleston under the occupation. "It isn't really so bad most
of the time. But yesterday, Balfour put two of my mother's
friends in jail because they refused to sign the loyalty
pledge. He charged them with spying, but everybody knows
the accusation is unfounded." Erin sat on the divan.
"Personally, I think the two women were probably just
being nosy, and it made Balfour angry."

"You're joking, aren't you? He jailed them for nothing?"
Noelle dropped the soft cloth she was using to wash her
face. The rose fragrance had filled the room, and she loved
it. "I don't know if I can live in a place that allows that to
go on."

Erin watched Noelle for a moment and then shook her
head. "You do what you have to do. Noelle, let me give you
some advice. Regardless of how you feel about the British,
pretend that you're on their side, at least while you're here.
It's . . . well, it's extremely important to the Patriot effort
for—"

A knock interrupted her, and Erin went to the door. She
swung it open, and Cammie entered. "Miss Hawkins be on
her way."

"Thank you, Cammie. Bring up some little cakes and
chocolate a little while after Miss Hawkins arrives." Erin
closed the door and returned to her seat. She glanced at
Noelle and then bolted to the door. "Cammie," she called
and waited for the woman to return to view. "Bring up a
glass of milk, some bread, and cheese right now."

Noelle started to protest, but her stomach rumbled and
she thought better of it. "You were saying?"

"Oh, don't get excited. We don't have much. Most of the
supplies that come into the wharf are for the British troops
garrisoned here, but I manage to hide a few items for us."
Erin sat down again. "Noelle, I was saying that
I . . . how shall I put this?"

She stood and began pacing in front of the tub. After glancing at the time, she turned to Noelle. "You'd better hurry. We have to finish the cheese and bread before Miss Hawkins arrives."

Cammie brought in the food, and Noelle pulled on Erin's dressing gown. Until she'd mentioned food, Noelle hadn't realized how hungry she was. She sat on the divan and bit into the cheese. "Oh, this is perfect."

"I thought you might be hungry." Erin snacked on a piece of cheese but took no bread. When Noelle had eaten enough, Erin took the tray to her room next door. "No need in running into Miss Hawkins carrying a platter like this. She's sure to suspect."

"Don't you trust Miss Hawkins?" Noelle asked and wondered why Erin would use the woman's services if she was so untrustworthy.

"Heavens, no. I don't really trust anyone . . . except you. I have to trust you because I can't have you staying here unless you know everything." Erin leaned toward the door and held her fingers to her lips. "So, Noelle, tell me about that exciting Captain Hastings."

"Drake?" Noelle asked and wondered why her cousin had changed the subject so quickly. Drake, in reality, defied description. Noelle knew so little about her feelings and their origin. How could she try to tell someone else, particularly someone she didn't know very well? She was saved from answering when a loud knock on her door interrupted their conversation.

"Come in," Erin called and then looked at Noelle. "I suppose I should have let you answer the door, since this is your room."

"It's perfectly fine. Don't worry about it," Noelle answered as the door swung open.

Cammie walked in. "Miss Hawkins here."

Erin smiled. "Please send her up."

"No need of that." A woman wearing a navy gabardine dress popped her head in. "I knew you'd want to see me immediately, so I persuaded Cammie to bring me right up."

Erin stood and greeted the seamstress and her assistant, then introduced them to Noelle. After a few pleasantries, Miss Hawkins opened the little cloth bag she carried.

"Let's get started. I understand from Cammie that we need something right away." Miss Hawkins unrolled a measuring tape and placed a pen and paper on the table. "Miss Wainwright, would you be so kind as to record the measurements I call out?"

The younger woman sat down near the table with Miss Hawkins's paper and pen. "Yes, ma'am."

Noelle looked at the girl. She was hardly more than fourteen or fifteen and was already apprenticed to Miss Hawkins. Even though Noelle's own circumstances weren't much better, she did have more freedom than would be afforded an apprentice. When she recalled the pouch of money Drake had given her, she felt free and equal to the task of ordering dresses.

After the measurements were taken, Noelle and Erin pored over the sketchbook Miss Hawkins had brought. Then they studied swatches of fabric, ribbons, lace, buttons, and decorations. By the time they'd decided on three gowns for evening and two for day, Noelle was exhausted. She never realized buying clothes could be so tiring, but she'd never ordered anything as fancy as these dresses.

"Put those on my account, Miss Hawkins," Erin instructed as she walked to the door with the seamstress.

Noelle jumped up. "Oh, no. Please charge them to me. I have money to pay for my own clothes."

Erin gazed at Noelle for a moment before turning back to the seamstress. "Please do as my cousin wishes."

Miss Hawkins left, assuring the girls that on the following day one of the gowns would be finished. The others would follow within the week.

Noelle dropped into the chair. "I'm exhausted."

"I'm sorry, Noelle," Erin said and patted Noelle's hand.

"I know you'll need these clothes immediately. I hated to have you go through all that so soon after your arrival, but it couldn't be helped. You can wear some of my clothes, but I fear your bosom will strain the fabric of my gowns."

Blushing, Noelle yawned. "I don't want to damage your clothes."

"Nonsense." Erin stood and walked toward the adjoining door. "I'll have Cammie wake you in time to dress for dinner."

Noelle peered through heavy eyelids at her cousin. "Are you having guests?"

Erin smiled and winked. "Colonel Balfour's assistant, Walter Martin, is billeted here."

CHAPTER
16

NOELLE'S EYES FLEW OPEN AS ERIN'S DOOR CLOSED. COULD she be joking? No, she would never joke about a thing like that. What could Noelle do? If she pranced downstairs to dinner with the infamous Balfour's assistant, she'd be arrested for sure.

She jumped up and raced to the adjoining door. Without knocking, she flung it open. "Erin, I can't possibly have dinner with Balfour's assistant."

"Why not?" Erin pulled her gown over her head and dropped it on the chair. "He won't eat you."

"I know, but—but—" Noelle stammered. Suddenly she wished she'd signed the pledge when Drake asked her to do so, but it was too late now. "I haven't signed the oath. He'll arrest me."

"Oh, don't be silly. He won't ask for your paper at dinner." Erin grinned and put her arm around Noelle's shoulders. "Noelle, don't worry. He thinks I'm the sweetest, most loyal Tory in the city."

"Why would he think such a thing?" Noelle asked, stunned to hear Erin speak that way.

"Because I make him believe it." Erin walked back to Noelle's door with her. "Now, you just take a nice nap. Tonight at dinner we'll bedazzle Walter."

Noelle didn't think she could sleep for worrying about her meeting with Walter Martin, Balfour's assistant. Although she felt sure that she would spend the remainder of her natural life in jail, she fell asleep quickly and rested peacefully.

When Noelle awoke, she glanced around and almost fell out of bed. The room was totally unfamiliar to her. When she remembered where she was, she sat on the edge of the down mattress and held her hands to her breast. She didn't know when she'd been so scared over nothing.

She heard a light tapping on the door that adjoined Erin's room. "Yes?" she called.

"Noelle, may I come in?" Erin asked and opened the door a crack.

"Sure. I was awake." Noelle laughed and told Erin about being so disoriented. "I didn't know what had happened. How long have I been asleep?"

"About three hours. I waited as long as I could to wake you." She stepped in and spun around. "How do you like this?"

"Oh, that's gorgeous. I've never had anything that lovely." Noelle fingered the watered silk. Its apple green color was perfect with Erin's auburn hair and green eyes. "That dress is perfect for you."

"Thanks. I love it. I've never had anything this pretty either. Or this revealing." Erin leaned close and whispered, "I ordered it especially for Walter Martin."

"Erin!" Noelle exclaimed. "How could you?"

"Easy," she whispered and held her head close to Noelle's. "Walter's room is across the corridor, so don't talk too loud."

Noelle stared at her pretty cousin. "Why didn't you tell me before? I might have said something foolish."

"He's just arrived home." Erin pulled Noelle toward the fireplace, the farthest spot from the door. "He's really nice. It's a pity he's British."

"Do you love him?" Noelle asked, feeling a sudden kinship with her cousin.

Erin laughed and then clapped her hands over her mouth.

"Not in the least, but I don't allow him to know how I really feel. He's a part of my plan."

"What plan?" Noelle asked and started to change into her borrowed gown. "Will you stop teasing me with bits of information and tell me what's going on?"

"Okay. Here's the truth." Erin sat down beside Noelle and in a low voice began to tell her story. "Father gets in a shipment of goods and sends them up the wagon trail to our Colonial fighting men. We're trying to keep them supplied with goods they can't get from around the country."

"How can Uncle Arlen do that with Balfour's man billeted right here in his own house? And isn't he ill?" Noelle studied Erin for a few seconds. "Erin, your father's not home, is he?"

Erin stood up and paced for a little while. "Noelle, promise me you won't tell Captain Hastings. He's nice, but I'm afraid he can do as much harm as Balfour."

Noelle considered what Erin said. Did she know something Noelle did not? "What do you know about Drake?"

"Nothing much, really. Just that he's handsome and kind." Erin grinned and raised her eyebrows. "And that Tarleton doesn't like him."

"Tarleton? How would you know?" Noelle asked and edged forward on her chair.

"He's been here for dinner with Walter," Erin confided and shook her head. "Now there's a real nasty man. He hates all Americans. He and his Green Jacket Brigade are nothing more than murderers."

Noelle's eyes widened as she listened. She'd heard a little about Tarleton, but not much. Drake never talked about him, and until this moment Noelle didn't know for sure whether the two officers knew each other. "I'm glad he doesn't like Drake. It makes it easier for me to like Drake."

Erin giggled. "So you do like the handsome captain."

"Of course. He saved my life more than once." Noelle still didn't know how much to tell Erin. Talking about Drake was difficult. "He is nice."

"He's more than nice. I think you love him." Erin hugged Noelle. "Are you in love with him? That's so romantic."

Grimacing, Noelle shook her head. "You're as bad as my friend Kathleen. She said the same thing."

"Well, she's right." Erin came closer and whispered, "Has he ever kissed you?"

Noelle's face flamed, and she stepped away from Erin. How could she relate the intimate details of her relationship with Drake to Erin, even though she was a cousin? To do so would ruin her reputation beyond repair.

"Well, yes, but—"

"Oh, how wonderful. I dream of the day when the man I love will take me into his arms and—"

"Erin!" Noelle exclaimed, burning with embarrassment at Erin's suggestion. She was too near the truth to suit Noelle. "Don't even say such things."

"Oh, don't be such a prude, Noelle. Times are changing," Erin scolded her cousin. "I'm impressed, not shocked. And I'm not suggesting that anything . . . well, that anything exciting happened, but, oh, it's wonderful to dream about."

"You've never been kissed?" Noelle asked, feeling suddenly superior to her stylish cousin."

"Of course I've been kissed," Erin confided and sighed wistfully. "But never by the man of my dreams."

"I understand." Noelle felt relieved that Erin hadn't guessed at the depth of her relationship with Drake. Even though she wasn't ashamed of what she'd done, she realized that her reputation would be ruined forever if Erin told anybody. "Now get back to the subject. We were talking about Uncle Arlen's secret business."

"Oh, yes. Well, he and my mother don't receive guests anymore because my father is gone so frequently." Erin peered around the room and listened intently. She knew she could trust Noelle, but the trust wasn't reciprocated—yet.

"So we let out the story that my father is ill and that Mother never leaves his bedside."

"How does Aunt Vevila like keeping to her room?" Noelle asked, wondering how her aunt could remain inside and hidden from the world.

"Confidentially, Mother is the one who is not really well. She's very frail, and the doctor doesn't know why." Erin's face changed from gaiety to distress over her mother's condition. "I fear she won't last very long. She bore a son several years ago. Little Arlen died shortly after birth, and she never recovered."

"I'm sorry. Was that after Papa and I visited?" Noelle remembered her aunt, a pale and gentle woman who said little. Papa had remarked that she was the ideal wife because of her quiet demeanor.

"No, but at that time she still managed to entertain visitors on occasion. I believe . . ." Erin said and paused. This was one secret she'd never told anyone. She didn't even know if it was true, but she believed it. "I really think Mother has grieved for little Arlen all these years. She's grieving herself to death, and there's nothing I can do about it."

"Oh, Erin, how awful for you. I always thought I had the meanest life imaginable because my mother died when I was so young, but your life must be pure agony, knowing she is there but refuses to get well." Noelle wrapped her arms around her cousin for the first time. They came together in mutual understanding and sympathy. "How do you manage to keep this large household operating properly?"

Erin shook her head and smiled. "I have not only this household to maintain, but also Bluffwood, our small plantation up at Goose Creek."

Noelle wondered how Erin could keep the two homes running efficiently. "Since Aunt Vevila is so ill, why don't you sell Bluffwood?"

Erin's eyes regained their twinkle. "Father uses the

plantation as a reason for coming and going in and out of Charleston so frequently."

Both girls giggled. Noelle really liked her cousin, more than she remembered. "Do you ever see Uncle Jonathan?" she asked.

Erin rolled her eyes and groaned. "I can't believe it. Uncle Jonathan is toddling along after Balfour like a puppy after meat drippings. Honestly, I never thought a member of our family would act like this. I mean, he's a Tory, for conscience's sake."

Noelle's eyes widened, and she was glad Aunt Thera wasn't here to see how Jonathan was acting. "What about Lilly? Does she support the British, like Uncle Jonathan?"

"Lilly's so timid. She does everything he says." Erin shook her head and grimaced. "I really think he beats her. I mean, the last time I saw her, she was dressed like one of the wharf women."

"No, not sweet little Lilly." Noelle couldn't imagine poor Lilly with such a lack of decency. The women who frequented the wharf were shockingly dressed and called out lewdly to all the men who passed by. "But surely she chooses her own clothes."

"She doesn't. She told me that Uncle Jonathan buys everything for her." Erin stood and strode to the door to listen. "I'm sure Lilly's afraid of him. I know *I* am. He frightens me. To think that our mothers' sister could have stooped so low as to marry that oaf."

Noelle giggled. "Well, he is my father's brother, too."

"I'm sorry. I didn't mean to offend you. But you know what I mean," Erin apologized and went back to the divan. "Who knows what that man will do next?"

"Don't worry about offending me. I never liked him either. My father never liked him. How can one brother be so different from another?" Noelle asked and listened. She looked at Erin a moment and whispered, "Do you hear something?"

"I thought I did. Sounded like somebody outside the

door." For a few seconds, both were silent. "I think we'd better finish getting you ready for dinner."

"Erin," Noelle whispered as she pulled the ice-blue gown over her head, "I'm afraid I won't know how to act with a British officer at dinner. What will he think of me staying here?"

"Oh, I told him all about you when he came by earlier while you were sleeping. I explained that your friend Captain Hastings had brought you here for your protection." Erin lifted her eyebrows and smiled. "Surely you can pretend to be sympathetic to the British cause for one evening, can't you? Or better still, act like one of these twits who doesn't know a honking goose from politics."

Noelle giggled and batted her eyelashes. "Oh, sir, you are such a smart man. How can a simple country girl like me ever hope to understand such complicated matters?"

Erin groaned and fell back on the divan. "I may be sick if you do that all evening, but it'll convince Walter."

After taking a last look in the mirror, the cousins linked arms and went down to the parlor. To Noelle's surprise, Drake awaited their arrival.

"Drake!" Noelle exclaimed with unmasked delight. "What are you doing here?"

"It seems I'm to be billeted here for a few days," Drake answered with a smile. "Walter and I are friends, and I spoke to him about needing lodging for the time I'm in Charleston, and he brought me here. Imagine my surprise."

With a grin she couldn't suppress, Noelle nodded. She knew as well as Drake that his good luck was very well planned.

"Excuse me, Miss Arledge. Allow me to present my friend, Walter Martin, a civilian who is in the employ of the British." Drake moved toward Noelle and took her arm. "Mr. Martin, Miss Noelle Arledge, late of Ninety-Six District."

Walter Martin eyed Noelle and smiled. "I see why you've taken such care to bring her to safety, Drake. Miss Arledge is one of the loveliest ladies I've had the opportunity to meet in Charleston. I'm delighted to make your acquaintance, Miss Arledge."

"Why, Mr. Martin, you're just teasing me because I'm a country girl. You'll have me blushing like a beet before I know it." Noelle smiled at Walter Martin as she tried to keep from gritting her teeth.

Drake gazed at her with amusement. He realized the show was for Walter. "See, Walter, I told you she was worth the trip."

Erin listened to the small talk for a minute and then said, "Shall we dine?"

Everyone agreed. Before Walter could reach Noelle, Drake tucked her hand in the crook of his arm and escorted her to dinner. Noelle glanced at Drake and thought his neck looked a little red. As she smiled shyly at him, she wondered if he might be a little jealous.

Erin's cook set a fine table. The food, procured from British kitchens, was excellent. Fresh fish stuffed with crab, rice, and greens made Noelle feel like a rich woman. She ate until she realized that she must look foolish to the others. When the cook brought in a flummery, Noelle groaned. "How can I eat any more?"

Drake grinned at her. "Well, if you don't want your dessert, I'll be delighted to—"

Interrupting him, Noelle smiled wickedly. "There's not a chance of your eating my dessert, sir, unless you clap me in irons first."

Drake saw the glint in her eyes and raised his hands in defeat. "You win this round, Miss Arledge."

After dinner Noelle listened politely to the conversation for a while. She felt tired, so tired that she could hardly keep her mind on the discussion. Winking at Erin, she stood and said after a particularly eloquent speech by Walter, "Oh, sir, you are such a smart man. How can a simple country girl like me ever hope to understand such complicated matters?"

Walter beamed at the compliment and rose. "You're not leaving us, Miss Arledge?"

"I'm afraid I've experienced a rather difficult and extensive journey. If you'll be so kind as to forgive me, I'm going to retire." Noelle smiled at Drake and Erin to include them in her apology.

Drake leapt to his feet. "Miss Arledge, please allow me to escort you to your room."

The smile on Erin's face told Noelle what her cousin was thinking. Noelle returned the knowing look and took Drake's arm. The deflated look on Walter's face amused her, but she didn't want to encourage him at all, not if there was a chance Erin might love him. They could talk about that later.

When Drake and Noelle reached her room, he opened the door and hesitated. "Noelle, I'm not sure this is going to work. I never realized that the Bannings' house was used to billet officers until after I left you this afternoon. And Walter works for Balfour. You and I need to discuss this at length."

"What is there to talk about?" she asked and leaned against the wall. "You brought me here for my safety. Are you saying I'm not safe with Walter in the house?"

"It's partly that, but more. Many of Charleston's leading citizens have been jailed. Some of the wealthier planters have been sent to St. Augustine. The charge is usually spying." He looked down into her eyes and saw the sparkle change from sapphire to amethyst, a sign he recognized as an indication of her excited condition. "Now, Noelle, what are you thinking?"

"Spying? Charleston's leading citizens? Clinton ought to be thrown in jail. If I ever meet—"

"Shhh! You don't want Walter to hear." Drake touched his fingers to her lips. "You can do nothing here, Noelle. You've got to sign that loyalty oath and act like a staunch supporter of the king."

Noelle's eyes flashed. "Drake, you know I'm no good at

fooling people. My temper would flare up, and then where would I be? At least let me—"

"I can see now that Charleston is no place for you. Before I could ride out of the city, you would be in jail for treason." Drake shook his head.

Noelle felt the relief wash over her. "Oh, Drake, does that mean you're going to take me home?"

"No, it just means that we need to discuss this and make plans." He glanced in both directions down the hallway and kissed her lightly on the lips. She smelled of roses in spring, like the ones in his mother's garden. He felt a flash of homesickness, but it was fleeting. "Good night, my dear Miss Arledge."

With a feeling of giddiness, Noelle slipped into her room. After some difficulty, she succeeded in removing Erin's gown and petticoats. Exhaustion made her eyelids heavy, and she fell into bed and was soon asleep.

Drake wandered back downstairs and spent the remainder of the evening listening to tales told by Walter Martin. The younger official had seemed genuinely friendly last year when they'd met, but now Drake found his attitude toward the Colonists vastly changed, more hostile. His concern for Noelle grew as he heard more tales of the atrocities inflicted by Clinton and Balfour on the Charlestonians. He knew that Noelle couldn't keep up her ruse of being a simple country girl much longer, particularly if Walter regaled her with the details of the imprisonment of innocent persons, some of whom were genteel women.

Erin watched Drake Hastings. She sensed his concern for Noelle and thought that he was an honest, caring man. That her cousin had fallen in love with him was obvious to her. How deep the relationship went, she couldn't tell. At first she hadn't known if Drake returned Noelle's feelings, but after he spent the entire meal gazing at her, hardly paying attention to anyone else, Erin now believed he did.

A staunch Patriot, Erin had once thought she could never accept a romance between a British officer and an American woman. Now she realized that every affair should be judged on its own merit. Noelle and Drake were made for each other. She wasn't sure whether they knew it yet or not.

Drake yawned, then looked embarrassed. "I apologize. I've been on the trail for a week, too. Since I had no help, I spent a great deal of my time on guard duty and I'm worn out."

"Forgive me, Captain." Erin rose and extended her hand. "I am delighted to have you with us for a few days, and let me thank you once again for your gallantry in bringing our sweet Noelle to us. If my father wasn't so ill, I'm sure he would thank you personally."

"You're very kind and hospitable. I do hope Mr. Banning recovers soon." Drake took her hand and kissed it lightly. "You are truly a lady of character, Miss Banning."

"Thank you, Captain Hastings." Erin blushed at his compliment. "I believe it's time we all turned in for the evening."

Walter jumped up and looked from Drake to Erin. "Yes, well, I'm off to bed, too, then."

The three of them walked up the stairs together. Erin left them outside their rooms and strolled to her own room. She'd hoped to hear something about the war but could hardly ask questions. Drake Hastings seemed angry about some of the things Balfour had done. Maybe he wasn't as loyal a British officer as she originally thought. It was too bad he wasn't fighting on the Colonists' side.

Noelle dozed fitfully. In her dreams she kept seeing the face of Walter Martin, angry and red. It fused with that of Sergeant Niven, and his demeanor became abusive. When she awakened, the room was dark except for the dim glow of the logs in the fireplace.

Rising, she discovered she'd gone to bed in her chemise, so now she changed into her nightgown. The light batiste garment did little to protect her from the cold, so she put another log on the fire and scrambled back into bed. She decided to order some flannel nightgowns when Miss Hawkins brought her new dress.

As she lay there, waiting to go back to sleep, Noelle heard a sound. She listened intently for a moment before deciding that she had imagined the noise. After all, she wasn't in the backwoods where the Indians raided every night.

Closing her eyes, she dozed off again, but was awakened by another noise. She resolved to lie awake until she could discover the origin of the sounds. After a few minutes of quiet, Noelle closed her eyes, only to hear a door creak and moan.

Immediately alert, she lay there trying to determine if the sound came from upstairs in the servants' quarters or across the hall. Her question was answered quickly.

Noelle's door opened, and someone stepped inside, then closed the door so fast she just had time to sit up in bed. In the dim light, she could hardly make out Drake's face. "Drake!" she whispered in surprise.

"Shhh!" Drake, barefoot and in his robe, hurried across the floor and sat on the edge of the bed. He leaned down and kissed her forehead.

"What are you doing here?" She didn't really care, but she wanted to find out before making a fool of herself.

"I came to see you. Cover up. It's freezing in here." Drake looked at the fire and noticed the blaze. "How can this room be so cold when you have such a big fire?"

"I threw a log on the fire just before you came in." Noelle noted happily that the fresh log had caught and was burning cheerfully. "What do you want at this hour?"

Drake lifted the covers and slid between them. "It's awfully cold."

"You should have dressed for cold weather," Noelle teased as he wrapped his arms around her.

"You, too." Drake felt the flimsy gown and kissed Noelle's lips gently. "Before I get too involved, I'll tell you why I came in here."

"I thought you came to see me." Noelle pretended to pout and crossed her arms over her breasts.

"I did. But I wanted to talk to you," he explained and then added, "first."

"I'm listening, Captain Hastings." Noelle tried to look thoughtful as he began his story.

Drake shook his head. Noelle was as saucy as any girl he'd ever met, but as bright or brighter than most men. "I'm afraid to leave you here with Walter in the house. He's a real ladies' man, and I think he may—"

Noelle interrupted him before he could make his point. "Why do you care if he's a ladies' man?"

"I don't. For all I care, he can make love to every woman in Charleston over the age of seventeen and under the age of ninety. That's not what I'm trying to say to you." Drake sensed her mood and grinned. "I don't care what he does as long as he doesn't get around to you. Trouble is, if he's smart, he'll start with you and stop before going any further. That's when he'll get into trouble with me."

Laughing, Noelle clapped her hands over her mouth. "If we wake Erin, we'll both be in trouble. That girl has the ears of a mouse when a cat's in the house."

"Look, I want you to get out of here as soon as possible. What about your other uncle? Can you stay with him?" Drake asked, hoping for an affirmative answer.

"No. There's no way I can stay with him." Noelle shook her head. "I refuse to have anything to do with him. He's . . . he's a lecher and a knave if ever I met one."

"But you haven't seen him in years. Maybe he's changed," Drake said, trying to find a solution to his problem. He realized that if he left Noelle with Walter Martin she'd be arrested before the week was out. Her temper would be the source of her downfall. "Don't you have another cousin, his daughter?"

Noelle nodded. "Yes, but, Drake, I can't stay with him. He's almost made a harlot of Lilly. Erin and I were talking about her this afternoon. Erin says poor Lilly walks around dressed like a woman from the wharves. You know, one—"

"I know, I know." He rubbed his chin thoughtfully. "Who else? Is there anyone you can think of?"

"There's nobody else. My mother had two sisters. One, Erin's mother, and the other Lilly's. Lilly's mother married my father's brother, although I don't know why. He's always been a ne'er-do-well."

"I need to think about this. We've got a problem that can't be resolved without taking you back home," he finally conceded and sighed. "Well, as long as I'm here . . ."

When he kissed her, Noelle was ready for him. All along, she thought that was why he'd come to her room. She snuggled into his embrace, and he held her close for a long time.

"Noelle, are you angry with me for forcing you to come here?" he asked, inhaling her sweet fragrance and hugging her closer.

"No. Actually, I'm delighted," she admitted.

"You mean you want to stay? You know you'll be throwing things at Walter within the week. He'll have you arrested—"

"Careful. The walls have ears." Noelle covered his mouth with her fingers. "I don't want to stay, but I'm glad I got to spend some time with Erin. She's going to be disappointed when she learns I'm leaving tomorrow."

"No, we can't leave tomorrow." Drake turned slightly and nibbled on her ear. "As much as I'd like to leave, I'm afraid I have to stay for a few days. I'm meeting with someone the day after tomorrow, and then we can leave."

"Good. That'll give me time for a nice visit." Noelle turned and kissed him. She tired easily of all this chatter about others. She wanted to concentrate on Drake.

He returned her kiss as a hungry man attacks food. Their kiss deepened, and he forgot everything and everybody else. He removed Noelle's gown, a thin barrier, threw it into the air, and let it fall beside the bed. His robe followed.

"Noelle, sweet Noelle," he whispered against her hair and then left a trail of kisses down her neck to her breast.

Taking one taut nipple into his mouth, he nibbled lightly and sucked it gently. Gratified to hear the resulting moan, he turned Noelle on her back and continued to caress her until her body moved beneath him.

Noelle arched and wriggled, moaning until he covered her mouth with his. Their joining was easier than ever before, but no less breathtaking.

Feeling like a ship floating on an undulating ocean, Noelle allowed herself to drift where Drake would guide her. His gentle touch sent shivers of delight through her and awakened her sleeping passion. Urging him on, she moved and squirmed with pleasure as he increased his pace like a sail suddenly catching a strong wind.

Her body moved without direction from her and found ways to crest the waves of desire. Drake's caresses sent exciting surges through her.

Noelle moaned and bit her bottom lip as the moment expanded into a torrent of vivid images and colors, swelling and overflowing from fantasy into reality and back until the difference existed no more. Her body, bathed in his kisses, ached with exhilaration, and she opened her eyes to look at Drake's pensive face.

After kissing her again, he slid to one side and cradled her in his arms. He waited until her breathing indicated that she had fallen asleep and then slipped back to his room.

"I must go, Erin," Noelle stated finally. She and Erin had been discussing her situation and disagreed on the solution. "Drake and I both agree that to remain here with Walter would be folly."

"But you handle him so well," Erin argued and looked at

her face in the mirror. "He's quite gullible. You'll see at the party tonight."

"I can't risk that, Erin. My temper is too quick," Noelle admitted grudgingly. "I fly into a rage before I stop to think why I'm doing it."

"The Arledge temper, eh? Well, maybe you're right." Erin turned on the little stool before the dressing table. "But I'll miss you. We could have had such fun together."

Sighing, Noelle nodded. She slipped her new sapphire-colored gown over her head and allowed it to slide down her shoulders and settle in place. Erin helped her fasten the buttons and arrange the panel in back.

Erin stepped back and cast a critical gaze at the effect. "That gown is perfect for you. Drake will be positively panting after you like a hound after a possum."

Noelle laughed and preened before the long mirror. The color complemented her hair and eyes. She whirled around, testing the width of the skirt and was pleased with the picture she presented. "That sounds like something I should say instead of you."

"Well," Erin said, "it's true, whoever says it. I'll bet Walter and Drake will both stumble over themselves to escort you in to dinner."

Making a face, Noelle turned to her cousin. "I hope not. I don't really like Walter that much. I'd much rather sit with Drake."

Nodding emphatically, Erin put her arm around Noelle. "Me, too."

When they reached the parlor, Drake and Walter both jumped to their feet. Several other soldiers rose as well, although not as quickly. At first Noelle saw only Drake. He looked handsome in his cleaned and pressed uniform, and the stubble that had grown during the journey had been neatly shaved away.

He smiled and strode over to her. Lifting her hand, he pressed a lingering kiss on her knuckles. "How nice to see you again, Miss Arledge. If it's possible, you look even lovelier than you did last night."

Noelle caught the emphasis of his words, and color bloomed in her cheeks. "Thank you, Captain Hastings, and may I take the liberty of saying that you are much more handsome in your uniform than . . ." She hesitated and caught his panicky expression. "Than almost anything I can think of."

Walter Martin rushed to kiss her hand and offered a compliment that meant nothing after Drake's words. Both men greeted Erin and fawned over her beautiful russet gown.

Erin introduced her to the other guests, and Noelle took a seat near the fireplace. Drake stood as near as possible and hardly took his eyes off her. Noelle knew that when the meal was announced, he intended to pounce on her to keep Walter from escorting her to dinner.

Seated by Erin, Walter looked a little disgruntled. From his appearance, Noelle could tell that he had wanted to sit with her if possible. She wondered why he had such an interest in her when Erin was beside him.

He was after information, Noelle decided and sat more erect in the chair. Well, he'd have a hard time finding out anything from her. Making a point of being particularly sweet and innocent, Noelle soon had all the men in the room watching her every move.

Drake appeared amused by her performance. He paid little attention to the other ladies present, but listened well to the soldiers. He, too, understood Walter's interest in Noelle.

Dinner passed without a crisis. Later, in the corner of the ballroom, a chamber orchestra began to play a minuet.

Bowing with a flourish, Drake smiled and took her hand. "Will you do me the honor of dancing with me, Miss Arledge?"

Noelle played the game as well as he. With a smile that

promised him an amusing evening, she cocked her head. "It is I who am honored, Captain Hastings."

As they pointed their toes, dipped, and swayed to the music of the minuet, Drake whispered, "Everyone is watching us. Should I scowl as if you had stepped on my toes?"

The smile left Noelle's face momentarily until she realized that Drake was teasing her. "Go ahead. Or perhaps I should really stamp on them. I feel sure that would give the kind folk of Charleston something to discuss for weeks."

Drake laughed. Noelle was as good a dancer as anyone else in the room. He didn't know why he was surprised. She constantly amazed him with her skills and talents. "What about Walter? Will you dance with him?"

Noelle glanced at Lieutenant Martin, who was watching them glide around the floor. Erin was dancing with another officer. Walter looked thoroughly unhappy. Noelle considered Drake's question. "I don't see any way of getting out of one dance. After all, he's a guest in my uncle's home."

"Tell him you can't talk and dance at the same time." Drake gazed down at her. "Step on *his* feet."

Laughing, Noelle and Drake walked off the dance floor when the music ended. From the corner of her eye, she could see Walter making his way toward them. Wondering what she should do, she turned, and a young officer stopped beside her.

"Miss Arledge? Would you dance with me?" he asked, his face flushed with color.

"I'd be delighted." Noelle had avoided Walter once again, but she knew she couldn't continue to do so. Dancing with British soldiers other than Drake made her stomach queasy, but she managed to smile. She expected them to ask some question that she would decline to answer, and then they would throw her in jail. The threat almost took the enjoyment out of dancing—almost.

One after another, the officers came and asked her to dance. Drake watched her carefully, dancing with Erin and then one other girl. After that, he stood along the wall near the punch table and sipped punch while talking to another man.

Noelle could evade Walter no longer. When she completed a dance, he rushed up to her before anyone else could and asked for a dance. "I'd be delighted," she lied.

As they danced, he chatted amiably. He asked her about people they might know. Noelle honestly answered that she knew none of them. When he asked if she knew anything about a man named Francis Marion, she felt the color rise in her cheeks. "Well, of course I've heard of him. Isn't he the man who rescued about one hundred fifty American Patriots who were being herded off to prison by British troops?"

"Yes. That's the man. When have you seen him?" he asked, a glint in his eyes.

"I? I know him by reputation only." Noelle felt her anger rise, and warning bells began to peal as loudly as the bells of St. Michael's Church. "I wouldn't know him if I were dancing with him right now."

"I can assure you that I am not Francis Marion. He's . . . well, he's a renegade if ever I heard of one. He hides in the swamps and—" Walter looked at Noelle. She had a peculiar expression on her face. "Well, I'm sure you aren't interested in anything so tedious as the war."

"No . . . no. I'm not." Noelle hoped the color was draining from her face. She'd come close to screaming at Walter that everyone in South Carolina above the age of three months could recite the exploits of Francis Marion, the Swamp Fox. "I'm afraid I'm not very good at talking and dancing. I can't seem to master doing both at the same time."

"You're a fine dancer. Better than anyone else here tonight," Walter said and flashed her a smile.

"You're just saying that to make me feel good. I'm as clumsy as . . . as a boar." Noelle wanted to say that Walter was as clumsy as a boar—or perhaps a bore—but she didn't. Their dance was finally over, and she felt the tension recede as they left the ballroom floor.

She'd come too close to giving herself away. Glancing around, she tried to signal Drake with her eyes. Noelle knew she had to leave Charleston as soon as possible or become a permanent resident at the jail.

CHAPTER
17

SINCE THE PARTY, NOELLE HAD MET NEARLY EVERY BRITISH officer in Charleston. She had learned to curb her tongue, smile, and act as dim-witted with all of them as she did with Walter. But she couldn't have done it forever. In the last few days, Noelle felt herself very close to speaking her mind to those pompous soldiers who felt that the Carolinians were nothing more than a bunch of criminals who had eluded them but were soon to be caught and imprisoned.

Matters were further complicated by three events that Noelle heard about by listening to the officers' gossip. Lord Cornwallis had sent a detachment of men to Fishdam Ford about twenty-five miles north of the British Headquarters at Winnsboro. Brigadier General Thomas Sumter's militia had fought hard, and the British losses were severe.

In private, Erin and Noelle giggled about the British defeat. In public, they merely nodded sympathetically when the soldiers talked about it.

The second event of interest to Noelle was the appointment of General Nathanael Greene to the command of the Southern Department of the Continental army. When he arrived, there were only 2,500 men in the division, and only a third of them were properly equipped and clothed, but optimism was high among the Patriots remaining in Charleston.

A third event sent Noelle and Erin into fits of giggles that took a long time to subside. Colonel William Washington used a fake cannon to procure the surrender of one hundred Tories in a fortified log barn at Rudgeley's Mill.

"A fake cannon!" Noelle hooted with laughter and hugged Erin. She could enjoy herself while the two of them were together.

Drake spent as much time as possible at the Banning house, but was gone quite often for days at a time. Noelle knew that he was desperately trying to arrange for the time to take her back to Tyger Rest, but the appointment of Greene caused quite a stir among the British and prevented Drake from leaving as planned.

At last the day came when Drake announced that they could leave. After tearful good-byes, Noelle and Drake departed, with Erin standing on the veranda of her beautiful home. Heading away from the city, they traveled past the outpost where Drake had left her when he went in to Charleston alone on the day of their arrival.

From the set of his jaw, Noelle knew that something terrible was bothering Drake, something that she didn't know about and that he would probably never tell her. Bowing to his wishes, she rode quietly, not disturbing his thoughts.

They rode for several miles before he spoke. "You know, I'm really glad you're going back home. After seeing the . . . the treatment of the Whigs in this city under Balfour's leadership, I realize now that you could never live here happily."

Noelle nodded. "I really hated to leave Erin, though. She's . . . she's got her hands full."

Without meaning to do so, Noelle had almost told Drake about Erin's real problems. As much as Noelle trusted Drake, he was still the enemy as far as the war was concerned. She considered this for a moment and then gazed at him. Unable to remember when she had last thought of him as her enemy, she smiled broadly. Maybe she was growing up, mellowing with age! She hadn't hated him for the past few days, ever since she'd consented to go to Tyger Rest with him.

She knew he was still the enemy of her people, but she felt none of her former anger with him. Life was much more pleasant when they were happy together.

The trip home took less time than the journey to Charleston. Brisk air stirred them to move quickly through woods now bereft of leaves.

Though they didn't have the rain to contend with on the return trip, their cover was scarcer and lighter as they traveled at night. The cold bit through their warm clothing and found little places to torment. Noelle felt that her nose would freeze and fall off; her ears were perpetually burning with the cold air, in spite of her hood; inside her boots, her toes were numb.

As they came closer to home, Noelle got more excited. "I can't wait to see Mandy and Lard. I never realized how much I missed them. I wonder if he's done anything else to Tyger Rest. He's really a good worker, you know. That's why Papa made him the overseer. Not many slaves are given that distinction."

Drake laughed, looked at her, and raised his eyebrows thoughtfully. "I hope you don't intend for me to respond to all that chatter. My goodness, have you been storing all this inside you? Has the dam burst?"

Noelle joined in his laughter. Over the past few days, they had enjoyed a wonderful relaxed relationship. Their conversation, while kept at a minimum to prevent discovery by their enemies, was light and teasing. The tension that had predominated their friendship seemed to have disappeared.

"It's just that I'm so excited about coming home. I really belong at Tyger Rest. I feel that I can do more to . . ." Noelle glanced at Drake and hoped that as they rode up the drive, he would place no significance on her words. "I belong here."

"Noelle, you aren't planning to do anything foolish, are you?" he asked and gazed directly at her.

Under his appraising stare, Noelle knew that she'd have to answer carefully. If he suspected anything at all, he would drag her right back to Charleston. "Drake, I do a lot of foolish things, but I seldom plan them in advance."

"Are you up to something I should know about?" He reached out and pulled on Sunshine's reins, forcing her to stop.

"Something you should know about?" Noelle asked innocently. Her answer was honest at least, even though she knew she was evading his real question. "Of course not. Don't be silly."

"I knowed it was you," Lard called, running toward them at full speed. "My missy done come home. Thank the Lord you're safe."

Drake and Noelle went to meet Lard. Drake dismounted and helped Noelle down from her saddle.

She ran to greet Lard. "Oh, I'm glad to see you."

Lard caught her and swung her in the air as if she were a tiny weightless doll. Over his shoulder, Noelle could see Mandy scurrying as fast as her rheumatic legs could carry her. "Mandy!" she called.

Mandy reached them and clasped her arms around all three of them. "The Lawd does answer prayers. I've been worried to death 'bout you down there with all them green Tories in that city of sin, women hangin' all over men and things. I heard what goes on there. And you is home before Christmas."

Drake drew back his head in laughter. "By the powder in my guns, Mandy, you're right. That's a city of sin if ever I saw one. Why, I even saw one woman, down near the wharves, who was wearing nothing—"

"Hush your mouth, Mr. Drake. Don't you be sayin' nothin' like that around my baby." Mandy clung to Noelle protectively. "You didn't let her go down there with them evil women, did you?"

"Of course not, Mandy," Noelle exclaimed, glaring at Drake for putting such an idea in Mandy's head. "He's just funning you."

"Is that right, Mr. Drake?" Mandy asked, eyeing him suspiciously. "You teasin' ole Mandy?"

"I'm sorry, Mandy," Drake admitted, hugging the slave. "I *was* just teasing you."

"Evil ain't nothin' to tease about," Mandy scolded and turned to look at Noelle. "You look all right. I know you is hungry. I got a fresh apple pie waitin' on you."

Within minutes they were seated at the table in the kitchen eating Mandy's apple pie. Noelle cooed, "I'm in heaven. This is better than anything I've eaten since we left."

Drake stared at Noelle for a few seconds and then turned to Mandy. "Did you know this girl is a good cook? Why, she cooked some fried apple pies that were mouth-watering good."

"I know she can cook. Ever' plantation mistress knows how to cook. If'n they can't cook, how they goin' tell their cook how to do?" Mandy reasoned. She picked up the thick plates and took them to her washpan.

Noelle waited while Drake and Lard brought her valise into the house. Erin had insisted that Noelle take her new dresses and the ice-blue one. They looked so beautiful on her that she couldn't refuse. Cammie had wrapped them in tissue and then rolled them as tightly as she could. She'd packed them in the valise that Erin gave Noelle, along with food and other items.

The first thing Noelle did at Tyger Rest was unpack the dresses. They were wrinkled, and she knew she'd have little opportunity to wear such fine clothes, but she loved them. Shaking the wrinkles out, she walked into her father's bedroom. It had the only real closet in the house. The little space beneath the staircase had been converted for use as a closet, and Noelle took advantage of it.

She hung up the dresses and hoped the wrinkles would

fall out. If not, Mandy could iron them, if Noelle ever needed to wear them again.

She decided that the time had come for her to move into her father's room. As an adult, she should have put her childish fears behind her long ago. Her father was gone; she was the mistress of the plantation. Her place was here in this big bedroom.

Noelle spent most of the afternoon moving her things downstairs while Drake and Lard worked outside. The hole in the dormitory roof had been repaired so well that it didn't leak at all. Noelle removed all the bedclothes and gave them to Mandy to be washed.

She looked at the windows, which were uncurtained. Unlike the Banning home, the plantations in the up-country had no draperies or window hangings. Noelle resolved to change that. She scrambled around and located some soft linen. It wouldn't be the same as the fine silk that graced the windows of Erin's home, but it was a start. Maybe one day Noelle's home would be as large and grand as her cousin's.

For now, Noelle didn't care. Being home counted most. Finishing the last touches on her new bedroom, Noelle smiled. She liked the way it looked. The old bed draperies with the wildlife scenes were gone and were replaced by a delicate white linen that had hung on Noelle's bed. She went outside and picked a few deep pink camelias and put them in a vase on her dressing table. "There, now, that looks more feminine."

"Indeed it does," Drake said from behind her. "What are you doing?"

Noelle felt the color rising in her cheeks. "I've decided to move downstairs. This was my father's bedroom, and I could never bring myself to sleep here after he died."

"Well, I'm sure you're doing the right thing." Drake looked around and nodded. "Yes, the right thing." Lard and I have gathered the last of the apples. There weren't many left. Mandy dried most of them. We found a few odds and ends in the garden and put them in the root cellar along with the items Erin gave us, so you should be pretty well stocked for winter."

Noelle turned to face him. The significance of his words began to sink in: Drake was leaving Tyger Rest. "You sound as if you're leaving and never coming back."

Drake moved closer and took her in his arms. "I'll be back, but I've been gone too long. I have to leave at first light."

Sighing with relief, Noelle repeated, "First light? Then you can stay the night? It's Christmas Eve."

"Yes," he whispered against her hair. Drake would miss her sweet fragrance and her gentle touch. During the past few days, he'd noticed a change in her, a maturity that hadn't been there before. Her fits of rage had stopped altogether; her moods were less diverse and more predictable. Noelle had grown up.

Had their shared intimacy caused the change? Had her innocent seduction changed both their lives so radically? He realized that he was a different man now. When morning came, he would find parting extremely difficult. He'd be leaving a piece of himself behind.

Without warning, Noelle broke away. She spun around and studied the room critically. "Drake, are you done with Lard?"

"Not quite. We're going to go hunting for a little while. I think I can shoot a turkey or two. Maybe bring back some fresh venison." Drake wondered at her abrupt change. Had he been too hasty in his estimation of her?

"Go on. I have too much to do to stand around talking." Noelle bustled past him and strode through the sitting room and dining room. She swung the back door open and called, "Mandy! Come over here. I need you."

Returning to her father's room, she bumped into Drake. "Are you still here? Out! Out! I have a lot to do this afternoon."

By the time Drake and Lard returned, the sun was setting. They stopped at the kitchen and told Mandy about their luck.

Lard held up a turkey and a duck. "And there's venison outside to be cured."

"This is a lucky day all right," mumbled Mandy. "I don't know nothin' bout curin' a animal. Somebody will have to help me."

Drake laughed and slapped Lard on the shoulder. "Just as you said, she's a house servant." Looking around, Drake noticed that Noelle was nowhere to be seen. "Where's Noelle?"

Mandy perked up and grinned. "You wash up for supper. She's waitin' on you. And I've got a fine Christmas supper ready. Lard, me and you goin' to eat right here after we serve Missy Noelle and Mr. Drake."

Lard smiled, showing his perfect white teeth. "Well, let's git to servin' cause I'm powerful hungry this evenin'."

Watching the expression on Mandy's face, Drake realized that the old slave was up to something. "What's going on, Mandy?"

Mandy's face told a story of delightful deceit. "Why you askin' old Mandy a question like that? Git yourself over to that pitcher and wash. Don't be botherin' me. Missy be waitin' on you."

Drake knew that asking questions would do him no good, so he did as directed. When he finished washing, Mandy handed him a clean shirt and breeches. Shaking his head in confusion, he went behind the cloth partition and dressed. While he was changing, he heard Mandy instruct Lard to inform Noelle that Drake would be there shortly.

Lard returned and called to Drake who was tucking his shirt in his breeches. "Mr. Drake, Miss Noelle say just come on in when you get ready."

Drake stepped from behind the curtain. He glanced at Lard. "Well, do I look good enough to dine with the lady of the house?"

"Well, sir, I got to be honest. Don't nobody look good enough to eat with Miss Noelle." Lard shook his head ruefully. "No, sir, nobody ain't good enough for Miss Noelle."

Drake smiled at Lard's assessment of his mistress. "You may be right, Lard."

Drake walked to the back door of the house and hesitated. What was Noelle up to? he wondered. He decided to surprise her and enter through the sitting room.

In the dark, Drake walked carefully around the house and up the steps. Through the window, he could see the soft glow of candlelight. Smiling, he strode up to the door and opened it without knocking.

"Oh!" Noelle exclaimed from the Chippendale chair by the fireplace. Her fingers were busy embroidering dainty stitches on a piece of linen. "I thought you'd come in through the dining room. Do come on in."

Drake didn't move for a minute. Noelle's hair hung in long soft curls about her face with a few gathered in a fluffy pompon on the crown, topped with a cluster of holly with berries the color of her lips. Dressed in the lovely gown she had worn on their last night in Charleston, she looked like a princess awaiting her prince. Lard was right.

"You look beautiful tonight, lovelier than I've ever seen you." Drake crossed the room and took her in his arms. "I often wondered how it would feel coming home to a woman like you, dressed in her finery and diligently pursuing her stitching."

"And how does it feel?" she purred, fingering the lacy edging on her gown.

For a moment Drake didn't know how to answer. This was a dream he'd never thought to realize. A confirmed bachelor, he hadn't considered the warmth of watching a woman who loved him working at something peaceful and domestic. He'd been foolish to avoid marriage all these years. Drake could deny it no longer. As soon as this war was over, he would come back home to Noelle.

"Well? How does it feel?" she asked when he seemed to be in a daze. Now wondering if she should have taken his silence to mean he didn't want to answer, she played with the pearls Irene had given her.

"Oh, I never imagined how wonderful it would be. I couldn't. Every man I know became miserable after getting married." Drake hesitated. He'd said too much. He couldn't afford to mention marriage to her until his life was no longer in jeopardy with every step he took. Feeling a little awkward, he searched for another subject to discuss. "Those are lovely pearls."

"Thank you. These were Irene's. She gave them to me because she had no daughter. I tried to give them back, but when I mentioned you, she thought that you and I . . . well, she insisted that I keep them."

He glanced at the pearls around her neck. Apparently they meant a great deal to Noelle. "Irene must have loved you very much. She always told me that when I married, she'd give those pearls to my wife." He held her close, inhaled her fresh fragrance mixed with the scent of cedar, and kissed her forehead. "Are you too busy to talk?"

Noelle put her embroidery in a sewing basket and placed it on the cabinet. Drake's explanation of Irene's intent for the pearls embarrassed her, but she was glad he had told her about it. "No. What shall we talk about?"

"Well, we can start with—"

"Time for supper," Mandy announced from the doorway.

Drake gazed down at Noelle and smiled. "May I escort you to supper, Miss Arledge?"

"Why, I'd be delighted, Captain Hastings," Noelle cooed. "And might I say that you look rather dashing in that shirt."

Noelle could go no further with her compliment. If she had, she would have mentioned the intriguing thatch of hair visible above the open shirt. She would have told him that his breeches fit quite snugly and that it warmed her cheeks just to look at him. His black boots reached his knees, completing the elegantly simple costume.

"You all goin' eat or stand and look at each other?"

Mandy asked and placed her hands on her hips. "The rest o' the world got to eat, too."

"I'm sorry, Mandy," Noelle apologized. "We're coming."

"It smells delicious. What's for dinner?" Drake took Noelle's arm and led her into the dining room.

He noticed the room for the first time. A hurricane chimney surrounded a single candle on the table. Tucked down inside at the base of the candle were a few sprigs of holly like the one Noelle wore in her hair. The table was set with gleaming pewter plates and cutlery. Cups of tea steamed beside tall glasses of fresh milk.

Drake seated Noelle and then moved to his own chair at the other end of the table. As he sat down, he saw Mandy take a kettle from Lard. After a few moments, Lard passed her a second kettle, and then a third. Mandy ladled soup from the first kettle into bowls and brought them into the dining room.

Startled at the formality of the meal, Drake ate silently for a few minutes. The soup, a beef broth with vegetables, was delicious. He suspected that if he turned up his bowl to drink the last of it, Mandy would rap his knuckles with a serving spoon.

Noelle smiled sweetly as she sipped her soup delicately. Drake seemed surprised that she could have arranged such a fine meal on short notice. He knew nothing of the hurried planning and executing of this evening. Like the lord of the manor, he knew only what he was told or saw for himself. But Noelle saw the appreciation in his eyes as he carved the baked chicken and poured a liberal amount of gravy over it before passing it on to her.

Playacting, that's what they were doing, she thought. They had only one evening together, and they would want to make it last. There was no time for unpleasant conversation. "Are you enjoying your meal, Captain Hastings?"

"Miss Arledge, this is the best meal I've ever eaten,"

Drake admitted honestly. "You employ the finest cook in the Colonies."

"In America," she corrected, but smiled to remove the sting of her words. "I believe you'll enjoy the dessert, too."

Mandy entered with a plate of apple dumplings. Drake's eyes grew large as he watched her spoon one onto his plate.

"Really, Mandy," he began and inhaled the wonderful scent of the apples and spices. "This is too good to be true."

When Mandy left the room beaming with pleasure, he gazed at Noelle. "This entire evening is too good to be true."

Noelle felt her face warm with the sincerity of his compliment. "I believe you're right."

When they finished eating, Drake escorted her to the sitting room. "What next, Miss Arledge?"

"Do you play chess, Captain?" she asked and indicated the marble pieces arranged on the board. Sitting down at the Queen Anne table, she smiled. "Would you like to wager on the outcome of this game?"

Drake dropped into the chair opposite her and studied her lovely face. "I'd like to, but I doubt if I can believe the sweet innocence of your face. I fear I'd be taken in by your beauty."

"Come now, sir," Noelle purred and touched his hand. "Surely you don't believe a simple country girl like me could beat an Oxford-educated man such as yourself?"

"Now, now, Noelle, don't play the innocent country girl. I know how ruthless you can be when the mood strikes." Drake tilted his head to one side to observe her. "You may have the honor of making the first move, Miss Arledge."

Noelle made her move. While Drake was a more skilled player than her father or anyone else she'd played, he lacked her superior talent for the game. She beat him three times in a row.

He rose and took a churchwarden from the rack and tucked a small bit of tobacco into the clay bowl. All along the mantel, Noelle had strewn sprigs of cedar and holly to add a fresh scent to the room. "Indeed, Miss Arledge, your skill is far more advanced than mine. Perhaps you would be interested in sharing this pipe of peace with me?"

"Drake Hastings, you know I'd never do anything as horrible as smoking one of those silly things." Noelle tossed her head and rose from the game table. She seated herself on the divan and watched him take drafts from the long white pipe. With his brash demeanor, he sat back down on his chair and hung one leg over the padded arm.

"Sit still, I have something for you." Noelle jumped up and scurried into the bedroom. She returned with a box and handed it to Drake.

"What is it?" he asked. He felt the excitement he saw in her violet eyes.

"A gift." Noelle sat on the edge of her chair.

Drake opened the box and stared in disbelief. "Heavens. Where did you get this?"

"Charleston. Miss Hawkins made it for you." Noelle smiled and then hung her head. "I'm sorry. I spent all of the money you gave me. The last of it went for your new shirt."

Mandy raced into the room and nearly knocked the pipe from Drake's hand. "Lawd have mercy, Miss Noelle, it's them Injuns again!"

Noelle jumped to her feet. "Indians? Are you sure?"

Lard ran into the room. "Mr. Drake, git your guns. We gotta whole mess of Injuns to shoot."

Noelle dashed into her father's room and up the stairs. Above the stairwell hung her last gun, a Brown Bess. Without hesitating, she sprinted back down the stairs, cursing the full skirt of her gown as she jumped down the last three stairs. "I'll show them this time."

When she reached the sitting room, Soaring Eagle stood talking to Drake. Noelle leveled her gun and aimed.

"No!" Drake shouted, dropped his new shirt, and stepped between the gun and Soaring Eagle. "Don't shoot, Noelle. He's my brother!"

The words reached Noelle but made no sense. How could Soaring Eagle be Drake's brother? Without realizing what she was doing, she lowered the gun, and Drake took it from her hands. "How can that be?"

Drake stood the gun in the corner and returned to Noelle's side. He drew her into the circle of his arms and held her at his side as he spoke to Soaring Eagle. "Why are you here?"

Soaring Eagle stared at Noelle with obsidian eyes that almost matched Drake's, and she could see Drake's jaw clenched in anger. She noticed the similarity of their faces for the first time, but still couldn't believe what Drake had said.

"My braves say beautiful woman return. I bring her gift." Soaring Eagle held out a clay pot and a basket. "When I say to Running Fox that Drake Hastings marry little white woman at edge of village, he say bring marriage gift. Offer peace to little sister."

Drake looked at Noelle and noticed her questioning eyes. "Soaring Eagle's father, Running Fox, kidnapped my mother. They fell in love. Soon after I was born, my mother was returned to Ash Meadow by my uncle and his friends, along with a few men from Ninety Six."

Noelle glanced from Drake to Soaring Eagle, still trying to confirm in her mind that what the two men said was true. Soaring Eagle still held the clay pot and basket out in front of him. With a tense smile, she took them from him. "I thank you for your gift and will remember it always."

Being so enthralled with the revelation she'd just heard, she didn't see another Indian step through the door. Soaring Eagle crossed his arms and stood facing Noelle and Drake.

"Say what I told you," came the voice of a white-haired Indian.

"Father," Drake said and took a step forward, almost dragging Noelle with him. "It has been many years since I've seen you."

"You very small boy." Chief Running Fox smiled with

pleasure as he took in Drake's appearance. "You have look of my people. How say little Crouching Deer to that?"

Drake closed his eyes briefly, then looked again at his father, and handed him the church warden. "Mother, Crouching Deer, is dead, but she was always proud of my appearance. She often told people that I looked like my father."

"I have great sorrow that my wife is dead." Running Fox broke off the tip of the pipe, puffed twice, and turned to Noelle. "You are to be wife of Thunder Hawk? Will make beautiful grandchildren for Chief Running Fox. When you marry?"

Blushing at Running Fox's suggestion of children, Noelle glanced at Drake for help in answering the question. They hadn't discussed any plans for a wedding. A smile touched her lips as she recalled the wedding of her friend Flora Johnson whose father had held a Brown Bess aimed at her fiancé's head during the ceremony. Noelle wondered if Running Fox would do the same for her.

"Father, we cannot marry until the war is over," Drake explained and hoped that Noelle didn't notice the scarlet color he felt sure was creeping up his neck.

"White man have strange law. First take wife and son of Chief Running Fox. Then say son of Running Fox not marry while making war. Customs confuse Running Fox." The chief reached out to touch Noelle's hair. He puffed on the pipe once more and handed it back to Drake. "Son Soaring Eagle say woman of Thunder Hawk have hair of gold from sun. He say truth.

"Soaring Eagle also tell Chief Running Fox that brother of Crouching Deer dead." Running Fox shook his head sadly and grasped Drake's arm. "I cannot have sorrow for brother who take sister from happy home. I have sorrow for my son who love uncle in spite of evil doing."

Drake looked at his father and nodded. "I understand Chief Running Fox. But my uncle didn't know that my mother loved you until he took her to England. It was too late then."

"Now too late to bring back wife of Running Fox. Father of little golden girl friend of Running Fox." The old Indian smiled at Noelle. "Running Fox feel sorrow that golden girl's father has joined the spirits."

"Thank you, Chief Running Fox." Noelle felt the tears sting her eyes, but she blinked them back and smiled. Somewhere behind her, Mandy and Lard were whispering to each other. They were still afraid of the Cherokee.

"Time for Chief Running Fox take Soaring Eagle home. Soaring Eagle fight no more for Redcoats." Running Fox embraced Drake. "Dodge bullet well, my son."

When the Indians were gone, Noelle dropped onto the divan and hung her head. The shock of seeing Soaring Eagle had drained her, but the fact that he and Drake were brothers astounded her. No wonder Drake had been able to communicate so easily with Soaring Eagle.

"Why didn't you tell me?" she asked finally and glanced up at Drake, who stood at the door watching the Indians retreat to their side of the Tyger River.

He turned to study her face. She looked tired but still beautiful. "How could I? After I found him here, burning your house, could I have risked telling you that he was my brother? After he shot my aunt and uncle and burned their house, could I tell you? Even now I find it hard to talk to you about him."

"Drake, it isn't your fault." Noelle rose and rushed to his side. "You couldn't have prevented either event."

"Yes, I could have. When I saw you that night outside Ash Meadow, I could have remained to help you." Drake brushed her arms aside and strode to the fireplace. He tapped the pipe against a log and placed it in the rack with the others. "I could have stopped him if I'd been there."

Noelle closed her eyes to blot out the sight of his agony. Her heart almost split like the embers in the dying fire when she saw how much he ached for not staying that night. "You couldn't have known he would go there. Drake, for the sake of all that's good, you couldn't know that he would attack your uncle's home."

"Maybe not, but—"

"No. Don't torture yourself like this." Noelle turned to Mandy and Lard who were watching the entire scene from the doorway to the dining room. "Lard, go get Drake a glass of warm milk."

Now that they'd been noticed, Mandy took the opportunity to speak for the first time. "My baby goin' to git married to a Redcoat. Lawd have mercy. But he a good 'un. Dis been a revealin' night, Lawd, a revealin' night for ole Mandy."

Noelle watched as Mandy and Lard disappeared through the back door. Stooping to pick up Drake's new shirt, she tried to smile. "Now, it's off to bed with you. Go on. I'll make sure everything's locked up for the night."

Drake disappeared into Charles Arledge's bedroom. Noelle looked on, as tenderness welled up inside her. Grandchildren for Running Fox. Did she carry a grandson for him already?

CHAPTER
18

NOELLE WAITED UNTIL LARD BROUGHT DRAKE'S MILK, AND then she locked the back door. She poked her head into the bedroom to see if Drake had fallen asleep. His dark eyes were glittering in the flickering light supplied by a single candle.

"Here," she said and held the cup out to him. "Drink this."

Noelle waited while Drake sipped his milk. "I feel very foolish," he said.

She chuckled a little and sat down on the edge of the bed. "I think I know how you feel. I felt somewhat the same way after I flew into a rage over nothing. I mean, I didn't think it was nothing at the time, but in retrospect, I can see that it was. And one day you'll look back on this and realize you could have done nothing to prevent anyone's death."

"Maybe I'll look back and feel that way, but I don't right now. Everything is wrong. I seem to be fighting within myself more than with the enemy. And I don't know who the enemy is. It could be me."

"Not you, but the people who started this war." Noelle took his cup and put it on the dining room table. The ring in the bottom would be hard to wash out in the morning, but Noelle didn't want to walk out to the kitchen and rinse it now. Smiling, she glanced at the chessboard. Her last victory hadn't been cleared yet. She would look at it in the morning and remember the fun they had. All in all, this had been a Christmas Eve that they would talk about for a long time.

The embers in the fireplace hardly glimmered, but the night wasn't so cold that she wanted to keep a fire burning. Noelle blew out the candles in the sitting room and looked around.

Drake lay propped on the pillows and watched her as she puttered around, and for a moment she let herself pretend they were married and that within her grew his child. A cozy feeling of rightness pervaded the atmosphere, and Noelle almost feared speaking would break the spell.

She went into the closet beneath the stairs and removed her beautiful gown. The cramped space made changing clothes difficult, but she couldn't use the bedroom. As intimate as she and Drake had been, she still hid when she was naked.

Drake grew impatient. Noelle's sweet domesticity caused powerful feelings of possessiveness in him. He wanted to claim her as his own, to keep her within sight at all times. The next few months would be difficult, but he had no choice where she was concerned. Other choices had been made this day and in the past few days since his visit to Charleston and since the atrocities he'd seen and heard of. But he couldn't ask Noelle to be his wife.

Until now his part in this war had been dangerous. Now, it would become doubly so.

He watched Noelle come from the tiny closet. In her thin nightgown, she was even prettier than when she was dressed in her finery for dinner. She walked past the cradle at the foot of the bed and drew her hand across it as she passed.

Noelle rounded the bed and slipped between the covers. Her feet were freezing, and she tucked them up close to Drake.

"Watch it, woman," he exclaimed. "That's a hanging offense."

Noelle giggled and snuggled closer to him. "Do your worst, sir, but wait until my feet get warm first."

Lifting his head and shoulders, Drake blew out the candle. Then he drew Noelle into his arms. "I give you clemency this once."

"Drake," she whispered and toyed with the thatch of dark hair on his chest. "I wish this evening could last forever."

He crushed her to him and kissed her gently. "I wish I could grant you that wish, Noelle, but we don't know what tomorrow will bring in these uncertain times. Perhaps when the war is over . . ."

When Noelle awoke, Drake was not in the bed with her. The sun sent squares of light across the dark patches of her quilt. Where could he be? On the table by the bed she saw a glittering object and scooted over to see it better.

It was a ring. She picked it up and looked at it closely. She'd seen the ring once before—at Erin's party.

Noelle slipped the ring on her finger. An amethyst glimmered in the sunlight and twinkled gaily. A piece of paper lay folded on the table. With trembling fingers, she picked it up and read: "Dearest Noelle, This ring has belonged to my family for years. Wear it and think of me often. Every time I look at it, I see your eyes. Merry Christmas and happy birthday, darling Noelle. With love, Drake Hastings."

Clutching the ring to her heart, she threw back the covers and leapt from the bed. She'd forgotten that today was her birthday. Without bothering to change or put on shoes, Noelle ran to the kitchen.

Lard and Mandy were working over some tool that needed mending. When she burst into the room, both of them looked astonished.

Excusing himself, Lard almost fell out of his chair as he left the cabin. Mandy shook her head. "Chile, when you goin' learn to act like a lady?"

"Where's Drake? When I got up, he was gone." Noelle

hurried to the window and looked out, but saw nobody other than Lard. "Did you see him? He didn't say good-bye."

"That man left this mornin' at the crack of dawn." Mandy shook her head. "For two book-learned folks, you two sure is a passel of foolish."

"What do you mean he left? Is he coming back? What did he say?" Questions tumbled out of Noelle's mouth, one on top of the other. "Where did he go?"

"Hold on, chile, you gonna git yourself in a misery." Mandy moved to Noelle's side. "You jus' march back to your room and git on your clothes. Then I tell you everthing he say."

Noelle knew that Mandy wouldn't change her mind, so she raced back to change. In the closet, she paused a moment to finger the soft silk of her blue gown. She was glad she had chosen to wear it last night.

Mandy had washed and ironed several of Noelle's winter dresses, so she put one on. Since today would be a workday for her, she put on a cotton chemise and pulled the back hem through her legs to tuck under the cord at the waist in front. She found an indigo wool petticoat skirt, drew it down over her head to rest on her hips, and tied the bands in back. A red jacket for day wear seemed appropriate and was handy, so she put it on and laced it with shaking fingers.

When she was finally dressed, she pulled on cotton stockings and tied the garters above the knee. Everything seemed to be taking away her precious time. She wanted to catch Drake and tell him good-bye. She had to see him before he got too far away.

Without bothering to buckle her shoes, she scampered back to the kitchen. Mandy had put a cup of coffee and a small bowl of hominy on the small table, but Noelle paid little attention to them. "Now, where is he?"

"Chile, that man done left to go back to the war. He say for you don't to worry. He be back when he can." Mandy shook her head gravely. "He shoulda stayed here with us."

The words sank in. Drake had really left without saying

good-bye. Maybe he thought it would be easier on her, but she couldn't let him get away before she told him she loved him. The words sang out in her mind as she stumbled toward the door. "Oh, fiddle," she grumbled and sat down to buckle her shoes before she tripped on them.

"I'll be back soon," she called as she hurried out the door.

"You come back here. Where you goin' without your breakfast? I says for you to come back." Mandy shook her head and went back into the kitchen.

Noelle found Sunshine in the barn. "Lard, saddle Sunshine."

"Where you goin' this early?" Lard asked and rose to do her bidding.

"I'm going after Drake. Now, hurry," Noelle urged and paced back and forth.

When Lard was done, he helped her into the saddle. "I'm goin' take the mule and ride with you. You ain't got no business ridin' 'round the country by yourself with a war a goin' on."

"No time. Stay with Mandy." Noelle flicked the reins, and Sunshine cantered out of the barn. When they reached open ground, Noelle coaxed the filly into a gallop. She had no time to lose.

When Noelle arrived at the end of the drive, she hesitated. Which way would he have gone? She noticed fresh scars on the hard mud of Blackstock Road and decided they must be from Nightmare's hooves.

She and Sunshine followed them. In some places, she couldn't see the tracks at all. In others, they were very clear. Then she lost them altogether. After riding back and forth along the road, Noelle finally gave up and returned to Tyger Rest.

The New Year came in uneventfully for Noelle. She sat up most of the night, waiting for Drake to return. She knew now that she didn't carry his child, but she felt the need to be near him. Dawn found her slumped against the arm of the divan.

Two weeks passed, and Drake didn't come back. Noelle began to worry about him. Every day she wandered around the grounds of Tyger Rest, looking for signs of him but found nothing.

One day she did find Kathleen Foster's brother, Geoffrey. "What are you doing here? I thought you were in Virginia."

"I was looking for Father. I'm going to join Daniel Morgan and his men. They're running north from Tarleton and should reach the Broad River within a few days." Geoffrey looked at her and smiled. "You sure are a pretty sight."

Noelle felt her heart go out to him. He'd come looking for his parents and found their plantation deserted. "Kathleen was here in the fall. She told me that she and your mother were going to Ninety Six because of all the Indian raids."

"Oh, that's where they are." Geoffrey nodded and sighed. "Well, I guess I'm out of luck."

"How about a hot meal before you go?" Noelle offered. When he agreed, they rode side by side back to Tyger Rest.

He told her what he'd witnessed and described Tarleton's heinous rein of terror over the South Carolina countryside. "Oh, did you hear about Benedict Arnold?"

"No, who's he?" she asked as they rode past the crepe myrtles.

"He was the commandant at West Point." Geoffrey shook his head gravely. "That bas . . . sorry. That man is now a brigadier general with the British. He's been leading attacks around the James River in Virginia. I heard he captured Richmond."

"No! That traitor." Noelle was appalled that a Patriot could do such a thing to his own country. Then she remembered. That was exactly what she wished Drake would do!

Geoffrey could stay only long enough to eat. Noelle

watched him leave and felt a tremendous burden from the news he'd brought.

Another two days came and went. By this time, Noelle could stand the confines of her plantation no longer. She decided to go to Ash Meadow to see if any of the Brookses' servants had returned.

She found Lard feeding the cow. "Saddle Sunshine for me. I need to ride over to Ash Meadow."

"No'm, you ain't goin' over there by yourself." Lard placed the saddle on the filly's back and turned to Noelle. "I'm goin' with you."

"Lard, stay here with Mandy. You know how skittish she is when she's alone. I'll be fine." Noelle mounted Sunshine. "Don't worry about me."

She rode out to Blackstock Road and turned east. Cantering along at a pleasant pace, she spotted the hoofprints of another horse. Nobody rode here anymore. There was nobody left to ride this far northwest.

"It must be Drake!" she exclaimed aloud and prodded Sunshine on. "Hurry, girl." The horse was headed toward Ash Meadow.

Noelle knew a shortcut. Her favorite path to Kathleen's led across Tyger Rest and through Ash Meadow.

Across the fields they went. The path was strewn with rocks and shrubs, but Noelle urged Sunshine on. In no time, she had crossed the creek that fed into the Tyger. At the top of the bank, she heard something and stopped, thinking it might be Drake. As she dismounted, she felt a surge of anticipation and recalled being in his arms and his loving her, warming every part of her. She tied Sunshine to a low-hanging tree limb and hurried along the path by the creek.

Noelle saw Drake standing some distance away. Nightmare was drinking from the stream. Noelle was about to call out when a man in a green jacket appeared. She hesitated. What was a Tory doing here at Ash Meadow? Why was Drake talking to him so urgently?

He was a British officer, she reminded herself, but she felt like a scorned woman. She had believed that if Drake really loved her, he would find the first Patriot encampment and join it. Her reasoning became cloudy. Did that mean if she loved Drake, she would convert to the Loyalist point of view? Why did life have to be so difficult?

Noelle watched the two men walk away, Drake leading Nightmare by the reins. They were headed in the direction from which she'd just come. She couldn't risk being seen.

A thought jarred her. Why couldn't she relay this information to Dan Morgan? He and his troops were in the area.

Waiting until the two men were out of sight, Noelle felt the agony of her discovery in full. No matter what happened between them, Drake was a British soldier and she was a Patriot. What common ground could bring the two together?

Where did her duty lie? To her country? To Drake? She glanced at the ring on her finger, and tears formed in her eyes. Drake had given her the ring as a gift and had signed the note "with love."

Slowly she walked back to Sunshine.

Without returning home, Noelle rode for Morgan's camp. She wasn't sure exactly where it was, nor was she prepared to make the journey, but she had to try. After riding for hours, she came upon what she thought was Morgan's encampment.

Hurrying to convey her message, she soon found herself in the middle of a British encampment. Everywhere the green of Tories surrounded her.

"Stop, miss," an officer commanded. "What are you doing here?"

"I'm sure it's none of your business." Noelle tried to move on, but the man grabbed Sunshine's reins.

"Not so fast, miss." He reached up and pulled Noelle from her saddle. Turning to another man, he yelled, "Put the horse with the others."

Noelle squirmed and wiggled to free herself. "How dare you?" she screamed. Everywhere men turned to stare at her. Would nobody come to her rescue?

An officer stepped from a cabin. His bright red hair curled across his forehead, and he stared at her with questioning eyes. After a moment he snapped, "Bring the girl to me."

The soldier who held her now half dragged the kicking and squirming Noelle to the cabin. She fought to keep from going into the cabin, but the officer reached out and jerked her inside. "Find a rope, Sergeant."

Noelle stood and faced her captor. His face was long and narrow, quite unattractive, and his nose was crooked. "I demand that you release me at once."

The officer laughed. "And why should I do that?"

He took the rope from the sergeant's hand and dismissed the soldier immediately. He stared directly at Noelle as he crossed the room and stopped in front of her.

Noelle's eyes widened with fright as the officer approached her. Backing away, she lifted her chin in defiance. "Who are you?"

"I am Major Banastre Tarleton," he replied and grabbed her hand. "Now, if you will cooperate, this will be easier for all of us."

Banastre Tarleton! The name conjured images of horror in Noelle's mind as she recalled the tales told in gory detail by the soldiers who had visited Erin's house. None of the stories were pretty. All told of his butchery. In fact, his own men referred to him as the Butcher.

Finding her voice, Noelle asked, "What do you want with me?"

"Information, my dear."

Tarleton wrapped the rope around her wrists so tightly that Noelle knew the circulation would be cut off. When he was satisfied with his work, he pushed her down into a chair and bound her to it.

"You can't do this to me." Noelle tried to wriggle free, but her bonds were too secure.

"Oh? I not only can do it to you, I have." Tarleton settled into a chair behind a table and stared at her.

Noelle refused to avert her eyes. She realized that he was trying to intimidate her. She lashed out with her only weapon—words. "Does it give you pleasure to bind young women who happen into your camp?"

"Many things give me pleasure, Miss . . ." He continued to stare at her, eyes narrowing to slits. "What is your name?"

"Why should I tell you anything?" she asked with more courage than she felt.

"Because if you don't tell me what I wish to know, I have ways of making you talk." He stood and rounded the table. Once more in front of her, he leaned against the heavy wooden surface. "Now, tell me who you are."

"Never." Noelle lifted her chin and glared back at him. She could be as difficult to deal with as he made her. His green jacket signified his Tory affiliation, his Green Jacket Brigade as they were called. To her, the green signified a challenge. He'd never find out anything from her. "We seem to be at a stalemate, Major."

He arched his eyebrows as if intrigued by her assessment of the situation. "In a stalemate there is no victor. I can assure you that this game will see me as the winner. Your defeat can be as easy or as difficult as you choose, but I remind you that I am a soldier. I make my decisions as a soldier. The fact that you are a woman is of no concern to me."

"I have no reason to tell you anything," Noelle said defiantly. "Untie me and let me go."

"Dreadfully sorry. That is not going to happen." He stood up and strode over to her. Looking down at her with a strange gleam in his eyes, he demanded, "Tell me who you are this instant or you will regret your decision."

Fear welled up inside Noelle, but she closed her lips and

continued to stare at him. Her hands were growing numb, but she couldn't allow him to bully her.

"So you continue to play the martyr, eh? So be it," he said and moved closer still. Leaning down, he stared directly into her eyes.

Noelle could smell the foulness of his breath and turned her face away from his. Nothing could have prepared her for his next move.

With a ferocity matched only by his reputation, Tarleton slapped her across the cheek. "Tell me who you are before I become angry."

Her cheek stung and ached, and Noelle's chin touched her chest as she bowed her head. Her eyes stung, but she bit her lip to prevent the tears from falling. Nobody had ever struck her in the face before. Summoning her courage, she faced him again. "Beat me if you will, but I'll never tell you anything. I'm an innocent woman who entered your camp unwittingly. You may kill me for it, but I won't answer your questions."

Fury registered in his eyes. Tarleton struck her chair so hard that it fell over. "You will talk, or I'll kill you," he screamed. "You're a spy, and I know it. You'll tell me where you're headed and why."

Noelle's vision grew fuzzy. Her head had struck the wall as she fell, and a knot rose on her forehead. She began to wonder how long she could endure such abuse.

"Major, I heard you had captured a young woman. As I have been scouting the area, I might be able to help you—"

Through the haze of her disorientation, Noelle thought she recognized Drake's voice. Her eyes refused to focus clearly, but from her vantage point on the floor she could see that the newcomer wore a red jacket.

"Yes, yes, tell me who she is and then get out." Tarleton clenched his fists in anger. "She refuses to talk, but she's a spy. I know it. I feel it. Have your say and get out so I can complete my interrogation."

Drake righted the chair and gazed into Noelle's eyes.

Only rigid discipline kept him from turning and shooting Tarleton between the eyes. Leveling his gaze at Tarleton, he declared, "This is Noelle Arledge, my fiancée."

Tarleton's eyes grew large as he glanced from Drake to Noelle. Disbelief flickered across his face, but Drake knew the bastard dared not question him. "She is no spy. I've stayed at her plantation on many occasions as I passed through the area. You, sir, are gravely mistaken."

"Mistaken? Never." Tarleton pounded on the desk and returned to his seat. "How is it I've heard nothing of your engagement?"

"The engagement was made official only recently. My uncle, John Brooks, lived near Miss Arledge. We were acquainted through him." Drake glanced back at Noelle to assure himself that she wasn't badly injured. He would find a way to deal with Tarleton later, but for now Drake had to appear to be a reasonable, loyal British officer. "As her guardian, he gave us his blessing shortly before his death."

"Get rid of her, then. Take her from my sight." Tarleton spat the words in disgust.

"Sir, I request permission to take her home. She lives on a plantation on the Tyger River. It's not too far and—"

"Permission denied. Put her on her horse and be thankful I don't confiscate the animal." Tarleton slapped the table and glared at Drake. "Get her out of here before I change my mind."

Drake untied her and helped her to stand. Hatred bubbled in him like oil in a cauldron, but he kept his counsel. He could do no good if he was court-martialed for killing Major Tarleton.

Drake lifted Noelle into his arms and carried her out to the corral. "Noelle, are you badly injured? If you are, give me time to kill that bastard and then—"

"No, Drake, you mustn't. I . . . I'll be fine. I'm just bruised, I think." Feeling as weak as poor-man's tea, Noelle clung to him and sighed. Somehow she would find a way to get even with Tarleton. She just didn't know how. "Oh,

Drake, I wanted to say . . . to thank you for the ring. And thank you for rescuing me. It seems that's all you have time to do."

"It's the most joyful task I ever had. I'm dreadfully sorry I was too late to prevent . . . That bastard, Noelle, I swear to you—"

"No, don't swear. Don't think it. When will you come to Tyger Rest again?" she asked and snuggled more closely into his embrace.

"I cannot say, but I'll be back as soon as I can." With a good-bye kiss, Drake lifted her as gently as possible into the saddle. "Go straight home and take care of those bruises. I can't protect you if he finds you wandering about again."

Noelle merely nodded. She couldn't lie to Drake, but she had to find General Daniel Morgan and tell him that Tarleton was on his heels.

Somehow she summoned the strength to urge Sunshine into a gallop. She headed west for a while in case she was being followed and then circled back around Tarleton's camp. From Geoffrey's information, she knew that Morgan and his men were somewhere along the Broad River near Cowpens.

Charles Arledge had often spoken of Daniel Morgan, the Old Waggoner, the great general, who because of political differences had resigned his commission early in the war. After Charleston fell, he'd resumed his post and now commanded his own company.

Noelle knew that if she could find Morgan, she could warn him and perhaps prevent a slaughter by the superior strength of Tarleton's forces. But she had to get past Tarleton first.

CHAPTER
19

NOELLE VOWED TO EXERCISE MORE CAUTION WHEN SHE approached an encampment of men. Her whole head ached now as a result of Tarleton's abuse, and she understood the epithets attached to the officer's name.

The weight of her task rode heavily on her. In doing her duty to her country, she was condemning Drake. Her information concerning Tarleton's whereabouts might prove fatal to the man she loved. Noelle felt the tears drizzling down her cheeks, leaving cold trails to be chapped by the wind, but nothing could make her shirk her duty. She had to stop thinking of Drake and do what she'd come to do.

Nearing the area where Geoffrey had said that Morgan and his men would be, Noelle slowed down. She dismounted and walked Sunshine into the camp.

A young man dressed in buckskin stopped her as she neared Thicketty Creek, barring her path with his gun. "Halt, miss. What business have you in this area?"

She didn't know him. Noelle knew that if she had, her chances of meeting with Daniel Morgan would have been better. "I've come to see General Morgan."

"And why would General Morgan want to see you?" the youth asked. "He's a busy man with that butcher Tarleton on our trail."

"That's exactly why I want to see him." Noelle wondered what she could say that would convince this man to let her pass. "Do you know Geoffrey Foster? From over at the Tyger River?"

"Seems I know him. Black hair? About five feet seven?" the young man asked and regarded Noelle oddly.

"No. Geoffrey has red hair, as red as the uniforms worn by the British, as red as that butcher Tarleton's. And he's six feet tall at least." Noelle was exasperated. This young man didn't seem to know Geoffrey at all. Perhaps he knew another Geoffrey Foster. "His sister, Kathleen, is my best friend."

"Yes, sir, that's Geoff all right." The young man grinned and relaxed. "Sorry, miss, just doin' my duty."

"Please, my message is urgent." Noelle tried to persuade the guard to take her to Morgan right away.

"Colonel Pickens just rode in. I doubt Morgan's goin' to want to talk to you." The young man looked as if he didn't know what to do.

"Look, I take full responsibility. Do you want to lose a battle because you refused to allow vital information to get through? Do you want that on your head?"

"Well, bein' as you put it that way, I'll take you and see what he says." The young man led the way into the camp.

Noelle followed, leading Sunshine through the crowded and bustling campgrounds of the Cowpens. Something was clearly about to happen, and Noelle felt that she was contributing to the success of the upcoming campaign.

The young man stopped outside a tent. "Wait here, miss. I'll see if General Morgan will hear your tale."

The young man was gone no more than a few minutes. When he returned, he said, "The general's busy, but if you can wait, he'll see you."

Nodding, Noelle sat down on the ground, since there was nothing else to sit on. She watched as the men built fires and prepared their noon meal.

Finally the tent flap opened and a soldier called, "Miss?"

"Yes." She jumped up and dusted off her skirt. "Here I am."

"Come in." He held the flap open for her.

Noelle entered the large tent and found herself in the

presence of several officers. The young officer introduced them as General Morgan, Colonel Pickens, and Colonel William Washington, a cousin of George Washington.

General Morgan said, "I understand you have some news for me."

"Yes, General Morgan, I do. My name is Noelle Arledge." When her name made no impression, she added, "Daughter of Charles Arledge of Tyger Rest."

"Ah, yes." The general nodded. "Continue."

"Sir, I was captured by a Tory and taken to Tarleton's encampment."

Concern registered on the three men's faces simultaneously. General Morgan stepped forward. "Please sit down, Miss Arledge."

Noelle sat in the chair he indicated and realized how exhausted she was. "As you can see, sir, I fared poorly with Colonel Tarleton."

"He deserves every vile name he's called." Colonel Pickens slammed his hand on the table.

"I agree." Noelle tried to smile, but her cheeks hurt. "He's just over the Pacolet River."

"That close?" Morgan looked from Pickens to Washington. "Anything else, Miss Arledge?"

"No, sir, I guess not," Noelle admitted. "Tarleton isn't the sort of man to discuss military secrets with a woman he beat and accused of being a spy."

"Then we thank you for your courage. I apologize for not having a man to spare to escort you home." Morgan stood. "How is your father?"

"He passed away last summer, sir." Noelle tried once again to smile. She was glad General Morgan remembered her father. It made her story more credible. "Good-bye, sir."

Noelle left the tent. The young man who had invited her into the tent escorted her to the edge of the encampment. As she was about to mount Sunshine, a disturbance attracted her attention. She turned to see a British officer being thrust into Morgan's tent. The officer was Drake.

"Uh, I forgot something." Noelle turned and ran back toward Morgan's tent. The officer caught her before she could get inside.

"Sorry, miss. We have a prisoner to interrogate." He gripped her arm and pulled her back toward her horse.

"Interrogate?" Noelle remembered her interrogation and shuddered. She had to stop Morgan before he could hurt Drake. At risk of being branded a British spy, she kicked the young officer in the shin and raced back to the tent.

Glancing over her shoulder, she noticed the man close on her heels. Running with all her power, she almost fell through the flaps of the tent. "Stop!" she yelled, hoping to prevent any harm befalling Drake.

She looked at him. His bruised face had several shallow cuts, and his hands were bound. "No. Oh, Drake, I'm so sorry."

"Miss Arledge, I presume you're acquainted with this man." General Morgan moved to her side.

"Yes, I am, sir." Noelle didn't know what to tell the general. She knew whatever she told him had to be convincing. "This is the man I was going after when I was captured by Tarleton," she said.

Morgan gazed at Drake. "Captain, what is your interest in this young lady?"

Noelle thought as fast as she could. "We are betrothed, sir."

"Is that right, Captain Hastings?" Morgan asked Drake.

"Sir, if the lady says we're engaged, we're engaged," Drake answered and gazed at Noelle. He could see that she was trying her best to rescue him as he had rescued her. Smiling at the irony, he continued, "And I'm proud of it."

This time Noelle did smile. She put her arms around Drake and tried to comfort him. "Please, sir, release him. I'm sure he wasn't spying. He was looking for me, to see if

I sustained any injury at the hands of Tarleton. He's innocent."

Noelle hoped that Morgan couldn't tell she was lying. Drake Hastings had been in the area far too long to be innocent of spying charges, but Noelle couldn't let him hang no matter what he'd done. "I'll vouch for his character, sir."

"You must be some man, Hastings, to have this lovely girl begging us to spare your life. What do you say to that?" Morgan asked and smiled a little.

Suddenly hating Morgan for toying with her, she stepped between him and Drake. "I've told you he's innocent, sir. I have one other thing to say. You must let him go. I may be carrying his child."

Morgan stared at Noelle as if to ascertain the truth of her words. "That's quite a charge. Perhaps we should hang him for trifling with the affections of one of our fair maidens."

At Noelle's stricken expression, Morgan bellowed with laughter. "I'm sorry, my dear. I apologize for having a bit of fun at your expense."

"Fun? Is this what you call fun?" Noelle pointed to the bruises and cuts on Drake's face.

"Noelle, don't—"

"Drake, leave me alone. I want an answer to my question." She planted her hands on her hips in anger. "I never thought the Old Waggoner would stoop so low as to—"

"Miss Arledge, I assure you that I didn't do this." Morgan motioned for her to sit down. When she refused, he continued, "Captain Hastings is indeed a spy. We have irrefutable evidence of that fact. He is *our* spy."

Noelle dropped into the chair next to Drake. "*Our* spy, sir? I don't understand."

"After Captain Hastings returned from Charleston, he came to my encampment and confessed that he'd seen more than he could take as a loyal subject of the king. He asked if I would accept him as a soldier under my command," Morgan explained.

Whirling around, she stared at Drake in disbelief. "Why didn't you tell me?"

"Miss Arledge, as you well know, an officer is not allowed to divulge information to civilians, regardless of their, er, relationship." Pickens stepped forward and touched her shoulder. "And, miss, if you are with child, I suggest you return home immediately to await that event."

Drake stared at her. Could she be expecting his child? Physically, she could, but was she? He found the thought intriguing. "Noelle—"

"No, Colonel Pickens, I . . . I made that up to help persuade General Morgan to free Drake," Noelle confessed.

"Well, that's a mercy," declared Morgan. "Colonel Hastings, I suggest we untie you so you can escort this young lady home."

"Colonel?" Noelle repeated.

"In the Continental army, he is Colonel Hastings." Morgan moved around the table again.

Washington untied Drake. He stood and wrung his wrists to revive the circulation. "Thank you, sir."

Noelle looked from Morgan to Drake. Both men were inches taller than Pickens and Washington, and nearly a foot taller than Noelle.

Feeling happy with herself for doing the right thing, Noelle strode purposefully alongside Drake as they moved toward the corral. "Drake, I'm sorry if I embarrassed you. I thought I was doing the right thing."

"You were, Noelle. And you didn't embarrass me. I thought you'd ridden to safety." Drake remembered the moment of joy he'd experienced when he thought that she might be telling the truth about carrying his child. He glanced at her. "You are not with child?"

Noelle looked up at him. "I said I wasn't."

"Were you saying that to save yourself embarrassment, or is it true?" Drake asked, half hoping that she had lied to protect her reputation. He rather enjoyed the idea of having a child.

"I assure you I am not with child," Noelle stated flatly. "Do not concern yourself."

Drake nodded, vaguely disappointed. They reached the corral, and a young sergeant found their mounts. "We need to be as quick as possible. I must return."

Noelle's heart swelled with pride. She'd wanted Drake to convert to the Patriot side all along, and he'd done just that. "I'm delighted that you have seen the right of the matter."

Laughing, Drake led the way from the encampment. By the time they reached Tyger Rest, the sun was down.

"I must return immediately, Noelle." Drake held her close for a few seconds and then looked down at her. "I don't know when I'll be able to return. After this night's work . . . I don't know."

With a kiss that seemed almost chaste after their intimacy, Drake rode away, leaving Noelle standing on the veranda of Tyger Rest. She watched until he disappeared at the end of the boxwoods and crepe myrtles.

"Too bad he hasn't a good luck charm," Noelle murmured as she entered the house and dropped onto the divan. He would need one tomorrow. If Tarleton saw him at Morgan's encampment, nothing would stop that butcher from killing Drake.

Feeling dusty and dirty, Noelle removed the pins from her hair and twisted it between her fingers. She went into the bedroom and started to brush out the tangles. "He really needs a good luck charm. What better than a lock of his true love's hair?"

She found a pair of scissors and clipped a curl to give to him. Next she found a locket her father had given her mother and put the lock of hair inside it.

Noelle poked her good luck charm in her pocket and ran out the back door. "Mandy! Lard! Saddle up Sunshine."

Lard peeked out of the blacksmith shop and stared at Noelle. "Where you fixin' to go this late in the evenin'?"

"I've got to catch Drake," she explained and hurried into the barn. "I have something to give him."

Riding as quickly as she could in spite of the briars catching at her, Noelle finally reached the creek. The steep bank forced her to dismount and walk Sunshine down. As she started up the other side, she heard voices.

She stopped and listened. Nobody should be here at this time of night, or at all for that matter. Noelle tied Sunshine's reins to a limb and crept along the bank toward the voices.

When she could hear what was being said, she stopped. After a few minutes, she knew that one of the men was Drake, so she listened more carefully and peered around the stone she hid behind.

"That's right. Tell Tarleton that Morgan's men are encamped at the Cowpens. If he marches early, he can catch them before they cross the Broad River." Drake mounted his horse and looked down at the other man.

Noelle sank down into the sand by the boulder. Drake had fooled them all. Her heart ached with the agony of knowing that she loved a traitor. Hours ago she'd thought he had pledged his loyalty to the Patriots. Now it seemed that his sudden conversion was merely a ruse to entrap Morgan's army, and she had encouraged the general to believe Drake's story.

If Morgan's men lost the battle that was sure to ensue, it would be her fault. Never, she thought angrily and stood up. Drake Hastings was a fine-talking man, but he wouldn't outsmart this country girl.

Hurrying as fast as she could without making a lot of noise, Noelle returned to Sunshine. Somehow she had to reach Morgan's encampment again without causing Drake to suspect her. It would be early morning by the time she arrived, but she didn't care. She was surprising even herself with her impulsive behavior!

Sunshine cantered along with Noelle holding her back. The filly sensed Noelle's excitement and tried to gallop, but Noelle refused to allow her free rein. She couldn't allow herself to catch up with Drake, but she wanted to arrive at the Cowpens minutes after he did.

Tears refused to fall, even though Noelle wanted to shed tears for her loss and for her vulnerability. Had he intentionally cultivated her friendship and then her love, hoping to cause an incident such as this? Was she to be his alibi all along?

Questions bombarded Noelle's mind until she felt like holding her hands against her temples and crying, "No more, please, no more."

She hung back, knowing what a good scout Drake was. To be caught now would prove disastrous—for her and for the Patriots. Noelle thought the seventeen miles or so would never pass before morning, but they did. The wee hours of January 17 were cold and damp, but the temperature didn't compare to her frozen heart.

When she reached the spot where the young officer had accosted her on her previous visit, she hesitated. Would she be stopped again? She was. This time, however, the sentry was a friend. Geoffrey Foster challenged her right to enter the compound.

"Geoff, it's me, Noelle Arledge," she whispered for fear that Drake might be near. She didn't know where he would have gone when he entered camp.

"Noelle?" Geoff asked, squinting to see her in the dim light. "Is that really you?"

"Yes, take me to General Morgan immediately," she instructed him.

"I can't do that. Anybody not attached to one of our units must be taken to Colonel Hastings before being given the freedom to enter." Geoff didn't move.

Noelle had thought Geoff would let her pass because he knew her. She was wrong, but she had to persuade him not to take her to Drake. Understandably, Morgan had put Drake in charge of admitting strangers because he could point out Loyalists posing as Patriots. Noelle glared at Geoff. "Geoff Foster, if you don't take me to Morgan this instant, I'm going to jerk that rifle from your arms and beat you over the head with it. I came here once before to speak with him, and I insist that you escort me there now."

Geoff hesitated. "Disobeying orders is a hanging offense, Noelle. I can't—"

"Geoff, this is a matter of life and death—yours as well as everyone else's. Take me now," Noelle demanded and grabbed his arm. Studying her carefully, Geoff handed the reins of her horse to a young soldier.

Apparently her message sank in, for Geoff led the way. Noelle could have gone herself, but she didn't want to rouse suspicion. She realized that there were camp followers who were allowed to roam about the camp, but she didn't want the soldiers to think she was one of them.

When they reached Morgan's tent, Noelle paused. Would Morgan believe her story after all the things she'd said during her previous visit? They knew she would lie for Drake. Would they believe she could also lie *about* him?

Noelle decided she'd just have to try. In spite of Geoff's attempt to stop her, she marched straight into the tent. Drake was seated across the table from Morgan, while Washington and Pickens sat on opposite ends.

They all looked up when she walked in. Drake jumped to his feet, as did the others. "Noelle!" he exclaimed, rushing around the table to her side. "What are you doing here?"

She glared at him a moment and with a chill in her voice that rivaled that of the early morning hours, said, "I'm here to see General Morgan, and I wish to see him in private."

"What is the meaning of this?" Morgan asked.

"General, I need to speak with you. It's a matter of life and death." She ignored the puzzled look on Drake's face and moved closer to Morgan. "Please don't deny me this request. I need but a minute of your time."

"Miss Arledge, we're in the middle of a planning session! One of our riders has just arrived with the news that Tarleton began his march at three o'clock this morning. I haven't time to play games with you." Morgan appeared to be upset. He returned to his chair. "You may speak to all of us or none."

Noelle didn't know if she could tell him her news with Drake in the tent, but she had no choice. Closing her heart to the pain she felt, she began. "General, when I was here earlier, I pled for Colonel Hasting's life. I'm here to tell you that I did so in error."

"Noelle!" Drake cried, taking her arm. "What are you saying?"

"Yes, Miss Arledge, tell us what you mean." Pickens sat down, clearly confused by her words.

"After Drake escorted me home, I decided to give him a good luck charm." Noelle glanced at each of the men to gauge their reaction. "A lock of hair."

She reached into her pocket and pulled out the locket. "You see? I rode after him to give him the charm. Knowing how quickly he rides, I took a path through the woods and thought to catch up with him."

Drake looked at her, confusion written across his face. Noelle averted her eyes. "Anyway, I heard someone talking and stopped to see who it could be. It was Drake and one of Tarleton's dragoons. Drake told the man everything."

Morgan smiled and nodded. "Now, Miss Arledge, you don't understand the complexities of war and–"

"I understand when military secrets are being given to the enemy. I heard him clearly. There is no mistake." Noelle inhaled deeply and closed her eyes for a few seconds. Her next words would seal Drake's fate. "Drake Hastings is a traitor. He has betrayed all of us to Tarleton."

Morgan gazed at Drake for a moment. "Colonel Hastings, is Miss Arledge's information accurate?"

Drake glanced at Noelle and then back at General Morgan. "Yes, sir, it is."

"You told this man all of our plans, as she stated?" Morgan questioned, nodding his head slightly as if understanding had begun to permeate his mind.

"Yes, sir, I did," Drake admitted without flinching.

"I see. Under whose orders did you report this information to Tarleton's man?" came the final question that would reveal all.

"Yours, sir," Drake confessed.

"His?" Noelle sat in the empty seat she'd used earlier. "You expect us to believe—"

"He's telling the truth, Miss Arledge," Morgan conceded with a smile. "Sometimes if your enemy knows your plans, it's much easier to trap him."

"I don't understand, sir." Noelle shook her head. Once again she had bumbled into a situation that was beyond her.

"If we know what Tarleton is expecting us to do, we can predict what he will do to compensate. Therefore we can plan against such an attack," Morgan explained and rose again. "And now, Miss Arledge. I'm going to send Colonel Hastings with you to a safe place. He may not remain with you. I presume that eventually you two will draw some conclusions about your future, but for now we have a war to tend to!"

Noelle and Drake walked to a tent near the back of the encampment. "Drake, I'm really sorry. I know war is serious business. I shouldn't have meddled where I didn't belong."

Drake shook his head in exasperation. "I suppose it's something I'll get used to."

He held the flap of the tent open, and they went inside. This tent was much smaller than Morgan's, and Drake had to bend over. They sat down on a blanket.

"I'm such a fool." Noelle hung her head, ashamed of the accusations she'd made and her unladylike impetuous behavior. But she was more ashamed of not trusting Drake.

"Noelle, I have to return to the strategy meeting. *Stay here*, especially when the battle begins." He held her close for a minute and then returned to his men.

CHAPTER
20

NOELLE WAITED FOR HOURS, IT SEEMED, BEFORE THE BATTLE began. She heard the sound of horses before they ever reached the encampment, and she stepped outside the tent. From her vantage point on a slight incline, she could see some of the action. She never expected to be so close to the fighting!

She saw Pickens place some riflemen about one hundred fifty yards ahead of the Virginia Continentals. Washington deployed his men flanking the Green River Road. Morgan stood within sight of his men, watching the battle instead of retiring to his tent. Noelle realized that Morgan knew the value of his presence to his men and capitalized on that knowledge.

The fighting began. Noelle watched the Carolina militiamen fire. Each man fired two or three shots and then ran. Oh, no, she thought as she watched the men in buckskin turn and race toward Colonel Howard's Continentals. They were running away. She almost couldn't look. The battle plan was obviously falling apart. A second row of riflemen did the same thing.

Noelle began to watch more closely. Tarleton's men charged ahead after the fleeing riflemen. A third row of sharpshooters fired three shots and dropped back. Now she understood. Morgan had told them to do so. Unsure of their ability to withstand a bayonet charge, Morgan had given them the task of firing three shots and retreating. Tarleton's men, unaware of this strategy, sensed an easy victory and gave eager chase. Washington's men swarmed in behind and around Tarleton's superior force. The Tories were surrounded.

Many of the Loyalists lay dead or injured on the battlefield. Noelle tried to determine who was winning. Easily, the Patriot forces were outwitting Tarleton's men, and few Patriots lay dead on the field.

Noelle felt buoyed by her observations. Morgan's men were going to win quickly. Washington had somehow gotten about thirty yards ahead of his men and was fighting with a sword against Tarleton, his red hair easily visible. Washington was surrounded. Biting her knuckles, she kept her eye on him as he fought bravely. When she thought he could fight no longer, a small slave fired a pistol and saved Colonel Washington's life.

Sensing victory, Noelle began to run. She didn't know where Drake was, but she wanted to be at Morgan's side when he declared victory. When she arrived at his tent, Morgan grinned at her and shook his head slightly. He reached down and picked up his young drummer, a boy of about nine, and kissed him on both cheeks.

Morgan's men were rounding up the prisoners. Some of the Continentals yelled, "Give them Tarleton's quarter."

Noelle sobered. They referred to Tarleton's battle at Waxhaw, where many regulars and Continentals were slaughtered after surrendering. She saw Morgan ride into the unit and prevent a massacre from occurring.

Two doctors moved from soldier to soldier, giving what aid they could to men of both sides. Many men were dead, mostly British, but the victory had been won. Noelle smiled with pride to know that the Americans were more humane toward injured prisoners than the British.

When Drake returned, he picked Noelle up and swung her around.

"Victory is all the sweeter." He hugged her close and kissed her. "Tarleton is furious, but he's gone. Pickens and

Washington are giving chase. I believe Washington sliced off several of Tarleton's fingers."

On the journey back to Tyger Rest, Noelle rode silently. She knew that Morgan's men were heading into North Carolina and that Drake would have to join them. Fear gripped her. She knew of Tarleton's vengeful mind. How far would he go?

When they arrived at Tyger Rest once again, Lard and Mandy ran to meet them, and both spoke at once. "Where you been?" "How come you didn't come home?"

"I had to go to Cowpens," Noelle answered and linked arms with Drake. "Lard, Mandy, I'd like you to meet Colonel Drake Hastings of Morgan's men. He's no longer in the king's army."

After fielding questions, Noelle and Drake retired to the house. Soon Drake would have to leave, and Noelle wanted to discuss their future. She had realized that part of Drake's reluctance to make a commitment was due to his participation in the war. How could she explain her feelings to him?

Snuggled into the crook of his arm before the fireplace, she rested her head on his shoulder and dreamed of days when he wouldn't have to leave her. "Drake, will you come back?"

Astonished by her question, Drake gazed down at her. "Will I come back? How can you ask such a question? Have I not returned every time I promised?"

"Yes, but . . ." Noelle couldn't voice her reservations and fears. Raising her head to look at him, she wondered if he understood how she felt. After all they'd been through together, Drake should know her as well as he knew himself.

He knew what she was asking and what she wanted to hear. He'd vowed not to make a commitment until this war was over, but a greater need existed now, one for which only he could provide. "Noelle, I love you. I adore you."

Drake kissed her gently and then hungrily. "I can't make promises because my life is not my own right now, but when this war is over, we'll be together forever and give my father all the grandchildren he can handle."

"I love you, too, Drake," she said as she realized how thoroughly satisfying it was to tell him what was in her heart.

They'd come a long way together and because of their commitment to the new America and to each other, she finally believed their road would lead to a glory that only they could share.

If you enjoyed *Crimson Sunrise*, you'll look forward to reading the second book in *The Charleston Women* trilogy, *Midnight Star*, coming soon from Diamond Books.

Turn the page for a sample of this glorious new novel by Kristie Knight, *Midnight Star*.

CHAPTER
1

December 25, 1780
Charleston, South Carolina

UNEASINESS KEPT ERIN BANNING AWAKE. FOR HOURS SHE had tossed and turned until she could stand no more. Sleep usually came easily to her—but not tonight. Where could Papa be? she wondered. Rising from her bed, she slipped into a wrapper and peeked out the window, knowing she would see nothing to relieve her apprehension. After pitching another log onto the fire, she curled up on the divan and tucked her feet beneath her to keep them warm.

Her father, Arlen Banning, should have been home last night, and Erin worried about him. The British patrols that were so prevalent around Charleston could have caught him and shipped him off to St. Augustine without her ever finding out. Erin felt that something awful had happened, but outside her bedroom her manner had to remain confident or the whole household would be in grave danger.

"Why did this horrible war ever start?" she whispered aloud, then clapped her hands over her mouth and glanced around.

Sleeping across the hall, Walter Martin, Colonel Balfour's civilian assistant, compounded her problems. Life in a city under siege was difficult enough without having a British official billeted in her house—particularly since her father ran a supply route that provided necessities to the Continental Army.

The bells of St. Michael's broke the silence. One, two, three . . . five times. Too early for most people to be about. Erin glanced around. Something was wrong. Papa had promised to be home in time for Christmas. He never broke a promise to her, and today was Christmas Day.

A clatter startled her as she worried about her father. Listening intently, she waited to see if she heard the sound again. Unable to identify the single noise, she went to the window and looked out again. She could see nothing.

The sound had come from her backyard. Erin left her room, hurried noiselessly along the dark passageway, descended the servants' staircase, and paused at the back door. With the sliver of a moon veiled by thick clouds, nothing of the yard was visible when she peeked through the lace curtains.

Biting her lip, she waited, wondering what she should do. She knew it couldn't be her father; he wouldn't make so much noise.

Her eyes finally adjusted to the darkness, and she saw a shape moving from the carriage house toward the piazza. Whoever was there had found the wooden bucket that Toby used to water Arlen Banning's horse. As the figure neared, she discovered that two men were stumbling along together, barely able to walk.

Unable to stand the tension any longer, she opened the door and stepped outside. One man seemed to be almost dragging the other along, and she hurried down the steps to help.

"Thank God we're here!" a male voice said, heavy with anxiety. "Help me get him into the house. If anyone sees him, we're all bound for the prison ships."

Erin stared in stunned disbelief. The stranger was dragging her father. Dark clots stained the left side of her father's face, and Erin was so shocked she couldn't move.

"Don't just stand there! Help me." The whispered pleas became urgent.

Taking her father's arm, Erin helped the strange man drag

him to the piazza. For a moment, questions bombarded her mind. What had happened? Who did this? Would Papa die? Nothing coherent or useful came to her.

The shock wore off a little, and she motioned to the door. "This way."

She held the door open, and they went quickly inside. Noticing the scent of spices, she absently wondered what kind of Christmas they would have if her father was injured as badly as he appeared to be. The man supporting her father was tall, but she couldn't see his face. Erin knew he was staring at her and felt the color rise in her cheeks. No man other than her father had ever seen her in a dressing gown. "We . . . we'll use the servants' staircase," she explained and pointed the way. Pausing only long enough to take a candle, she moved forward. "Some of the servants may be up already, so go quietly. Our day starts early."

"Lead the way." The man shifted Arlen Banning's weight slightly to get a better grip, adjusted a leather satchel on his shoulder, and moved as quietly as possible down the dark hallway.

With every step up the staircase, Erin cringed as she felt her father recoil with pain. The smell of blood caused her stomach to turn, but she never wavered in her assistance. Terrified, she struggled on and tried to ignore the bitter gall rising in her throat. Questions tumbled in her mind, but she refused to voice them until she knew he was out of sight. Fortunately, his room was at the rear of the house near the servants' stairs.

When they reached the top of the steps, she paused. "Wait here."

Tiptoeing down the corridor, she prayed that Walter Martin still slept. Outside his door, she stopped and listened. Soft snores greeted her, so she returned to her father's side.

For once Erin was glad her father snored so loudly that her parents had been forced to sleep in separate rooms. Waking her mother with the news of Arlen Banning's injury would be disastrous—and that could be postponed for now.

Always a featherhead, her mother, Vevila Banning, would surely swoon at the sight of blood and screech at the top of her lungs about Arlen Banning's injury. For some time now, Erin had expected her mother to die of grief, but somehow Vevila Banning lived on although she seldom made any pretense of knowing what was going on around her. Erin knew that their safety depended on secrecy. Her mother never could keep secrets.

Fear for her family assailed Erin as they reached her father's room, but she opened the door without hesitating, and they hurried inside. Leaving the stranger to support her father's weight, she closed the door quickly.

Throwing back the bedclothes with one hand, she motioned with the other for the man to bring her father forward. Erin allowed Arlen to fall back on the pillows while she removed his muddy shoes. Blood caked one side of his head, shoulder, and left leg. The fabric of his shirt had hardened around the shoulder wound, while the woolen breeches formed a crusty circle around the injury to his leg. A shiver racked his deathly still body. "We'll need a fire. He's freezing."

"So am I, miss. Here, Arlen insisted that I give this to you. We were almost killed trying to salvage it."

Bowie Gallagher handed the leather satchel to her and waited while the young woman hurried around the room and lit several candles. This had been a long night, too long, and he felt the exhaustion seep through his muscles and bones until they threatened to give way. In the golden glow of candlelight, the room came to life. For the first time he noticed the slight stature of his hostess. Nearly a foot shorter than he, she'd nonetheless upheld her part of Arlen's weight when they brought him upstairs.

When she turned to face the stranger, he was taken aback. Pulled severely away from her face, her auburn hair hung in a single braid across her shoulder like a spike of flame on the soft white of her dressing gown. Looking closer, he saw that her square face betrayed a strength most Charleston women worked hard to hide. He sensed that this young woman would never be so petty as to hide her inner strength.

She strode to the mantel and lit the candles over the hearth. Extending her other hand to point to the fireplace, she turned to him. "Can you light the fire? I've got to send Nero for the doctor."

He took the kindling from her hand and felt the impact of the scent of rosewater and her penetrating eyes and found himself unable to look away. Deep green, they sparkled with the reflection of the candle she carried in her other hand. Her skin was creamy, and the fine planes of her face were highlighted by a hint of pink on her cheeks. Bowie found that he could hardly speak. "Miss . . ."

"Banning. Erin Banning," she supplied, looking up into his eyes. Color crept into her cheeks under his penetrating gaze, and she broke the silence. "I am Arlen Banning's daughter."

"Oh, yes. Arlen speaks of you often." Bowie stared for a moment and then realized how foolish he must look. "I'm Bowie Gallagher, your father's partner. I'd be delighted to start the fire."

"Pleased to meet you, Mr. Gallagher. Papa has mentioned you as well." Erin watched as he arranged the kindling and then placed a sizable log on top. More than a little curious, she shifted the leather satchel to her other hand, but she hadn't time to look inside now, nor did she wish to do so in view of this man.

For the past year she'd wondered about this phantom partner of her father's, but she understood the need for secrecy. In these uncertain times few people could be trusted, and Papa always avoided public contact with Mr. Gallagher. He had spoken enthusiastically of his partner's daring, but had never mentioned his name or described him to Erin. Mr. Gallagher's broad shoulders, snugly covered by his coat, tapered to a narrow waist, and she found herself wondering how he looked without the garment. She soon found out.

He removed his damp jacket and hung it over the back of a chair by the fire. He walked back to Arlen's side and looked down.

Feeling a bit flustered, Erin jerked into action. "I'll send Nero for Dr. Rutledge."

Erin hastened as quietly as possible up the servants' stairs to the third floor, taking two or three at a time. She wanted to send Nero on his way before questioning Mr. Gallagher about her father's injuries. Reaching the servants' quarters, she gasped for breath before striding to the second door. She listened quietly, hoping to hear sounds that would indicate Nero was awake. She heard nothing.

"Not a good day to oversleep, Nero," she muttered and tapped lightly on the door.

As she was about to knock a second time, the door flew open, and Nero appeared completely dressed. "Yes'm, Miss Erin?"

Erin sighed with relief and silently thanked the Lord. "Nero, Father's been injured. Hurry to Dr. Rutledge's. You'll have to go around the long way to Tradd Street to keep from waking Widow Jenkins's dogs. You know it won't do for you to be caught. And be careful when you come back. We don't want to awaken Mr. Martin if we don't have to."

"What I say if anybody ask where I'm goin' this early?" Nero asked as he pulled on his cloak.

"Tell them you're headed for the fish market," she answered without thinking. "No, no. That won't do. Anybody with a pea for a brain would know that Toby would do that. Uh, tell them you're . . . Why, tell them you're going for the doctor. Everybody in Charleston knows how ill Mother is. Tell the truth."

"Yes'm. Don't you worry none. I bring back Dr. Rutledge lickety-split. An' I sure ain't gonna go near them dogs," he answered and donned his black hat.

Nero followed Erin down the stairs and exited through the back door. She watched him go down the steps and called, "Nero, please be careful and hurry."

Erin watched until he was out of sight, then went to the kitchen to look in the satchel. She pulled out a jar of preserves and a duck. Papa had promised her a duckling for Christmas dinner! Grinning, she raced back upstairs. She found Bowie tucking her father in bed. "Is he conscious?"

"Off and on. I removed his clothing to make him more comfortable. The injuries to his head and shoulder aren't as bad as his leg. There's a bullet lodged in the leg, and he cut his head when he fell against a sharp stick. It looks like a second bullet passed through his upper arm." Bowie gazed at the concern in her face. From the things Arlen had told him, Erin Banning was a fearless, spirited young woman. He hoped it was true. She would need courage during the next few days.

"What happened, Mr. Gallagher?" Erin could refrain from asking no longer. She sat on the edge of her father's bed and took his hand in hers. It was cold, too cold. She jumped up. "Just a minute. I'll get him some more covers. He's still freezing."

"Can you bring me a blanket, too?" Bowie glanced at her as he rubbed his hands together over the fire. "You look as if you may need . . . uh, I mean, it's too cold for that . . . you need something warmer, to wear."

Erin gazed at him for a moment, not understanding what he meant. She wasn't the least bit cold. Then she looked down. She'd forgotten that she was wearing her wrapper. "Oh, I apologize. I never thought . . . I mean, I'll be right back."

Erin hurried to her room and took a few minutes to pull on a suitable dress and shawl before collecting several quilts from the armoire.

Wondering if Mr. Gallagher had been shocked by her attire, she squared her shoulders and strode into her father's room. She had neither the time nor the inclination to be embarrassed about appearing in her dressing gown. It was, after all, still the middle of the night. "Here, Mr. Gallagher. Wrap up in this."

Bowie took a quilt from her and draped it around himself. The chill he'd gotten from hiding for several days on damp ground beneath bushes and in the rushes at the edge of streams made him feel as though he'd never be warm again. He glanced at Arlen as Erin spread two more quilts over him. The man's skin was gray.

Bowie shook his head and wondered if his partner would die. "My thanks, Miss Banning. I'm freezing."

"Sit by the fire to get warm. I'll take care of Papa." Erin ran back down the servants' stairs to get the kettle of water left simmering on the back coals and returned quickly. She hadn't time to awaken the other servants. After hanging the kettle over the fire to keep it warm until the doctor arrived, she cast a furtive glance at Bowie Gallagher. He wasn't handsome in the sense of the foppish men she knew here in Charleston, but his strong profile silhouetted in the firelight intrigued her.

When he caught her staring, he raised his eyebrows questioningly. "Have I done something wrong?"

Erin thought quickly. What could she answer? "No, you were going to tell me what happened."

"Oh, yes. Some British soldiers ambushed us," Bowie answered and tugged the quilt closer around his shoulders. He felt foolish sitting here with this lovely young woman while he looked like an Indian squaw, but he was too cold to care. "I think it was blind luck on the part of the Tories, but I can't be sure. Someone could have informed them of our whereabouts."

"But who? No one knows about the supply route." Erin dipped a cloth in the hot water. Wringing it out carefully, she winced at the sting of the scalding water and looked up at her guest. He was clearly concerned both for her father and for their business—and for the Patriot cause as well. Luckily he cared for her father. Otherwise, Arlen Banning might have been left to die by the wayside. Tears stung her eyes as she considered losing her father to the British. "You have my undying gratitude, Mr. Gallagher."

"Bowie. Call me Bowie." He leaned forward in the chair. "I'm afraid we're going to become acquainted rather quickly because of this incident."

"What do you mean?" Erin asked, letting the steaming water drizzle through her fingers into the kettle as she wrung out the cloth again. Watching Bowie, she crossed to her father's bed and began to bathe his face with the cloth. He hadn't moved since they'd placed him on the bed. "I don't understand."

"Well, I'll have to stay here in Charleston for a few days until I can find someone to take Arlen's place." Bowie unwrapped himself and walked over to Arlen's bed. He tried to think of something else, something that would allow him to forget that his very best friend, his partner, a man who was more than a father to him, might die while he stood there. "Can you trust this doctor that you sent for?"

Erin gazed at him before answering. "I trust him with my life. It's Dr. Rutledge. Do you know him?"

"I know of him." He came closer to Erin. When she gazed up at him, he whispered, "Arlen told me you have a British official billeted here."

"Yes," she murmured. For the past few minutes, as she raced up and down the stairs, she'd hoped that Walter was still asleep, but he would be up soon, if he hadn't already risen. She couldn't risk having him see her father in his present condition. "We'll have to be very quiet. I'll have to find a way to tell Mama about this without upsetting her. She isn't well, you know."

"I understand. Your father said he hadn't told her about the nature of our business venture. Will that be a problem?" Bowie turned his back to the fire and watched her working with her father. By the time the doctor arrived, she would have most of the blood washed away.

Erin stopped and turned to look at Bowie. How could she

tell a stranger that if her mother knew something, all of Charleston would know it? Keeping secrets had never been one of Vevila Banning's strong points. "It may be. I suppose I could lie to her."

"To your mother? Surely she will notice Arlen's injuries. What does he tell her when he leaves?" Bowie asked, stepping away from the crackling fire.

Erin concentrated on his questions. "Papa always tells her he's away on plantation business. As for his injuries, she will notice them, but I can very easily tell her he fell from a horse or something."

"I see. He also tells the British soldiers he's on plantation business." Bowie nodded and grinned. "It's a good thing she's as gullible as they are."

With a twinkle in her eye, Erin returned his smile. "I wouldn't go that far, but she's quite gullible. Walter Martin probably suspects something, but he never mentions it because he eats better here than he could anywhere else. Walter brings us food, and Papa smuggles in ham and fresh fish."

"That helps me to understand your boarder a little better." Bowie looked at her, again struck by the courage she needed to live in such a dangerous situation. "Now, how are we going to explain me to Walter?"

Erin's mouth fell open, and she stared in disbelief at Bowie's words. "You can't be meaning to present yourself at breakfast, can you? Walter is willing to ignore certain things, but I don't think he'd risk his post over you."

Bowie nodded his understanding. He needed to come and go freely, but he couldn't put the Banning family in further danger by openly showing himself to Balfour's assistant. "I suppose you're right. Is there a place in this house where Walter never goes? I have a place to stay, but I can't get there for a few days. And I'd like to be able to consult with Arlen about the route. You know, I've never actually been up the supply route."

"I understand. Hmmm. Let me think about that." Erin

considered the situation and cast a worried glance at her father. "I probably can hide you in here for today. Tonight I can help you get away."

"Thank you, Miss Banning." Bowie smiled, thinking that he'd have the day to get acquainted with this fascinating woman. The idea intrigued him, but his work was too vital for him to remain any longer than was absolutely necessary. "If you recall, I've been riding all night and—"

"Forgive me, Mr. Gallagher." Erin tilted her head and gazed into his eyes. "Mr. Martin has the run of the house—except the sleeping rooms. I'll take you to my room where you may sleep safely for the day."

Bowie suddenly felt his spirits lift. "I understand some of the officers billeted here in town really enjoy life. They throw elaborate parties and dances while the townspeople starve." He considered the situation and shook his head.

Erin gazed at him. His light brown hair framed a strong face and bright blue eyes. He stood almost a foot taller than she, but his powerful presence, more than his height, seemed to dwarf her. "Can I help?"

Bowie considered her offer. Spending time with Erin Banning, using the excuse of working for the cause, seemed to him an appealing notion. Thinking quickly, he opened his mouth to speak, but closed it without uttering a word.

A noise from the street distracted them. Bowie glanced at her as if to seek a place to hide immediately. "Who do you suppose that is?"

"It's probably Dr. Rutledge. I can't imagine why they're making so much noise." Erin glanced around the room and then at Bowie who seemed reluctant to be found in the Banning home at this hour. "I told you Dr. Rutledge can be trusted. Stay here. I'll let him in."

Thankful that Dr. Rutledge hadn't tarried, Erin raced out the door and tiptoed down the stairs. Outside, the streets were still quiet; the citizens of Charleston had not yet arisen.

Dr. Rutledge's carriage stood at the end of the walkway. Nero carried the doctor's bag, and the two men moved quickly toward the steps.

Erin drew her shawl closer and gazed over their heads for a moment. The sun was rising over the bay. Glorious shades of scarlet, pink, and lavender blended to produce a spectacular sunrise. A few puffy clouds drifted lazily over the Ashley River; the day would be cold but splendid.

As the physician approached, she smiled and extended her hands in greeting. "Thank you for coming, Dr. Rutledge."

"You know I'm always available when you need me." Dr. Rutledge took her hands and clasped them for a moment. "I'm sorry about the noise, but I felt that my being quiet would cause speculation we can ill afford. People are accustomed to my habits and see my carriage here too often to question my comings and goings."

"I'm sure you're right, but every sound echoes in my head like a cannon," Erin explained. "It seems that the quieter I try to be, the more noise I make."

"Is Arlen conscious?"

Erin shook her head. Her father had regained consciousness briefly, but not when she was present. "No. But, Bowie . . . Mr. Gallagher said he was conscious for a few moments. I fear he's lost a great deal of blood."

"Take me to your father, Erin my dear. We can talk later."

Erin nodded and removed her hands from his grasp. Nero followed the two of them up the stairs, but Dr. Rutledge stopped the servant at the door to Arlen Banning's room. "Thank you, Nero. I'll take this from here."

As Nero sauntered back to the staircase, Erin opened the door and led Dr. Rutledge into the room. Bowie sat by the fireplace and nodded when Dr. Rutledge closed the door and followed her to the bed.

The doctor glanced at Arlen Banning and opened his black leather case. After taking his coat off, he said to Erin,

"Please bring the light closer. Where is that confounded boarder of yours?"

Erin moved the candelabrum to the side of the bed. "I haven't heard him stirring. He had rather a late night last night."

"Thank the gods for that." Dr. Rutledge opened each of Arlen's eyes briefly and looked at them. As he examined the cut on his patient's head, he turned to Erin. "Good job, my dear. I need you to work with me. You make a good nurse."

"Will he be all right?" Hoping to see some sign of recovery, she gazed at her father's limp body.

"Can't say, my dear, can't say." Dr. Rutledge continued his examination and finally turned to her. "The leg wound is serious." He continued probing the ragged bullet hole until he found the ball and removed it. "I'm amazed he survived this long. He's lost a lot of blood. He'll have to be handled carefully during the next day or so if he's to recover."

Stunned, Erin could only stare. Her mouth opened, but nothing came out. Dr. Rutledge was saying that Papa might die. Feeling suddenly cold and alone, she looked at her father. He was too young to die, too vital. Suddenly she was struggling to hold back tears.

She'd known his condition was serious from the moment she saw the injury, but to have Dr. Rutledge confirm it aloud was something for which she wasn't prepared. She watched as Dr. Rutledge sewed up the leg and then bandaged both wounds. Erin felt the strong touch of a hand on her shoulder and turned to see whose it was. Bowie slid his arm around her and held her straight when she wished she could faint to black out the possibilities. But she needed to be strong and had never fainted in her life.

The comfort of Bowie's arm around her helped a little. She realized he was suffering, too, but nobody felt the way she did. Erin Banning had always been Papa's little girl.

"Erin my dear." Dr. Rutledge patted her arm. "Your

father is going to need you during the next few days. You must care for him yourself during this critical period."

Lifting her gaze to his, Erin tried to smile. "Then, you think he may not . . . that he may . . . live?"

Dr. Rutledge nodded. "He's tough. It'll take more than the British to kill him, I believe. Although his condition is quite serious, I think he'll make it with the proper care."

"Anything, I'll do anything." Erin's smile widened with hope. "Just tell me what to do."

"Sir, I'll be glad to help if I may," Bowie put in, tightening his grip on Erin's shoulders slightly. He wasn't about to let Arlen die without a fight.

"Oh! I wasn't thinking clearly," Erin apologized hastily, feeling better now that Dr. Rutledge had given her some hope for her father's recovery. "Dr. Rutledge, allow me to introduce my father's partner, Bowie Gallagher."

"Ah, I thought you were the daring Mr. Gallagher." Dr. Rutledge extended his hand and clapped Bowie on the shoulder. "Arlen has spoken of you often. Delighted to meet you."

"You can't imagine how happy I am to meet you, sir. I thought Arlen would die before I could get him here," Bowie admitted and looked down at Erin. "This young lady is quite a bit like her father, don't you think?"

Dr. Rutledge laughed. "More than Arlen would ever have wanted. And I imagine poor Vevila wishes Erin had taken after the Teagues rather than the Bannings. She does look a bit like her mother, though, with that auburn hair."

Bowie glanced at Erin. In the soft candlelight, her hair appeared to be tinged with gold. "Her mother must be a beautiful woman."

"Quite handsome, quite," Dr. Rutledge agreed, picked up his black bag, and turned to Erin. "My dear, I'll stop by again late this afternoon. If Arlen wakes up, give him a few sips of beef broth. Needs to build up his blood. Don't try to force too much down him, though. Might make him sick."

Erin thought the two men had forgotten she was there.

They had talked over her head as if she were invisible, but she felt almost giddy with the knowledge that her father had a chance to live. "I'll do my best."

"Are you staying in Charleston, son?" Dr. Rutledge asked Bowie when he stopped at the door. "Yes, sir. I need to find someone to fill in for Arlen." Bowie didn't move his arm but let it continue to rest comfortingly around Erin's shoulders. At first he had comforted her, but now her nearness and the wonderful scent of roses lifted his spirits.

The next few days might prove interesting, he thought and hugged her a little closer. Earlier, when he'd asked where he could remain out of sight, he'd intended the question to be innocent. But when she offered him her room, his mind had drifted toward a purpose far different from hiding out for a few days.

Erin Banning intrigued him. As Dr. Rutledge had observed, she was remarkably like Arlen. Her courage and strength seemed as great as Arlen's, and Bowie wondered how living with a woman with such fortitude would be.

Beginning to feel a bit embarrassed by the strong arm around her shoulders, Erin glanced up at Bowie. He stared down at her in such an intense way that she blushed.

When she turned to speak to Dr. Rutledge again, he was gone. She would have followed him, but Arlen stirred and her attention immediately focused on him. She broke free of Bowie's embrace and ran to her father's side. Watery eyes met hers, and a wan smile teased at the corners of Arlen's mouth, but speech was impossible. "I'll get you something to drink, Papa."

Erin raced down the stairs as if fleeing for her life. At the bottom of the curved staircase, she paused to catch her breath. She realized that she had no choice but to let Bowie stay, but she wondered how long she could endure those clear blue questioning eyes without wilting where she stood.

"No time to think about him," she muttered and turned toward the kitchen. As she whirled around, she found herself face to face with Walter Martin. "Mr. Martin,

I . . . I didn't realize you were up. I'm sorry if we awakened you."

"No, I've been up for quite some time. I awoke early. Some noise outside startled me." Walter eyed her closely.

"Yes, I had to send for Dr. Rutledge," Erin admitted, hoping that Walter hadn't been awakened by the noise of Bowie bringing her father home. "Mother has taken a turn for the worse."

"The noise that awakened me occurred before Dr. Rutledge arrived," Walter remarked and leaned against the railing at the bottom of the stairs. "Something in back of the house, I believe."

Erin felt the strain of trying to act calm when her heart had almost stopped, but she shrugged noncommittally. "Cats or dogs, I suppose. Or perhaps Papa's return. If you'll excuse me, I need to hurry into the kitchen to warm some broth."

Hurrying past him, Erin felt his eyes on her but didn't turn around. If he knew something, there was nothing she could do about it now. If he didn't, she might let information slip if she continued to talk to him. Anyhow, she could do nothing now but wait. Her father couldn't be moved, and Bowie couldn't leave now that the sun had risen.

Once in the kitchen, she closed the door and leaned on it for a minute. Nero had stoked the fire, and she found a bowl of leftover beef stew. She ladled out some and put it in a pot over the fire. Several moments crept by as she watched the pot in silence.

Her thoughts drifted to her father's partner. Bowie Gallagher was different from the other men she'd met, and Erin found that she liked that difference very much.

351

HISTORICAL
ROMANCE –

—send in the coupon below—

To get your FREE historical romance and start saving, fill out the coupon below and mail it today. As soon as we receive it we'll send you your FREE book along with your first month's selections.

Mail to: 1-55773-507-B

True Value Home Subscription Services, Inc.
P.O. Box 5235
120 Brighton Road
Clifton, New Jersey 07015-5235

YES! I want to start previewing the very best historical romances being published today. Send me my FREE book along with the first month's selections. I understand that I may look them over FREE for 10 days. If I'm not absolutely delighted I may return them and owe nothing. Otherwise I will pay the low price of just $3.50 each; a total of $14.00 (at least a $15.80 value) and save at least $1.80. Then each month I will receive four brand new novels to preview as soon as they are published for the same low price. I can always return a shipment and I may cancel this subscription at any time with no obligation to buy even a single book. In any event the FREE book is mine to keep regardless.

Name _____

Address _____ Apt. _____

City _____ State _____ Zip _____

Signature _____
                 (if under 18 parent or guardian must sign)
Terms and prices subject to change.